LAST SEEN
WEARING
&
LAST BUS TO
WOODSTOCK

THE INSPECTOR MORSE NOVELS

Last Bus to Woodstock
Last Seen Wearing
The Silent World of Nicholas Quinn
Service of All the Dead
The Dead of Jericho
The Riddle of the Third Mile
The Secret of Annexe 3
The Wench is Dead
The Jewel That Was Ours
The Way Through The Woods
The Daughters of Cain
Death is Now My Neighbour
The Remorseful Day

Also available in Pan Books

Morses Greatest Mystery and other stories
The First Inspector Morse Omnibus
The Second Inspector Morse Omnibus
The Third Inspector Morse Omnibus
The Fourth Inspector Morse Omnibus

Colin Dexter

LAST SEEN WEARING

&

LAST BUS TO WOODSTOCK

PAN BOOKS

Last Seen Wearing first published 1976
by Macmillan and first published by Pan Books 1977
Last Bus to Woodstock first published 1975
by Macmillan and first published by Pan Books 1977

This omnibus edition published 2002 by Pan Books
an imprint of Pan Macmillan Ltd
Pan Macmillan, 20 New Wharf Road, London N1 9RR
Basingstoke and Oxford
Associated companies throughout the world
www.panmacmillan.com

ISBN 0 330 41817 3

1 3 5 7 9 8 6 4 2

A CIP catalogue record for this book is available from
the British Library.

Typeset by SetSystems Ltd, Saffron Walden, Essex
Printed and bound in Great Britain by
Mackays of Chatham plc, Chatham, Kent

LAST SEEN
WEARING

For J.C.F.P. and J.G.F.P.

PRELUDE

The Train Now Standing at Platform One

HE FELT QUITE pleased with himself. Difficult to tell for certain, of course; but yes, quite pleased with himself really. As accurately as it could his mind retraced the stages of the day's events: the questions of the interviewing committee – wise and foolish; and his own answers – carefully considered and, he knew, well phrased. Two or three exchanges had been particularly satisfactory and, as he stood there waiting, a half-smile played across his firm, good-humoured lips. One he could recall almost verbatim.

'You don't think you may perhaps be a bit young for the job?'

'Well, yes. It will be a big job and I'm sure that there will be times – that is if you should appoint me – when I should need the experience and advice of older and wiser heads.' (Several of the older and wiser heads were nodding sagely.) 'But if my age is against me, there isn't much I can do about it, I'm afraid. I can only say that it's a fault I shall gradually grow out of.'

It wasn't even original. One of his former colleagues had recounted it to him and claimed it for his own. But it was a good story: and judging from the quietly controlled mirth and the muted murmurs of appreciation, apparently none of the thirteen members of the selection committee had heard it before.

Mm.

Again the quiet smile played about his mouth. He looked at his watch. 7.30 p.m. Almost certainly he would be able to catch the 8.35 from Oxford, reaching London at 9.42; then over to Waterloo; and home by midnight perhaps. He'd be a bit lucky if he managed it, but who cared? It was probably those two double whiskies that were giving him such a glowing sense of elation, of expectancy, of being temporarily so much in tune with the music of the spheres. He would be offered the job, he felt – that was the long and the short of it.

February now. Six months' notice, and he counted off the months on his fingers: March, April, May, June, July, August. That would be all right: plenty of time.

His eyes swept leisurely along the rather superior detached houses that lined the opposite side of the road. Four bedrooms; biggish gardens. He would buy one of those prefabricated greenhouses, and grow tomatoes or cucumbers, like Diocletian ... or was it Hercule Poirot?

He stepped back into the wooden shelter and out of the raw wind. It had begun to drizzle again. Cars swished intermittently by, and the surface of the road gleamed under the orange streetlights ... Not quite so good, though, when they had asked him about his short time in the army.

You didn't get a commission, did you?'

'No.'

'Why not, do you think?'

'I don't think that I was good enough. Not at the time. You need special qualities for that sort of thing.' (He was getting lost: waffle on, keep talking.) 'And I was er . . . well I just hadn't got them. There were some extremely able men joining the army at that time – far more confident and competent than me.' Leave it there. Modest.

An ex-colonel and an ex-major nodded appreciatively. Two more votes, likely as not.

It was always the same at these interviews. One had to be as honest as possible, but in a dishonest kind of way. Most of his army friends had been ex-public schoolboys, buoyed up with self-confidence, and with matching accents. Second lieutenants, lieutenants, captains. They had claimed their natural birthright and they had been duly honoured in their season. Envy had nagged at him vaguely over the years. He, too, had been a public schoolboy . . .

Buses didn't seem very frequent, and he wondered if he would make the 8.35 after all. He looked out along the well-lit street, before retreating once more into the bus shelter, its wooden walls predictably covered with scrawls and scorings of varying degrees of indecency. Kilroy, inevitably, had visited this shrine in the course of his infinite peregrinations, and several local tarts proclaimed to prospective clients their nymphomaniac inclinations. Enid loved Gary and Dave loved Monica. Variant readings concerning Oxford United betrayed the impassioned frustrations of the local football fans: eulogy and urination. All Fascists should go home immediately and freedom should be granted forthwith to Angola, Chile and Northern Ireland. A window had been smashed and slivers of glass sparkled sporadically amid the orange peel, crisp packets and Cola tins. Litter! How it appalled him. He was far more angered by obscene litter than by obscene literature. He would pass some swingeing litter laws if they ever made him the supremo. Even in this job he could do something about it. Well, if he got it . . .

Come on, bus. 7.45. Perhaps he should stay in Oxford for the night? It wouldn't matter. If freedom should be granted to Angola and the rest, why not to him? It had been a long time since he had spent so long away from home. But he was losing nothing – gaining in fact; for the expenses were extremely generous. The whole thing must have cost the Local Authority a real packet. Six of them short-listed – one from Inverness! Not that *he* would get the job, surely. Quite a strange experience, though, meeting people like that. One couldn't get too friendly. Like the contestants in a beauty competition. Smile and scratch their eyes out.

Another memory glided slowly back across his mind. 'If you were appointed, what do you think would be your biggest headache?'

'The caretaker, I shouldn't wonder.'

He had been amazed at the uproariously delighted reception given to this innocent remark, and only afterwards had he discovered that the current holder of the sinecure was an ogre of quite stupendous obstinacy – an extraordinarily ill-dispositioned man, secretly and profoundly feared by all.

Yes, he would get the job. And his first tactical

triumph would be the ceremonial firing of the wicked caretaker, with the unanimous approbation of governors, staff and pupils alike. And then the litter. And then . . .

'Waitin' for a bus?'

He hadn't seen her come in from the far side of the shelter. Below her plastic hat tiny droplets of drizzle winked from the carefully plucked eyebrows. He nodded. 'Don't seem very frequent, do they?' She walked towards him. Nice-looking girl. Nice lips. Difficult to say how old she was. Eighteen? Even younger, perhaps.

'There's one due about now.'

'That's good news.'

'Not a very nice night.'

'No.' It seemed a dismissive reply, and feeling a desire to keep the conversation going, he wondered what to say. He might just as well stand and talk as stand and be silent. His companion was clearly thinking along similar lines and showed herself the slicker practitioner.

'Goin' to Oxford?'

'Yes. I'm hoping to catch the 8.35 train to London.'

'You'll be all right.'

She unfastened her gleaming plastic mac and shook the raindrops to the floor. Her legs were thin, angular almost, but well proportioned; and the gentlest, mildest of erotic notions fluttered into his mind. It was the whisky.

'You live in London?'

'No, thank goodness. I live down in Surrey.'

'You goin' all that way tonight?'

Was he? 'It's not far really, once you've got across London.' She lapsed into silence. 'What about you? You going to Oxford?'

'Yeah. Nothing to do 'ere.'

She must be young, surely. Their eyes met and held momentarily. She had a lovely mouth. Just a brief encounter, though, in a bus shelter, and pleasant – just a fraction more pleasant than it should have been. Yet that was all. He smiled at her, openly and guilelessly. 'I suppose there's plenty to do in the big wicked city of Oxford?'

She looked at him slyly. 'Depends what you want, don't it?' Before he could ascertain exactly what she wanted or what extramural delights the old university city could still provide, a red double-decker curved into the lay-by, its near front wheel splattering specks of dirty-brown water across his carefully polished black shoes. The automatic doors rattled noisily open, and he stepped aside for the girl to climb in first. She turned at the handrail that led to the upper deck.

'Comin' upstairs?'

The bus was empty, and when she sat down on the back seat and blinked at him invitingly, he had little option or inclination to do otherwise than to sit beside her. 'Got any cigarettes?'

'No, I'm sorry. I don't smoke.'

Was she just a common slut? She almost acted like one. He must look a real city gent to her: immaculate dark suit, new white shirt, a Cambridge tie, well-cut heavy overcoat, and a leather brief-case. She would probably expect a few expensive drinks in a plush four-star lounge. Well, if she did, she was in for a big disappointment. Just a few miles on the top of a Number 2 bus. And yet he felt a subdued, magnetic attraction towards her. She took off her transparent plastic hat and shook out her long dark-brown hair. Soft, and newly washed.

A weary-footed conductor slowly mounted the circular staircase and stood before them.

'Two to Oxford, please.'

'Whereabouts?' The man sounded surly.

'Er, I'm going to the station . . .'

She said it for him. 'Two to the station, please.' The conductor wound the tickets mechanically, and disappeared dejectedly below.

It was completely unexpected, and he was taken by surprise. She put her arm through his, and squeezed his elbow gently against her soft body. 'I 'spect he thinks we're just off to the pictures.' She giggled happily. 'Anyway, thanks for buying the ticket.' She turned towards him and gently kissed his cheek with her soft, dry lips.

'You didn't tell me you were going to the station.'

'I'm not really.'

'Where are you going then?'

She moved a little closer. 'Dunno.'

For a frightening moment the thought flashed across his mind that she might be simple-minded. But no. He felt quite sure that for the present time at least she had an infinitely saner appreciation of what was going on than he. Yet he was almost glad when they reached the railway station. 8.17. Just over a quarter of an hour before the train was due.

They alighted and momentarily stood together in silence beneath the *Tickets: Buffet* sign. The drizzle persisted.

'Like a drink?' He said it lightly.

'Wouldn't mind a Coke.'

He felt surprised. If she was on the look-out for a man, it seemed an odd request. Most women of her type would surely go for gin or vodka or something with a bigger kick than Coke. Who was she? What did she want?

'You sure?'

'Yes thanks. I don't go drinkin' much.'

They walked into the buffet, where he ordered a double whisky for himself, and for her a Coke and a packet of twenty Benson & Hedges. 'Here we are.'

She seemed genuinely grateful. She quickly lit herself a cigarette and quietly sipped her drink. The time ticked on, the minute hand of the railway clock dropping inexorably to the half hour. 'Well, I'd better get on to the platform.' He hesitated a moment, and then reached beneath the seat for his brief-case. He turned towards her and once again their eyes met. 'I enjoyed meeting you. Perhaps we'll meet again one day.' He stood up, and looked down at her. She seemed more attractive to him each time he looked at her.

She said: 'I wish we could be naughty together, don't you?'

God, yes. Of course he did. He was breathing quickly

and suddenly the back of his mouth was very dry. The loudspeaker announced that the 8.35 shortly arriving at Platform One was for Reading and Paddington only; passengers for . . . But he wasn't listening. All he had to do was to admit how nice it would have been, smile a sweet smile and walk through the buffet door, only some three or four yards away, and out on to Platform One. That was all. And again and again in later months and years he was bitterly to reproach himself for not having done precisely that.

'But where could we go?' He said it almost involuntarily. The pass at Thermopylae was abandoned and the Persian army was already streaming through.

CHAPTER ONE

Beauty's ensign yet
Is crimson in thy lips and in thy cheeks,
And death's pale flag is not advanced there.
Shakespeare, *Romeo and Juliet*, Act V

THREE AND A half years later two men were seated together in an office.

'You've got the files. Quite a lot of stuff to go on there.'

'But he didn't get very far, did he?' Morse sounded cynical about the whole proposition.

'Perhaps there wasn't very far to go.'

'You mean she just hopped it and – that was that.'

'Perhaps.'

'But what do you want me to do? Ainley couldn't find her, could he?'

Chief Superintendent Strange made no immediate answer. He looked past Morse to the neatly docketed rows of red and green box-files packed tightly along the shelves.

'No,' he said finally. 'No, he didn't find her.'

'And he was on the case right from the start.'

'Right from the start,' repeated Strange.

'And he got nowhere.' Strange said nothing. 'He wasn't a fool, was he?' persisted Morse. What the hell did it matter anyway? A girl leaves home and she's never seen again. So what? Hundreds of girls leave home. Most of them write back to their parents before long – at least as soon as the glamour rubs off and the money has trickled away. Some of them don't come home. Agreed. Some of them never do; and for the lonely waiters the nagging heartache returns with the coming of each new day. No. A few of them never come home . . . Never.

Strange interrupted his gloomy thoughts. 'You'll take it on?'

'Look, if Ainley . . .'

'No. *You* look!' snapped Strange. 'Ainley was a bloody sight better policeman than you'll ever be. In fact I'm asking you to take on this case precisely because you're *not* a very good policeman. You're too airy-fairy. You're too . . . I don't know.'

But Morse knew what he meant. In a way he ought to have been pleased. Perhaps he was pleased. But two years ago. Two whole years! 'The case is cold now, sir – you must know that. People forget. Some people need to forget. Two years is a long time.'

'Two years, three months and two days,' corrected Strange. Morse rested his chin on his left hand and rubbed the index finger slowly along the side of his nose. His grey eyes stared through the open window and on to the concrete surface of the enclosed yard. Small tufts of grass were sprouting here and there. Amazing. Grass growing through concrete. How on earth? Good place to hide a body – under concrete. All you'd need to do . . . 'She's dead,' said Morse abruptly.

12

Strange looked up at him. 'What on earth makes you say that?'

'I don't know. But if you don't find a girl after all that time – well, I should guess she's dead. It's hard enough hiding a dead body, but it's a hell of a sight harder hiding a living one. I mean, a living one gets up and walks around and meets other people, doesn't it? No. My guess is she's dead.'

'That's what Ainley thought.'

'And you agreed with him?'

Strange hesitated a moment, then nodded. 'Yes, I agreed with him.'

'He was really treating this as a murder inquiry, then?'

'Not officially, no. He was treating it for what it was – a missing-person inquiry.'

'And unofficially?'

Again Strange hesitated. 'Ainley came to see me about this case several times. He was, let's say, uneasy about it. There were certain aspects of it that made him very . . . very worried.'

Surreptitiously Morse looked at his watch. Ten past five. He had a ticket for the visiting English National Opera performance of *Die Walküre* starting at half-past six at the New Theatre.

'It's ten past five,' said Strange, and Morse felt like a young schoolboy caught yawning as the teacher was talking to him . . . School. Yes, Valerie Taylor had been a schoolgirl – he'd read about the case. Seventeen and a bit. Good looker, by all accounts. Eyes on the big city, like as not. Excitement, sex, drugs, prostitution, crime, and then the gutter. And finally remorse. We all felt remorse in the end. And then? For the first time since he had been sitting in Strange's office Morse felt his brain becoming engaged. What *had* happened to Valerie Taylor?

He heard Strange speaking again, as if in answer to his thoughts.

'At the end Ainley was beginning to get the feeling that she'd never left Kidlington at all.'

Morse looked up sharply. 'Now I wonder why he should think that?' He spoke the words slowly, and he felt his nerve-endings tingling. It was the old familiar sensation. For a while he even forgot *Die Walküre*.

'As I told you, Ainley was worried about the case.'

'You know why?'

'You've got the files.'

Murder? That was more up Morse's alley. When Strange had first introduced the matter he thought he was being invited to undertake one of those thankless, inconclusive, interminable, needle-in-a-haystack searches: panders, pimps and prostitutes, shady rackets and shady racketeers, grimy streets and one-night cheap hotels in London, Liverpool, Birmingham. Ugh! Procedure. Check. Recheck. Blank. Start again. *Ad infinitum.* But now he began to brighten visibly. And, anyway, Strange would have his way in the end, whatever happened. Just a minute, though. Why now? Why Friday, 12 September – two years, three months and two days (wasn't it?), after Valerie Taylor had left home to return to afternoon school? He frowned. 'Something's turned up, I suppose.'

Strange nodded. 'Yes.'

That was better news. Watch out you miserable

sinner, whoever you are, who did poor Valerie in! He'd ask for Sergeant Lewis again. He liked Lewis.

'And I'm sure,' continued Strange, 'that you're the right man for the job.'

'Nice of you to say so.'

Strange stood up. 'You didn't seem all that pleased a few minutes ago.'

'To tell you the truth, sir, I thought you were going to give me one of those miserable missing-person cases.'

'And that's exactly what I am going to do.' Strange's voice had acquired a sudden hard authority. 'And I'm not *asking* you to do it – I'm *telling* you.'

'But you said . . .'

'*You* said. I didn't. Ainley was wrong. He was wrong because *Valerie Taylor is very much alive.*' He walked over to a filing cabinet, unlocked it, took out a small rectangular sheet of cheap writing paper, clipped to an equally cheap brown envelope, and handed both to Morse. 'You can touch it all right – no fingerprints. She's written home at last.'

Morse looked down miserably at the three short lines of drab, uncultured scrawl:

Dear Mum and Dad,
    Just to let you know I'm alright so don't worry. Sorry I've not written before, but I'm alright. Love Valerie.'

There was no address on the letter.

Morse slipped the envelope from the clip. It was postmarked Tuesday, 2 September, London, EC4.

CHAPTER TWO

We'll get excited with Ring seat (10).
Clue from a Ximenes crossword puzzle

ON THE LEFT-HAND side sat a man of vast proportions,
who had come in with only a couple of minutes to
spare. He had wheezed his way slowly along Row J like
a very heavy vehicle negotiating a very narrow bridge,
mumbling a series of breathless 'thank yous' as each of
the seated patrons blocking his progress arose and
pressed hard back against the tilted seats. When he had
finally deposited his bulk in the seat next to Morse, the
sweat stood out on his massive brow, and he panted
awhile like a stranded whale.

On the other side sat a demure, bespectacled young
lady in a long purple dress, holding a bulky opera score
upon her knee. Morse had nodded a polite 'good
evening' when he took his seat, but only momentarily
had the lips creased before reassuming their wonted,
thin frigidity. Mona Lisa with the guts ache, thought
Morse. He had been in more exhilarating company.

But there was the magnificent opera to relish once
again. He thought of the supremely beautiful love duet
in Act 1, and he hoped that this evening's Siegmund
would be able to cope adequately with that noble tenor
passage – one of the most beautiful (and demanding)

in all grand opera. The conductor strode along the orchestra pit, mounted the rostrum, and suavely received the plaudits of the audience. The lights were dimmed, and Morse settled back in his seat with delicious anticipation. The coughing gradually sputtered to a halt and the conductor raised his baton. *Die Walküre* was under way.

After only two minutes, Morse was conscious of some distracting movement on his right, and a quick glance revealed that the bespectacled Mona Lisa had extricated a torch from somewhere about her person and was playing the light laterally along the orchestrated score. The pages crinkled and crackled as she turned them, and for some reason the winking of the flashlight reminded Morse of a revolving lighthouse. Forget it. She would probably pack it up as soon as the curtain went up. Still, it was a little annoying. And it was hot in the New Theatre. He wondered if he should take his jacket off, and almost immediately became aware that one other member of the audience had already come to a firm decision on the same point. The mountain on his left began to quiver, and very soon Morse was a helpless observer as the fat man set about removing his jacket, which he effected with infinitely more difficulty than an ageing Houdini would have experienced in escaping from a straitjacket. Amid mounting shushes and clicking of tongues the fat man finally brought his monumental toils to a successful climax and rose ponderously to remove the offending garment from beneath him. The seat twanged noisily against the back rest, was restored to its horizontal position, and groaned heavily as it sank once more beneath the mighty load. More shushes, more clickings – and finally a blissful suspension of hostilities in Row J, disturbed only for Morse's sensitive soul by the lighthouse flashings of the Lady with the Lamp. Wagnerites were a funny lot!

Morse closed his eyes and the well-known chords at last engulfed him. Exquisite . . .

For a second Morse thought that the dig in his left rib betokened a vital communication, but the gigantic frame beside him was merely fighting to free his handkerchief from the vast recesses of his trouser pocket. In the ensuing struggle the flap of Morse's own jacket managed to get itself entrapped, and his feeble efforts to free himself from the entanglement were greeted by a bleak and barren glare from Florence Nightingale.

By the end of Act 1, Morse's morale was at a low ebb. Siegmund had clearly developed a croaking throat, Sieglinde was sweating profusely, and a young philistine immediately behind him was regularly rustling a packet of sweets. During the first interval he retreated to the bar, ordered a whisky, and another. The bell sounded for the start of Act 2, and he ordered a third. And the young girl who had been seated behind Morse's shoulders during Act 1 had a gloriously unimpeded view of Act 2; and of Act 3, by which time her second bag of Maltesers had joined the first in a crumpled heap upon the floor.

The truth was that Morse could never have surrendered himself quite freely to unadulterated enjoyment that night, however propitious the circumstances might have been. At every other minute his mind was reverting to his earlier interview with Strange – and then to Ainley. Above all to Chief Inspector Ainley. He had not known him at all well, really. Quiet sort of fellow. Friendly enough, without ever being a friend. A loner. Not, as Morse remembered him, a particularly interesting man at all. Restrained, cautious, legalistic. Married, but no family. And now he would never have a family, for Ainley was dead. According to the eye-witness it was largely his own fault – pulling out to overtake and failing to notice the fast-closing Jaguar looming in the outside lane of the M40 by High Wycombe. Miraculously no one else was badly hurt. Only Ainley, and Ainley had been killed. It wasn't like Ainley, that. He must have been thinking of something else . . . He had gone to London in his own car and in his own free time, just eleven days ago. It was frightening really – the way other people went on living. Great shock – oh yes – but there were no particular friends to mourn too bitterly. Except his wife . . . Morse had met her only once, at a police concert the previous year. Quite young, much younger than he was; pretty enough, but nothing to set the heart a-beating. Irene, or something like that? Eileen? Irene, he thought.

His whisky was finished and he looked around for the barmaid. No one. He was the only soul there, and the linen wiping-towels were draped across the beer pumps. There was little point in staying.

He walked down the stairs and out into the warm dusking street. A huge notice in red and black capitals covered the whole of the wall outside the theatre: ENGLISH NATIONAL OPERA Mon. 1 Sept – Sat. 13 Sept. He felt a slight quiver of excitement along his spine. Monday the first of September. That was the day Dick Ainley had died. And the letter? Posted on Tuesday, the second of September. Could it be? He mustn't jump to conclusions though. But why the hell not? There was no eleventh commandment against jumping to conclusions, and so he jumped. Ainley had gone to London that Monday and something must have happened there. Had he perhaps found Valerie Taylor at last? It began to look a possibility. *The very next day* she had written home – after being away for more than two years. Yet there was something wrong. The Taylor case had been shelved, not closed, of course; but Ainley was working on something else, on that bomb business, in fact. So why? So why? Hold it a minute. Ainley had gone to London on his day off. Had he . . .?

Morse walked back into the foyer, to be informed by a uniformed flunkey that the house was sold out and that the performance was half-way through anyway. Morse thanked him and stepped into the telephone kiosk by the door.

'I'm sorry, sir. That's for patrons only.' The flunkey was right behind him.

'I *am* a bloody patron,' said Morse. He took from his pocket the stub for Row J 26, stuck it under the flunkey's nose and ostentatiously and noisily closed the kiosk door behind him. A large telephone directory was stuck awkwardly in the metal pigeon-hole, and Morse opened it at the As. Addeley ... Allen ... back a bit ... Ainley. Only one Ainley, and in next year's directory even he would be gone. R. Ainley, 2 Wytham Close, Wolvercote.

Would she be in? It was already a quarter to nine. Irene or Eileen or whatever she was would probably be staying with friends. Mother or sister, most likely. Should he try? But what was he dithering about? He knew he would go anyway. He noted the address and walked briskly out past the flunkey.

'Goodnight, sir.'

As Morse walked to his car, parked in nearby St Giles', he regretted his childish sneer of dismissal to this friendly valediction. The flunkey was only doing his job. Just as I am, said Morse to himself, as he drove without enthusiasm due north out of Oxford towards the village of Wolvercote.

CHAPTER THREE

A man is little use when his wife's a widow.
Scottish proverb

AT THE WOODSTOCK roundabout, on the northern
ring-road perimeter of Oxford, Morse took the sharp
left fork, and leaving the motel on his right drove over
the railway bridge (where as a boy he had so often
stood in wonder as the steam locomotives sped thunder-
ously by) and down the hill into Wolvercote.

The small village consisted of little more than the
square stone-built houses that lined its main street, and
was familiar to Morse only because each of its two
public houses boasted beer drawn straight from the
wood. Without being too doctrinaire about what he was
prepared to drink, Morse preferred a flat pint to the
fizzy keg most breweries, misguidedly in his view, were
now producing; and he seldom passed through the
village without enjoying a jug of ale at the King Charles.
He parked the Lancia in the yard, exchanged a few
pleasantries with the landlady over his beer, and asked
for Wytham Close.

He soon found it, a crescented cul-de-sac no more than
a hundred yards back along the road on the right-hand
side, containing ten three-storey terraced residences
(pompously styled 'town houses'), set back from the

adopted road, with steep concreted drives leading up to the built-in garages. Two street lamps threw a pale phosphorescence over the open-plan, well-tended grass, and a light shone from behind the orange curtains in the middle-storey window of No 2. The bell sounded harsh in the quiet of the darkened close.

A lower light was switched on in the entrance hall and a vaguely-lineated shadow loomed through the frosted glass of the front door.

'Yes?'

'I hope I'm not disturbing you,' began Morse.

'Oh. Hullo, Inspector.'

'I thought . . .'

'Won't you come in?'

Morse's decision to refuse the offer of a drink was made with such obvious reluctance that he was speedily prevailed upon to reverse it; and sitting behind a glass of gin and tonic he did his best to say all the right things. On the whole, he thought, he was succeeding.

Mrs Ainley was small, almost petite, with light-brown hair and delicate features. She looked well enough, although the darkness beneath her eyes bore witness to the recent tragedy.

'Will you stay on here?'

'Oh, I think so. I like it here.'

Indeed, Morse knew full well how attractive the situation was. He had almost bought a similar house here a year ago, and he remembered the view from the rear windows over the green expanse of Port Meadow across to the cluster of stately spires and the dignified dome of the Radcliffe Camera. Like an

Ackerman print, only alive and real, just two or three miles away.

'Another drink?'

'I'd better not,' said Morse, looking appealingly towards his hostess.

'Sure?'

'Well, perhaps a small one.'

He took the plunge. 'Irene, isn't it?'

'Eileen.'

It was a bad moment. 'You're getting over it, Eileen?' He spoke the words in a kindly way.

'I think so.' She looked down sadly, and picked some non-existent object from the olive-green carpet. 'He was hardly marked, you know. You wouldn't really have thought . . .' Tears were brimming, and Morse let them brim. She was quickly over it. 'I don't even know why Richard went to London. Monday was his day off, you know.' She blew her nose noisily, and Morse felt more at ease.

'Did he often go away like that?'

'Quite often, yes. He always seemed to be busy.' She began to look vulnerable again and Morse trod his way carefully. It had to be done.

'Do you think when he went to London he was, er . . .'

'I don't know what he went for. He never told me much about his work. He always said he had enough of it at the office without talking about it again at home.'

'But he was worried about his work, wasn't he?' said Morse quietly.

'Yes. He always was a worrier, especially . . .'

'Especially?'

'I don't know.'

'You mean he was more worried – recently?'

She nodded. 'I think I know what was worrying him. It was that Taylor girl.'

'Why do you say that?'

'I heard him talking on the phone to the headmaster.' She made the admission guiltily as if she really had no business to know of it.

'When was that?'

'About a fortnight, three weeks ago.'

'But the school's on holiday, isn't it?'

'He went to the headmaster's house.'

Morse began to wonder what else she knew. 'Was that on one of his days off . . .?'

She nodded slowly and then looked up at Morse. 'You seem very interested.'

Morse sighed. 'I ought to have told you straight away. I'm taking over the Taylor case.'

'So Richard found something after all.' She sounded almost frightened.

'I don't know,' said Morse.

'And . . . and that's why you came, I suppose.' Morse said nothing. Eileen Ainley got up from her chair and walked briskly over to a bureau beside the window. 'Most of his things have gone, but you might as well take this. He had it in the car with him.' She handed to Morse a Letts desk diary, black, about six inches by four. 'And there's a letter for the accountant at the station. Perhaps you could take it for me?'

'Of course.' Morse felt very hurt. But he often felt hurt – it was nothing new.

Eileen left the room to fetch the envelope and Morse quickly opened the diary and found Monday, 1 September. There was one entry, written in neatly-formed, minuscule letters: 42 Southampton Terrace. That was all. The blood tingled, and with a flash of utter certitude Morse knew that he hardly needed to look up the postal district of 42 Southampton Terrace. He *would* check it, naturally; he would look it up immediately he got home. But without the slightest shadow of doubt he knew it already. It would be EC4.

He was back in his North Oxford bachelor home by a quarter to eleven, and finally discovered the street map of London, tucked neatly away behind *The Collected Works of Swinburne* and *Extracts from Victorian Pornography*. (He must put that book somewhere less conspicuous.) Impatiently he consulted the alphabetical index and frowned as he found Southampton Terrace. His frown deepened as he traced the given coordinates and studied the grid square. Southampton Terrace was one of the many side-streets off the Upper Richmond Road, south of the river, beyond Putney Bridge. The postal district was SW12. He suddenly decided he had done enough for one day.

He left the map and the diary on top of the bookshelf, made himself a cup of instant coffee and selected from his precious Wagner shelf the Solti recording of *Die Walküre*. No fat man, no thin-lipped woman, no raucous tenor, no sweaty soprano distracted his mind as Siegmund and Sieglinde poured forth their souls in an ecstasy of recognition. The coffee remained untouched and gradually grew cold.

But even before the first side was played through, a fanciful notion was forming in his restless brain. There was surely a very simple reason for Ainley's visit to London. He should have thought of it before. Day off; busy, preoccupied, uncommunicative. He'd bet that was it! 42 Southampton Terrace. Well, well! *Old Ainley had been seeing another woman, perhaps.*

CHAPTER FOUR

As far as I could see there was no connection between them beyond the tenuous nexus of succession.

Peter Champkin

IN DIFFERENT PARTS of the country on the Monday following Morse's interview with Strange, four fairly normal people were going about their disparate business. What each was doing was, in its own way, ordinary enough – in some cases ordinary to the point of tediousness. Each of them, with varied degrees of intimacy, knew the others, although one or two of them were hardly worthy of any intimate acquaintanceship. They shared one common bond, however, which in the ensuing weeks would inexorably draw each of them towards the centre of a criminal investigation. For each of them had known, again with varied degrees of intimacy, the girl called Valerie Taylor.

Mr Baines had been second master in Kidlington's Roger Bacon Comprehensive School since its opening three years previously. Before that time he had also been second master, in the very same buildings, although then they had housed a secondary modern school, now incorporated into the upper part of a three-tier comprehensive system – a system which in their wisdom or unwisdom (Baines wasn't sure) the Oxfordshire Education Committee had adopted as its answer to the problems besetting the educational world in general and the children of Kidlington in particular. The pupils would be returning the following day, Tuesday, 16 September, after a break of six and a half weeks, for much of which time, whilst some of his colleagues had motored off to Continental resorts, Baines had been wrestling with the overwhelmingly complex problems of the timetable. Such a task traditionally falls upon the second master, and in the past Baines had welcomed it. There was a certain intellectual challenge in dovetailing the myriad options and combinations of the curriculum to match the inclinations and capacities of the staff available; and, at the same time (for Baines), a vicarious sense of power. Sadly, Baines had begun to think of himself as a good loser, a best man but never the groom. He was now fifty-five, unmarried, a mathematician. He had applied for many headships over the years and on two occasions had been the runner-up. His last application had been made three and a half years ago, for the headship of his present school, and he thought he'd had a fairly good chance; but even then, deep down, he knew that he was getting past it. Not that he had been much impressed by the man they appointed, Phillipson. Not at the time, anyway. Only thirty-four, full of new ideas. Keen on changing everything – as if change inevitably meant a change for the better. But over the last year or so he had learned to respect Phillipson a good deal more. Especially after that glorious showdown with the odious caretaker.

Baines was sitting in the small office which served as

a joint HQ for himself and for Mrs Webb, the head-master's secretary – a decent old soul who like himself had served in the old secondary modern school. It was mid-morning and he had just put the finishing touches to the staff dinner-duty roster. Everyone was neatly fitted in, except the headmaster, of course. And him-self. He had to pick up his perks from somewhere. He walked across the cluttered office clutching the hand-written sheet.

'Three copies, my old sugar.'

'Immediately, I suppose,' said Mrs Webb good-naturedly, picking up another sealed envelope and looking at the addressee before deftly slitting it along the top with a paperknife.

'What about a cup of coffee?' suggested Baines.

'What about your roster?'

'OK. I'll make the coffee.'

'No you won't.' She got up from her seat, picked up the kettle, and walked out to the adjacent cloakroom. Baines looked ruefully at the pile of letters. The usual sort of thing, no doubt. Parents, builders, meetings, insurance, examinations. *He* would have been dealing with all that if ... He poked haphazardly among the remaining letters, and suddenly a flicker of interest showed in his shrewd eyes. The letter was lying face down and on the sealed flap he read the legend 'Thames Valley Police'. He picked it up and turned it over. It was addressed to the headmaster with the words PRIVATE AND CONFIDENTIAL typed across the top in bold red capitals.

'What are you doing going through my mail?' Mrs Webb plugged in the kettle and with mock annoyance snatched the letter from him.

'See that?' asked Baines.

Mrs Webb looked down at the letter. 'None of our business, is it?'

'Do you think he's been fiddling his tax returns?' Baines chuckled deeply.

'Don't be silly.'

'Shall we open it?'

'We shall *not*,' said Mrs Webb.

Baines returned to his cramped desk and started on the prefects' roster. Phillipson would have to appoint half a dozen new prefects this term. Or, to be more precise, he would ask Baines to give him a list of possible names. In some ways the head wasn't such a bad chap.

Phillipson himself came in just after eleven. 'Morning, Baines. Morning, Mrs Webb.' He sounded far too cheerful. Had he forgotten that school was starting tomorrow?

'Morning, headmaster.' Baines always called him 'headmaster'; the rest of the staff called him 'sir'. It was only a little thing, but it was something.

Phillipson walked across to his study door and paused by his secretary's desk. 'Anything important, Mrs Webb?'

'I don't think so, sir. There's this, though.' She handed him the letter marked 'Private and Confidential', and Phillipson, with a slightly puzzled frown upon his face, entered his study and closed the door behind him.

In the newly-appointed county of Gwynedd, in a small semi-detached house on the outskirts of Caernarfon, another schoolmaster was acutely conscious that school restarted on the morrow. They had returned home only the previous day from a travesty of a holiday in Scotland – rain, two punctures, a lost Barclaycard and more rain – and there was a host of things to be done. The lawn, for a start. Benefiting (where he had suffered) from a series of torrential downpours, it had sprouted to alarming proportions during their absence, and was in urgent need of an instant crop. At 9.30 a.m. he discovered that the extension for the electric mower was not functioning, and he sat himself down on the back doorstep with a heavy heart and a small screwdriver.

Life seldom seemed to run particularly smoothly for David Acum, until two years ago assistant French master at the Roger Bacon Comprehensive School in Kidlington, and now, still an assistant French master, at the City of Caernarfon School.

He could find no fault with the fittings at either end of the extension wire, and finally went inside again. No sign of life. He walked to the bottom of the stairs and yelled, his voice betraying ill-temper and exasperation, 'Hey! Don't you think it's about time you got out of that bloody bed?'

He left it at that and, back in the kitchen, sat down

cheerlessly at the table where half an hour earlier he had made his own breakfast, and dutifully taken a tray of tea and toast upstairs. Ineffectually he tinkered once more with one of the wretched plugs. She joined him ten minutes later, dressing-gowned and beslippered.

'What's eating you?'

'Christ! Can't you see? I suppose you buggered this up the last time you hoovered – not that I can remember when that was!'

She ignored the insult and took the extension from him. He watched her as she tossed her long blonde hair from her face and deftly unscrewed and examined the troublous plugs. Younger than he was – a good deal younger, it seemed – he found her enormously attractive still. He wondered, as he often wondered, whether he had made the right decision, and once more he told himself he had.

The fault was discovered and corrected, and David felt better.

'Cup of coffee, darling?' All sweetness and light.

'Not just yet. I've got to get cracking.' He looked out at the overgrown lawn and swore softly as faintly dotted lines of slanting drizzle formed upon the window pane.

A middle-aged woman, blowzy, unkempt, her hair in cylindrical curlers, materialized from a side door on the ground floor; her quarry was bounding clumsily down the stairs.

'I want to speak to yer.'

'Not now, sweetheart. Not now. I'm late.'

'If yer can't wait now yer needn't come back. Yer things'll be in the street.'

'Now just a minute, sweetheart.' He came close to her, leaned his head to one side and laid a hand on each of her shoulders. 'What's the trouble? You know I wouldn't do anything to upset you.' He smiled pleasantly enough and there was something approaching an engaging frankness in his dark eyes. But she knew him better.

'Yer've got a woman in yer room, 'aven't yer?'

'Now there's no need for you to get jealous, you know that.'

She found him repulsive now, and regretted those early days. 'Get 'er out and keep 'er out – there's to be no more women 'ere.' She slapped his hands from her shoulders.

'She'll be going, she'll be going – don't worry. She's only a young chick. Nowhere to kip down – you know how it is.'

'Now!'

'Don't be daft. I'm late already, and I'll lose the job if I ain't careful. Be reasonable.'

'Yer'll lose yer bed an' all if yer don't do as I tell yer.'

The youth took a dirty five-pound note from his hip pocket. 'I suppose that'll satisfy you for a day or two, you old bitch.'

The woman took the money, but continued to watch him. 'It's got to stop.'

'Yeah. Yeah.'

'How long's she been 'ere?'

'A day or two.'

'Fortnight, nearer, yer bleedin' liar.'

The youth slammed the door after him, ran down to the bottom of the road, and turned right into the Upper Richmond Road.

Even by his own modest standards, Mr George Taylor had not made much of a success of his life. Five years previously, an unskilled manual worker, he had accepted 'voluntary redundancy' money after the shake-up that followed the reorganization of the Cowley Steel plant, had then worked for almost a year driving a bulldozer on the M40 construction programme and spent the next year doing little but casual jobs, and drinking rather too much and gambling rather too much. And then that terrible row and, as a result of it, his present employment. Each morning at 7.15 he drove his rusting, green Morris Oxford from his Kidlington council house into the city of Oxford, down past Aristotle Lane into Walton Street, and over the concreted track that led through the open fields, between the canal and the railway line, where lay the main city rubbish dump. Each morning of the working week for the past three years – including the day when Valerie had disappeared – he had made the same journey, with his lunchtime sandwiches and his working overalls beside him on the passenger seat.

Mr Taylor was an inarticulate man, utterly unable to rationalize into words his favourable attitude towards his present job. It would have been difficult for anyone. The foul detritus of the city was all around him, rotten food and potato peelings, old mattresses, piles of sheer filth, rats and always (from somewhere) the scavenger gulls. And yet he liked it.

At lunchtime on Monday the fifteenth, he was sitting with his permanent colleague on the site, a man with a miry face ingrained with dirt, in the wooden hut which formed the only semi-hygienic haven in this wilderness of waste. They were eating their sandwiches and swilling down the thick bread with a dirty brown brew of ugly-looking tea. Whilst his companion mused over the racing columns of the *Sun*, George Taylor sat silent, a weary expression on his stolid face. The letter had brought the whole thing back to the forefront of his mind and he was thinking again of Valerie. Had he been right to persuade the wife to take it to the police? He didn't know. They would soon be round again; in fact he was surprised they hadn't been round already. It would upset the wife again – and she'd been nothing but a bag of nerves from the beginning. Funny that the letter had come just after Inspector Ainley was killed. Clever man, Ainley. He'd been round to see them only three weeks ago. Not official, like, but he was the sort of bloke who never let anything go. Like a dog with a bone.

Valerie . . . He'd thought a lot of Valerie.

A corporation vehicle lumbered to a halt outside the hut, and George Taylor poked his head through the door. 'On the top side, Jack. Shan't be a minute.' He pointed vaguely away to the far corner of the tip, swallowed the last few mouthfuls of his tea and prepared for the afternoon's work.

At the far edge of the tip the hydraulic piston whirred into life and the back of the lorry tilted slowly down and its contents were deposited upon the sea of stinking refuse.

For Morse, this same Monday was the first day of a frustrating week. Another series of incendiary devices had been set off over the weekend in clubs and cinemas, and the whole of the top brass, including himself, had been summoned into urgent conclave. It was imperative that all available police personnel should be mobilized. All known suspects from Irish republicans to international anarchists were to be visited and questioned. The Chief Constable wanted quick results.

On Friday morning a series of arrests was made in a dawn swoop, and later that day eight persons were charged with conspiracy to cause explosions in public places. Morse's own contribution to the successful outcome of the week's inquiries had been virtually nil.

CHAPTER FIVE

She turned away, but with the autumn weather
Compelled my imagination many days,
Many days and many hours.

          T. S. Eliot, *La Figlia Che Piange*

As HE LAY abed on Sunday, 21 September, Morse was beset by the nagging feeling that there was so much to be done if only he could summon up the mental resolve to begin. It was like deferring a long-promised letter; the intention lay on the mind so heavily that the simple task seemed progressively to assume almost gigantic proportions. True, he had written to the headmaster of the Roger Bacon Comprehensive School – and had received an immediate and helpful reply. But that was all; and he felt reluctant to follow it up. Most of his fanciful notions about the Taylor girl had evaporated during the past week of sober, tedious routine, and he had begun to suspect that further investigation into Valerie's disappearance would involve little more than an unwelcome continuation of similar sober and tedious routine. But he was in charge now. It was up to him.

Half-past nine already. His head ached and he resolved on a day of total abstinence. He turned over, buried his head in the pillow, and tried to think of nothing. But for Morse such a blessed state of nihilism was utterly impossible. He finally arose at ten, washed and shaved and set off briskly down the road for a Sunday morning newspaper. It was no more than twenty minutes' walk and Morse enjoyed the stroll. His head felt clearer already and he swung along almost merrily, mentally debating whether to buy the *News of the World* or the *Sunday Times*. It was the regular hebdomadal debate which paralleled the struggle in Morse's character between the Coarse and the Cultured. Sometimes he bought one; sometimes he bought the other. Today he bought both.

At half-past eleven he switched on his portable to listen to Record Review on Radio Three, and sank back in his favourite armchair, a cup of hot, strong coffee at his elbow. Life was good sometimes. He picked up the *News of the World,* and for ten minutes wallowed in the Shocking Revelations and Startling Exposures which the researchers of that newspaper had somehow managed to rake together during the past seven days. There were several juicy articles and Morse started on the secret sex life of a glamorous Hollywood pussycat. But it began to pall after the first few paragraphs. Ill-written and (more to the point) not even mildly titillating; it was always the same. Morse firmly believed that there was nothing so unsatisfactory as this kind of halfway house pornography; he liked it hot or not at all. He wouldn't buy the wretched paper again. Yet he had made the same decision so many times before, and knew that next week again he would fall the same silly sucker for the same salacious front-page promises. But for this morning he'd had enough. So much so that he gave no more than a passing glance to a provocative photograph of a seductive starlet exposing one half of her million-dollar breasts.

After relegating (as always) the Business News Section to the wastepaper basket, he graduated to the *Sunday Times*. He winced to see that Oxford United had been comprehensively trounced, read the leading articles and most of the literary reviews, tried unsuccessfully to solve the bridge problem, and finally turned to the Letters. Pensions, Pollution, Private Medicine – same old topics; but a good deal of sound common sense. And then his eye caught a letter which made him sit bolt upright. He read it and a puzzled look came to his face. August 24? He couldn't have bought the *Sunday Times* that week. He read the short letter again.

To the Editor. Dear Sir,
My wife and I wish to express our deep gratitude to your newspaper for the feature 'Girls who run away from Home' (Colour Suppt. August 24). As a direct result of reading the article, our only daughter, Christine, returned home last week after being away for over a year. We thank you most sincerely.
Mr and Mrs J. Richardson (Kidderminster).

Morse got up and went to a large pile of newspapers neatly bundled in string, that lay in the hallway beside the front door. The Boy Scouts collected them once a month, and although Morse had never been a tenderfoot himself he gave the movement his qualified approval. Impatiently he tore at the string and delved into the pile. Thirty-first August. Fourteenth September. But no 24 August. It may have gone with the last pile. Blast. He looked through again, but it wasn't there. Now who might have a copy? He tried his next-door neighbour, but on reflection he might have saved himself the bother. What about Lewis? Unlikely, yet worth a try. He telephoned his number.

'Lewis? Morse here.'

'Ah. Morning, sir.'

'Lewis, do you take the *Sunday Times*?'

''Fraid not, sir. We have the *Sunday Mirror*.' He sounded somewhat apologetic about his Sabbath-day reading.

'Oh.'

'I could get you a copy, I suppose.'

'I've got today's. I want the copy for August the twenty-fourth.'

It was Sergeant Lewis's turn to say, 'Oh.'

'I can't really understand an intelligent man like you, Lewis, not taking a decent Sunday newspaper.'

'The sport's pretty good in the *Sunday Mirror*, sir.'

'Is it? You'd better bring it along with you in the morning, then.'

Lewis brightened. 'I won't forget.'

Morse thanked him and rang off. He had almost said he would swop it for his own copy of the *News of the World*, but considered it not improper to conceal from his subordinates certain aspects of his own depravity.

He could always get a back copy from the Reference Library. It could wait, he told himself. And yet it couldn't wait. Again he read the letter from the parents of the prodigal daughter. They would be extra-pleased now, with a letter in the newspaper, to boot. Dad would probably cut it out and keep it in his wallet – now that the family unit was functioning once more. We were all so vain. Cuttings, clippings and that sort of thing. Morse still kept his batting averages somewhere . . .

And suddenly it hit him. It all fitted. Four or five weeks ago Ainley had resurrected the Taylor case of his own accord and pursued it in his own spare time. Some reporter had been along to Thames Valley Police and got Ainley to spill the beans on the Taylor girl. Ainley had given him the facts (no fancies with Ainley!) and somehow, as a result of seeing the facts again, he had spotted something that he had missed before. It was just like doing a crossword puzzle. Get stuck. Leave it for ten minutes. Try again – and eureka! It happened to everyone like that. And, he repeated to himself, *Ainley had seen something new.* That must be it.

As a corollary to this, it occurred to Morse that if Ainley had taken a hand in the article, not only would Valerie Taylor have been one of the missing girls featured, but Ainley himself would almost certainly have kept the printed article – just as surely as Mr J. Richardson would be sticking his own printed letter into his Kidderminster wallet.

He rang Mrs Ainley. 'Eileen?' (Right this time.) 'Morse here. Look, do you happen to have kept that bit of the *Sunday Times* – you know, that bit about missing girls?'

'You mean the one they saw Richard about?' He *had* been right.

'That's the one.'

'Yes. I kept it, of course. It mentioned Richard several times.'

'Can I, er, can I come round and have a look at it?'

'You can have it with pleasure. I don't want it any more.'

Some half an hour later, forgetful of his earlier pledge, Morse was seated with a pint of flat beer and a soggy steak-and-mushroom pie. He read the article through with a feeling of anticlimax. Six girls were featured – after the preliminary sociological blurb about the problems of adolescence – with a couple of columns on each of them. But the central slant was on the parents the girls had left behind them. 'The light in the hall has been left on every night since she went,' as one of the anguished mothers was reported. It was pathetic and it was distressing. There were pictures, too. First, pictures of the girls, although (of necessity) none of the photographs was of a very recent vintage, and two or three (including that of Valerie herself) were of less than definitive clarity. And thus it was for the first time that Chief Inspector Morse looked down upon the face of Valerie Taylor. Of the six she would certainly be in the running for the beauty crown – though run close by a honey of a girl from Brighton. Attractive face, full mouth, come-hither eyes, nice eyebrows (plucked, thought Morse) and long dark-brown hair. Just the face – no figure to admire.

And then, over the page, the pictures of the parents. Mr and Mrs Taylor seemed an unremarkable pair, seated unnaturally forward on the shabby sofa: Mr wearing a cheap Woolworth tie, with his rolled-up sleeves revealing a large purple tattoo on his broad right forearm; Mrs wearing a plain cotton dress with a cameo brooch somewhat ostentatiously pinned to the collar. And on a low table beside them, carefully brought into the focus of the photograph, a cohort of congratulatory cards for their eighteenth wedding anniversary. It was predictable and posed, and Morse felt that a few tears might well have been nearer the truth.

He ordered another pint and sat down to read the commentary on Valerie's disappearance.

Two years ago, the month of June enjoyed a long, unbroken spell of sunny weather, and Tuesday 10 June was a particularly sweltering day at the village of Kidlington in the county of Oxfordshire. At 12.30 p.m. Valerie Taylor left the Roger Bacon Comprehensive School to walk to her home in Hatfield Way on the council estate nearby, no more than six or seven hundred yards from the school. Like many of her friends Valerie disliked school dinners and for the previous year had returned home each lunch-time. On the day of her daughter's disappearance Valerie's mother, Mrs Grace Taylor, had prepared a ham salad, with blackcurrant tart and custard for sweet, and together mother and daughter ate the meal at the kitchen table. Afternoon lessons began again at 1.45, and Valerie usually left the house at about 1.25. She did so on 10 June. Nothing seemed amiss that cloudless Tuesday afternoon. Valerie walked down the short front path, turned in the direction of the school, and waved a cheery farewell to her mother. She has never been seen again.

Mr George Taylor, an employee of the Oxford City Corporation, returned from work at 6.10 p.m. to find his wife in a state of considerable anxiety. It was quite unlike Valerie not to tell her mother if she was likely to be late, yet at that point there seemed little cause for immediate concern. The minutes ticked by; the quarters chimed on the Taylors' grandfather clock, and then the hours. At 8.00 p.m. Mr Taylor got into his car and drove to the school. Only the caretaker was still on the premises and he could be of no help. Mr Taylor then called at the homes of several of Valerie's friends, but they likewise could tell him nothing. None of them could remember seeing Valerie that afternoon, but it had been 'games' and it was nothing unusual for pupils to slip away quietly from the sports field.

When Mr Taylor returned home it was 9.00 p.m. 'There must be some simple explanation,' he told his wife; but if there was, it was not forthcoming, and the time pressed slowly on. 10.00 p.m. 11.00 p.m. Still nothing. George Taylor suggested they should notify the police, but his wife was terrified of taking such a step.

When I interviewed them this week both Mr and Mrs Taylor were reluctant (and understandably so) to talk about the agonies they suffered that night. Throughout the long vigil it was Grace Taylor who feared the worst and suffered the most, for her husband felt sure that Valerie had gone off with some boyfriend and would be back the next morning. At 4.00 a.m. he managed to persuade his wife to take two sleeping tablets and he took her upstairs to bed.

She was sleeping when he left the house at 7.30 a.m., leaving a note saying that he would be back at lunch-time, and that if Valerie still had not returned they would have to call the police. In fact the police were notified earlier than that. Mrs Taylor had awoken at about nine and, in a distraught state, had rung them from a neighbour's telephone.

Detective Chief Inspector Ainley of the Thames Valley Police was put in charge of the case, and intensive inquiries were immediately begun. During the course of the next week the whole of the area in the vicinity of Valerie's home and the area of woodland behind the school were searched with painstaking care and patience; the river and the reservoir were dragged ... But no trace was found of Valerie Taylor.

Inspector Ainley himself was frankly critical of the delay. At least twelve hours had been lost; fifteen, if the police had been notified as soon as the Taylors' anxiety had begun to deepen into genuine alarm.

Such delay is a common feature of the cases assembled here. Vital time lost; perhaps vital clues thrown to the wind – and all because parents think they will be wasting the time of the police and would seem to look foolish if the wayward offspring should suddenly turn up whilst the police were busy taking statements. It is a common human weakness, and it is only too easy to blame parents like the Taylors. But would we ourselves have acted all that differently? I knew exactly what Mrs Taylor meant when she said to me, 'I felt all the time that if we called the police something dreadful must have happened.' Illogical, you may say, but so very understandable.

Mr and Mrs Taylor still live on the council estate in Hatfield Way. For over two years now they have waited and prayed for their daughter to return. As in the five other cases discussed here, the police files remain open. 'No,' said Inspector Ainley, 'we shan't be closing them until we find her.'

Not bad reporting, thought Morse. There were several things in the article that puzzled him slightly, but he deliberately suppressed the fanciful notions that began to flood his mind. He had been right earlier. When Ainley had got the hard facts down on paper, he had spotted something that for over two years had lurked in the darkness and eluded his grasp. Some clue or other which had monopolized his attention and filled his spare time, and eventually, if indirectly, led to his death.

Just stick to the facts, Morse, stick to the facts! It would be difficult, but he would try. And tomorrow he and Lewis would start on the files wherein lay the facts as Ainley had gleaned them. Anyway, Christine was back in Kidderminster and, like as not, Valerie would be back in Kidlington before the end of the month. The naughty girls were all coming home and would soon be having the same sort of rows they'd had with mum and dad before they left. Life, alas, was like that.

Over his third pint of beer Morse could stem the flood of fancy no longer. He read the article through quickly once again. Yes, there was something wrong here. Only a small thing, but he wondered if it was the same small thing that had set Ainley on a new track . . . And the strangest notion began to formulate in the mind so recently dedicated to the pursuit of unembellished fact.

CHAPTER SIX

He certainly has a great deal of fancy, and a very good memory; but, with a perverse ingenuity, he employs these qualities as no other person does.

Richard Brinsley Sheridan

AS HE KNOCKED at the door of Morse's office Sergeant Lewis, who had thoroughly enjoyed the police routine of the previous week, wondered just what was in store for him now. He had worked with the unpredictable inspector before and got on fairly well with him; but he had his reservations.

Morse was seated in his black leather chair and before him on his untidy desk lay a green box-file.

'Ah. Come in, Lewis. I didn't want to start without you. Wouldn't be fair, would it?' He patted the box-file with a gesture of deep affection. 'It's all there, Lewis, my boy. All the facts. Ainley was a fact man – no day-dreaming theorist was Ainley. And we shall follow where the great man trod. What do you say?' And without giving his sergeant the slightest opportunity to say anything, he emptied the contents of the file face downwards upon the desk. 'Shall we start at the top or the bottom?'

'Might be a good idea to start at the beginning, don't you think, sir?'

'I think we could make out a good case for starting at either end – but we shall do as you say.' With some difficulty Morse turned the bulky sheaf of papers the right way up.

'What exactly are we going to do?' asked Lewis blankly.

Morse proceeded to recount his interview with Strange, and then passed across to Lewis the letter received from Valerie Taylor. 'And we're taking over, Lewis – you happy about that?' Lewis nodded half-heartedly. 'Did you remember the *Sunday Mirror*?'

Lewis dutifully took the paper from his coat pocket and handed it to Morse, who took out his wallet, found his football coupon and with high seriousness began to check his entry. Lewis watched him as his eyes alternately lit up and switched off, before the coupon was comprehensively shredded and hurled in the general direction of the waste-paper basket.

'I shan't be spending next week in the Bahamas, Lewis. What about you?'

'Nor me, sir.'

'Do you ever win anything?'

'Few quid last year, sir. But it's a million to one chance – getting a big win.'

'Like this bloody business,' mumbled Morse, distastefully surveying the fruits of Ainley's labours.

For the next two and a half hours they sat over the Taylor documents, occasionally conferring over an obscure or an interesting point – but for the most part in silence. It would have been clear to an independent witness of these proceedings that Morse read approximately five times as quickly as his sergeant; but whether he remembered five times as much of what he read would have been a much more questionable inference. For Morse found it difficult to concentrate his mind upon the documents before him. As he saw it, the facts, the bare unadulterated facts, boiled down to little more than he had read in the pub the previous day. The statements before him, checked and signed, appeared merely to confirm the bald, simple truth; after leaving home to return to school Valerie Taylor had completely vanished. If Morse wanted a fact, well, he'd got one. Parents, neighbours, teachers, classmates – all had been questioned at length. And amidst all their well-meaning verbosity they all had the same thing to say – nothing. Next, reports of Ainley's own interviews with Mr and Mrs Taylor, with the headmaster, with Valerie's form tutor, with her games mistress and with two of her boyfriends. (Ainley had clearly liked the headmaster, and equally clearly had disapproved of one of the boyfriends.) All nicely, neatly written in the small, rounded hand that Morse had already seen. But – nothing. Next, reports of general police inquiries and searches, and reports of the missing girl being spotted in Birmingham, Clacton, London, Reading, Southend, and a remote village in Moray. All wild-goose chases. All false alarms. Next, personal and medical reports on Valerie herself. She did not appear academically gifted in any way; or if she was, she had so far successfully concealed her scholastic potential from her teachers. School reports suggested a failure, except in practical subjects, to make the best of her limited abilities (familiar phrases!), but she seemed a personable enough young lady, well liked (Morse drew his own conclusions) by her fellow pupils of either sex. On the day of her disappearance she was attested by school records to be seventeen years and five months old, and five feet six inches in height. In her previous academic year she had taken four CSE subjects, without signal success, and she was at that time sitting three GCE O-level subjects – English, French and Applied Science. From the medical report it appeared that Valerie was quite remarkably healthy. There were no entries on her National Health medical card for the last three years, and before that only measles and a bad cut on the index finger of her left hand. Next, a report over which Ainley had obviously (and properly) taken considerable pains, on the possibility of any trouble on the domestic front which may have caused friction between Valerie and her parents, and led to her running away from home. On this most important point Ainley had gone to the trouble of writing out two sheets of foolscap in his own fair hand; but the conclusions were negative. On the evidence of Valerie's form tutor (among whose manifold duties something designated 'pastoral care' appeared a high priority), on the evidence of the parents themselves, of the neighbours and of Valerie's own friends, there seemed little reason to assume anything but the perfectly normal ups-and-downs in the relationship between the members of the Taylor clan. Rows, of course. Valerie had been home very late once or twice from dances and discos, and Mrs Taylor could use a sharp tongue. (Who couldn't?) Ainley's own conclusion was that he could find no immediate cause within the family circle to account for a minor squabble – let alone the inexplicable departure of an only daughter. In short – nothing. Morse thought of the old Latin proverb. *Ex nihilo nihil fit.* Out of nothing you'll get nothing. Not that it helped in any way.

Apart from the typed and handwritten documents, there were three maps: an ordnance-survey map of the Oxford district showing the areas covered by the search parties; a larger map of the Oxfordshire region on which the major road and rail routes were marked with cryptic symbols; and finally a sketch-map of the streets between the Roger Bacon School and the Taylors' house, with Valerie's route to and from her school carefully and neatly drawn in in red biro by the late chief inspector. Whilst Lewis was plodding along, several miles behind his master, the master himself appeared to be finding something of extraordinary interest in this last item: his right hand shaded his forehead and he seemed to Lewis in the throes of the deepest contemplation.

'Found something, sir?'

'Uh? What?' Morse's head jerked back and the idle daydream was over.

'The sketch-map, sir.'

'Ah, yes. The map. Very interesting. Yes.' He looked at it again, decided that he was unable to recapture whatever interest may have previously lain therein and picked up the *Sunday Mirror* once more. He read his horoscope: 'You're doing better than you realize, so there could be a major breakthrough as far as romance is concerned. This week will certainly blossom if you spend it with someone witty and bright.'

He looked glumly across at Lewis, who for the moment at least appeared neither very witty nor very bright.

'Well, Lewis. What do you think?'

'I've not quite finished yet, sir.'

'But you must have some ideas, surely.'

'Not yet.'

'Oh, come on. What do you think happened to her?'

Lewis thought hard, and finally gave expression to a conviction which had grown steadily stronger the more he had read. 'I think she got a lift and ended up in London. That's where they all end up.'

'You think she's still alive, then?'

Lewis looked at his chief in some surprise. 'Don't you?'

'Let's go for a drink,' said Morse.

They walked out of the Thames Valley HQ and at the Belisha crossing negotiated the busy main road that linked Oxford with Banbury.

'Where are we going, sir?'

Morse took Ainley's hand-drawn map from his pocket. 'I thought we ought to take a gentle stroll over the ground, Lewis. You never know.'

The council estate was situated off the main road, to their left as they walked away from Oxford, and very soon they stood in Hatfield Way.

'We going to call?'

'Got to make a start somewhere, I suppose,' said Morse.

The house was a neat, well-built property, with a circular rose-bed cut into the centre of the well-tended front lawn. Morse rang the bell, and rang again. It seemed that Mrs Taylor was out. Inquisitively Morse peered through the front window, but could see little more than a large, red settee and a diagonal line of ducks winging their inevitable way towards the ceiling. The two men walked away, carefully closing the gate behind them.

'If I remember rightly, Lewis, there's a pub just around the corner.'

They ordered a cheese cob and a pint apiece and Morse handed to Lewis the Colour Supplement of 24 August.

'Have a quick look at that.'

Ten minutes later, with Morse's glass empty and Lewis's barely touched, it was clear that the quick look was becoming a rather long look, and Morse replenished his own glass with some impatience.

'Well? What's troubling you?'

'They haven't got it quite right, though, have they?'

Morse looked at him sharply. 'What's that supposed to mean?'

'Well. It says here that she was never seen again after leaving the house.'

'She wasn't.'

'What about the lollipop man?'

'The *what?*'

'The lollipop man. It was in the file.'

'Oh, was it?'

'You did seem a bit tired, I thought, sir.'

'Tired? Nonsense. You need another pint.' He drained what was left in his own glass, picked up Lewis's and walked across to the bar.

An elegantly dressed woman with a full figure and pleasingly slim legs had just bought a double whisky and was pouring a modicum of water into it, the heavy diamond rings on the fingers of her left hand sparkling wickedly and bright.

'Oh, and Bert, twenty Embassy, please.' The landlord reached behind him, handed over the cigarettes, squinted his eyes as he calculated the tariff, gave her the change, said 'Ta, luv,' and turned his attention to Morse.

'Same again, sir?'

As the woman turned from the counter, Morse felt sure he had seen her somewhere before. He seldom forgot a face. Still, if she lived in Kidlington, he could have seen her anywhere. But he kept looking at her; so much so that Lewis began to suspect the inspector's intentions. She was all right – quite nice, in fact. Mid-thirties, perhaps, nice face. But the old boy must be hard up if . . .

Two dusty-looking builders came in, bought their ale and sat down to play dominoes. As they walked to the table one of them called over to the woman: 'Hallo, Grace. All right?' Morse showed little surprise. Hell of a sight better-looking than her photograph suggested, though.

*

At 1.20 Morse decided it was time to go. They walked back the way they had come, past the Taylors' house and down to the main road, busy at this time with a virtually continuous stream of traffic either way. Here they turned right and came up to the Belisha crossing.

'Do you think that's our lollipop man?' asked Morse. In the middle of the road stood a white-coated attendant in a peak cap, wielding the sceptre of his authority like an arthritic bishop with a crook. Several pupils of the Roger Bacon School were crossing under the aegis of the standard-bearer, the girls in white blouses, grey skirts and red knee-length socks, the boys (it seemed to Morse) in assorted combinations of any old garments. When the attendant returned from mid-stream, Morse spoke to him in what he liked to think of as his intimate, avuncular manner.

'Been doing this long?'

'Just over a year.' He was a small, red-faced man with gnarled hands.

'Know the chap who did it before?'

'You mean old Joe. 'Course I did. 'E did it for – oh, five or six year.'

'Retired now, has he?'

'Ah. S'pose you could say so. Poor old Joe. Got knocked ovver – feller on a motorbike. Mind you, old Joe were gettin' a bit slow. Seventy-two he were when he were knocked ovver. Broke 'is 'ip. Poor old Joe.'

'Not still in hospital, I hope?' Morse fervently prayed that poor old Joe was still limping along somewhere in the land of the living.

'No. Not 'im. Down at the old folkses place at Cowley.'

'Well, you be careful,' said Morse, as he and Lewis crossed over with another group of schoolchildren, and stood and watched them as they dawdled past the line of shops and the public lavatories, and reluctantly turned into the main drive leading to the school.

Back in the office Morse read aloud the relevant part of the testimony of Mr Joseph Godberry, Oxford Road, Kidlington:

> I almost always saw Valerie Taylor at dinner times, and I saw her on 10 June. She didn't cross by my Belisha because when I saw her she was on the other side of the road. She was running fairly quickly as if she was in a dickens of a hurry to meet somebody. But I remember she waved to me. I am quite sure it was Valerie. She would often stop and have a quick word with me. 'Joe' she called me, like most of them. She was a very nice girl and always cheery. I don't know what she did after I saw her. I thought she was going back to school.

Morse looked thoughtful. 'I wonder, now,' he said.

'Wonder what, sir?'

Morse was looking into the far distance, through the office window, and into the filmy blue beyond, excitement glowing in his eyes. 'I was just wondering if she

57

was carrying a bag of some sort when old Joe Godberry saw her.'

Lewis looked as mystified as he felt, but received no further elucidation. 'You see,' said Morse, his eyes gradually refocusing on his sergeant, 'you see, if she *was*, I'm beginning to think that you're wrong.'

'Wrong, sir?'

'Yes, wrong. You said you thought Valerie Taylor was still alive, didn't you?'

'Well, yes. I think she is.'

'And I think, *think*, mind you, that you're wrong, Lewis. I *think that Valerie Taylor is almost certainly dead.*'

CHAPTER SEVEN

And French she spak ful faire and fetisly,
After the scole of Stratford atte Bowe,
For French of Paris was to hir unknowe.
Geoffrey Chaucer, *Canterbury Tales*

DONALD PHILLIPSON ARRIVED in school at 8.00 on
Tuesday morning. The Michaelmas Term had been
under way for one full week now and things were going
well. The anti-litter campaign was proving moderately
successful, the new caretaker seemed an amenable sort
of fellow, and the Parent–Teacher Association had
(somewhat surprisingly, he thought) backed him up to
the hilt in his plea for a more rigid ruling on school
uniforms. On the academic side only four members of
staff had left in the summer (one quarter the previous
year's total), the GCE and CSE results had been mark-
edly better than before, and the present term saw the
first full intake of thirteen-plus pupils, among whom (if
junior-school headmasters could be believed) were
some real high-flyers. Perhaps in a few years' time there
would be one or two Open Awards at Oxbridge . . . Yes,
he felt more than a little pleased with himself and with
life this Tuesday morning. The only thing that marred
the immediate prospect was a cloud, rather larger than
a man's hand, on the not-so-distant horizon. But he felt

confident that he would be able to weather whatever storm might break from that quarter, although he must think things through rather more carefully than he had done hitherto.

At 8.20 the head boy and the head girl would be coming to his study, as they did each morning, and there were several matters requiring his prompt attention. He heard Mrs Webb come in at 8.15, and Baines at 8.30. Punctuality was sharper, too. He did a small amount of teaching with the sixth form (he was an historian), but he kept Tuesdays completely free. It had been his practice since he was appointed to take off Tuesday afternoons completely and he looked forward to a fairly gentle day.

The morning's activities went off well enough – even the singing of the hymns in assembly was improving – until 11.15 when Mrs Webb received the telephone call.

'Is the headmaster there?'

'Who shall I say is calling, please?'

'Morse. Inspector Morse.'

'Oh, just a minute, sir. I'll see if the headmaster's free.' She dialled the head's extension. 'Inspector Morse would like a word with you, sir. Shall I put him through?'

'Oh. Er. Yes, of course.'

Mrs Webb switched the outside call to the headmaster's study, hesitated a moment, and then quickly lifted the receiver to her ear again.

'. . . hear from you. Can I help?'

'I hope you can, sir. It's about the Taylor girl. There are one or two things I'd like to ask you about.'

'Look, Inspector. It's not really very convenient to talk at the minute – I'm interviewing some of the new pupils this morning. Don't you think it would be ...' Mrs Webb put the phone down quickly and quietly, and when Phillipson came out her typewriter was chattering along merrily. 'Mrs Webb, Inspector Morse will be coming in this afternoon at three o'clock, so I shall have to be here. Can you arrange some tea and biscuits for us?'

'Of course.' She made a note in her shorthand book. 'Just the two of you?'

'No. Three. He's bringing a sergeant along – I forget his name.'

The anonymous sergeant himself was spending the same morning at the old people's home in Cowley, and finding Mr Joseph Godberry (in small doses) an interesting sort of fellow. He had fought at Mons in the '14–'18 War, had slept, by his own account, with all the tarts within a ten mile radius of Rouen, and had been invalided out of the army in 1917 (probably from sexual fatigue, thought Lewis). He reminisced at considerable length as he sat by his bed in D ward, accepting his present confinement with a certain dignity and good humour. He explained that he could hardly walk now and recounted to Lewis in great detail the circumstances and consequences of his memorable accident.

In fact the 'accident', together with Mons and Rouen, had become one of the major incidents of his life and times; and it was with some difficulty that Lewis managed to steer Joe's thoughts to the disappearance of Valerie Taylor. Oh, he remembered her, of course. Very nice girl, Valerie. In London, bet your bottom dollar. Very nice girl, Valerie.

But could Joe remember the day she disappeared? Lewis listened carefully as he rambled on, repeating with surprising coherence and accuracy most of what he had said in his statement to the police. In Lewis's opinion, he was a good witness, but he was becoming tired and Lewis felt the moment had come to put the one question which Morse had been so eager for him to ask.

'Do you remember by any chance if Valerie was carrying anything when you saw her that day – the day she disappeared?'

Joe moved uneasily in his chair and slowly turned his rheumy old eyes on Lewis. Something seemed to be stirring there and Lewis pressed home the point.

'You know what I mean, a carrier bag, or a case, or anything like that?'

'Funny you should say that,' he said at last. 'I never thought about it afore.' He looked as though he were about to haul out some hazy memory on to the shores of light, and Lewis held his breath and waited. 'I reckon as you're right, you know. She were carryin' something. That's it. She were carryin' a bag of some sort; carryin' it in 'er left hand, if me memory serves me correck.'

*

In Phillipson's study formalities were exchanged in friendly fashion. Morse asked polite questions about the school – quite at his best, thought Lewis. But the mood was to change swiftly.

Morse informed the headmaster that he had taken over the Taylor case from Chief Inspector Ainley, and the cease-fire was duly observed for a further few minutes, whilst the proper commiserations were expressed. It was only when he produced the letter from Valerie that Morse's manner appeared to Lewis to become strangely abrasive.

Phillipson read through the letter quickly.

'Well?' said Morse.

Lewis felt that the headmaster was more surprised by the sharp tone in the inspector's voice than by the arrival of a letter from his troublesome, long-lost ex-pupil.

'Well what?' Phillipson clearly was not a man easily bullied.

'Is it her writing?'

'I can't tell. Don't her parents know?'

Morse ignored the question. 'You can't tell me.' The statement was flat and final, with the tacit implication that he had expected something better.

'No.'

'Have you got some of her old exercise books we could look at?'

'I don't really know, Inspector.'

'Who would know?' Again the astringent impatience in his voice.

'Perhaps Baines would.'

'Ask him in, please,' snapped Morse.

'I'm sorry, Inspector, but Baines has this afternoon off. Tuesday is games afternoon and . . .'

'I know, yes. So Baines can't help us either. Who can?'

Phillipson got up and opened the study door. 'Mrs Webb? Will you come in here a minute, please.'

Was Lewis mistaken, or did she throw a rather frightened glance in Morse's direction?

'Mrs Webb, the inspector here wonders if any of Valerie Taylor's old exercise books may have been kept somewhere in the school. What do you think?'

'They may be in the store-room, I suppose, sir.'

'Would it be the usual practice for pupils themselves to keep them?' Morse addressed himself directly to the secretary.

'Yes, it would. But in this case I should think her desk would have been turned out at the end of term and the books would be . . .' She was getting lost and looked helplessly towards the headmaster.

'I'm sure Mrs Webb is right, Inspector. If the books are anywhere, they will be in the store-room.'

Mrs Webb nodded, swallowed hard and was given leave to withdraw.

'We'd better have a look in the store-room, then. You've no objections?'

'Of course not. But it's in a bit of a mess, I should think. You know how things are at the beginning of term.'

Morse smiled weakly and neither confirmed nor refuted his knowledge of such matters.

They walked along the corridor, down some steps, and turned off right through a classroom, wherein all the chairs were neatly placed upon the tops of the desks. The school was virtually deserted, but intermittent shrieks of joyous laughter from the direction of the sports field seemed to belie the view that games were too unpopular with the majority of pupils.

The headmaster unlocked the door to the large unwindowed, unventilated store-room, and when the three men entered Lewis found himself facing with some foreboding the piles of dusty textbooks, files and stationery.

'I'm afraid it may be a longish job,' said Phillipson, with some irritation in his voice. 'If you like, I could get some of the staff to go through all the old exercise books here.' He pointed vaguely to great piles of books stacked on wooden shelves along the far wall.

'That's very kind of you, headmaster, but we can deal with this all right. No problem. If we can call back to your office when we've finished here?' It was an unmistakable hint that the presence of the headmaster would not profit the present stage of the investigation, and Morse listened carefully as Phillipson retraced his steps to his study. 'He's a bit worried, wouldn't you say, Lewis?'

'I don't blame him, sir. You've been pretty sharp with him.'

'Serve him right,' said Morse.

'What's he done wrong?'

'I spoke to him on the phone this morning and he said he was interviewing some new pupils.'

'Perhaps he was,' suggested the honest Lewis.

'I had the feeling he didn't want to talk just then, and I was right.' Lewis looked at him quizzically. 'I heard a click on the line while we were talking. You can guess who was listening in.'

'Mrs Webb?'

'Mrs Webb. I rang again later and asked her why she'd been eavesdropping. She denied it, of course; but I told her I'd forget all about it if she told me the truth about who had been in the headmaster's study. She was scared – for her job, I suppose. Anyway, she said that nobody had been in with Phillipson when I rang.'

Lewis opened his mouth to say something but Morse was already pouncing on the piles of textbooks.

'Ah, Keats. Fine poet, Keats. You should read him, Lewis ... Well, well, well. *Travels with a Donkey*.' He picked up a copy and began to read under the cobwebbed central light bulb.

Lewis made for the far wall of the room, where whole stacks of exercise books, used and unused, mauve, green, blue and orange, were heaped upon the shelves, some bundled neatly, but the majority in loose disarray. Lewis, as always, tackled his task with systematic thoroughness, although he doubted whether he would find anything. Fortunately, it was a good deal easier going than he had thought.

Half an hour later he found them. A pile of loose books, eight of them, each with the name Valerie Taylor inscribed in capitals on the front cover. He blew the dust off the edges and savoured his brief moment of triumph.

'I've found them, sir.'

'Well done. Leave them where they are – don't touch them.'

'I already have, I'm afraid, sir.'

'Was there any dust on the top book?'

The sweet taste of success had already turned sour. 'I don't know.'

'Give 'em here.' Morse was clearly very cross and muttered angrily under his breath.

'Pardon, sir?'

'I said I think someone else may well have been looking at these books recently. That's what I said!'

'I don't think the top book *was* dusty, sir. Just the edges.'

'And where's the dust on the edges?'

'I blew it off.'

'You blew it off! Christ, man. We've got a murder on our hands here, and we're supposed to be investigating it – not blowing all the bloody clues away!'

He gradually calmed down, and with a silent Lewis returned to Phillipson's study. It was now 4.30 and apart from the headmaster and Mrs Webb the school was empty.

'I see you found the books.'

Morse nodded curtly, and the three men sat down once more. 'Bit of luck, really,' continued Phillipson. 'It's a wonder they weren't thrown away.'

'Where *do* you throw old books away?' It seemed an odd question.

'Funnily enough they get buried – down on the rubbish dump. It's a difficult job burning a whole lot of books, you know.'

'Unless you've got a fiery furnace,' said Morse slowly.

'Well, yes. But even . . .'

'You've got a furnace here?'

'Yes, we have. But . . .'

'And that would burn just about anything, would it?'

'Yes. But as I was going . . .' Again Morse cut him short.

'Would it burn a body all right?' His words hung in the air, and Lewis shivered involuntarily. Phillipson's eyes were steady as he looked directly at Morse.

'Yes. It would burn a body, and it wouldn't leave much trace, either.'

Morse appeared to accept the remark without the slightest surprise or interest. 'Let's get back to these books a minute, sir, if we may. Are there any missing?'

Phillipson hadn't the remotest idea and breathed an inner sigh of relief as Baines (answering an earlier urgent summons) knocked on the study door, was ushered in and introduced.

It was immediately clear that the second master was a mine of information on all curricular queries, and within ten minutes Morse had copies of the information he required: Valerie's timetable for the summer term in which she disappeared, her homework schedule for the same period, and a list of her subject teachers. No books, it seemed, were missing. He made some complimentary remarks on Baines's efficiency, and the second master's shrewd eyes blinked with gratification.

After they had all gone Phillipson sat behind his desk and groaned inwardly. In the space of one short afternoon the cloud on the horizon had grown to menacing proportions. What a bloody fool he had been!

As a husband and a father, Sergeant Lewis experienced the delights and despondencies, the difficulties and the duties of family life, and with Morse's blessing returned home at 5.45 p.m.

At the same time Morse himself, with no such responsibilities, returned to his office at Police HQ. He was quite looking forward to his evening's work.

First he studied Valerie's timetable for each of her Tuesday mornings during that last summer term.

9.15–10.00	Environmental Studies
10.00–10.45	Applied Science
10.45–11.00	Break
11.00–11.45	Sociology
11.45–12.30	French

He contemplated with supercilious disdain the academic disciplines (sub-disciplines, he would call them) which were now monopolizing the secondary school curricula. 'Environmental Studies', he doubted, was little more than a euphemism for occasional visits to the gasworks, the fire-station and the sewage installations; whilst for Sociology and Sociologists he had nothing but sour contempt, and could never discover either what was entailed in its subject matter or how its practitioners deployed their dubious talents. With such a plethora of non-subjects crowding the timetable there was no room for the traditional disciplines taught in his own day ... But French now. At least that had a bit of backbone, although he had always felt that a language which sanctioned the pronunciation of *donne, donnes* and *donnent* without the slightest differentiation could hardly deserve to be taken seriously. Anyway, she was studying French and it was French which won the day. He consulted the homework schedule and found that French was set on Friday evenings and (he guessed) it might be collected in and marked on the following Monday. He checked to see that French appeared on Monday's timetable. It did. And then handed back to the pupils on the Tuesday, perhaps? That is, if the teacher had remembered to set the homework and if the teacher had been conscientious enough to mark it straightaway. Who was the teacher, anyway? He looked at the list. Mr D. Acum. Well, a little inspection of Mr Acum's discharge of duty was called for, and Morse flicked through the orange exercise book until he came to the last entry. He found the day, Friday, 6 June, carefully filled in and neatly underlined. He then turned his attention to Valerie's efforts, which had entailed the translation from English into French of ten short sentences. Judging, however, from the enormous quantity of red ink the despairing D. Acum had seen fit to squander upon her versions, judging from the treble underlinings, and the pathetic 'Oh dear' written beside one particularly heinous blunder, Valerie's linguistic prowess seemed extraordinarily limited. But Morse's eye was not on the exercise itself. He had spotted it as soon as he turned to the page. Beneath the exercise Acum had written: 'See me immediately after the lesson.' Morse felt a shiver of excitement. 'After the lesson.' 12.30 p.m. Acum must have been one of the very last people to have seen Valerie before she ... Before she what? He looked through his office window at the pale blue sky gradually edging into dusk – and he wondered. Had Ainley got on to Acum? Why had Acum wished to see Valerie Taylor that far-off Tuesday morning? The most likely answer, he supposed, was that Valerie would be ticked off good and proper for such disgusting work. But the simple fact remained: Acum had been one of the very last people to see Valerie alive.

Before leaving for home Morse looked once again at the short letter from Valerie and compared its handwriting with that of the exercise books. On the face of it, certainly, there seemed an undeniable similarity. But for a definitive opinion he would have to wait until the forensic experts had considered the specimens; and that would mean waiting until fairly late tomorrow evening, for he and Lewis had a trip to London in the morning. Would he believe them if their report stated categorically that the letter was written by Valerie Taylor? Yes. He would have no choice but to accept such a conclusion. But he thought he need have little worry on that score: for it was now his firm conviction that the letter had not been written by Valerie at all, but by someone who had carefully copied her writing – copied it rather *too* well, in fact. Further, Morse felt he knew who had copied it, although the reasons for the deception he could, at this stage, only dimly descry. Quite indubitably now, in his own mind, the case was one of wilful murder.

CHAPTER EIGHT

Gypsy Rose Lee, the strip-tease artist, has arrived in
Hollywood with twelve empty trunks.

> Harry P. Wade, American Columnist

DOUBTLESS IN ITS heyday a fine example of neo-
Georgian elegance, the sturdily and attractively built
house was now fallen on seedier times, the stuccoed
front dirty and chipped. Stuck to one of the stout pillars
which flanked the peeling front door was an outdated
poster announcing the arrival of Maharaj Ji, and on the
other, in black figures, the number 42.

The door was opened by a blowzy, middle-aged
woman, a cigarette drooping from her lips and a
headscarf half hiding the hair-curlers – like a caricature
of the screen charlady. She seemed to eye them
shrewdly, but it may have been nothing more than the
effect of avoiding the smoke from her cigarette.

'Police. It's Mrs er?'

'Gibbs. What can I do for yer?'

'Can we come in?'

She hesitated, then moved aside. The door was
closed and the two men stood awkwardly in the
entrance hall, where they saw neither seats nor chairs
of any description, only a grandfather clock showing
the correct time (10.30), an overloaded coat-rack, and

an umbrella stand incongruously housing a set of ancient golf clubs. It became clear that they were not to be invited into the cosiness of any inner sanctum.

'About three weeks ago, you had a call I think from one of my colleagues – Inspector Ainley.' She considered the statement guardedly, nodded, and said nothing. 'You may have read in the papers that after he left here he was killed in a road accident.'

Mrs Gibbs hadn't, and the lady's latent humanity stirred to the extent of a mumbled phrase of commiseration if not to the removal of the cigarette from her lips, and Morse knew that he would have to chance his arm a bit.

'He wrote, of course, a full report of his visit here and, er, I think you will have a good idea why we've called again today.'

'Nothing to do with me, is it?'

Morse seized his opportunity. 'Oh, no, Mrs Gibbs. Nothing at all. That was quite clear from the report. But naturally we need your help, if you'll be kind enough . . .'

''E's not 'ere. 'E's at work – if yer can call it work. Not that 'e'll be 'ere much longer, anyway. Caused me quite enough trouble 'e 'as.'

'Can we see his room?'

She hesitated. 'Yer got the authority?'

It was Morse's turn to hesitate, before suddenly producing an official-looking document from his breast pocket.

Mrs Gibbs fiddled in her apron pocket for her spectacles. 'That other policeman – 'e told me all about the legal position. Said as 'ow I shouldn't let anyone in 'ere as 'adn't got the proper authority.'

Trust Ainley, thought Morse. 'He was quite right of course.' Morse directed the now bespectacled lady's attention to an impressive-looking signature and beneath it, in printed capitals, CHIEF CONSTABLE (OXON). It was enough, and Morse quickly repocketed the cyclostyled letter about the retirement pensions of police officers at and above the rank of Chief Inspector.

They made their way up three flights of dusty stairs, where Mrs Gibbs produced a key from her multi-purpose apron pocket and opened a dingy, brown-painted door.

'I'll be downstairs when yer've finished.'

Morse contented himself with a mild 'phew' as the door closed, and the two men looked around them. 'So this was where Ainley came.' They stood in a bed-sitting room, containing a single (unmade) bed, the sheets dirty and creased, a threadbare settee, an armchair of more recent manufacture, a huge, ugly wardrobe, a black-and-white TV set and a small underpopulated bookcase. They passed through a door in the far wall, and found themselves in a small, squalid kitchen, with a greasy-looking gas cooker, a Formica-topped table and two kitchen stools.

'Hardly an opulent occupant?' suggested Morse. Lewis sniffed and sniffed again. 'Smell something?'

'Pot, I reckon, sir.'

'Really?' Morse beamed at his sergeant with delight, and Lewis felt pleased with himself.

'Think it's important, sir?'

'Doubt it,' said Morse. 'But let's have a closer look round. You stay here and sniff around – I'll take the other room.'

Morse walked straight to the bookcase. A copy of the *Goon Show Scripts* appeared to be the high-water mark of any civilized taste in the occupant's reading habits. For the rest there was little more than a stack of Dracula comics and half a dozen supremely pornographic magazines, imported from Denmark. The latter Morse decided to investigate forthwith, and seated in the armchair he was contentedly sampling their contents when Lewis called from the kitchen.

'I've found something, sir.'

'Shan't be a minute.' He thought guiltily of sticking one of the magazines in his pocket, but for once his police training got the better of him. And with the air of an Abraham prepared to sacrifice an Isaac upon the altar, he replaced the magazines in the bookcase and went through to his over-zealous sergeant.

'What about that, sir?' Morse nodded unenthusiastically at the unmistakable paraphernalia of the pot-smoker's paradise. 'Shall we pack this little lot up, sir?'

Morse thought for a while. 'No, we'll leave it, I think.' Lewis's eagerness wilted, but he knew better than to argue. 'All we need to find out now is who he is, Lewis.'

'I've got that, too, sir.' He handed the inspector an unopened letter from Granada TV Rental Service addressed to Mr J. Maguire.

Morse's eyes lit up. 'Well, well. We might have known it. One of the boyfriends, if I remember rightly. Well done, Lewis! You've done a good job.'

'You find anything, sir?'

'Me? Oh, no. Nothing, really.'

Mrs Gibbs, who was waiting for them as they reached the bottom of the stairs, expressed the hope that the visit was now satisfactorily terminated, and Morse said he hoped so, too.

'As I told yer, 'e won't be 'ere much longer, the trouble 'e's caused me.'

Sensing that she was becoming fractionally more communicative Morse kept the exchanges going. He had to, anyway.

'Great pity, you know, that Inspector Ainley was killed. You'd have finished with this business by now. It must be a bit of a nuisance . . .'

'Yes. He said as 'ow 'e 'oped he needn't come bothering me again.'

'Was, er, Mr Maguire here when he called?'

'No. 'E called about the same time as you gentlemen. 'Im' (pointing aloft) ' – 'e were off to work. Well, some people'd call it work, I s'pose.'

'Where does he work now?' Morse asked the question lightly enough, but the guarded look came back to her eyes.

'Same place.'

'I see. Well, we shall have to have a word with him, of course. What's the best way to get there from here?'

'Tube from Putney Bridge to Piccadilly Circus – least, that's the way 'e goes.'

'Could we park the car there?'

'In Brewer Street? Yer must be joking!'

Morse turned to Lewis. 'We'd better do as Mrs Gibbs says, sergeant, and get the tube.'

On the steps outside Morse thanked the good lady profusely and, almost as an afterthought it seemed, turned to speak to her once more.

'Just one more thing, Mrs Gibbs. It may be lunchtime before we get up there. Have you any idea where Mr Maguire will be if he's not at work?'

'Like as not the Angel – I know 'e often 'as a drink in there.'

As they walked to the car Lewis decided to get it off his chest. 'Couldn't you just have asked her straight out where he worked?'

'I didn't want her to think I was fishing,' replied Morse. Lewis thought she must be educationally subnormal if she hadn't realized that by now. But he let it go. They drove down to Putney Bridge, parked the car on a TAXIS ONLY plot, and caught the tube to Piccadilly Circus.

Somewhat to Lewis's surprise, Morse appeared to be fairly intimately conversant with the geography of Soho, and two minutes after emerging from the tube in Shaftesbury Avenue they found themselves standing in Brewer Street.

'There we are then,' said Morse, pointing to the Angel, Bass House, only thirty yards away to their left. 'Might as well combine business with a little pleasure, don't you think?'

'As you wish, sir.'

Over the beer, Morse asked the barman if the

manager was around, and learned that the barman was the manager. Morse introduced himself, and said he was looking for a Mr J. Maguire.

'Not in any trouble, is he?' asked the barman.

'Nothing serious.'

'Johnny Maguire, you say. He works over the way at the strip club – the Penthouse. On the door, mostly.'

Morse thanked him, and he and Lewis walked over to the window and looked outside. The Penthouse was almost directly opposite.

'Ever been to a strip club, Lewis?'

'No. But I've read about 'em, of course.'

'Nothing like first-hand experience, you know. C'mon, drink up.'

Outside the club Morse surveyed the pictorial preview of the erotic delights to be savoured within. 18 GORGEOUS GIRLS. The sexiest show in London. 95p only. NO OTHER ADMISSION CHARGE.

'The real thing this is, gentlemen. Continuous performance. No G-strings.' The speaker was a ginger-haired youth, dressed in a dark green blazer and grey slacks, who sat in a small booth at the entrance lobby.

'Bit expensive, isn't it?' asked Morse.

'When you've seen the show, sir, you'll think it's cheap at the price.'

Morse looked at him carefully, and thought there was something approaching honesty in the dark eyes. Maguire – almost certainly; but he wouldn't run away. Morse handed over two pound-notes and took the tickets. To the young tout the policemen were just another couple of frustrated middle-aged voyeurs, and he had already spotted another potential customer studying the stills outside.

'The real thing this is, sir. Continuous performance. No G-strings.'

'You owe me 10p,' said Morse.

They walked through a gloomy passage-way and heard the music blaring from behind a screened partition, where sat a smallish, swarthy gentleman (Maltese, thought Morse) with a huge chest and bulging forearms.

He took the tickets and tore them across. 'Can I see membership cards, please?'

'What membership cards?'

'You must be members of the club, sir.' He reached for a small pad, and tore off two forms. 'Fill in, please.'

'Just a minute,' protested Morse. 'It says outside that there's no other admission charge and . . .'

'One pown each, please.'

'. . . We've paid our 95p and that's all we're paying.'

The small man looked mean and dangerous. He rose to his meagre height and moved a thick arm to Morse's jacket. 'Fill in, please. That will be one pown each.'

'Will it buggery!' said Morse.

The Maltese advanced slightly and his hands glided towards Morse's wallet-pocket.

Neither Morse nor Lewis were big men, and the last thing that Morse wanted at this juncture was a rough-house. He wasn't in very good condition anyway . . . But he knew the type well. Courage, Morse! He brushed the man's hand forcibly from his jacket and stepped a menacing pace forward.

'Look, you miserable wog. You want a fight? That's fine. I wouldn't want to bruise my fist against your ugly chops, myself, but this pal of mine here will do it with the greatest pleasure. Just up his street. Army middle-weight champion till a year ago. Where shall we go, you dirty little squit?'

The little man sat back and sagged in his chair like a wilting balloon, and his voice was a punctured whine.

'You got to be members of the club. If you not I get prosecuted by police.'

'F—— off,' said Morse, and with the ex-boxing champion behind him walked through the screen partition.

In the small auditorium beyond sat a sprinkling of males, dotted around on the three rows of seats facing the small, raised stage, on which a buxom blonde stripper had just, climactically, removed her G-string. At least one of the management's promises had been honoured. The curtains closed and there was a polite smatter of half-hearted applause.

'How did you know I was a boxing champion?' whispered Lewis.

'I didn't,' said Morse, with genuine surprise.

'You might get it right, though, sir. *Light* middle-weight.'

Morse grinned happily, and a disembodied voice from the wings announced the advent of The Fabulous Fiona. The curtains opened jerkily to reveal a fully-clothed Fiona; but it was immediately apparent that her

fabulous body, whatever delights were soon to be un-
veiled, was signally bereft of any rhythmic suppleness as
she struggled amateurishly to synchronize a few elementary dance steps with the languorously suggestive music.

After The Sexy Susan and The Sensational Sandra
even Morse was feeling a trifle blasé; but, as he
explained to an unenthusiastic Lewis, there might be
better things to come. And indeed The Voluptuous
Vera and The Kinky Kate certainly did something to
raise the general standard of the entertainment. There
were gimmicks aplenty: fans, whips, bananas and
rubber spiders; and Morse dug Lewis in the ribs as an
extraordinarily shapely girl, dressed for a fancy-dress
ball, titillatingly and tantalizingly divested herself of all
but an incongruously ugly mask.

'Bit of class there, Lewis.'

But Lewis remained unimpressed; and when the
turn came round for the reappearance of The Fabulous
Fiona Morse reluctantly decided they had better go.
The little gorilla was fleecing a thin, spotty-faced young
man of his one pown membership fee as they walked
out of the club into the dazzling sunshine of the
London street. After a few breaths of comparatively
clean air, Morse returned to the entrance and stood by
the young man.

'What's your name, lad?'

'William Shakespeare. What's yours?' He looked at
Morse with considerable surprise. Who the hell did he
think he was? It was over two years ago since anyone
had spoken to him in that tone of voice. At school, in
Kidlington.

'Can we go and talk somewhere?'

'What *is* this?'

'John Maguire, if I'm not mistaken? I want to talk to you about Miss Valerie Taylor – I think you may have heard of her. Now we can do it quietly and sensibly, or you can come along with me and the sergeant here to the nearest police station. Up to you.'

Maguire was obviously worried. 'Look. Not here, please. I've got half an hour off at four o'clock. I'll meet you then. I'll be in there.' He pointed anxiously to a sleazy-looking snack bar across the road next to the Angel.

Morse pondered what to do.

'Please,' urged Maguire. 'I'll be there. Honest, I will.'

It was a difficult decision, but Morse finally agreed. He thought it would be foolish to antagonize Maguire before he'd even started on him.

Morse gave quick instructions to Lewis as they walked away. He was to take a taxi back to Southampton Terrace and wait until Morse returned. If Maguire did decide to scuttle (it seemed unlikely, though) he would almost certainly go back there for some of his things.

At the end of the street Lewis found a cab almost immediately, and Morse guiltily strolled back to the Penthouse.

'You'd better give me another ticket,' demanded Morse brusquely. He walked once more down the murkily-lit passage, gave his ticket to a surprised and silent dwarf, and without further trouble re-entered the auditorium. He recognized The Voluptuous Vera without difficulty and decided that it would be no more than a minimal hardship thus to while away the next hour and a half. He just hoped the masked young lady was still on the bill . . .

At 4.00 p.m. they sat opposite each other in the snack bar.

'You knew Valerie Taylor then?'

'I was at school with her.'

'Her boyfriend, weren't you?'

'One of 'em.'

'Like that, was it?' Maguire was non-committal. 'Why did Inspector Ainley come to see you?'

'You know why.'

'Did you know he was killed in a road accident the day he saw you?'

'No, I didn't.'

'I asked you why he came to see you.'

'Same reason as you, I suppose.'

'He asked you about Valerie?'

Maguire nodded, and Morse had the feeling that the boy was suddenly feeling more relaxed. Had Morse missed the turning?

'What did you tell him?'

'What could I tell him? Nothing more to tell, is there? They got me to write out a statement when I was at school, and I told them the truth. Couldn't do much more than that, could I?'

'You told the truth?'

'Course, I did. I couldn't have had anything to do with it. I was in school all day, remember?'

Morse did remember, although he cursed himself for not bringing the boy's statement with him. Maguire had stayed at school for dinner and had been playing cricket the whole afternoon. At the time he must have seemed a peripheral figure in the investigation. Still was, perhaps. But why, then, *why* had Ainley come to London just to see him again – after all that time? There must have been *something*, something big. Morse finished the last dregs of his cold coffee and felt a bit lost. His devious manoeuvrings of the day began to look unnecessarily theatrical. Why couldn't he be a straight policeman for once in his life? Still, he had a couple of trump cards, and one never knew. He prepared to play the first.

'I'll give you one more chance, Maguire, but this time I want the truth – all of it.'

'I've told you . . .'

'Let's get one thing straight,' said Morse. 'I'm interested in Valerie Taylor – that's all. I'm not worried about any of those other things . . .' He left the words in the air, and a flash of alarm glinted in the boy's eyes.

'What other things? I don't know what you're talking about.'

'We've been to your flat today, lad.'

'So?'

'Mrs Gibbs doesn't seem too happy, does she, about one or two things . . .?'

'Old cow.'

'She didn't have to *tell* us anything, you know.'

'What am I supposed to have done? Come on – lèt's have it.'

'How long have you been on drugs, lad?'

It hit him solidly between the eyes, and his effort at recovery was short of convincing. 'What drugs?'

'I just told you, lad. We've been to your flat today.'

'And I suppose you found some pot. So what? Just about everybody smokes pot here.'

'I'm not talking about everybody.' Morse leaned forward and let him have it. 'I'm talking about you, lad. Smoking pot's illegal, you know that, and I could frogmarch you out of here and ship you to the nearest police station – remember that! But I've just told you, lad, I'm quite prepared to let it ride. Christ, why do you have to make it so hard for yourself? You can go back to your bloody flat and pump yourself with heroin for all I care. I'm just not bothered, lad – not if you co-operate with me. Can't you get that into your thick skull?'

Morse let it sink in a minute before continuing. 'I want to know just one thing – what you told Inspector Ainley, that's all. And if I can't get it out of you here, I'll take you in and I'll get it out of you somewhere else. Please yourself, lad.'

Morse picked up his overcoat from the seat beside him and draped it across his knees. Maguire stared dejectedly at the table-top and played nervously with a bottle of tomato ketchup. There was indecision in his eyes, and Morse timed what he hoped was his second trump card perfectly.

'How long had you known that Valerie was pregnant?' he asked quietly.

Bull's-eye. Morse replaced his coat on the seat beside

him, and Maguire spoke more freely. 'About three weeks before.'

'Did she tell anyone else?'

Maguire shrugged his shoulders. 'She was a real sexy kid – everyone was after her.'

'How often did you go to bed with her?'

'Ten – dozen times, I suppose.'

'The truth, please, lad.'

'Well, three or four times, maybe. I don't know.'

'Where was this?'

'My place.'

'Your parents know?'

'No. They were out working.'

'And she said you were the father?'

'No. She wasn't like that. Said I could have been, of course.'

'Did you feel jealous?' Morse had a suspicion that he did, but Maguire made no answer. 'Was she very upset?'

'Just scared.'

'What of? Scandal?'

'More scared of her mum, I think.'

'Not her dad?'

'She didn't say so.'

'Did she talk about running away?'

'Not to me.'

'Who else might she have spoken to?' Maguire hesitated. 'She had another boyfriend, didn't she,' persisted Morse, 'apart from you?'

'Pete?' Maguire could relax again. 'He didn't even touch her.'

'But she might have spoken to him?' Maguire was

amused, and Morse felt that his questioning had lost its impetus. 'What about her form tutor? She might have gone to her, perhaps?'

Maguire laughed openly. 'You don't understand.'

But suddenly Morse realized that he was beginning to understand, and as the dawn was slowly breaking in his mind, he leaned forward and fixed Maguire with grey eyes, hard and unblinking.

'She could have gone to the headmaster, though.' He spoke the words with quiet, taut emphasis, and the impact upon Maguire was dramatic. Morse saw the sudden flash of burning jealousy and knew that gradually, inch by inch, he was moving nearer to the truth about Valerie Taylor.

Morse took a taxi to Southampton Terrace where he found a patient Lewis awaiting him. The car was ready and they were soon heading out along the M40 towards Oxford. Morse's mind was simultaneously veering in every direction, and he lapsed into uncommunicative introversion. It wasn't until they left the three-lane motorway that he broke the long silence.

'Sorry you had such a long wait, Lewis.'

'That's all right, sir. You had a long wait, too.'

'Yes,' said Morse. He made no mention of his return to the Penthouse. He must have gone down a good deal already in his sergeant's estimation; he had certainly sunk quite low enough in his own.

It was five miles outside Oxford that Lewis exploded the minor bombshell.

'I was having a talk with Mrs Gibbs, sir, while you were with Mr Maguire.'

'Well?'

'I asked her why he'd been such a nuisance.'

'What did she say?'

'She told me that until recently he'd had a girl in the flat.'

'She *what?*'

'Yes, sir. Almost a month, she said.'

'But why the hell didn't you tell me before, man? You surely realize . . .?' He glared at Lewis, incredulous and exasperated, and sank back in despair behind his safety belt.

His stubborn conviction that Valerie was no longer alive would (one had thought) have been sorely tested when he looked back into his office at 8.00 p.m. Awaiting him was a report from the forensic laboratory, short and to the point.

'Sufficient similarities to warrant positive identification. Suggest that investigation proceed on firm assumption that letter was written by signatory, Miss Valerie Taylor. Please contact if detailed verification required.'

But Morse seemed far from impressed. In fact, he looked up from the report and smiled serenely. Reaching for the telephone directory, he looked up Phillipson, D. There was only one Phillipson: 'The Firs', Banbury Road, Oxford.

CHAPTER NINE

We hear, for instance, of a comprehensive school in Connecticut where teachers have three pads of coloured paper, pink, blue and green, which are handed out to pupils as authority to visit respectively the headmaster, the office or the lavatory.

Robin Davis, *The Grammar School*

SHEILA PHILLIPSON WAS absolutely delighted with her Oxford home, a four-bedroomed detached house, just below the Banbury Road roundabout. Three fully grown fir trees screened the spacious front garden from the busy main road, and the back garden, with its two old apple trees and its goldfish pond, its beautifully conditioned lawn and its neatly tended borders, was an unfailing joy. With unimaginative predictability she had christened it 'The Firs'.

Donald would be late home from school; he had a staff meeting. But it was only a cold salad, and the children had already eaten. She could relax. At a quarter to six she was sitting in a deck-chair in the back garden, her eyes closed contentedly. The evening air was warm and still . . . She felt so proud of Donald; and of the children, Andrew and Alison, now contentedly watching the television. They were both doing so well at their primary school. And, of course, if they didn't really get the chances they deserved, they could always go to private schools; and Donald would probably send them there – in spite of what he'd told the parents at the last speech day. The Dragon, New College School, Oxford High, Headington – one heard such good reports. But that was all in the future. For the moment everything in the garden was lovely. She lifted her face to catch the last rays of the sloping sun and breathed in the scent of thyme and honeysuckle. Lovely. Almost too lovely, perhaps. At half-past six she heard the crunch of Donald's Rover on the drive.

Later in the evening Sheila did not recognize the man at the door, a slimly built man with a clean, sensitive mouth and wide light-grey eyes. He had a nice voice, she thought, for a police inspector.

In spite of Morse's protests that Tom and Jerry ranked as his very favourite TV programme, the children were immediately sent upstairs to bed. She was cross with herself for not having packed them off half an hour ago: toys littered the floor, and she fussily and apologetically gathered together the offending objects and took them out. On her return she found her visitor gazing with deep interest at a framed photograph of herself and her husband.

'Press photograph, isn't it?'

'Yes. We had a big party in Donald's, er, in my husband's first term here. All the staff, husbands and wives – you know the sort of thing. The *Oxford Mail* took that. Took a lot of photographs, in fact.'

'Have you got the other photographs?'

'Yes. I think so. Would you like to look at them? My husband won't be long. He's just finishing his bath.'

She rummaged about in a drawer of the bureau, and handed to Morse five glossy, black-and-white photographs. One of them, a group photograph, held his keen attention: the men in dinner jackets and black bow ties, the ladies in long dresses. Most of them looked happy enough.

'Do you know some of the staff?' she asked.

'Some of them.'

He looked again at the group. 'Beautifully clear photograph.'

'Very good, isn't it?'

'Is Acum here?'

'Acum? Oh yes, I think so. Mr Acum left two years ago. But I remember him quite well – and his wife.' She pointed them out on the photograph; a young man with a lively, intelligent face and a small goatee beard; and, her arm linked through his, a slim, boyish-figured girl, with shoulder-length blonde hair, not unattractive perhaps, but with a face (at least on this evidence) a little severe and more than a little spotty.

'You knew his wife, you say?' asked Morse.

Sheila heard the gurgling death-rattle of the bath upstairs, and for some inexplicable reason felt a cold shudder creeping along her spine. She felt just as she did as a young girl when she had once answered the phone for her father. She recalled the strange, almost frightening questions . . .

A shiningly-fresh Phillipson came in. He apologized

for keeping Morse waiting, and in turn Morse apologized for his own unheralded intrusion. Sheila breathed an inward sigh of relief, and asked if they'd prefer tea or coffee. With livelier brews apparently out of the question, Morse opted for coffee and, like a good host, the headmaster concurred.

'I've come to ask about Acum,' said Morse, with brisk honesty. 'What can you tell me about him?'

'Acum? Not much really. He left at the end of my first year here. Taught French. Well-qualified chap. Exeter – took a second if I remember rightly.'

'What about his wife?'

'She had a degree in Modern Languages, too. They met at Exeter University, I think. In fact she taught with us for a term when one of the staff was ill. Not too successfully, I'm afraid.'

'Why was that?'

'Bit of a tough class – you know how it is. She wasn't really up to it.'

'They gave her a rough ride, you mean?'

'They nearly took her pants down, I'm afraid.'

'You're speaking metaphorically, I hope?'

'I hope so, too. I heard some hair-raising rumours, though. Still, it was my fault for taking her on. Too much of a blue-stocking for that sort of job.'

'What did you do?'

Phillipson shrugged. 'I had to get rid of her.'

'What about Acum himself? Where did he go?'

'One of the schools in Caernarfon.'

'He got promotion, did he?'

'Well no, not really. He'd only been teaching the

one year, but they could promise him some sixth-form work. I couldn't.'

'Is he still there?'

'As far as I know.'

'He taught Valerie Taylor – you know that?'

'Inspector, wouldn't it be fairer if you told me why you're so interested in him? I might be able to help more if I knew what you were getting at.'

Morse pondered the question. 'Trouble is, I don't really know myself.'

Whether he believed him or not, Phillipson left it at that. 'Well, I know he taught Valerie, yes. Not one of his brightest pupils, I don't think.'

'Did he ever talk to you about her?'

'No. Never.'

'No rumours? No gossip?'

Phillipson took a deep breath, but managed to control his mounting irritation. 'No.'

Morse changed his tack. 'Have you got a good memory, sir?'

'Good enough, I suppose.'

'Good enough to remember what you were doing on Tuesday 2nd September this year?'

Phillipson cheated and consulted his diary. 'I was at a headmasters' conference in London.'

'Whereabouts in London?'

'It was at the Café Royal. And if you must know the conference started at . . .'

'All right. All right.' Morse held up his right hand like a priest pronouncing the benediction, as a flush of anger rose in the headmaster's cheeks.

'Why did you ask me that?'

Morse smiled benignly. 'That was the day Valerie wrote to her parents.'

'What the hell are you getting at, Inspector?'

'I shall be asking a lot of people the same question before I've finished, sir. And some of them will get terribly cross, I know that. But I'd rather hoped that you would understand.'

Phillipson calmed down. 'Yes, I see. You mean . . .'

'I don't mean anything, sir. All I know is that I have to ask a lot of awkward questions; it's what they pay me for. I suppose it's the same in your job.'

'I'm sorry. Go ahead and ask what you like. I shan't mind.'

'I shouldn't be too sure of that, sir.' Phillipson looked at him sharply. 'You see,' continued Morse, 'I want you to tell me, if you can, exactly what you were doing on the afternoon that Valerie Taylor disappeared.'

Mrs Phillipson brought in the coffee, and after she had retired once more to the kitchen the answer was neatly wrapped and tied.

'I had lunch at school that day, drove down into Oxford, and browsed around in Blackwells. Then I came home.'

'Do you remember what time you got home?'

'About three.'

'You seem to remember that afternoon pretty well, sir?'

'It *was* rather an important afternoon, wasn't it, Inspector?'

'Did you buy any books?'

'I don't remember that much, I'm afraid.'

'Do you have an account with Blackwells?'

Momentarily Phillipson hesitated. 'Yes. But . . . but if I'd just bought a paperback or something I would have paid in cash.'

'But you might have bought something more expensive?' Morse looked along the impressive rows of historical works that covered two walls of the lounge from floor to ceiling, and thought of Johnny Maguire's pathetic little collection.

'You could check up, I suppose,' said Phillipson curtly.

'Yes. I suppose we shall.' Morse felt suddenly very tired.

At half-past midnight Sheila Phillipson tiptoed quietly down the stairs and found the codeine bottle. It kept coming back to her mind and she couldn't seem to push it away from her – that terrible night when Donald had been making love to her, and called her Valerie. She'd never mentioned it, of course. She just couldn't.

Suddenly she jumped, a look of blind terror in her eyes, before subsiding with relief upon a kitchen stool.

'Oh, it's only you, Donald. You frightened me.'

'Couldn't you sleep either, darling?'

CHAPTER TEN

> Not a line of her writing have
> I,
> Not a thread of her hair.
>   Thomas Hardy, *Thoughts of Phena*

MORSE SEEMED RELUCTANT to begin any work when he arrived, late, in his office on Thursday morning. He handed Lewis the report on Valerie's letter and started on *The Times* crossword puzzle. He looked at his watch, marked the time exactly in the margin of the newspaper and was soon scribbling in letters at full speed. Ten minutes later he stopped. He allowed himself only ten minutes, and almost always completed it. But this morning one clue remained unsolved.

'What's this, Lewis? Six letters. Blank A – Blank S – Blank N. *Eyes had I – and saw not?*'

Lewis jotted down the letters and pretended to think. He just hadn't a crossword mind. 'Could it be "parson", sir?'

'Why on earth should it be "parson"?'

'Well, it fits.'

'So do a hundred and one other words.'

'Such as?' Morse struggled hard before producing 'damson'. 'I'd rather have my parson, sir.'

Morse put the paper aside. 'Well. What do you think?'

'Seems to be her writing, doesn't it?'

There was a knock on the door and a pretty young office girl deposited the morning post into the in-tray. Cursorily and distastefully Morse looked through the correspondence.

'Nothing urgent here, Lewis. Let's go along to the lab. I think Old Peters must be getting senile.'

Now in his early sixties, Peters had previously worked for twenty years as a Home Office pathologist, and somewhere along the line the juices of human fallibility had been squeezed from his cerebral processes. His manner was clinical and dry, and his words seemed to be dictated by a minicomputer installed somewhere inside his brain. His answers were slow, mechanical, definitive. He had never been known to argue with anyone. He just read the information-tapes.

'You think this is Valerie Taylor's writing, then?'

He paused and answered. 'Yes.'

'Can you ever be certain about things like hand-writing, though?'

He paused and answered. 'No.'

'How certain are you?'

He paused and answered. 'Ninety per cent.'

'You'd be surprised then if it turned out that she didn't write it?'

He paused and the computer considered its reaction to the improbability. 'Yes. Surprised.'

'What makes you think she wrote it?'

He paused and lectured briefly and quietly on the evidence of loops and quirks and whorls. Morse battled on against the odds. 'You can forge a letter, though, can't you?'

He paused and answered. 'Of course.'

'But you don't think this was forged?'

He paused and answered. 'I think it was written by the girl.'

'But a person's handwriting changes over the years, doesn't it? I mean the letter's written in almost exactly the same way as the exercise books.'

He paused and answered. 'There's a basic built-in style about all our handwriting. Slopes change, certainly, and other minor things. But whatever changes, there is still the distinctive style, carrying with it the essential features of our personal characteristics.' He paused again, and Lewis had the impression he was reading it all out of a book. 'In Greek, the word "character" means handwriting, they tell me.'

Lewis smiled. He was enjoying himself.

Morse put a penultimate problem to the computer. 'You wouldn't go into the witness box and say it definitely *was* her writing, would you?'

He paused and answered. 'I would tell a jury what I've told you – that the order of probability is somewhere in the region of ninety per cent.'

Morse turned as he reached the door. 'Could *you* forge her handwriting convincingly?'

The desiccated calculating-machine actually smiled and the hesitation this time was minimal. 'I've had a lot of experience in this field, you know.'

'You *could* then?'

He paused and answered. '*I* could, yes.'

Back in his office Morse brought Lewis up to date with his visit the previous evening to the Phillipson residence.

'You don't like him much, do you, sir?'

Morse looked aggrieved. 'Oh, I don't dislike him. It's just that I don't think he's completely above-board with me, that's all.'

'We've all of us got things we'd like to hide, haven't we, sir?'

'Mm.' Morse was staring through the window. *Eyes had I – and saw not.* Six letters. It still eluded him. Like the answer to this case. A whole orchestra of instruments and some of them playing just slightly out of tune.

'Did you know that "orchestra" was an anagram of "carthorse", Lewis?'

Lewis didn't. He idly wrote down the letters and checked. 'So it is. Perhaps the clue you can't get is an anagram, sir.'

The light dawned in Morse's eyes. 'You're a genius. SAW NOT.' Sherlock Holmes picked up *The Times* again, wrote in the answer and beamed at his own Doctor Watson.

'Now let's consider the case so far.' Lewis sat back and listened. Morse was away.

'We can say, can we not, that the letter was either written by Valerie herself or by another person. Agreed?'

'With odds of nine to one on Valerie.'

'Yes, with strong odds on Valerie. Now if Valerie herself wrote the letter, we can reasonably assume that she is still alive, that she probably ran off to London, that she's still there, that she's quite happy where she is, doesn't want to come back to Kidlington – and that we're wasting our bloody time.'

'Not if we find her.'

'Of course we are. What do we do if we find her? Bring her back home to mummy and tell her what a naughty girl she's been? What's the point of that?'

'It would clear up the case, though.'

'If she wrote the letter, there *is* no case.'

Something had been troubling Lewis sorely since the previous evening and he got it off his conscience. 'Do you think what Mrs Gibbs told me was important, sir – you know, about the girl in Maguire's flat?'

'Doubt it,' said Morse.

'You don't think it could have been Valerie?'

'I keep telling you, Lewis. *She's dead* – whatever that pettifogging Peters says, *she couldn't have written that letter.*'

Lewis groaned inwardly. Once the chief got an idea stuck firmly in his brain, something cataclysmic was needed to dislodge it.

'Let's just assume for a minute that the letter was *not* written by Valerie. In that case it was written by someone who copied her writing, and copied it with enormous care and skill. Yes?'

'But why should anyone . . .'

'I'm coming to that. Why should anyone want to

make us believe that Valerie was still alive *if in fact she was dead*? Well, as I see it, there is one simple and overwhelmingly convincing answer to that question. Someone wants us to believe Valerie is still alive because he or she sees a very real danger that further police investigation in the Taylor girl affair is likely to uncover the truth, Lewis – which is that Valerie is dead and that someone murdered her. I think that for some reason this someone began to get very scared, and wrote that letter to put us off the scent. Or more specifically, perhaps, to put Ainley off the scent.'

Lewis felt he could make no worthwhile contribution to such a weird hypothesis, and Morse continued.

'There is another possibility, though, and we mustn't discount it. The letter could have been written by someone for *precisely the opposite reason* – to put the police back on the scent. And if you think about it, that's precisely what has happened. Ainley was still working on the case – but unofficially. And when he was killed, if it hadn't been for the letter, the case would have been left where it was – unsolved and gradually forgotten. But once the letter arrived, what happened? Strange called me in and told me to take over, to reinvestigate the case officially. Precisely what we're doing now. Now let's follow this line of reasoning a bit further. Who would want the police to reopen the case? Not the murderer – that's for sure. Who then? It could be the parents, of course. They might think that the police weren't really doing much about things . . .'

Lewis looked stupefied. 'You don't honestly think the Taylors wrote the letter, do you?'

'Had the possibility not occurred to you?' asked Morse quietly.

'No.'

'Well it should have done. After all, they're as likely as anyone to make a good job of forging a letter in their daughter's handwriting. But there's a much more interesting possibility, I think. The letter could have been sent by someone who knew that Valerie had been murdered, who had a jolly good idea of who murdered her, and who wanted the murderer brought to justice.'

'But why . . .'

'Just a minute. Let's assume that such a person knew that Ainley was getting perilously close to the truth, had perhaps even helped Ainley towards the truth. What happens then? Tragedy. Ainley is killed and everything is back at square one. Look at it this way. Let's assume that Ainley went to London on the Monday and actually found Valerie Taylor alive. You with me? All right – the cat's out of the bag; she's been found. The next day she writes to her parents. There's no point in covering up any longer. If she doesn't tell them, Ainley will.'

'That seems to fit, sir.'

'Ah. But there's another interpretation, isn't there? Let's now assume that Ainley *didn't* find Valerie – and I don't think he did. Let's suppose he found something rather more sinister than Valerie Taylor alive and well. Because remember, Lewis, *something* took Ainley to London that day. We shall perhaps never know what, but he was getting nearer and nearer the truth all the time. And when he was killed someone, Lewis, *someone* desperately wanted his work to be followed up. And so the day after Ainley's death, a letter is written. It was written precisely because *Valerie Taylor was dead* – not alive, and it had exactly the effect it was intended to have. The case was reopened.'

The convolutions of Morse's theories were beginning to defeat Lewis's powers of logical analysis. 'I don't quite follow some of that, sir, but . . . you're still basing it all on the assumption that she didn't write the letter, aren't you? I mean if what Peters says is . . .'

The pretty office girl came in again and handed to Morse a buff-coloured file.

'Superintendent Strange says you may be interested in this, sir. It's been tested for fingerprints – no good, he says.'

Morse opened the file. Inside was a cheap brown envelope, already opened, posted the previous day in central London, and addressed to the Thames Valley Police. The letter inside was written on ruled, white note-paper.

Dear Sir,
    I heard you are trying to find me, but I don't want you to because I don't want to go back home.
               Yours truly, Valerie Taylor.

He handed the letter to Lewis. 'Not the most voluminous of correspondents, our Valerie, is she?'

He picked up the phone and dialled the lab, and from the slight pause at the other end of the line he knew he must be speaking to the computer itself.

CHAPTER ELEVEN

All women become like their mothers. That is their
tragedy.

Oscar Wilde

FOR THE SECOND time within twenty-four hours Morse
found himself studying a photograph with more than
usual interest. Lewis he had left in the office to make a
variety of telephone calls, and he himself stood, arms
akimbo, staring fixedly at the young girl who stared back
at him, equally fixedly, from the wall of the lounge. Slim,
with dark-brown hair and eyes that almost asked if you'd
dare and a figure that clearly promised it would be
wonderful if you found the daring. She was a very
attractive girl and, like the elders in Troy who looked
for the first time upon Helen, Morse felt no real surprise
that she had been the cause of so much trouble.

'Lovely-looking girl, your daughter.'

Mrs Taylor smiled diffidently at the photograph. 'It's
not Valerie,' she said, 'it's me.'

Morse turned with undisguised astonishment in his
eyes. 'Really? I didn't realize you were so much alike. I
didn't mean to er . . .'

'I used to be nice-looking, I suppose, in those days. I
was seventeen when that was taken – over twenty years
ago. It seems a long time.'

Morse watched her as she spoke. Her figure was a good deal thicker round the hips now, and her legs, though still slim, were faintly lined with varicose veins. But it was her face that had changed the most: a few wisps of greying hair trailed over the worn features, the teeth yellowing, the flesh around the throat no longer quite so firm. But she was still . . . Men were luckier, he thought; they seemed to age much less perceptibly than women. On a low cupboard against the right-hand wall behind her stood an elegant, delicately proportioned porcelain vase. Somehow it seemed to Morse so incongruously tasteful and expensive in this drably furnished room, and he found himself staring at it with a slightly puzzled frown.

They talked for half an hour or so, mostly about Valerie; but there was nothing she could add to what she had told so many people so many times before. She recalled the events of that far-off day like a nervous well-rehearsed pupil in a history examination. But that was no surprise to Morse. After all, as Phillipson had reminded him the previous evening, it *was* rather an important day. He asked her about herself and learned she had recently taken a job, just mornings, at the Cash and Carry stores – stocking up the shelves mostly; tiring, on her feet most of the time, but it was better than staying at home all day, and nice to have some money of her own. Morse refrained from asking how much she spent on drink and cigarettes but there was something that he had to ask.

'You won't be upset, Mrs Taylor, if I ask you one or two rather personal questions, will you?'

'I shouldn't think so.'

She leaned back on the crimson settee and lit another cigarette, her hand shaking slightly. Morse felt he ought to have realized it before. He could see it in the way she sat, legs slightly parted, the eyes still throwing a distant, muted invitation. There was an overt if faded sensuality about the woman. It was almost tangible. He took a deep breath.

'Did you know that Valerie was pregnant when she disappeared?'

Her eyes grew almost dangerous. 'She wasn't pregnant. I'm her mother, remember? Whoever told you that was a bloody liar.' The voice was harsher now, and cheaper. The façade was beginning to crack, and Morse found himself wondering about her. Husband away; long, lonely days and daughter home only at lunchtimes – and that only during Valerie's last year at school.

He hadn't meant to ask his next question. It was one of those things that wasn't really anyone else's business. It had struck him, of course, the first time he had glanced at the Colour Supplement: the cards for the eighteenth wedding anniversary, and Valerie at the time almost twenty – or would have been, had she still been alive. He took another deep breath.

'Was Valerie your husband's child, Mrs Taylor?'

The question struck home and she looked away. 'No. I had her before I knew George.'

'I see,' said Morse gently.

At the door she turned towards him. 'Are you going to see him?' Morse nodded. 'I don't mind what you ask him but ... but please don't mention anything about ... about what you just asked me. He was like a father to her always but he ... he used to get teased a lot about Valerie when we were first married especially ... especially since we didn't have any kids ourselves. You know what I mean. It hurt him, I know it did, and ... and I don't want him hurt, Inspector. He's been a good man to me; he's always been a good man to me.'

She spoke with a surprising warmth of feeling and as she spoke Morse could see the lineaments of an erstwhile beauty in her face. He heard himself promise that he wouldn't. Yet he found himself wondering who Valerie's real father had been, and if it might be important for him to find out. If he *could* find out. If anyone knew – including Valerie's mother.

As he walked slowly away he wondered something else, too. There had been something, albeit hardly perceptible, something slightly off-key about Mrs Taylor's nervousness; just a little more than the natural nervousness of meeting a strange man – even a strange policeman. It was more like the look he had several times witnessed on his secretary's face when he had burst unexpectedly into her office and found her hastily and guiltily covering up some personal little thing that she hoped he hadn't seen. Had there been someone else in the house during his interview with Mrs Taylor? He thought so. In an instant he turned on his heel and spun round to face the house he had just left – and he saw it. The right-hand curtain of an upstairs window twitched slightly and a vague silhouette glided back against the wall. It was over in a flash. The curtain was still; all sign of life was gone. A cabbage-white butterfly stitched its way along the privet hedge – and then that, too, was gone.

CHAPTER TWELVE

Even the dustbin lid is raised mechanically
  At the very last moment
You could dispose of a corpse like this
  Without giving the least offence.
                    D. J. Enright, *No Offence: Berlin*

IT OCCURRED TO Morse as he drove down the Woodstock Road into Oxford that although he had done
most things in life he had never before had occasion to
visit a rubbish tip. In fact, as he turned into Walton
Street and slowed to negotiate the narrowing streets
that led down to Jericho, he could not quite account
for the fact that he knew exactly where to go. He passed
Aristotle Lane and turned right into Walton Well Road,
over the hump-backed bridge that spanned the canal,
and stopped the Lancia beside an open gate, where a
notice informed him that unauthorized vehicles were
not allowed to drive further and that offenders would
be prosecuted by an official with (it seemed to Morse)
the portentous title of Conservator and Sheriff of Port
Meadow. He slipped the car into first gear and drove
on, deciding that he would probably qualify in the
'authorized' category, and rather hoping that someone
would stop him. But no one did. He made his way
slowly along the concreted pathway, a thin belt of trees

on his right and the open green expanse of Port Meadow on his left. Twice when corporation lorries came towards him he was forced off the track on to the grass, before coming finally to the edge of the site, where a high wooden gate over a deep cattle-grid effectively barred all further progress. He left the car and proceeded on foot, noting, as he passed another sign, that members of the public would be ill-advised to touch any materials deposited on the tip, treated as they were with harmful insecticides. He had gone more than 200 yards before he caught his first sight of genuine rubbish. The compacted surface over which he walked was flat and clear, scored by the caterpillar tracks of bulldozers and levellers, with only the occasional partially submerged piece of sacking to betray the burial of the thousands of tons of rubbish beneath. Doubtless grass and shrubs would soon be burgeoning there, and the animals would return to their old territories and scurry once more in the hedgerows amid the bracken and the wild flowers. And people would come and scatter their picnic litter around and the whole process would begin again. Sometimes *Homo sapiens* was a thoroughly disgusting species.

He made his way towards the only observable sign of life – a corrugated-iron shack, once painted green but ramshackle now and rusty, where an indescribably grimy labourer directed him deeper into the network of filth. Two magpies and an ominous-looking crow reluctantly took to flight as he walked by, and flapped their slow way across the blighted wilderness. At last

Morse came to the main area of the tip: Pepsi and Coca-Cola tins, perished household gloves, lengths of rusting wire, empty cartons of washing-up liquid, and a disintegrating dart-board; biscuit tins, worn-out shoes, a hot-water bottle, ancient car seats and a comprehensive collection of cardboard boxes. Morse swatted away the ugly flies that circled his head, and was glad to find he had one last cigarette left. He threw the empty packet away; it didn't seem to matter much here.

George Taylor was standing beside a yellow bull-dozer, shouting to its driver above the deep-throated growl of the engine, and pointing towards a great mound of earth and stones piled like a rampart along the side of the shallow tip. Morse idly conjured up the image of some archaeologist who, some thousand years hence, might seek to discover the life-style of twentieth-century man, and Morse commiserated with him on the dismal debris he would find.

George was a heavily built, broad-shouldered man, not too intelligent, perhaps, but, as Morse saw him, honest and likeable enough. He sat down upon a ten-gallon paraffin tin, Morse himself having declined the offer of similar accommodation, supposing that by this time George's trousers were probably immune from the harmful effects of all insecticides. And so they talked, and Morse tried to picture the scene as it must have been each night in the Taylor household: George arriving home, dirty and tired, at 6.15 or thereabouts; Mrs Taylor cooking the evening meal and washing up the pots; and Valerie – but what did he know of Valerie? Occasionally condescending to do a modicum of homework? He didn't know. Three isolated personalities, under the same roof, somehow brought and kept together by that statistical unit beloved by the sociologists – the family. Morse asked about Valerie – her life at home, her life at school, her friends, her likes and her dislikes; but he learned little that was new.

'Have you ever thought that Valerie may have run away because she was expecting a baby?'

George slowly lit a Woodbine and contemplated the broken glass that littered the ground at his feet. 'You think of most things, don't you, when summat like that happens. I remembered when she were a young gal she were a bit late sometimes – and I used to think all sorts of things had happened.' Morse nodded. 'You got a family, Inspector?'

Morse shook his head and, like George, contemplated the ground about his feet.

''S funny, really. You think of the most terrible things. And then she'd come back and you'd feel all sort of happy and cross at the same time, if you know what I mean.'

Morse thought he knew; and for the first time in the case he saw something of the heartache and the sorrow of it all, and he began to hope that Valerie Taylor was still alive.

'Was she often late coming home?'

George hesitated. 'Not really. Well, not till she were about sixteen, anyway.'

'And then she was?'

'Well, not too late. Anyway, I allus used to wait up for her.'

Morse put it more bluntly. 'Did she ever stay out all night?'

'Never.' It was a firm and categorical answer, but Morse wondered if it were true.

'When was the latest she came in? After midnight?' George nodded rather sadly. 'Much after?'

'Sometimes.'

'Rows, were there?'

'The wife got cross, of course. Well, so did I, really.'

'She often stayed out late, then?'

'Well, no. Not often. Just once every few weeks, like, she'd say she was going to a party with her friends, or summat like that.' He rubbed his hand across his stubbled chin and shook his head. 'These days it's not like it was when we was boys. I don't know.'

They brooded silently and George kicked a flattened Coca-Cola tin a few yards further away.

'Did you give her much pocket money?' asked Morse.

'Quid a week – sometimes a bit more. And at weekends she used to work on the till down the super-market. Used to spend it on clothes mostly – shoes, that sort of thing. She was never short of money.'

With a powerful snarl the bulldozer shovelled a few more cubic yards of earth across a stinking stretch of refuse, and then slowly retreated to manoeuvre diag-onally into position behind the next heap, criss-crossing the ground with the patterned tracks that Morse had noticed earlier. And as the gleaming teeth of the scoop dug again into the crumbling soil, something stirred vaguely in the back of Morse's mind; but George was speaking again.

'That inspector what was killed, you know, he came to see me a few weeks back.'

Morse stood very still and held his breath, as if the slightest movement might be fatal. His question would appear, he hoped, to spring from casual curiosity.

'What did he want to see you about, Mr Taylor?'

''S funny really. He asked me the same as you. You know, about Valerie staying out at nights.'

Morse's blood ran slightly cold, and his grey eyes looked into the past and seemed to catch a glimpse of what had happened all that time ago ... Another corporation lorry rumbled up the slight incline, ready to stock-pile the latest consignment of rubbish, and George stood up to direct proceedings.

'Not been much help, I'm afraid, Inspector.'

Morse shook George's dirty, calloused hand, and prepared to leave.

'Do you think she's alive, Inspector?'

Morse looked at him curiously. 'Do you?'

'Well, there's the letter, isn't there, Inspector?'

For some strange, intuitive reason Morse felt the question had somehow been wrong, and he frowned slightly as he watched George Taylor walk over to the lorry. Yes, there was the letter, and he hoped now that Valerie had written it, but ...

He stood where he was and looked around him.

How would you like to be stuck in a filthy hole like this, Morse – probably for the rest of your life? And when anyone calls to see you, all you can offer is an old ten-gallon paraffin tin sprayed with harmful insecticide. You've got your own black leather chair and the white carpet and the desk of polished Scandinavian oak. Some people are luckier than others.

As he walked away the yellow bulldozer nudged its nose into another pile of earth; and soon the leveller would come and gradually smooth over the clay surface, like a passable cook with the chocolate icing on a cake.

CHAPTER THIRTEEN

Man kann den Wald nicht vor Baümen sehen.
German proverb

LEWIS HAD GONE home when Morse returned to his office at 5.30, and he felt it would probably be sensible for him to do the same. Many pieces of the jigsaw were now to hand, some of them big ugly pieces that looked as if they wouldn't fit anywhere; but they would – if only he had the time to think it all out. For the moment he was too much on top of things. Some of the trees were clear enough, but not the configuration of the forest. To stand back a bit and take a more synoptic view of things – that's what he needed.

He fetched a cup of coffee from the canteen, and sat at his desk. The notes that Lewis had made, and left conspicuously beneath a paperweight, he deliberately put to one side. There were other things in life than the Taylor case, although for the moment he couldn't quite remember what they were. He went through his in-tray and read through reports on the recent spate of incendiary bombings, the role of the police at pop festivals, and the vicious hooliganism after Oxford United's last home game. There were some interesting points. He crossed through his initials and stuck the reports in his out-tray. The next man on the list would do exactly the same; quickly glance through, cross through his initials, and stick them in his out-tray. There were too many reports, and the more there were the more self-defeating the whole exercise became. He would vote for a moratorium on all reports for the next five years.

He consulted his diary. The following morning he would be in the courts, and he'd better get home and iron a clean shirt. It was 6.25 and he felt hungry. Ah well. He'd call at the Chinese restaurant and take-away ... He was pulling on his overcoat and debating between King Prawns and Chicken Chop Suey when the phone went.

'Personal call from a Mr Phillipson. Shall I put him through, sir?' The girl on the switchboard sounded weary too.

'You're working late tonight, Inspector?'

'I was just off,' said Morse with a yawn in his voice.

'You're lucky,' said Phillipson. 'We've got a Parents' Evening – shan't be home till ten myself.'

Morse was unimpressed and the headmaster got to the point.

'I thought I'd just ring up to say that I checked up at Blackwells – you remember? – about buying a book.'

Morse looked at Lewis's notes and completed the sentence for him.

'. . . and you bought Momigliano's *Studies in Historiography* published by Weidenfeld and Nicolson at £2.50.'

'You checked, then?'

'Yep.'

'Oh well. I thought, er, I'd just let you know.'

'Thoughtful of you, sir. I appreciate it. Are you speaking from school?'

'From my study, yes.'

'I wonder if you've got a phone number for Mr Acum there?'

'Just a minute, Inspector.'

Morse kept the receiver to his ear and read through the rest of Lewis's notes. Nothing from Peters yet about that second letter; nothing much from anybody . . .

To anyone with less than extremely acute hearing it would have been quite imperceptible. But Morse heard it, and knew once again that someone had been eavesdropping on the headmaster's telephone conversations. Someone in the office outside the head's study; and Morse's brain slid easily along the shining grooves.

'Are you there, Inspector? We've got two numbers for Acum – one at school, one at home.'

'I'll take 'em both,' said Morse.

After cradling the receiver, he sat and thought for a moment. If Phillipson wanted to use the phone in his study, he would first dial 9, get an outside line automatically, and then ring the code and the number he wanted. Morse had noticed the set-up when he had visited the school. But if he, Morse, wanted to ring Phillipson, he wouldn't be able to get him unless someone were sitting by the switchboard in the outer office; and he doubted that the faithful Mrs Webb would be required that evening for the Parents' Evening.

He waited a couple of minutes and rang.

Brr. Brr. It was answered almost immediately.

'Roger Bacon School.'

'That the headmaster?' enquired Morse innocently.

'No. Baines here. Second master. Can I help you?'

'Ah, Mr Baines. Good evening, sir. As a matter of fact it was you I was hoping to get hold of. I, er, wonder if we might be able to meet again fairly soon. It's this Taylor girl business again. There are one or two points I think you could help me with.'

Baines would be free about a quarter to ten, and he could be in the White Horse soon after that. No time like the present.

Morse felt pleased with himself. He would have been even more pleased had he been able to see the deeply worried look on Baines's face as he shrugged into his gown and walked down into the Great Hall to meet the parents.

There was little point in going home now and he walked over to the canteen and found a copy of the *Telegraph*. He ordered sausages and mash, wrote the precise time in the right-hand margin of the back page and turned to 1 across. *Has been known to split under a grilling* (7). He smiled to himself. It was too many letters for BAINES, so he wrote SAUSAGE.

Back in the office he felt he was in good form. Crossword finished in only seven and a half minutes. Still, it was a bit easier than *The Times*. Perhaps this case would be easy if only he could look at it in the right way, and as Baines had said there was no time like the present. A long, quiet, cool, detached look at the case.

But it never worked quite like that. He sat back and closed his eyes and for more than an hour his brain seethed in ceaseless turmoil. Ideas, ideas galore, but still the firm outline of the pattern eluded him. One or two of the pieces fitted firmly into place, but so many wouldn't fit at all. It was like doing the light-blue sky at the top of a jigsaw, with no clouds, not even a solitary sea-gull to break the boundless monochrome.

By nine o'clock he had a headache. Leave it. Give it a rest and go back later. Like crosswords. It would come; it would come.

He consulted the STD codes and found that he would have to get Caernarfon through the operator. It was Acum who answered.

As succinctly as he could Morse explained the reason for his call, and Acum politely interjected the proper noises of understanding and approval. Yes, of course. Yes, of course he remembered Valerie and the day she had disappeared. Yes, he remembered it all well.

'Did you realize that you were one of the very last people to see Valerie before she, er, before she disappeared?'

'I must have been, yes.'

'In fact, you taught her the very last school lesson she ever had, I think?'

'Yes.'

'I mention this, sir, because I have reason to believe that you asked Valerie to see you after the lesson.'

'Ye-es. I think I did.'

'Remember why, sir?' Acum took his time and Morse wished that he could see the schoolmaster's face.

'If I remember rightly, Inspector, she was due to sit her O-level French the next week, and her work was, well, pretty dreadful, and I was going to have a word with her about it. Not that she had much chance in the exam, I'm afraid.'

'You said, sir, you were *going* to see her.'

'Yes, that's right. As it happened I didn't get a chance. She had to rush off, she said.'

'Did she say why?'

The answer was ready this time, and it took the wind out of Morse's sails. 'She said she'd got to see the head.'

'Oh, I see.' Another piece that didn't fit. 'Well, thank you, Mr Acum. You've been most helpful. I hope I've not interrupted anything important.'

'No. No. Just marking a few books, that's all.'

'Well, I'll leave you to it. Thanks very much.'

'Not at all. If I can help in any other way, don't hesitate to ring me, will you?'

'Er, no. I won't. Thanks again.'

Morse sat still for many minutes and began to wonder if he ought not to turn the jigsaw upside down and work the blue sky in at the bottom. There was no doubt about it: he ought to have gone home as he'd promised himself earlier. He was just walking blindly in the forest bumping into one wretched tree after another. But he couldn't go home yet; he had an appointment.

Baines was there already and got up to buy the inspector a drink. The lounge was quiet and they sat alone in a corner and wished each other good health.

Morse tried to size him up. Tweed jacket, grey slacks, balding on top and rather flabby in the middle, but obviously nobody's fool. His eyes were keen and Morse imagined the pupils would never take too many liberties with Baines. He spoke with a slight North Country accent and as he listened to Morse he picked away at his lower nostrils with his index finger. Irritating.

What was the routine on Tuesday afternoons? Why was there no register taken? Was there any likelihood that Valerie had, in fact, returned to school that afternoon, and only later disappeared? How did the pupils work the skiving that was obviously so widespread? Was there any sort of skivers' den where the reluctant athletes could safely hide themselves away? Have a smoke perhaps?

Baines seemed rather amused. He could give the boys and girls a few tips about getting off games! By jove, he could. But it was the staff's fault. The PE teachers were a bloody idle lot – worse than the kids. Hardly bothered to get changed, some of them. And anyway there were so many activities: fencing, judo, table-tennis, athletics, rounders, netball – all this self-expression nonsense. No one really knew who was expected when and where. Bloody stupid. Things had tightened up a bit with the new head, but – well. Baines gave the impression that for all his possible virtues Phillipson had a long way still to go. Where they went to? Plenty of places. He'd found half a dozen smoking in the boiler room one day, and the school itself was virtually empty. Quite a few of them just sloped off home though, and some didn't turn up at all. Anyway, like the headmaster, he wasn't really involved on Tuesday afternoons. It wasn't a bad idea, though, to get away from school occasionally – have a free afternoon. The headmaster had tried to do it for all the staff. Put all their free periods together and let them have a morning or an afternoon off. Trouble was that it meant a hell of a lot of work for the chap who did the timetabling. Him!

As he talked on Morse wondered whether he still felt bitter towards Phillipson; whether he would be all that eager to throw out a life-line to the drowning helmsman. He casually mentioned that he knew of Baines's ill luck in being pipped for the job; and bought more beer. Yes (Baines admitted), he'd been a bit unlucky perhaps, and more than once. He thought he could have run a school as well as most, and Morse felt he was probably right. Greedy and selfish (like most men), but shrewdly competent. Above all, thought Morse, he would have enjoyed power. And now that there no longer seemed much chance of power, perhaps a certain element of dark satisfaction in observing the inadequacies of others and quietly gloating over their misfortunes. There wasn't a word for it in English. The Germans called it *Schadenfreude*. Would Baines get the job if Phillipson left or if for some reason he *had* to leave? Morse thought he would be sure to. But how far would he go in actively promoting such a situation? Perhaps though, as usual, Morse was attributing too much cynical self-seeking to his fellow men, and he brought his attention back to the fairly ordinary man who sat opposite him, talking openly and amusingly about life in a comprehensive school.

'Did you ever teach Valerie yourself?' asked Morse.

Baines chuckled. 'In the first form – just for a year. She didn't know a trapezium from a trampoline.'

Morse grinned, too. 'Did you like her?'

It was a sobering question, and the shrewdness gleamed again in Baines's eyes.

'She was all right.' But it was an oddly unsatisfactory answer and Baines sensed it. He went on glibly about her academic prowess, or lack of it, and veered off into an anecdote about the time he'd found forty-two different spellings of 'isosceles' in a first-year examination.

'Do you know Mrs Taylor?'

'Oh, yes.' He stood up and suggested there was just time for another pint. Morse knew that the momentum had been broken, quite deliberately, and he felt very tempted to refuse. But he didn't. Anyway, he was going to ask Baines a rather delicate favour.

Morse slept fitfully that night. Broken images littered his mind, like the broken glass strewn about the rubbish tip. He tossed and turned; but the merry-go-round was out of control, and at 3.00 a.m. he got up to make himself a cup of tea. Back in bed, with the light left on, he tried to concentrate his closed, swift-darting eyes on to a point about three inches in front of his nose, and gradually the spinning mechanism began to slow down, slower and slower, and then it stopped. He dreamed of a beautiful girl slowly unbuttoning her low-cut blouse and swaying her hips sensuously above him as she slid down the zip at the side of her skirt. And then she put her long slim fingers up to her face and moved the mask aside, and he saw the face of Valerie Taylor.

CHAPTER FOURTEEN

I am a man under authority.
Matthew, viii, 9

IT WASN'T TOO bad working with Morse. Odd sort of chap, sometimes, and should have got himself married long ago; everybody said that. But it wasn't too bad. He'd worked with him before, and enjoyed it most of the time. Sometimes he seemed a very ordinary sort of fellow. The real trouble was that he always had to find a complex solution to everything, and Lewis had enough experience of police work to know that most criminal activity owed its origins to simple, cheap, and sordid motives, and that few of the criminals themselves had sufficiently intelligent or tortuous minds to devise the cunning stratagems that Morse was wont to attribute to them. In Morse's mind the simple facts of any case seemed somewhere along the line to get fitted out with hooks and eyes which rendered the possibility of infinite associations and combinations. What the great man couldn't do, for all his gifts, was put a couple of simple facts together and come up with something obvious. The letters from Valerie were a case in point. The first one, Peters had said, was pretty certainly written by Valerie herself. Why then not work on the assumption that it *was*, and go on from there? But no. Morse had to believe the letter was forged, just because it would fit better with some fantastical notion that itself owed its abortive birth to some equally improbable hypothesis. And then there was the second letter. Morse hadn't said much about that; probably learned his lesson. But even if he had to accept that Valerie Taylor had written the letters, he would never be prepared to believe anything so simple as the fact that she'd got fed up with home and with school, and had just gone off, as hundreds of other girls did every year. Then why not Valerie? The truth was that Morse would find it all too easy; no fit challenge for that thoroughbred mind of his. Yes, that was it.

Lewis began to wish he could have a few days on his own in London; use his own initiative. He might find *something*. After all, Ainley probably had – well, according to Morse he had. But there again the chief was only guessing. There was no evidence for it. Wasn't it far more likely that Ainley hadn't found anything? If he was killed on the very day that he'd actually found some vital clue – after well over two years of finding nothing – it would be a huge coincidence. Too big. But no. Morse himself took such coincidences blithely in his stride.

He went to the canteen for a cup of tea and sat down by Constable Dickson.

'Solved the murder yet, sarge?'

'What murder?'

Dickson grinned. 'Now don't tell me they've put old

Morse on a missing persons case, 'cause I shan't believe you. Come on, sarge, spill the beans.'

'No beans to spill,' said Lewis.

'Come off it! I was on the Taylor business, too, you know. Searched everywhere we did – even dragged the reservoir.'

'Well, you didn't find the body. And if you don't have the body, Dickson boy, you don't have a murder, do you?'

'Ainley thought she was bumped off, though, didn't he?'

'Well, there's always the possibility, but ... Look here, Dickson.' He swivelled round in his chair and faced the constable. 'You kill somebody, right? And you've got a body on your hands, right? How do you get rid of it? Come on, tell me.'

'Well, there's a hundred and one ways.'

'Such as?'

'Well, for a start, there's the reservoir.'

'But that was dragged, you say.'

Dickson looked mildly contemptuous. 'Yes, but I mean. A bloody great reservoir like that. You'd need a bit of luck, wouldn't you, sarge.'

'What else?'

'There was that furnace in the school boiler room. Christ, you wouldn't find much trace if they stuck you in there.'

'The boiler room was kept locked.'

'Come off it! S'posed to have been, you mean. Anyway, *somebody's* got keys.'

'You're not much help, are you, Dickson?'

129

'Could have been buried easy enough, couldn't she? It's what usually happens to dead bodies, eh, sarge?' He was inordinately amused by his own joke, and Lewis left him alone in his glory.

He returned to the office and sat down opposite the empty chair. Whatever he thought about Morse it wasn't much fun without him . . .

He thought about Ainley. *He* hadn't known about the letters. If he had . . . Lewis was puzzled. Why *hadn't* Morse worried more about the letters? Surely the two of them should be in London, not sitting on their backsides here in Kidlington. Morse was always saying they were a team, the two of them. But they didn't function as a team at all. Sometimes he got a pat on the back, but mostly he just did what the chief told him to. Quite right and proper, too. But he would dearly love to try the London angle. He could always suggest it, of course. Why not? Why indeed not? And if he found Valerie and proved Morse wrong? Not that he wanted to prove him wrong really, but Morse was such an obstinate blighter. In Lewis's garden ambition was not a weed that sprouted freely.

He noted that Morse had obviously read the notes he had made, and felt mildly gratified. Morse must have come back to the office after seeing the Taylors; and Lewis wondered what wonderful edifice his superior officer had managed to erect on the basis of those two interviews.

The phone rang and he answered it. It was Peters.

'Tell Inspector Morse it's the same as before. Different pen, different paper, different envelope, different postmark. But the verdict's the same as before.'

'Valerie Taylor wrote it, you mean?'

Peters paused. 'I didn't say that, did I? I said the verdict's the same as before.'

'Same odds as before, then?'

He paused. 'The degree of probability is just about the same.'

Lewis thanked him and decided to communicate the information immediately. Morse had told him that if anything important came up, a message would always get through to him. Surely this was important enough? And while he was on the phone he would mention that idea of his. Sometimes it was easier on the phone.

He learned that Morse was in the witness box, but that he should be finished soon. Morse would ring back, and did so an hour later.

'What do you want, Lewis? Have you found the corpse?'

'No, sir. But Peters rang.'

'Did he now?' A note of sudden interest crept into Morse's voice. 'And what did the old twerp have to say, this time?' Lewis told him and felt surprised at the mild reception given to this latest intelligence. 'Thanks for letting me know. Look, Lewis, I've finished here now and I'm thinking of taking the afternoon off. I had a bloody awful night's sleep and I think I'll go to bed. Look after my effects, won't you?'

To Lewis, he seemed to have lost interest completely. He'd tried his best to make a murder out of it; and now he'd learned he'd failed, he'd decided to go to bed! It was as good a time as any to mention that other little thing.

'I was just wondering, sir. Don't you think it might be a good idea if I went up to London. You know – make a few inquiries, have a look round—'

Morse interrupted him angrily from the other end of the line. 'What the hell are you talking about, man? If you're going to work with me on this case, for God's sake get one thing into that thick skull of yours, d'you hear? Valerie Taylor isn't living in London or anywhere else. You got that? She's dead.' The line was dead, too.

Lewis walked out of the office and slammed the door behind him. Dickson was in the canteen; Dickson was always in the canteen.

'Solved the murder yet, sarge?'

'No I have not,' snarled Lewis. 'And nor has Inspector bloody Morse.'

He sat alone in the farthest corner and stirred his coffee with controlled fury.

CHAPTER FIFTEEN

'Tis a strange thing, Sam, that among us people can't agree the whole week because they go different ways upon Sundays.

George Farquhar

THE BRIEF INDIAN summer, radiant and beneficent, was almost at an end. On Friday evening the forecast for the weekend was unsettled, changeable weather with the possibility of high winds and rain; and Saturday was already appreciably cooler, with dark clouds from the west looming over North Oxfordshire. Gloomily the late-night weatherman revealed to the nation a map of the British Isles almost obliterated by a series of close, concentric millibars with their epicentrum somewhere over Birmingham, and prophesied in minatory tones of weak fronts and associated depressions. Sunday broke gusty and raw, and although the threatened rain storm held its hand, there was, at 9.00 a.m., a curiously deadened, almost dreamlike quality about the early morning streets, and the few people there were seemed to move as in a silent film.

From Carfax (at the centre of Oxford) Queen Street leads westwards, very soon changing its name to Park End Street; and off Park End Street on the left-hand side and just opposite the railway station, is Kempis

Street, where stands a row of quietly senescent terraced houses. At five minutes past nine the door of one of these houses is opened, and a man walks to the end of the street, opens the faded-green doors of his garage and backs out his car. It is a dull black car, irresponsive, even in high summer, to any glancing sunbeams, and the chrome on the front and rear bumpers is rusted to a dirty brown. It is time he bought a new car, and indeed he has more than enough money to do so. He drives to St Giles' and up the Woodstock Road. It would be slightly quicker and certainly more direct to head straight up the Banbury Road; but he wishes to avoid the Banbury Road. At the top of the Woodstock Road he turns right along the ring-road for some three or four hundred yards and turns left at the Banbury Road roundabout. Here he increases his speed to a modest 45 m.p.h. and passes out of Oxford and down the long, gentle hill that leads to Kidlington. Here (inconspicuously, he hopes) he leaves his car in a side street which is only a few minutes' walk from the Roger Bacon Comprehensive School. It is a strange decision. It is more than that; it is an incomprehensible decision. He walks fairly quickly, pulling his trilby hat further over his eyes and hunching deeper into his thick, dark overcoat. He walks up the slight incline, passing the prefabricated hut in which the Clerk of Works directs (and will direct) the perpetual and perennial alterations and extensions to the school, and as deviously as he can he penetrates the sprawling amalgam of outbuildings, permanent and temporary, wherein the pupils of secondary school age are initiated into the mysteries of the Sciences and the

134

Humanities. Guardedly his eyes glance hither and thither, but there is no one to be seen. Thence over the black tarmac of the central play area and towards the two-storeyed, flat-roofed central administrative block, newly built in yellow brick. The main door is locked; but he has a key. He enters quietly and unlocks the door. Within, there is a deathly silence about the familiar surroundings; his footsteps echo on the parquet flooring, and the smell of the floor polish takes him back to times of long ago. Again he looks around him and quickly mounts the stairs. The door to the secretary's office is locked; but he has a key, and enters and locks the door behind him. He walks over to the headmaster's study. The door is locked; but he has a key, and enters and feels a sudden fear. But there is no reason for the fear. He walks over to a large filing cabinet. It is locked; but he has a key, and opens it and takes out a file marked 'Staff Appointments'. He flicks through the thick file and replaces it; tries another; and another. At last he finds it. It is a sheet of paper he has never seen before; but it contains no surprises, for he has known its contents all along. In the office outside he turns on the electric switch of the copying machine. It takes only thirty seconds to make two copies (although he has been asked for only one). Carefully he replaces the original document in the filing cabinet, relocks the study door, unlocks and relocks the outer door, and makes his way down the stairs. Stealthily he looks outside. It is five minutes to ten. There is no one in sight as he lets himself out, relocks the main door and leaves the school premises. He is lucky. No one has seen him and he retraces his steps. A man is standing on the pavement by the car, but moves on, guiltily tugging a small white dog along the pavement and momentarily deferring the imminent defecation.

This same Sunday morning Sheila Phillipson is picking up the windfalls under the apple trees. The grass needs cutting again, for in spite of the recent weeks of sunshine a few dark ridges of longish grass are sprouting in dark-green patches; and with rain apparently imminent, she will mention it to Donald. Or will she? He has been touchy and withdrawn this last week – almost certainly because of that girl! It is unlike him, though. Hereto he has assumed the duties and responsibilities of the head-ship with a verve and a confidence that have slightly surprised her. No. It isn't like him to worry. There must be something more to it; something wrong somewhere.

She stands with the basket of apples on her arm and looks around: the tall fencing that keeps them so private, the bushes and shrubs and ground-cover that blend so wonderfully with their variegated greens. It is almost terrifyingly beautiful. And the more she treasures it all the more frightened she is that she may lose it all. How she wants to keep everything just as it is! And as she stands beneath the apple-heavy boughs her face grows hard and determined. She *will* keep it all – for Donald, for the children, for herself. She will let nothing and no one take it from her!

Donald comes out to join her and says (praise be!) that it's high time he cut the grass again, and greets the promise of apple pie for dinner with a playfully loving kiss upon her cheek. Perhaps after all she is worrying herself over nothing.

At midday the beef and the pie are in the oven, and as she prepares the vegetables she watches him cutting the lawn. But the shaded patterns of the parallel swaths seem not so neat as usual – and suddenly she bangs her hands upon the window and shouts hysterically: 'Donald! For God's—' So nearly, so very nearly has he chewed up the electric flex of the lead with the blades of the mower. She has read of a young boy doing just that only a week ago: instantly and tragically fatal.

The Senior Tutor's secretary has had to come into Lonsdale College this Sunday morning. In common with many she feels convinced there are far too many conferences, and wonders whether the Conference for the Reform of French Teaching in Secondary Schools will significantly affect the notorious inability of English children to learn the language of any other nation. So many conferences, especially before the start of the Michaelmas Term! She is efficient and has almost everything ready for the evening's business: lists of those attending, details of their schools, programmes for the following two days' activities, certifications of attendance and the menus for the evening's banquet. There remain only the name-tags, and using the red ribbon and the upper case she begins typing the name and provenance of each of the delegates. It is a fairly simple and quick operation. She then cuts up the names into neat rectangles and begins to fit them into the small celluloid holders: MR J. ABBOTT, The Royal Grammar School, Chelmsford; MISS P. ACKROYD, High Wycombe Technical College; MR D. ACUM, City of Caernarfon School . . . and so on, to the end of the list.

She is finished by midday and takes all her bits and pieces to the Conference Room, where at 6.30 p.m. she will sit behind the reception desk and greet the delegates as they arrive. To be truthful, she rather enjoys this sort of thing. Her hair will be most cunningly coiffured, and on her name-tag she has proudly printed 'Lonsdale College' as her own academic provenance.

With the new stretch of the M40 blasted through the heart of the Chilterns, the journey to and from London is now quicker than ever; and Morse feels reasonably satisfied with his day's work when he arrives back in Oxford just after 4.00 p.m. Lewis was quite right: there were one or two things that could only be checked in London, and Morse thinks that he has dealt with them. On his return he calls in at Police HQ and finds an envelope, heavily sealed with Sellotape, and boldly marked for the attention of Chief Inspector Morse. The pieces are beginning to fall into place. He dials Acum's home number and waits.

'Hello?' It is a woman's voice.

'Mrs Acum?'

'Yes, speaking.'

'Could I have a word with your husband, please?'

'I'm afraid he's not here.'

'Will he be in later?'

'Well, no. He won't. He's away on a teachers' conference.'

'Oh, I see. When are you expecting him back, Mrs Acum?'

'He said he hoped to be back Tuesday evening – fairly late, though, I think.'

'I see.'

'Can I give him a message?'

'Er, no. Don't worry. It's not important. I'll try to ring him later in the week.'

'You sure?'

'Yes, that'll be fine. Thanks very much, anyway. Sorry to trouble you.'

'That's all right.'

Morse sits back and considers. As he's just said, it isn't really important.

Baines is not a man of regular habits, nor indeed of settled tastes. Sometimes he drinks beer, and sometimes he drinks Guinness. Occasionally, when a heavy burden weighs upon his mind, he drinks whisky. Sometimes he drinks in the lounge, and sometimes he drinks in the public bar; sometimes in the Station Hotel, and sometimes in the Royal Oxford, for both are near. Sometimes he doesn't drink at all.

Tonight he orders a whisky and soda in the lounge bar of the Station Hotel. It is a place with a very special and a very important memory. The bar is fairly small, and he finds he can easily follow long stretches of others' conversations; but tonight he is deaf to the chatter around him. It has been a worrying sort of day – though not worrying exactly; more a nervy, fluttery sort of day. Clever man, Morse!

Several of the customers are waiting for the London train; smartly dressed, apparently affluent. Later there will be a handful who have missed the train and who will book in for the night if there are vacancies; relaxed, worldly men with generous expense allowances and jaunty anecdotes. And just once in a while there is a man who deliberately misses his train, who rings his wife and tells his devious tale.

It had been a chance in a thousand, really – seeing Phillipson like that. Phillipson! One of the six on the short-list, a list that had included himself! A stroke of luck, too, that *she* had not seen him when, just after 8.30, they had entered arm-in-arm. And then they had actually appointed Phillipson! Well, well, well. And the little secret glittered and gleamed like a bright nugget of gold in a miser's hoard.

Phillipson, Baines, Acum; headmaster, second master, ex-Modern Languages master of the Roger Bacon School, and all thinking of Valerie Taylor as they lay awake that Sunday night listening as the wind howled and the rain beat down relentlessly. At last to each of them came sleep; but sleep uneasy and disturbed. Phillipson, Baines, Acum; and tomorrow night one of the three will be sleeping a sleep that is long and undisturbed; for tomorrow night at this same time one of the three will be dead.

CHAPTER SIXTEEN

They wish to know the family secrets and to be feared
accordingly.

Juvenal, *Satire III*, 113

MORSE WOKE FROM a deep, untroubled sleep at 7.30
a.m. and switched on Radio Oxford: trees uprooted,
basements flooded, outbuildings smashed to match-
wood. But as he washed and shaved, he felt happier
than he had done since taking over the case. He saw
things more clearly now. There was a long way still to
go but at least he had made the first big breakthrough.
He would have to apologize to Lewis – that was only fit
and proper; but Lewis would understand. He backed
out the Lancia and got out to lock the garage doors.
The rain had ceased at last and everywhere looked
washed and clean. He breathed deeply – it was good to
be alive.

He summoned Lewis to his office immediately, cleared
his desk, and cheated by having a quick preliminary
look at 1 across: *Code name for a walrus* (5). Ha! The
clue was like a megaphone shouting the answer at him.
It was going to be his day!

Lewis greeted his chief defensively; he had not seen

him since the previous Thursday morning. Where Morse had been he didn't know, and what he'd been doing he didn't really care.

'Look,' said Morse. 'I'm sorry I blasted your head off last week. I know you don't worry about things like that, but I do.'

It was a new angle, anyway, thought Lewis.

'And I feel I ought to apologize. It's not like me, is it, to go off the deep end like that.'

It was hardly a question and Lewis made no reply.

'We're a team, Lewis, you and me – you must never forget that . . .' He went on and on and Lewis felt better and better. 'You see, Lewis, the long and the short of it is that you were right and I was wrong. I should have listened to you.' Lewis felt like a candidate who learns that he has been awarded grade 1 although he was absent for the examination.

'Yes,' continued Morse, 'I've had the chance to stand back and see things a little more clearly, and I think we can now begin to see what really happened.'

He was becoming rather pompous and self-satisfied, and Lewis tried to bring him down to earth. As far as he knew, Morse had been nowhere near the office since Thursday morning.

'There's that report from Peters on Valerie's second letter, sir. You remember, I rang you about it.'

Morse brushed the interruption aside. 'That's not important, Lewis. But I'm going to tell you something that *is* important.' He leaned back in the black leather chair and commenced an analysis of the case, an analysis which at several points had Sergeant Lewis staring at him in wide-eyed amazement and despair.

'The one person who has worried me all along in this case has been Phillipson. Why? Because it's clear that the man is hiding something, and to keep things dark he's been forced to tell us lies.'

'He didn't lie about Blackwells, sir.'

'No. But I'm not worried so much about what happened on the day when Valerie disappeared. That's where we've been making our mistake. We should have been concentrating much more on what happened *before* she disappeared. We should have been looking into the past for some incident, some relationship, *something*, that gives a coherent pattern to all the rest. Because, make no mistake, there *is* something buried away back there in the past, and if we can find it everything will suddenly click into place. It's the key, Lewis – a key that slips easily into the lock and when it turns it's smooth and silky and – hey presto! So, let's forget for a while who saw Valerie last and what colour knickers she was wearing. Let's go back long before that. For if I'm right, if I'm right . . .'

'You think you've found the key?'

Morse grew rather more serious. 'I think so, yes. I think that what we've got to reckon with in this case is *power*, the power that someone, by some means or other, can exercise over someone else.'

'Blackmail, you mean, sir?'

Morse paused before answering. 'It may have been; I'm not sure yet.'

'You think someone's blackmailing Phillipson, is that it?'

'Let's not rush, Lewis. Just suppose for a minute. Suppose you yourself did something shady, and no one found out. No one, that is, except for one other person. Let's say you bribed a witness, or planted false evidence or something like that. All right? If you got found out, you'd be kicked out of the force on your ear, and find yourself in jug, as likely as not. Your career would be ruined, and your family, too. You'd give a lot to keep things dark, and just let's suppose that I was the one who knew all about this, eh?'

'You'd have me by the . . .' Lewis thought better of it.

'I would, indeed. But not only that. I could also do some shady things myself, couldn't I? And get you to cover up for me. It would be dangerous, but it might be necessary. I could get you to compound the original crime you'd committed, by committing another, but committing it for *me*, not for yourself. From then on we'd sink or swim together, I know that; but we'd be fools to split on each other, wouldn't we?'

Lewis nodded, he was getting a bit bored.

'Just think, Lewis, of the ordinary people we come across every day. They do the same sort of things we do and have the same sort of hopes and fears as everybody else. And they're not really villains at all, but some of them occasionally do things they'd be frightened to death of anyone else finding out about.'

'Pinching a bag of sugar from the supermarket – that sort of thing?' Morse laughed.

'Your mind, as always, Lewis leaps immediately to the limits of human iniquity! In the seventh circle of Dante's Hell we shall doubtless find the traitors, the mass murderers, the infant torturers, and the stealers of sugar from the supermarkets. But that's the sort of thing I mean, yes. Now just let that innocent mind of yours sink a little lower into the depths of human depravity, and tell me what you find.'

'You mean having another woman, sir?'

'How delicately you put things! Having another woman, yes. Jumping between the sheets with a luscious wench and thinking of nothing but that great lump of gristle hanging between your legs. And the little woman at home cooking a meal for you and probably pressing your pants or something. You make it all sound like having another pint of beer, Lewis; but perhaps you're right. It's not all that important in the long run. A quick blow-through, a bit of remorse and anxiety for a few days, and then it's all over. And you tell yourself you're a damned fool and you're not going to do it again. But what, Lewis, *what if someone finds out?*'

'Bit of hard luck.' He said it in such a way that Morse looked at him curiously.

'Have *you* ever had another woman?'

Lewis smiled. An old memory stirred and swam to the surface of his mind like a bubble in still water. 'I daren't tell you, sir. After all, I wouldn't want you to kick me out of the force, would I?'

The phone rang and Morse answered it. 'Good . . . Good . . . That's good . . . Excellent.' Morse's half of the conversation seemed singularly unenlightening and

Lewis asked him who it was. 'I'll come to that in a minute, Lewis. Now, where were we? Oh yes. I suspect – and, if I may say so, you tend to confirm my suspicion – that adultery is more widespread than even the League of Light would have us believe. And a few unlucky ones still get caught with their pants down, and a hell of a lot of others get away with it.'

'What are you getting at, sir?'

'Simply this.' He took a deep breath and hoped it wouldn't sound too melodramatic. 'I think that Phillipson had an affair with Valerie Taylor, that's all.'

Lewis whistled softly and slowly took it in. 'What makes you think that?'

'No one reason – just lots of little reasons. And above all, the fact that it's the only thing that makes sense of the whole wretched business.'

'I think you're wrong, sir. There's an old saying, isn't there – if you'll excuse the language – about not shitting on your own doorstep. Surely it would be far too risky? Her at the school and him headmaster? I don't believe it, sir. He's not such a fool as that, surely?'

'No, I don't think he is. But as I told you, I'm trying to look back further than that, to the time, let's say, before he became headmaster.'

'But he didn't know her then. He lived in Surrey.'

'Yes. But he came to Oxford at least once, didn't he?' said Morse slowly. 'He came up here when he was interviewed for the job. And in that sense, to use your own picturesque terminology, he wouldn't exactly be shitting on his own doorstep, would he?'

'But you just can't say things like that, sir. You've got to have some *evidence*.'

'Yes. We shall need some evidence, you're quite right. But just forgetting the evidence for a minute, what worries me is whether it's a *fact* or not; and I think that we've just got to assume that it *is* a fact. We *could* get the evidence – I'm sure of that. We could get it from Phillipson himself; and I think, Lewis, that there are one or two other persons who could tell us a good deal if they had a mind to.'

'You mean, sir, that you've not really got any evidence yet?'

'Oh, I wouldn't say that. One or two pointers, aren't there?'

'Such as?'

'Well, first of all there's Phillipson himself. *You* know he's hiding something as well as I do.' As was his wont, Morse blustered boldly through the weakest points in his argument. 'He doesn't talk about the girl in a natural way at all – not about the girl *herself*. It's almost as if he's frightened to remember her – as if he feels guilty about her in some way.' Lewis seemed stolidly unimpressed, and Morse left it. 'And then there's Maguire. By the way, I saw him again yesterday.'

Lewis raised his eyebrows. 'Did you? Where was that?'

'I, er, thought I ought to follow your advice after all. You were quite right, you know, about the London end. One or two loose ends to tie up, weren't there?'

Lewis opened his mouth, but got no further.

'When I first saw him,' continued Morse, 'it was obvious that he was jealous – plain miserably jealous. I think Valerie must have dropped the odd hint; nothing too specific, perhaps. And I tackled Maguíre about it again yesterday, and – well, I'm sure there was a bit of gossip, at least among some of the pupils.'

Lewis continued to sit in glum silence.

'And then there was George Taylor. According to him it was just about that time – when Phillipson first came for the job, that is – that Valerie began staying out late. Again I agree, nothing definite, but another suggestive indication, wouldn't you say?'

'To be truthful, sir, I wouldn't. I think you're making it all up as you're going along.'

'All right. I'll not argue. Just have a look at this.' He handed to Lewis the document that Baines had so carefully packaged for him. It was a photocopy of the expenses form that Phillipson had submitted to the Governors after the headship interviews. From the form it was immediately apparent that he had not reached home that evening; he had claimed for B and B at the Royal Oxford, and had arrived home at lunchtime on the following day.

'He probably missed his train,' protested Lewis.

'Don't think so,' said Morse. 'I've checked. The last of the interviews was over by a quarter to six, and there was a good train for Phillipson to catch at 8.35. And even if he'd missed that, there was another at 9.45. But he wouldn't miss it, would he? Two and three-quarter hours to get from Kidlington to Oxford? Come off it!'

'He probably felt tired – you know how it is.'

'Not too tired to cock his leg around Valerie Taylor.'

'It's just not fair to say that, sir.'

'Isn't it, now? Well, let me tell you something else, Lewis. I went to the Royal Oxford yesterday and found the old register. Do you know something? *There is no entry for any Phillipson that night.*'

'All right. He just tried to claim a few extra quid for nothing. He caught the train after all.'

'I bet he wouldn't like me to check up with his wife about that!' Morse was now regaining his momentum.

'You've not checked with her, then?'

'No. But I checked up on something else. I went round to the Station Hotel just opposite. Very interesting. They looked out their old register for me, and I'll give you one guess who the last entry on the list was.'

'He probably just got the names of the hotels muddled. They're pretty near each other.'

'Could be. But you see, Lewis, *there's no Phillipson there either.* Let me show you what there was, though.'

He passed over a photocopied sheet of paper and Lewis read what Morse had found:

'Mr E. Phillips, 41 Longmead Road, Farnborough.' He sat silently, and then looked again at the copy of the expenses form that Morse had given him earlier. It was certainly odd. Very, very odd.

'And,' continued Morse, 'I've checked on something else. There's no Mr Phillips who lives in Longmead Road, Farnborough, for the very simple reason there *is* no Longmead Road in Farnborough.'

Lewis considered the evidence. Initials? Move on one from D to E. Easy. Phillipson? Just leave off the last two letters. Could be. But something else was staring him in the face. The home address (as given on the expenses form) of Mr D. Phillipson was 14 Longmead Road, Epsom. Transpose the 1 and the 4, and move on one from E to F: Epsom to Farnborough.

'I should think Peters ought to be able to give us a line on the handwriting, sir.'

'We'll leave him out of it.' It sounded final.

'It's a bit suspicious, all right,' admitted Lewis. 'But where does Valerie Taylor fit in? Why her?'

'It's got to be her,' said Morse. 'It all adds up, don't you see?'

'No.'

'Well, let's just assume that what I suspect is the truth. Agreed? *Assume*, nothing more. Now, where are we? For some reason Phillipson meets Valerie, probably in Oxford, probably at the station buffet. He chats her up and – Bob's your uncle. Off they go to the Station Hotel – a bit of a roll round the bed, and she goes off home with a few quid in her pocket. I don't think she'd stay all night; probably a couple of hours or so – no more. It wouldn't be easy for her to leave the hotel after midnight, would it? Not without causing a bit of comment.'

'I still don't see why it should be Valerie, though. And even if you're right, sir, what's it all got to do with Valerie disappearing?'

Morse nodded. 'Tell me, Lewis. If *anyone* got to know about this little bit of philandering, who do you think it would be?'

'Phillipson could have told his wife, I suppose. You know, he would have felt guilty about it—'

'Mm.' It was Morse's turn to display a lack of enthusiasm and Lewis tried again.

'I suppose Valerie could have told someone?'

'Who?'

'Her mum?'

'She was a bit scared of her mum, wasn't she?'

'Her dad, then?'

'Could be.'

'I suppose someone could have seen them,' said Lewis slowly.

'I'm pretty sure someone did,' said Morse.

'And you think you know who it was?'

Again Morse nodded. 'So do you, I think.'

Did he? In such situations Lewis had learned to play it cleverly. 'You mean . . .?' He tried to look as knowing as his utter lack of comprehension would permit, and mercifully Morse took up his cue.

'Yes. He's the only person connected with the case who lives anywhere near there. You don't make an excursion to the Station Hotel if you live in Kidlington, do you? Come to think of it, you don't make an excursion to the Station Hotel wherever you live. The beer there's bloody awful.'

Lewis understood now, but wondered how on earth they'd ever managed to get this far on such a flimsy series of hypotheses. 'He found out, you think?'

'Saw 'em, most probably.'

'You've not tackled him about it yet?'

'No, I want to get a few things straight first. But I shall be seeing him, have no fear.'

'I still don't see why you think it was Valerie.'

'Well, let's look at things from her point of view for a minute. She gets herself pregnant, right?'

'So you say, sir.'

'And so does Maguire.'

'We've got no real evidence.'

'No, not yet, I agree. But we may well have some fairly soon – you'll see. For the minute let's just assume she's pregnant. I'm pretty sure that Phillipson himself wouldn't have been the proud daddy; in fact, I shouldn't think he ever dreamed of touching her again. But if she were in trouble, daren't tell her parents, say – who would she go to? As I see it, she may well have gone to someone who owed her a favour, someone who had some sort of moral duty to help her, someone in fact who daren't *not* help her. In short she'd probably go to Phillipson. And, as I see it, they cooked up something between 'em. The Taylors – they'd almost certainly have to be in on it – the Taylors, Phillipson and Valerie. I should think that Phillipson arranged a place for her to go to in London, paid the abortion clinic, and let the whole thing look like a runaway schoolgirl lark. The Taylors are saved any local scandal and disgrace. Phillipson has paid his pound of flesh, and Valerie is let off lightly for her sins. Yes, I think that's roughly what might have happened; only roughly, mind you.'

'But how did she disappear?'

'Again I'm guessing. But I suspect that when she left

home after lunch she took a minimum of things with her – hence the bag or basket, whatever it was; it had to look, you see, as if she was going off to school in the normal way – the neighbours and so on might see her. As it happens, they didn't – but that was pure chance. I should think she went down the main road, probably nipped into the ladies' lavatory by the shops and changed her school uniform for something a bit trendier (don't forget the bag, Lewis!), and met Phillipson who was waiting for her in his car further down the road near the roundabout. They've probably got her case in the boot already. He drove her down to the station in Oxford, gave her full instructions, parked somewhere in town, bought a book at Blackwells and got home by three o'clock. Easy.' He stopped and looked hopefully at Lewis. 'Well, something like that. What do you think?'

'And I suppose she just gets rid of the baby like you say, finds she likes London, gets in with a swinging set, and forgets all about mum and dad and everything at home.'

'Something like that,' said Morse, without conviction.

'They put the police to a dickens of a lot of trouble for nothing, then, didn't they?'

'Probably never thought we'd make so much fuss.'

'They'd have a good idea.'

Morse was looking increasingly uneasy. 'As I told you, Lewis, it's only a rough outline. Just remember that if Valerie had wanted to, she could have ruined Phillipson's career in a flash. Just think of the headlines! It'd be dynamite! And think of Valerie, too. She certainly wouldn't want to be carting a kid around at her age. And her parents . . .'

'A lot of parents don't seem to mind too much these days, sir.'

Morse was feeling cross and showed it. 'Well *they* did! They minded enough to go through with the whole bloody business; still are going through with it . . .'

Somewhere along the line the euphoria had turned to a saddened exasperation. He knew far better than Lewis could have told him that he hadn't really thought things through.

'You know, Lewis, something must have turned sour somewhere, mustn't it? Perhaps something went wrong . . .' He suddenly brightened. 'We shall have to find out, shan't we?'

'You think Valerie's still alive then, sir?'

Morse backed down with commendable grace. 'I suppose so, yes. After all she wrote home, didn't she? Or so you tell me.'

He had a cheek, this man Morse, and Lewis shook his head in dismay. Everything had pointed to a straightforward case of a girl running away from home. As everyone (including Morse) had said, it happens all the time. And what a dog's breakfast he'd made of it all!

But Lewis had to concede that there might be something worth salvaging from all that complicated nonsense. Valerie and Phillipson. *Could* be true, perhaps. But why did he have to invent all that fanciful stuff about changing in ladies' lavatories? Oh dear. But something else was worrying him.

'You said, sir, that you thought Baines might have found out about Phillipson and this girl – whoever she was.'

'I think he did. In fact, I think Baines knows a hell of a lot more about the whole caboodle than anybody.'

'More than you, sir?'

'God, yes. He's been watching and waiting, has Baines; and I suspect he'd be very happy for the truth – or most of it – to come out. Phillipson would be a dead duck then, and they'd have to appoint a new headmaster, wouldn't they? And they've got Baines – a faithful servant who's been there all these years, runner-up at the last appointment ... why, I shouldn't think the Governors would even advertise.'

'They'd have to, sir. It's the law.'

'Oh ... Anyway, he'd get the job – sure as eggs are eggs. And he'd love it. The thought of all that power, Lewis – power over other people's lives. That's what Baines is hankering after.'

'Don't you think,' said Lewis gently, 'that it would be a good idea to get things on to a bit of a firmer footing, sir? I mean, why not question Phillipson and Baines and the Taylors? You'd probably get the truth out of one of them.'

'Perhaps.' Morse stood up and flexed his arms. 'But you're going to be pleased with me, Lewis. At the beginning of this case I promised myself I'd stick to *facts*, and so far I've not done very well. But you see a reformed character before you, my friend. First, I've arranged to see Phillipson and Baines – together, mind you! – tomorrow afternoon. Good touch, eh, Lewis? *Tuesday* afternoon. Should be good, I reckon. No holds barred! And then – that phone call you heard. Metropolitan Police, no less. They're going to help us if they can; and they think they can. If Valerie did go up to London for an abortion, she'd have to go to some sort of clinic, wouldn't she? And we know exactly *when* she went. She might have changed her name and address and God knows what. But those boys in London are pretty sharp. If she *did* go to a clinic – even a shady, back-street clinic – I reckon we've got her on toast. And if they don't trace anything – well we shall have to think again, I suppose. But if we do find out where she went – and I think we shall – well, we're there, aren't we? She had no money of her own, that's for sure, and somebody, *somebody*, Lewis, had to fork out pretty handsomely. And then? Then we take it from there.' Morse sat down again. He was trying hard, but was convincing no one, not even himself.

'You're not really very interested in finding her at all, are you, sir?'

The sparkle had gone from Morse's eyes: Lewis was right, of course. 'To tell you the truth, I shan't give two buggers if we never find her. Perhaps we've found her, anyway. She may have been the girl sharing Maguire's flat. I don't think so. But if she was – so what? She may have been one of those strippers we saw; you remember, the one with the mask and the bouncy tits. So what? You know, Lewis, this whole case is beginning to get one almighty bore, and if all we're going to do is stir up a load of trouble and get poor old Phillipson the sack – I'd rather pack it up.'

'It's not like you to back out of anything, sir.'

Morse stared morosely at the blotting paper. 'It's just not my sort of case, Lewis. I know it's not a very nice thing to say, but I just get on better when we've got a body – a body that died from unnatural causes. That's all I ask. And we haven't got a body.'

'We've got a living body,' said Lewis quietly.

Morse nodded. 'I suppose you're right.' He walked across the room and stood by the door, but Lewis remained seated at the desk. 'What's the matter, Lewis?'

'I just can't help wondering where she is, sir. You know, at this very minute she must be somewhere, and if only we knew we could just go along there and find her. Funny, isn't it? But we can't find her, and I don't like giving up. I just wish we *could* find her, that's all.'

Morse walked back into the room and sat down again. 'Mm. I'd not thought of it quite like that before . . . I've been so cocksure she was dead that I haven't really thought of her as being alive. And you're right. She's somewhere; at this very second she's sitting *somewhere*.' The grey eyes were beginning to glow once more and Lewis felt happier.

'Could be quite a challenge, couldn't it, sir?'

'Ye-es. Perhaps it's not such a bad job after all – chasing a young tart like Valerie Taylor.'

'You think we should try, then?'

'I'm beginning to think we should, yes.'

'Where do we start?'

'Where the hell do you think? She's almost certainly sitting somewhere in a luxury flat plucking her eyebrows.'

'But where, sir?'

'Where? Where do you think? London, of course. What was that postmark? EC4 wasn't it? She's within a few miles' radius of EC4. Sure to be!'

'That wasn't the postmark on the second letter she wrote.'

'Second letter? Oh yes. What was the postmark on that?'

Lewis frowned slightly. 'W1. Don't you remember?'

'W1, eh? But I wouldn't worry your head about that second letter, Lewis?'

'You wouldn't?'

'No, I wouldn't bother about it at all. You see, Lewis, I wrote that second letter myself.'

CHAPTER SEVENTEEN

And all the woe that moved him so
    That he gave that bitter cry,
And the wild regrets, and the bloody sweats,
    None knew so well as I:
For he who lives more lives than one
    More deaths than one must die.
        Oscar Wilde, *The Ballad of Reading Gaol*

THERE WERE OVER one hundred and twenty of them, and it was too many. Why, if each of them were given leave to speak only for a minute, that would be two hours! But anyway, Acum didn't think he wanted to say anything. The great majority of the delegates were in their forties and fifties, senior men and women who, judging from their comments and their questions, sent forth an annual stream of gifted linguists to assume their natural Oxbridge birthrights.

He had felt tired after his five-and-a-half-hours' drive the previous day, and this morning's programme, conducted in a genteel atmosphere of rarefied intellectuality, had hardly succeeded in fostering any real *esprit de corps*. Speaking on 'Set Texts in the Sixth Form' the Senior Tutor had given voice softly and seriously to the delicate rhythms of Racine, and Acum began to wonder if the premier universities were not growing further and further out of touch with his own particular brand of comprehensive school. His main problem in the sixth was to recruit a handful of pupils who had just about reached the minimum requirement of a grade C in O-level French, and who, in the wake of their qualified triumphs, had promptly mislaid the substance of their erstwhile knowledge during two long months of carefree summer freedom. He wondered if other schools were different; if he himself, in some way, were to blame.

Fortunately the post-lunch discussion on the merits of the Nuffield French experiment was infinitely lighter and brighter, and Acum felt slightly more at home with his co-delegates. The Senior Tutor, the rhythms of Racine still rippling along through his mind, testified evangelically to the paramount need for a formal grammatical discipline in the teaching of all languages, including modern languages. And if Racine and Molière were not worth reading, reading with accuracy, and reading without the remotest possibility of misunderstanding arising from mistranslation – then we all might just as well forget literature and life. It sounded magnificent. And then that burly, cheerful fellow from Bradford had brought the academic argument down to earth with a magnificent thud: give him a lad or a lass with t'gumption to order t'pound of carrots at t'French greengrocer's shop, any dair! The conference exploded in glorious uproar. Slyly, a dignified old greybeard suggested that no Englishman, even one who had the good fortune to learn his native tongue in Yorkshire, had ever been confronted with an insuperable language-barrier in finding his way to a *pissoir* in Paris.

It was all good stuff now. The conference should have passed a vote of thanks to the burly Bradfordian and his pound of carrots. Even Acum nearly said something; and almost every other member of the silent majority nearly said something, too. There were just far too many there. Ridiculous, really. No one would notice if you were there or not. He was going out tonight, anyway. No one was going to miss him if he slipped away from the conference hall. He would be back long before the porters' lodge was shut at 11.00 p.m.

The school bell rang at 4.00 p.m., and the last lesson of the day was over. Streams of children emerged from classrooms and, like a nest of ants uncovered, bewilderingly crossed and re-crossed to cloakrooms, to bicycle sheds, to societies, to games practices and to sundry other pursuits. More leisurely, the teachers threaded their way back through the milling throngs to the staff room; some to smoke, some to talk, some to mark. And very soon most of them, teachers and pupils alike, would be making their way home. Another day was done.

Baines returned from teaching a fourth-year mathematics set and dropped a pile of thirty exercise books on to his table. Twenty seconds each – no more; only ten minutes the lot. He might as well get them marked straight away. Thank the Lord it wasn't like marking English or History, with all that reading to do. His practised eye had learned to pounce upon the pages in a flash. Yes, he would dash them off now.

'Mr Phillipson would like a word with you,' said Mrs Webb.

'Oh. Now?'

'As soon as you came in, he said.'

Baines knocked perfunctorily and entered the study.

'Have a seat a minute, Baines.'

Warily the second master took a seat. There was a serious edge to Phillipson's voice – like a doctor's about to inform you that you've only a few months more to live.

'Inspector Morse will be in again tomorrow afternoon. You know that, don't you?' Baines nodded. 'He wants to talk to us both – together.'

'He didn't mention that to me.'

'Well, that's what he's going to do.' Baines said nothing. 'You know what this probably means, don't you?'

'He's a clever man.'

'No doubt. But he won't be getting any further, will he?' The tone of Phillipson's voice was hard, almost the tone of a master to his pupil. 'You realize what I'm saying, don't you, Baines? Keep your mouth shut!'

'Yes, you'd like me to do that, wouldn't you?'

'I'm warning you!' The latent hatred suddenly blazed in Phillipson's eyes. No pretence now; only an ugly, naked hatred between them.

Baines got up, savouring supremely the moment of his power. 'Don't push me too far, Phillipson! And just remember who you're talking to.'

'Get out!' hissed Phillipson. The blood was pounding in his ears, and although a non-smoker he longed to light a cigarette. He sat motionless at his desk for many minutes and wondered how much longer the nightmare could go on. What a relief it would be to end it all – one way or another . . .

Gradually he grew calmer, and his mind wandered back again. How long ago was it now? Over three and a half years! And still the memory of that night came back to haunt him like a ghost unexorcized. That night . . . He could picture it all so vividly still . . .

He felt quite pleased with himself. Difficult to tell for certain, of course; but yes, quite pleased with himself really. As accurately as it could his mind retraced the stages of the day's events; the questions of the interviewing committee – wise and foolish; and his own answers – carefully considered . . .

CHAPTER EIGHTEEN

In philological works ... a dagger † signifies an obsolete word. The ... sign, placed before a person's name, signifies deceased.

Rules for Compositors and Readers, OUP

THIS SAME MONDAY night or, to be accurate, Tuesday morning, Morse was not in bed until 2.00 a.m., overtired and underbeered. The euphoria of the earlier part of the day had now completely passed, partly as a result of Lewis's sceptical disparagement, but more significantly because of his own inability ever to fool himself for very long. He still believed that some of the pieces had clicked into place, but knew that many didn't fit at all; and a few didn't even look like pieces of the same jigsaw. He recollected how in the army he had been given a test for colour-blindness. A sheet of paper on which a chaotically confused conglomeration of colour blocks were printed had been magically metamorphosed when looked at through differently-coloured filter slides; a red filter, and there appeared an elephant; a blue filter, and a lion leaped out at the eyes; a green filter, and behold the donkey! Donkey ... He'd been reading something about a donkey only a few days ago. Where had he read it? Morse was not a systematic reader; he was a dipper-in. He looked at the small pile of books on his bedside table underneath the alarm clock. *The Road to Xanadu, A Selection of Kipling's Short Stories, The Life of Richard Wagner* and *Selected Prose of A. E. Housman.* It was in Housman, surely, that bit about the donkey who couldn't make up its asinine mind which bundle of hay to start on first. Hadn't the stupid animal finally died of starvation? He soon found the passage:

> An editor of no judgement, perpetually confronted with a couple of MSS to choose from, cannot but feel in every fibre of his being that he is a donkey between two bundles of hay.

Two MSS, and no judgement! That summed it up perfectly. One MS told him that Valerie Taylor was alive, and the other told him she was dead. And he still didn't know which MS a man of judgement should settle for. Oh Lord! Which of the wretched MSS had the correct reading? Had either?

He knew that at this rate he would never go to sleep, and he told himself to forget it all and think of something else. He picked up Kipling and began re-reading his favourite short story, *Love O' Women.* He firmly believed that Kipling knew more about women than Kinsey ever had, and he came back to a passage marked with vertical lines in the margin:

> . . . as you say, sorr, he was a man with an educashin, an' he used ut for his schames; an' the same educashin an' talkin' an' all that made him able to do

fwhat he had a mind to wid a woman, that same wud turn back again in the long-run an' *tear him alive.*

Phew!

He thought back on what he'd learned about Valerie's sex life. Nothing much, really. He thought of Maguire, and half-remembered something Maguire had said that didn't quite ring true. But he couldn't quite get hold of it and the memory slipped away again like a bar of soap in the bath.

Educashin. Most people were more interesting for a bit of education. More interesting to women . . . some of these young girls must soon get tired of the drib-drab, wishy-washy drivel that sometimes passed for conversation. Some of them liked older men for just that reason; interesting men with some show of pretence for cultured pursuits, with a smattering of knowledge – with something more in mind than fiddling for their bra-straps after a couple of whiskies.

What *was* Valerie like? Had she gone for the older men? Phillipson? Baines? But surely not Baines. Some of her teachers, perhaps? Acum? He couldn't remember the other names. And then he suddenly caught the bar of soap. He'd asked Maguire how many times he'd been to bed with Valerie, and Maguire had said a dozen or so. And Morse had told him to come off it and tell him the truth, fully expecting a considerably increased count of casual copulations. But no. Maguire had come down, hadn't he? 'Well, three or four,' he'd said. Something like that. Probably hadn't slept with her at all? Morse sat up and considered. Why, ah why, hadn't he pressed this point with Maguire when he had seen him yesterday? Was she really pregnant after all? He had assumed so, and Maguire had seemingly confirmed his suspicions. But was she? It made sense if she was. But made sense of what? Of the preconceived pattern that Morse was building up, and into which, willy-nilly, the pieces were being forced into their places.

If only he knew what the problem *was*. Then he wouldn't be quite so restless, even if it proved beyond his powers. Problem! He remembered his old Latin master. Hm! Whenever *he* was confronted with an insoluble difficulty – a crux in the text, an absurdly complex chunk of syntax – he would turn to his class with a serious mien: 'Gentlemen, having looked this problem boldly in the face, we must now, I think, pass on.' Morse smiled at the recollection . . . It was getting very late. A crux in the Oxford Classical Text, marked by daggers . . . the daggered text . . . He was falling asleep. Texts, manuscripts, and a donkey in the middle braying and bellyaching, not knowing which way to turn . . . like Morse, like himself . . . His head fell to the right and his ear strained no more for the incomprehensible nocturnal clues. He fell asleep, the light still burning and Kipling's stories still held loosely in his hand.

Earlier the same evening Baines had opened his front door to find an unexpected visitor.

'Well, well! This *is* a surprise. Come in, won't you? Shall I take your coat?'

'No. I'll keep it on.'

'Well, at least you'll have a drop of something to cheer you up, eh? Can I offer you a glass of something? Nothing much in, though, I'm afraid.'

'If you like.'

His visitor following behind, Baines walked through to the small kitchen, opened the fridge, and looked inside. 'Beer? Lager?'

Baines squatted on his haunches and reached inside. His left hand lay on the top of the fridge, the fingernails slightly dirty; his right hand reached far in as he bent forward. There were two bald patches on the top of his head, with a greying tuft of hair between them, temporarily thwarting the impending merger. He wore no tie, and the collar of his light-blue shirt was grubbily lined. He would have changed it the next day.

CHAPTER NINETEEN

One morn I miss'd him on the custom'd hill.
Thomas Gray, *Elegy Written in a Country
Churchyard*

FULL MORNING ASSEMBLY at the Roger Bacon Comprehensive School began at 8.50. The staff stood at the back of the main hall, wearing (at least those authorized to do so) the insignia of their respective universities; it was something the head insisted on. Punctual to the second, and flanked at some short distance in the rear by the second master and the senior mistress, Phillipson, begowned and behooded, walked from the back of the hall, and the pupils rose to their feet as the procession made its way down the central gangway, climbed the short flight of steps at the side and mounted on to the stage itself. The routine seldom varied: a hymn sung, a prayer intoned, a passage read from Holy Writ – and paid for one more day were the proper respects to the Almighty. The last unsynchronized 'Amen' marked the end of morning devotions, and gave the cue to the second master to recall the attention of the assembled host to more terrestrial things. Each morning he announced, in clear, unhurried tones, any changes in the day's procedure necessitated by staff absences, house activities, the times and places of society meetings, and the results of the sports teams. And, always, reserved until the end, he read with doomsday gravity a list of names; the names of pupils who would report outside the staff room immediately after the assembly was finished: the recalcitrants, the anarchists, the obstructionists, the truants, the skivers, and the defectors in general from the rules that governed the corporate life of the establishment.

As the procession walked up the central aisle on Tuesday morning, and as the school rose en bloc from their seats, several heads turned towards each other and many whispered voices asked where Baines could be; not even the oldest pupils could remember him being away for a single day before. The senior mistress looked lopsided and lost: it was like the dissolution of the Trinity. Phillipson himself read the notices, referring in no way to the absence of his adjutant. The girls' hockey team had achieved a rare and decisive victory, and the school greeted the news with unwonted enthusiasm. The chess club would meet in the physics lab and 4C (for unspecified criminality) would be staying in after school. The following pupils, etc., etc. Phillipson turned away from the rostrum and walked out through the wings. The school chattered noisily and prepared to go to their classrooms.

At lunchtime Phillipson spoke to his secretary.

'No word from Mr Baines yet?'

'Nothing. Do you think we should give him a ring?'

Phillipson considered for a moment. 'Perhaps we should. What do you think?'

'Not like him to be away, is it?'

'No, it isn't. Give him a ring now.'

Mrs Webb rang Baines's Oxford number and the distant burring seemed to echo in a vaulted, ominous silence.

'There's no answer,' she said.

At 2.15 p.m. a middle-aged woman took from her handbag the key to Baines's house; she cleaned for him three afternoons a week. Oddly, the door was unlocked and she pushed it open and walked in. The curtains were still drawn and the electric light was still turned on in the living room, as well as in the kitchen, the door to which stood open wide. And even before she walked through to the kitchen she saw the slumped figure of Baines in front of the refrigerator, a long-handled household knife plunged deep into his back, the dried blood forming a horrid blotch upon the cotton shirt, like a deranged artist's study in claret and blue.

She screamed hysterically.

It was 4.30 p.m. before the fingerprint man and the photographer were finished, and before the hump-backed surgeon straightened his afflicted spine as far as nature would permit.

'Well?' asked Morse.

'Difficult to say. Anywhere from sixteen to twenty hours.'

'Can't you pin it down any closer?'

'No.'

Morse had been in the house just over an hour, for much of which time he had been sitting abstractedly in one of the armchairs in the living room, waiting for the others to leave. He doubted they could tell him much, anyway. No signs of forcible entry, nothing stolen (or not apparently so), no fingerprints, no blood-stained footprints. Just a dead man, and a deep pool of blood and a fridge with an open door.

A police car jerked to a halt outside and Lewis came in. 'He wasn't at school this morning, sir.'

'Hardly surprising,' said Morse, without any conscious humour.

'Do we know when he was murdered?'

'Between eight o'clock and midnight, they say.'

'Pretty vague, sir.'

Morse nodded. 'Pretty vague.'

'Did you expect something like this to happen?'

Morse shook his head. 'Never dreamed of it.'

'Do you think it's all connected?'

'What do you think?'

'Somebody probably thought that Baines was going to tell us what he knew.' Morse grunted noncommittally. 'Funny, isn't it, sir?' Lewis glanced at his watch. 'He'd have told us by now, wouldn't he? And I've been thinking, sir.' He looked earnestly at the inspector. 'There weren't many who knew you were going to see Baines this afternoon, were there? Only Phillipson really.'

'Each of them could have told somebody else.'

'Yes, but—'

'Oh, it's a good point. I see what you're getting at. How did Phillipson take the news, by the way?'

'Seemed pretty shattered, sir.'

'I wonder where he was between eight o'clock and midnight,' mumbled Morse, half to himself, as he eased himself out of the armchair. 'We'd better try to look like detectives, Lewis.'

The ambulance men asked if they could have the body, and Morse walked with them into the kitchen. Baines had been eased gently on to his right side, and Morse bent down and eased the knife slowly from the second master's back. What an ugly business murder was. It was a wooden-handled carving knife. 'Prestige, Made in England', some 35–36 centimetres long, the cutting blade honed along its entire edge to a razor-sharp ferocity. Globules of fresh pink blood oozed from the wicked-looking wound, and gradually seeped over the stiff clotted mess that once had been a blue shirt. They took Baines away in a white sheet.

'You know, Lewis, I think whoever killed him was bloody lucky. It's not too easy to stab a man in the back, you know. You've got to miss the spinal column and the ribs and the shoulder blades, and even then you've got to be lucky to kill someone straight off. Baines must have been leaning forward, slightly over to his right, and exposing about the one place that makes it comparatively easy. Just like going through a joint of beef.'

Lewis loathed the sight of death, and he felt his stomach turning over. He walked to the sink for a glass of water. The cutlery and the crockery from Baines's last meal were washed up and neatly stacked on the draining board, the dish cloth squeezed out and draped over the bowl.

'Perhaps the post-mortem'll tell us what time he had his supper,' suggested Lewis hopefully.

Morse was unenthusiastic. He followed Lewis to the sink and looked around half-heartedly. He opened the drawer at the right of the sink unit. The usual collection: teaspoons, tablespoons, wooden spoons, a fish slice, two corkscrews, kitchen scissors, a potato peeler, various meat skewers, a steel – and a kitchen knife. Morse picked up the knife and looked at it carefully. The handle was bone, and the blade was worn away with constant sharpening into a narrowed strip. 'He's had this a good while,' said Morse. He ran his finger along the blade; it had almost the same cruel sharpness as the blade that had lodged its head in Baines's heart.

'How many carving knives do you keep at home, Lewis?'

'Just the one.'

'You wouldn't think of buying another one?'

'No point, really, is there?'

'No,' said Morse. He placed the murder weapon on the kitchen table and looked around. There seemed singularly little point in any inspection, however intelligently directed, of the tins of processed peas and preserved plums that lined the shelves of the narrow larder.

'Let's move next door, Lewis. You take the desk; I'll have a look at the books.'

Most of the bookshelves were taken up with works on mathematics, and Morse looked with some interest at a comprehensive set of textbooks on the *School Mathematics Project*, lined up in correct order from Book 1 to Book 10, and beside them the corresponding Teacher's Guide for each volume. Morse delved diffidently into Book 1.

'Know anything about modern maths, Lewis?'

'Modern maths? Ha! I'm an acknowledged expert. I do all the kids' maths homework.'

'Oh.' Morse decided to puzzle his brain no more on how 23 in base 10 could be expressed in base 5, replaced the volume, and inspected the rest of Baines's library. He'd been numerate all right. But literate? Doubtful. On the whole Morse felt slightly more sympathy with Maguire's uncompromising collection.

As he stood by the shelves the grim, brutal fact of Baines's murder slowly sank into his mind. As yet it figured as an isolated issue; he'd had no chance of thinking of it in any other context. But he would be doing so soon, very soon. In fact some of the basic implications were already apparent. Or was he fooling himself again? No. It meant, for a start, that the donkey knew for certain which bundle of hay to go for, and that, at least, was one step forward. Baines must have known something. Correction. Baines must have known virtually everything. Was that the reason for his death, though? It seemed the likeliest explanation. But who had killed him? Who? From the look of things the murderer must have been known to Baines – known pretty well; must have walked into the kitchen and stood there as Baines reached inside the fridge for something. And the murderer had carried a knife – surely that was a reasonable inference? Had brought the knife into the house. But how the hell did anyone carry a knife as big as that around? Stuff it down your socks, perhaps? Unless . . .

From across the room a low-pitched whistle of staggering disbelief postponed any answers that might have been forthcoming to these and similar questions. Lewis's facial expression was one of thrilled excitement mingled with pained incredulity.

'You'd better come over here straight away, sir.'

Morse himself looked down into the bottom right-hand drawer of the desk; and he felt the hairs at the nape of his neck grow stiff. A book lay in the drawer, an exercise book; an exercise book from the Roger Bacon Comprehensive School; and on the front of the exercise book a name, a most familiar name, was inscribed in capital letters: VALERIE TAYLOR: APPLIED SCIENCE. The two men looked at each other and said nothing. Finally Morse picked up the book gently, placing the top of each index finger along the spine; and as he did so, two loose sheets of paper fell out and fluttered to the floor. Morse picked them up and placed them on the desk. The sheets contained drafts of a short letter; a letter which began Dear Mum and Dad and ended Love Valerie. Several individual words were crossed out and the identical words, but with minor alterations to the lettering, written above them; and between the drafts were whole lines of individual letters, practised and slowly perfected: w's, r's, and t's. It was Lewis who broke the long silence.

'Looks as if you're not the only forger in the case, sir.' Morse made no reply. Somewhere at the back of his mind something clicked smoothly into place. So far in the case he had managed to catch a few of the half-whispers and from them half-divine the truth; but now it seemed the facts were shouting at him through a megaphone.

Baines, it was clear, had written the letter to Valerie's parents; and the evidence for Valerie being still alive was down to zero on the scale of probabilities. In one way Morse was glad; and in another he felt a deep and poignant sadness. For life was sweet, and we each of us had our own little hopes, and few of us exhibited overmuch anxiety to quit this vale of misery and tears. Valerie had a right to live. Like himself. Like Lewis. Like Baines, too, he supposed. But someone had decided that Baines had forfeited his right to live any longer and stuck a knife through him. And Morse stood silently at Baines's desk and knew that everyone expected him to discover who that someone was. And perhaps he would, too. At the rate he was going he would be able to know the truth before the day was out. Perhaps all he had to do was look through the rest of the drawers and find the whole solution neatly copied out and signed. But he hardly expected to find much else, and didn't. For the next hour he and Lewis carefully and patiently vetted the miscellaneous con-tents of each of the other drawers; but they found nothing more of any value or interest, except a recent photocopy of Phillipson's expenses form.

The phone stood on the top of the desk, a white phone, the same phone that had rung at lunchtime when Mrs Webb had called a man who then lay cold and dead beside the opened fridge. And then, suddenly, Morse noticed it. It had been under his nose all the time but he had ignored it because it was an item so naturally expected: a plastic, cream-coloured rectangular telephone index-system, whereby one pressed the alphabetical letter and the index opened automatically at the appropriate place. Half expecting to find his own illustrious self recorded, Morse pressed the 'M'; but there was nothing on the ruled card. Clearly none of Baines's more intimate acquaintances boasted a surname beginning with 'M'. So Morse pressed 'N'; and again he found no entry. And 'O'; and with the same result. Probably Baines had only recently acquired the index? It looked reasonably new and maybe he had not yet transcribed the numbers from an older list. But no such list had yet been found. Morse pressed 'P', and a slight shiver ran along his spine as he saw the one entry: Phillipson, with the headmaster's Oxford telephone number neatly appended thereto. Morse continued systematically through the remainder of the alphabet. Under 'R' was the number of the Oxford branch of the RAC, but nothing more. And under 'S', the number of a Sun Insurance agent. And then 'T'; and once again the slight, involuntary shiver down the spine. Taylor. And somewhere at the back of Morse's mind something else clicked smoothly into place. 'U', 'V' – nothing. 'W',

Mr Wright, with an Oxford number: builder and decorator. On to 'x', 'y', 'z' – nothing. 'a'. Morse looked
carefully at the card and frowned, and whistled softly.
Only one entry: Acum, the personal number (not the
school's) written neatly in the appropriate column . . .

In all, there were fourteen entries only, most of
which were as innocently explicable as the RAC and
the interior decorator. And only three of the fourteen
names appeared to have the slightest connection with the
case: Acum, Phillipson, Taylor. Funny (wasn't it?) how
the names seemed to crop up in trios. First, it had been
Acum, Baines and Phillipson, and now Baines had got
himself crossed off the list and another name had
appeared almost magically in his place: the name of
Taylor. Somewhere, yet again, in the farthest uncharted
corners of Morse's mind, a little piece clicked smoothly
into place.

Although the curtains had been drawn back as soon
as the police arrived, the electric lights were still
switched on, and Morse finally switched them off as he
stood on the threshold. It was 5.30 p.m.

'What's next?' asked Lewis.

Morse pondered a while. 'Has the wife got the chips
on, Lewis?'

'I 'spect so, sir. But I'm getting rather fond of dried-
up chips.'

CHAPTER TWENTY

Alibi (L. alibi, elsewhere, orig. locative – alius, other);
the plea in a criminal charge of having been elsewhere
at the material time.

Oxford English Dictionary

'HE'S NOT GOING to like it much.'

'Of course he's not going to like it much.'

'It's almost as good as saying we suspect him.'

'Well? We do, don't we?'

'Among others, you mean, sir?'

'Among others.'

'It's a pity they can't be just a bit more definite about
the time.' Lewis sounded uneasy.

'Don't worry about that,' said Morse. 'Just get a
complete schedule – from the time he left school to the
time he went to bed.'

'As I say, sir, he's not going to like it very much.'

Morse got up and abruptly terminated the conversation. 'Well, he'll have to bloody well lump it, won't he?'

It was just after 6.30 p.m. when Morse pushed his way
through the glass doors, left Police HQ behind him and
made his way slowly and thoughtfully towards the
housing estate. He wasn't looking forward to it, either.

As Lewis had said, it was almost as good as saying you suspected them.

The Taylors' green Morris Oxford was parked along the pavement, and it was the shirt-sleeved George himself who answered the door, hastily swallowing a mouthful of his evening meal.

'I'll call back,' began Morse.

'No. No need, Inspector. Nearly finished me supper. Come on in.' George had been sitting by himself in the kitchen finishing off a plate of stew and potatoes. 'Cup o' tea?'

Morse declined and sat opposite George at the rickety kitchen table.

'What can I do for you, Inspector Morse?' He filled an outsize cup with deep-brown tea and lit a Woodbine. Morse told him of Baines's murder. The news had broken just too late for the final edition of the *Oxford Mail*, a copy of which lay spread out on the table.

George's reaction was flat and unconcerned. He'd known Baines, of course – seen him at parents' evenings. But that was all. It seemed to Morse curious that George Taylor had so little to say or (apparently) to feel on learning of the death of a fellow human being he had known; yet neither was there a hint of machination or of malice in his eyes, and Morse felt now, as on the previous occasion they had met, that he rather liked the man. But sooner or later he had to ask him, in the hallowed phrases, to account for all his movements on the previous evening. For the moment he stood on the brink and postponed the evil moment; and mercifully George himself did a good deal of the work for him.

'The missus knew him better'n me. I'll tell her when she gets in. Mondays and Tuesdays she's allus off at Bingo down in Oxford.'

'Does she ever win?' The question seemed oddly irrelevant.

'Few quid now and then. In fact she won a bit last night, I reckon. But you know how it is – she spends about a quid a night anyway. Hooked on it, that's what she is.'

'How does she go? On the bus?'

'Usually. Last night, though, I was playing for the darts team down at the Jericho Arms, so I took her down with me, and she called in at the pub after she was finished, and then came home with me. It's on the bus, though, usually.'

Morse took a deep breath and jumped in. 'Look, Mr Taylor, it's just a formality and I know you'll understand, but, er, I've got to ask you exactly where you were last night.'

George seemed not in the least put out or perturbed. In fact – or was it a nothing, an imperceptibility, a fleeting flash of Morse's imagination? – there might have been the merest hint of relief in the friendly eyes.

Lewis was already waiting when Morse arrived back in his office at 7.30 p.m., and the two men exchanged notes. Neither of them, it appeared, had been in too much danger of flushing any desperado from his lair. The alibis were not perfect – far from it; but they were good enough. Phillipson (according to Phillipson) had arrived home from school about 5.15 p.m.; had eaten, and had left home, alone, at 6.35 p.m. to see the Playhouse production of *St Joan.* He had left his car in the Gloucester Green car park and reached the theatre at 6.50 p.m. The play had lasted from 7.15 to 10.30 p.m., and apart from walking to the bar for a Guinness in the first interval he had not left his seat until just after 10.30 when he collected his car and drove back home. He remembered seeing the BBC2 news bulletin at 11.00 p.m.

'How far's Gloucester Green from Baines's house?' asked Morse.

Lewis considered. 'Two, three hundred yards.'

Morse picked up the phone and rang the path lab. No. The humpbacked surgeon had not yet completed the scrutiny of various lengths of Baines's innards. No. He couldn't be more precise about the time of death. Eight to midnight. Well, if Morse were to twist his arm it might be 8.30 to 11.30 – even 11.00, perhaps. Morse cradled the phone, stared up at the ceiling for a while, and then nodded slowly to himself.

'You know, Lewis, the trouble with alibis is not that some people have 'em and some people don't. The real trouble is that virtually no one's likely to have a really water-tight alibi. Unless you've been sitting all night handcuffed to a couple of high court judges, or something.'

'You think Phillipson could have murdered Baines, then?'

'Of course he could.'

Lewis put his notebook away. 'How did you get on with the Taylors, sir?'

Morse recounted his own interview with George Taylor, and Lewis listened carefully.

'So *he* could have murdered Baines, too.'

Morse shrugged noncommittally. 'How far's the Jericho Arms from Baines's place?'

'Quarter of a mile – no more.'

'The suspects are beginning to queue up, aren't they, Lewis?'

'Is Mrs Taylor a suspect?'

'Why not? As far as I can see, she'd have had no trouble at all. Left Bingo at 9.00 p.m. and called in at the Jericho Arms at 9.30 p.m. or so. On the way she walks within a couple of hundred yards of Baines's place, eh? And where does it all leave us? If Baines was murdered at about 9.30 last night – what have we got? Three of 'em – all with their telephone numbers on Baines's little list.'

'And there's Acum, too, sir. Don't forget him.'

Morse looked at his watch. It was 8.00 p.m. 'You know, Lewis, it would be a real turn-up for the books if Acum was playing darts in the Jericho Arms last night, eh? Or sitting at a Bingo board in the Town Hall?'

'He'd have a job wouldn't he, sir? He's in Caernarfon.'

'I'll tell you one thing for sure, Lewis. Wherever Acum was last night he wasn't in Caernarfon.'

He picked up the phone and dialled a number. The call was answered almost immediately.

'Hello?' The line crackled fitfully, but Morse recognized the voice.

'Mrs Acum?'

'Yes. Who is it?'

'Morse. Inspector Morse. You remember, I rang you up—'

'Yes, of course I remember.'

'Is your husband in yet?'

'No. I think I mentioned to you, didn't I, that he wouldn't be back until late tonight?'

'How late will he be?'

'Not too late, I hope.'

'Before ten?'

'I hope so.'

'Has he got far to travel?'

'Quite a long way, yes.'

'Look, Mrs Acum. Can you please tell me where your husband has been?'

'I told you. He's been on a teachers' conference. Sixth form French.'

'Yes. But where exactly was that?'

'Where? I'm not quite sure where he was staying.'

Morse was becoming impatient. 'Mrs Acum, you know what I mean. Where was the conference? In Birmingham?'

'Oh, I'm sorry. I see what you mean. It was in Oxford, actually.'

Morse turned to Lewis and his eyebrows jumped an inch. 'In Oxford, you say?'

'Yes. Lonsdale College.'

'I see. Well, I'll ring up again – about ten. Will that be all right?'

'Is it urgent, Inspector?'

'Well, let's say it's important, Mrs Acum.'

'All right, I'll tell him. And if he gets back before ten, I'll ask him to ring you.'

Morse gave her his number, rang off, and whistled softly. 'It gets curiouser and curiouser, does it not, Lewis? How far is Lonsdale College from Kempis Street?'

'Half a mile?'

'One more for the list, then. Though I suppose Acum's got just as good, or just as bad, an alibi as the rest of 'em.'

'Haven't you forgotten one possible suspect, sir?'

'Have I?' Morse looked at his sergeant in some surprise.

'Mrs Phillipson, sir. Two young children, soon in bed, soon asleep. Husband safely out of the way for three hours or so. She's got as good a motive as anybody, hasn't she?'

Morse nodded. 'Perhaps she's got a better motive than most.' He nodded again and looked sombrely at the carpet.

With a startling suddenness, a large spider darted across the floor with a brief, electric scurry – and, as suddenly, stopped – frozen into a static, frightening immobility. A fat-bodied, long-legged spider, the angular joints of the hairy limbs rising high above the dark squat body. Another scurry – and again the frozen immobility – more frightening in its stillness than in its

186

motion. It reminded Morse of a game he used to play at children's parties called 'statues'; the music suddenly stopped and – still! Freeze! Don't move a muscle! Like the spider. It was almost at the skirting board now, and Morse seemed mesmerized. He was terrified of spiders.

'Did you see that whopper in Baines's bath?' asked Lewis.

'Shut up, Lewis. And put your foot on the bloody thing, quick!'

'Mustn't do that, sir. He's got a wife and kids waiting for him somewhere.' He bent down and slowly moved his hand towards the spider; and Morse shut his eyes.

CHAPTER TWENTY-ONE

John and Mary are each given 20p.
John gives 1p to Mary.
How much more does Mary have than John?
Problem set in the 11+ examination

THE URGE TO gamble is so universal, so deeply embedded in unregenerate human nature that from the earliest days the philosophers and moralists have assumed it to be evil. *Cupiditas*, the Romans called it – the longing for the things of this world, the naked, shameless greed for gain. It is the cause, perhaps, of all our troubles. Yet how easy it remains to understand the burning envy, felt by those possessing little, for those endowed with goods aplenty. And gambling? Why, gambling offers to the poor the shining chance of something got for nothing.

Crude analysis! For to some it is gambling itself, the very process and the very practice of gambling that is so immensely pleasurable. So pleasurable indeed that gambling needs, for them, no spurious *raison d'être* whatsoever, no necessary prospect of the jackpots and the windfalls and the weekends in Bermuda; just the heady, heavy opiate of the gambling game itself with the promise of its thousand exhilarating griefs and dangerous joys. Win a million on the wicked spinning-wheel tonight, and where are you tomorrow night but back around the wicked spinning-wheel?

Every society has its games, and the games are just as revealing of the society as are its customs – for in a sense they are its customs: heads or tails, and *rouge ou noir,* and double or quits and clunk, clunk, clunk, in the pay-off tray as the triple oranges align themselves along the fruit machine; and odds of 10 to 1 as the rank outsider gallops past the post at Kempton Park; *and then came the first, saying, Lord, thy pound hath gained ten pounds. And he said unto him, Well done, thou good servant: because thou hast been faithful in a very little, have thou authority over ten cities.* And once a week, a hope a light-year distant, of half a million pounds for half a penny stake, where happiness is a line of Xs and a kiss from a buxom beauty queen. For some are lucky at the gambling game. And some are not, and lose more than they can properly afford and try to recoup their losses and succeed only in losing the little that is left; and finally, alas, all hope abandoned, sit them down alone in darkened garages and by the gas rings in the kitchens, or simply slit their throats – and die. And some smoke fifty cigarettes a day, and some drink gin or whisky; and some walk in and out of betting shops, and the wealthier reach for the phone.

But what wife can endure a gambling husband, unless he be a steady winner? And what husband will ever believe his wife has turned compulsive gambler, unless she be a poorer liar than Mrs Taylor is. And Mrs Taylor dreams she dwells in Bingo halls.

*

It had started some years back in the church hall at Kidlington. A dozen of them, no more, seated in rickety chairs with a clickety subfusc vicar calling the numbers with a dignified Anglican clarity. And then she had graduated to the Ritz in Oxford, where the acolytes sit comfortably in the curving tiers of the cinema seats and listen to the harsh metallic tones relayed by microphones across the giant auditorium. There is no show here of human compassion, little even of human intercourse. Only 'eyes down' in a mean-minded race to the first row, the first column, the first diagonal completed. Many of the players can cope with several cards simultaneously, a cold, pitiless purpose in their play, their mental antennae attuned only to the vagaries of the numerical combinations.

The game itself demands only an elementary level of numeracy, and not only does not require but cannot possibly tolerate the slightest degree of initiative or originality. Almost all the players almost win; the line is almost complete, and the card is almost full. Ye gods! Look down and smile once more! Come on, my little number, come! I'm *there*, if only, if only, if only . . . And there the women sit and hope and pray and bemoan the narrow miss and curse their desperate luck, and talk and think 'if only' . . .

Tonight Mrs Taylor caught the No 2 bus outside the Ritz and reached Kidlington at 9.35 p.m.; she decided she would call in at the pub.

*

It was 9.35 p.m., too, when Acum rang, a little earlier than expected. He had been fortunate with the traffic (he said); on to the A5 at Towcester and a good clear run for a further five uncomplicated hours. He had left Oxford at 3.15, just before the conference had officially broken up. Jolly good conference, yes. The Monday night? Just a minute; let's think. In hall for dinner, and then there had been a fairly informal question-and-answer session afterwards. Very interesting. Bed about 10.30; a bit tired. No, as far as he remembered – no, he *did* remember; he hadn't gone out at all. Baines dead? What? Could Morse repeat that? Oh dear; very sorry to hear it. Yes, of course he'd known Baines – known him well. When did he die? Oh, Monday. Monday evening? Oh, yesterday evening, the one they'd just been speaking about. Oh, he saw now. Well, he'd told Morse what he could – sorry it was so little. Not been much help at all, had he?

Morse rang off. He decided that trying to interview by telephone was about as satisfactory as trying to sprint in divers' boots. There was no option; he would have to go up to Caernarfon himself, if . . . if what? Was it really likely that Acum had anything to do with Baines's death? If he had, he'd picked a pretty strange way of drawing almost inevitable attention to himself. And yet . . . And yet Acum's name had been floating unobtrusively along the mainstream of the case from the very beginning, and yesterday he had seen Acum's telephone number in the index file on Baines's desk. Mm. He would have to go and see him. He ought to have seen him before now; for whatever else he was or wasn't Acum had been a central figure during that school summer when she'd disappeared. But . . . but you don't just come down to Oxford for a meeting and decide that while you're there you'll murder one of your ex-colleagues. Or do you? Who would suspect? After all, it was quite by accident that he himself had learned of Acum's visit to Oxford. Had Acum presumed . . .? Augrrh! It was suddenly cold in the office and Morse felt tired. Forget it! He looked at his watch. 10 p.m. Just time for a couple of pints if he hurried.

He walked over to the pub and pushed his way into the overcrowded public bar. The cigarette smoke hung in blue wreaths, head-high like undispersing morning mist, and the chatter along the bar and at the tables was raucous and interminable, the subtleties of conversational silence quite unknown. Cribbage, dominoes and darts and every available surface cluttered with glasses: glasses with handles and glasses without, glasses empty, glasses being emptied and glasses about to be emptied, and then refilled with the glorious, amber fluid. Morse found a momentary gap at the bar and pushed his way diffidently forward. As he waited his turn, he heard the fruit machine (to the right of the bar) clunking out an occasional desultory dividend, and he leaned across the bar to look more carefully. A woman was playing the machine, her back towards him. But he knew her well enough.

The landlord interrupted a new and improbable line of thought. 'Yes, mate?'

Morse ordered a pint of best bitter, edged his way a

little further along the bar, and found himself standing only a few feet behind the woman playing the machine. She pushed her glass over the bar.

'Stick another double in there, Bert.'

She opened an inordinately large leather handbag and Morse saw the heavy roll of notes inside. Fifty pounds? More? Had she had a lucky night at Bingo?

She had not seen Morse – he was sure of that – and he observed her as closely as he could. She was drinking whisky and swopping mildly ribald comments with several of the pub's *habitués*. And then she laughed – a coarse, common cackle of a laugh, and curiously and quite unexpectedly Morse knew that he found her attractive, dammit! He looked at her again. Her figure was still good, and her clothes hung well upon her. Yes, all right, she was no longer a beauty, he knew that. He noticed the fingernails bitten down and broken; noticed the index finger of her right hand stained dark-brown with nicotine. But what the hell did it matter! Morse drained his glass and bought another pint. The germ of the new idea that had taken root in his mind would never grow this night. He knew why, of course. It was simple. He needed a woman. But he had no woman and he moved to the back of the room and found a seat. He thought, as he often thought, of the attractiveness of women. There had been women, of course; too many women, perhaps. And one or two who still could haunt his dreams and call to him across the years of a time when the day was fair. But now the leaves were falling round him: mid-forties; unmarried; alone. And here he sat in a cheap public bar where life was beer and fags and crisps and nuts and fruit machines and ... The ashtray on the table in front of him was revoltingly full of stubs and ash. He pushed it away from him, gulped down the last of his beer and walked out into the night.

He was sitting in the bar of the Randolph Hotel with an architect, an older man, who talked of space and light and beauty, who always wore a bowler hat, who studied Greek and Latin verses, and who slept beneath a railway viaduct. They talked together of life and living, and as they talked a girl walked by with a graceful, gliding movement, and ordered her drink at the bar. And the architect nudged his young companion and gently shook his head in wistful admiration.

'My boy, how lovely, is she not? Extraordinarily, quite extraordinarily lovely.'

And Morse, too, had felt her beautiful and necessary, and yet had not a word to say.

Turning in profile as she left the bar the young girl flaunted the tantalizing, tip-tilted outline of her breasts beneath her black sweater, and the faded architect, the lover of the classical poets, the sleeper beneath the viaduct, stood up and addressed her with grave politeness as she passed.

'My dear young lady. Please don't feel offended with me, or indeed with my dear, young friend here, but I wish you to know that we find you very beautiful.'

For a moment a look of incredulous pleasure glazed the painted eyes; and then she laughed – a coarse and common cackle of a laugh.

'Gee, boys, you ought to see me when I'm washed!' And she placed her right hand on the shoulder of the architect, the nails pared down to the quick and the index finger stained dark brown with nicotine. And Morse woke up with a start in the early light of a cold and friendless dawn, as if some ghostly hand had touched him in his sleep.

CHAPTER TWENTY-TWO

Life can only be understood backwards,
but it must be lived forwards.
                                        Søren Kierkegaard

MORSE WAS IN his office by 7.30 a.m.

When he was a child, the zenith of terrestrial bliss
had been a long, luxuriating lie in bed. But he was no
longer a child, and the fitful bouts of sleep the night
before had left him tired and edgy. His thoughts as he
sat at his desk were becoming obsessive and his ability
to concentrate had temporarily deserted him. The drive
to the office had been mildly therapeutic, and at least
he had *The Times* to read. The leaders of the superpow-
ers had agreed to meet at Vladivostok, and the economy
continued its downhill slide towards inevitable disaster.
But Morse read neither article. He was becoming
increasingly less well-informed about the state of the
nation and the comings and goings of the mighty. It
was a cowardly frame of mind, he knew that, but not
entirely reprehensible. Certainly it wasn't very sensible
to know too much about some things, and he seemed to
be becoming peculiarly susceptible to auto-suggestion.
Even a casual reminder that a nervous breakdown was
no rarity in our society was enough to convince him
that he would likely as not be wheeled off into a

psychiatric ward tomorrow; and the last time he had braced himself to read an article on the causes of coronary thrombosis he had discovered that he exhibited every one of the major symptoms and had worked himself into a state of advanced panic. He could never understand why doctors could be anything but hyper-hypochondriacs, and supposed perhaps they were. He turned to the back page of *The Times* and took out his pen. He hoped it would be a real stinker this morning. But it wasn't. Nine and a half minutes.

He took a pad of paper and began writing, and was still writing when the phone rang an hour later. It was Mrs Lewis. Her husband was in bed with a soaring temperature. Flu, she thought. He'd been determined to go in to work, but her own wise counsels had prevailed and, much it appeared to her husband's displeasure, she had called the doctor. Morse, all sympathy, praised the good lady's course of action and warned her that the stubborn old so-and-so had better do as she told him. He would try to call round a bit later.

Morse smiled weakly to himself as he looked through the hurriedly written notes. It had all been for Lewis's benefit, and Lewis would have revelled in the routine. Phillipson: ticket office at the Playhouse; check row and number; occupants of seats on either side; check, trace, interview. The same with the Taylors and with Acum. The Ritz, the Jericho Arms and Lonsdale College. Ask people, talk to people, check and re-check, slowly and methodically probe and reconstruct. Yes, how Lewis would have enjoyed it. And, who knows? Something might have come of it. It would be irresponsible to neglect such obvious avenues of inquiry. Morse tore the sheets across the middle and consigned them to the waste-paper basket.

Perhaps he ought to concentrate his attention on the knife. Ah yes, the knife! But what the dickens was he supposed to do with the knife? If Sherlock were around he would doubtless deduce that the murderer was about five feet six inches tall, had tennis elbow and probably enjoyed roast beef every other Sunday. But what was *he* supposed to say about it? He walked to the cabinet and took it out; and summoning all his powers of logical analysis he stared at it with concentrated intensity, and discovered that into his open and receptive mind came nothing whatsoever. He saw a knife – no more. A household knife; and somewhere in the country, most probably somewhere in the Oxford area, there was a kitchen drawer without its carving knife. That didn't move forward the case one millimetre, did it? And could anyone really be sure whether a knife had been sharpened by a left- or a right-handed carver? Was it worth trying to find out? How fatuous the whole thing was becoming. But *how* the knife had been carried – now that was a much more interesting problem. Yes. Morse put the knife away. He sat back in the black leather chair, and once again he pondered many things.

The phone rang again at half-past ten, and Morse started abruptly and guiltily in his chair, and looked at the time in disbelief.

It was Mrs Lewis again. The doctor had called.

Pharyngitis. At least three or four days in bed. But could Morse come round? The invalid was anxious to see him.

He certainly looked ill. The unshaven face was pale and the voice little more than a batrachian croak.

'I'm letting you down, chief.'

'Nonsense. You get better that's all. And be a good boy and do as the quack tells you.'

'Not much option with a missus like mine.' He smiled wanly, and supporting himself on one arm reached for his glass of weakly pale orange juice. 'But I'm glad you've come, sir. You see, last night I had this terrible headache, and my eyes went all funny – sort of wiggly lines all the time. I couldn't recognize things very well.'

'You've got to expect summat to go wrong with you if you're ill,' said Morse.

'But I got to thinking about things. You remember the old boy on the Belisha crossing? Well, I didn't mention it at the time but it came back to me last night.'

'Go on,' said Morse quietly.

'It's just that I don't think he could see very well, sir. I reckon that's why he got knocked over and I just wondered if . . .'

Lewis looked at the inspector and knew instinctively that he had been right to ask him to come. Morse was nodding slowly and staring abstractedly through the bedroom window and on to the neatly kept strip of garden below, the beds trimmed and weeded, where a few late roses lingered languidly on.

Joe was still in the old people's home at Cowley, and lay in the same bed, half propped up on his pillows, his head lolling to the side, his thin mouth toothless and gaping. The sister who had accompanied Morse along the ward touched him gently.

'I've brought you a visitor.'

Joe blinked himself slowly awake and stared vaguely at them with unseeing eyes.

'It's a policeman, Mr Godberry. I think they must have caught up with you at last.' The sister turned to Morse and smiled attractively.

Joe grinned and his mouth moved in a senile chuckle. His hand groped feebly along the locker for his spectacle case, and finally he managed to hook an ancient pair of National Health spectacles behind his ears.

'Ah, I remember you, sergeant. Nice to see you again. What can I do fo' you this time?'

Morse stayed with him for fifteen minutes, and realized how very sad it was to grow so old.

'You've been very helpful, Joe, and I'm very grateful to you.'

'Don't forget, sergeant, to put the clock back. It's this month, you know. There's lots o' people forgits to put the clocks back. Huh. I remember once . . .'

Morse heard him out and finally got away. At the end of the ward he spoke again briefly to the sister.

'He's losing his memory a bit.'

'Most of them do, I'm afraid. Nice old boy, though. Did he tell you to put the clock back?'

Morse nodded. 'Does he tell everybody?'

'A lot of them seem to get a fixation about some little thing like that. Mind you, he's right, isn't he?' She laughed sweetly and Morse noticed she wore no wedding ring. *I hope you won't be offended, Sister, if I tell you that I find you very attractive.*

But the words wouldn't come, for he wasn't an architect who slept beneath the railway viaduct, and he could never say such things. Just as she couldn't. Morse wondered what she was thinking, and realized he would never know. He took out his wallet and gave her a pound note.

'Put it in the Christmas fund, Sister.'

Her eyes held his for a brief moment and he thought they were gentle and loving; and she thanked him nicely and walked briskly away. Fortunately the Cape of Good Hope was conveniently near.

Clocks! It reminded him. There was a good tale told in Oxford about the putting back of clocks. The church of St Benedict had a clock which ran by electricity, and for many years the complexities of putting back this clock had exercised the wit and wisdom of clergy and laity alike. The clock adorned the north face of the tower and its large hands were manoeuvred round the square, blue-painted dial by means of an elaborate lever device, situated behind the clock-face and reached via a narrow spiral staircase leading to the tower roof. The problem had been this. No one manipulating the lever immediately behind the clock-face could observe the effects of his manipulations, and so thick were the walls of the church tower that not even with a megaphone could an accomplice, standing outside the church, communicate to the manipulator the aforementioned effects. Each year, therefore, one of the churchwardens had taken upon himself to mount the spiral staircase, to manipulate the lever in roughly the right direction, to descend the staircase, to walk out of the church, to look upwards at the clock, to ascend the staircase once more, to give the lever a few more turns before descending again and repeating the process, until at last the clock was cajoled into a reluctant synchronization. Such a lengthy and physically daunting procedure had been in operation for several years, until a mild-looking thurifer, rumoured to be one of the best incense-swingers in the business, had with becoming diffidence suggested to the minister that to remove the fuse from the fuse-box and to replace it after exactly sixty minutes might not only prove more accurate but also spare the rather elderly churchwarden the prospect of a coronary thrombosis. This idea, discussed at considerable length and finally accepted by the church committee, had proved wonderfully effective, and was now a firmly established practice.

Someone had told Morse the story in a pub, and he recalled it now. It pleased him. Lewis, but for his illness, would even now be running up and down the spiral staircase looking at his alibis. But that was out – at least for several days. It was up to Morse himself now to take the fuse away and set the clock aright. But not just for an hour – for much, much longer than that. In fact for two years, three months and more, to the day when Valerie Taylor had disappeared.

Chapter Twenty-Three

For having considered God and himself
he will consider his neighbour.
    Christopher Smart, *My Cat Jeoffrey*

DETECTIVE CONSTABLE DICKSON soon realized he
was on to something and he felt as secretly excited as
the poor woman was visibly nervous. It was the sixth
house he had visited, a house on the opposite side of
the street from Baines's and nearer the main road.

'You know, madam, that Mr Baines across the way
was murdered on Monday night?' Mrs Thomas nodded
quickly. 'Er, did you know Mr Baines?'

'Yes, I did. He's lived in the street nearly as long as I
have.'

'I'm, er ... we're, er, obviously anxious to find any
witness who might have seen someone going into
Baines's house that night – or coming out, of course.'
Dickson left it at that and looked at her hopefully.

In her late sixties now, scraggy-necked and flat-
chested, Mrs Thomas was a widow who measured her
own life's joy by the health and happiness of her white
cat, which playfully and lovingly gyrated in undulating
spirals around her lower leg as she stood on the
threshold of her home. And as she stood there she was
almost glad that this young police officer had called,

for she *had* seen something; and several times the previous evening and again this Wednesday morning she had decided she ought to report it to someone. It would have been so easy in the first exciting hours when policemen had been everywhere; later, too, when they had come and placed their no-parking signs, like witches' hats, around the front of the house. Yet it was all so hazy in her mind. More than once she wondered if she could have imagined it, and she would die of shame if she were to put the police to any trouble for no cause. It had always been like that for Mrs Thomas; she had hidden herself unobtrusively away in the corners of life and seldom ventured forth.

But, yes; she had seen something.

Her life was fairly orderly, if nothing else, and each evening of the week, between 9.30 and 10.00 p.m., she put out the two milk bottles and the two Co-op tokens on the front doorstep before bolting the door securely, making herself a cup of cocoa, watching the News at Ten, and going to bed. And on Monday evening she had seen something. If only at the time she had thought it might be important! Unusual, certainly, but only afterwards had she realized exactly how unusual it had been: for never had she seen a woman knocking at Baines's door before. Had the woman gone in? Mrs Thomas didn't think so, but she vaguely remembered that the light was burning in Baines's front room behind the faded yellow curtains. The truth was that it had all become so very frightening to her. Had the woman she had seen been the one who . . .? Had she actually seen the . . . murderer? The very thought of it caused her to shiver throughout her narrow frame. Oh God, please not! Such a thing should never be allowed to happen to her – to her of all people. And as the panic rose within her, she again began to wonder if she'd dreamed it after all.

The whole thing was too frightening, especially since there was one thing that she knew might be very important. Very important indeed. 'You'd better come in, officer,' she said.

In the early afternoon she felt far less at ease than she had done with the constable. The man sitting opposite her in the black leather chair was pleasant enough, charming even; but his eyes were keen and hard, and there was a restless energy about his questions.

'Can you describe her, Mrs Thomas? Anything special about her – anything at all?'

'It was just the coat I noticed – nothing else. I told the constable . . .'

'Yes, I know you did; but tell me. Tell me, Mrs Thomas.'

'Well, that's all really – it was pink, just like I told the constable.'

'You're quite sure about that?'

She swallowed hard. Once more she was assailed by doubts from every quarter. She thought she was sure; she *was* sure, really, but could she just conceivably be wrong?

'I'm – I'm fairly sure.'

'What sort of pink?'

'Well, sort of . . .' The vision was fading rapidly now, had almost gone.

'Come on!' snapped Morse. 'You know what I mean. Fuchsia? Cyclamen? Er, lilac?' He was running out of shades of pink and received no help from Mrs Thomas. 'Light pink? Dark pink?'

'It was a fairly bright sort of . . .'

'Yes?'

It was no good, though; and Morse changed his tack and changed it again and again. Hair, height, dress, shoes, handbag – on and on. He kept it up for more than twenty minutes. But try as she might Mrs Thomas was now quite incapable of raising any mental image whatsoever of Baines's late-night caller. Suddenly she knew that she was going to burst into tears, and she wanted desperately to go home. And just as suddenly it all changed.

'Tell me about your cat, Mrs Thomas.'

How he knew she had a cat, she hadn't the faintest idea, but the tension drained away from her like the pus from an abscess lanced by the dentist. She told him happily about her blue-eyed cat.

'You know,' said Morse, 'one of the most significant physical facts about the cat is so obvious that we often tend to forget it. A cat's face is flat between the eyes and so the eyes can work together. Stereoscopic vision they call it. Now, this is very rare among animals. You just think. The majority of animals have . . .' He went on for several minutes and Mrs Thomas was enthralled. But more than that; she was excited. It was all so clear again and she interrupted his discourse on the facial structure of the dog and told him all about it. Cerise pink coat – it might have been a herring-bone pattern, no hat, medium height, brownish hair. About ten minutes to ten. She was pretty certain about the time because . . .

She left soon afterwards, happy and relieved, and a nice policeman saw her safely back to her own cosy front parlour, where the short-haired white cat lay indolently upon the sofa, momentarily opening the mysterious, stereoscopic eyes to greet his mistress's return.

Cerise. Morse got up and consulted the OED. 'A light, bright, clear red, like the colour of cherries.' Yes, that was it. For the next five minutes he stared vacantly through the window in the pose of Rodin's Aristotle; and at the end of that time he lifted his eyebrows slightly and nodded slowly to himself. It was time to get moving. He knew a coat like that, although he'd only seen it once – the colour of bright-pink cherries in the summer time.

CHAPTER TWENTY-FOUR

'Is there anybody there?' said the Traveller
Knocking on the moonlit door.
           Walter de la Mare, *The Listeners*

WITHIN THE PHILLIPSON family the financial arrangements were a matter of clear demarcation. Mrs Phillipson herself had a small private income accruing from interest received on her late mother's estate. This account she kept strictly separate from all other monies; and although her husband had known the value of the original capital inheritance, he had no more idea of his wife's annual income than she did of her husband's private means. For Phillipson himself also had a private account, in which he accumulated a not negligible annual sum from his examining duties with one of the national boards, from royalties on a moderately successful textbook, written five years previously, on nineteenth-century Britain, and from various incidental perks associated with his headship. In addition to these incomes there was, of course, Phillipson's monthly salary as a headmaster, and this was administered in a joint account on which both drew cash and wrote cheques for the normal items of household expenditure. The system worked admirably, and since by any standards the family was well-to-do, financial bickering had never blighted the Phillipsons' marriage; in fact financial matters had never caused the slightest concern to either party. Or had not done so until recently.

Phillipson kept his cheque book, his bank statements and all his financial correspondence in the top drawer of the bureau in the lounge, and he kept it locked. And in normal circumstances Mrs Phillipson would no more have dreamed of looking through this drawer than of opening the private and confidential letters which came through the letter-box week after week from the examination board. It was none of her business, and she was perfectly happy to keep it that way – in normal circumstances. But circumstances had been far from normal these last two weeks, and she had not lived with Donald for over twelve years without coming to know his moods and his anxieties. For she slept beside him every night and he was her husband, and she knew him. She knew with virtual certainty that whatever had lain so heavily upon his mind these last few days was neither the school, nor the inspector whose visit had been so strangely upsetting, nor even the ghost of Valerie Taylor that flitted perpetually across the twilit zone of his subconscious fears. It was a man. A man she had come to think of as wholly evil and wholly malignant. It was Baines.

No specific incident had led her to open her husband's drawer and to examine the papers within; it was more an aggregation of many minor incidents which had driven her lively imagination to the terminus – a terminus which the facts themselves may never have reached, but towards which (as she fearfully foresaw their implications) they seemed inevitably to be heading. Did he know that she had her own key to the drawer? Surely not. For otherwise, if there was something he was anxious to hide, he would have kept the guilty evidence at school and not at home. And she *had* looked – only last week, and many things were now so frighteningly clear. Assuredly she had heard the warning voices, and yet had looked and now could guess the truth: her husband was being blackmailed. And strangely enough she found that she could face the truth: it mattered less to her than she had dared to hope. But one thing was utterly certain. Never would she tell a living soul – never, never, never! She was his wife and she loved him, and would go on loving him. And if possible she would protect him; to the last ounce of her energy, to the last drop of her blood. She might even be able to do something. Yes, she might even be able to *do* something . . .

She seemed neither surprised nor dismayed to see him, for she had learned a great deal about herself the past few days. Not only was it better to face up to life's problems than to run away from them or desperately to pretend they didn't exist; it seemed far easier, too.

'Can we talk?' asked Morse.

She took his coat and hung it on the hall-stand behind the front door, beside an expensive-looking winter coat, the colour of ripening cherries.

They sat in the lounge, and Morse again noticed the photograph above the heavy mahogany bureau.

'Well, Inspector? How can I help you?'

'Don't you know?' replied Morse quietly.

'I'm afraid not.' She gave a little laugh and the hint of a smile played at the corners of her mouth. She spoke carefully, almost like a self-conscious teacher of elocution, the 'd' and the 't' articulated separately and distinctly.

'I think you do, Mrs Phillipson, and it's going to be easier for both of us if you're honest with me from the start because believe me, my love, you're going to be honest with me before we've finished.'

The niceties were gone already, the words direct and challenging, the easy familiarity almost frightening. As if she were looking in on herself from the outside, she wondered what her chances were against him. It depended, of course, on what he knew. But surely there was nothing he *could* know?

'What am I supposed to be honest about?'

'Can't we keep this between ourselves, Mrs Phillipson? That's why I've called now, you see, while your husband's still at school.'

He noted the first glint of anxiety in the light-brown eyes; but she remained silent, and he continued. 'If you're in the clear, Mrs Phillipson—' He had repeated her name with almost every question, and she felt uncomfortable. It was like the repeated blows of a battering ram against a beleaguered city.

'*In the clear?* What *are* you talking about?'

'I think you called at Mr Baines's house on Monday night, Mrs Phillipson.' The tone of his voice was ominously calm, but she only shook her head in semi-humorous disbelief.

'You can't really be serious, can you, Inspector?'

'I'm always serious when I'm investigating murder.'

'You don't think – you can't think that I had anything to do with *that*? On Monday night? Why, I hardly knew the man.'

'I'm not interested in how well you knew him.' It seemed an odd remark and her eyebrows contracted to a frown.

'What *are* you interested in?'

'I've told you, Mrs Phillipson.'

'Look, Inspector. I think it's about time you told me exactly why you're here. If you've got something you want to say to me, please say it. If you haven't . . .'

Morse, in a muted way, admired her spirited performance. But he had just reminded Mrs Phillipson, and now he reminded himself: he was investigating murder.

When he spoke again his words were casual, intimate almost. 'Did you like Mr Baines?'

Her mouth opened as if to speak and, as suddenly, closed again; and whatever doubts had begun to creep into Morse's mind were now completely removed.

'I didn't know him very well. I just told you that.' It was the best answer she could find, and it wasn't very good.

'Where were you on Monday evening, Mrs Phillipson?'

'I was here of course. I'm almost always here.'

'What time did you go out?'

'Inspector! I just told—'

'Did you leave the children on their own?'

'Of course I didn't – I mean I wouldn't. I could never—'

'What time did you get back?'

'Back? Back from where?'

'Before your husband?'

'My husband was out – that's what I'm telling you. He went to the theatre, the Playhouse—'

'He sat in row M seat 14.'

'If you say so, all right. But he wasn't home until about eleven.'

'Ten to, according to him.'

'All right, ten to eleven. What does—'

'You haven't answered my question, Mrs Phillipson.'

'What question?'

'I asked you what time *you* got home, not your husband.' His questions were flung at her now with breakneck rapidity.

'You don't think I would go out and leave—'

'Go out? Where to, Mrs Phillipson? Did you go on the bus?'

'I didn't go anywhere. Can't you understand that? How could I possibly go out and leave—'

Morse interrupted her again. She was beginning to crack, he knew that; her voice was high-pitched now amidst the elocutionary wreckage.

'All right – you didn't leave your children alone – I believe you – you love your children – of course you do

– it would be illegal to leave them on their own – how old are they?'

Again she opened her mouth to speak, but he pushed relentlessly, remorselessly on.

'Have you heard of a baby-sitter, Mrs Phillipson? – somebody who comes in and looks after your children while you go out – do you hear me? – while you go out – do you want me to find out who it was? – or do you want to tell me? – I could soon find out, of course – friends, neighbours – do you want me to find out, Mrs Phillipson? – do you want me to go and knock next door? – and the door next to that? – of course, you don't, do you? You know, you're not being very sensible about this, are you, Mrs Phillipson?' (He was speaking more slowly and calmly now.) 'You see, I *know* what happened on Monday night. Someone saw you, Mrs Phillipson; someone saw you in Kempis Street. And if you'd like to tell me why you were there and what you did, it would save a lot of time and trouble. But if you won't tell me, then I shall have to—'

Of a sudden she almost shrieked as the incessant flow of words began to overwhelm her. 'I told you! I don't know what you're talking about! You don't seem to understand that, do you? *I just don't know what you're talking about!*'

Morse sat back in the armchair, relaxed and unconcerned. He looked about him, and once more fastened his gaze on the photograph of the headmaster and his wife above the large bureau. And then he looked at his wristwatch.

'What time do the children get home?' His tone was suddenly friendly and quiet, and Mrs Phillipson felt the panic welling up within her. She looked at her own wristwatch and her voice was shaking as she answered him.

'They'll be home at four o'clock.'

'That gives us an hour, doesn't it, Mrs Phillipson. I think that's long enough – my car's outside. You'd better put your coat on – the pink one, if you will.'

He rose from the armchair, and fastened the front buttons of his jacket. 'I'll see that your husband knows if . . .' He took a few steps towards the door, but she laid her hand upon him as he moved past her.

'Sit down, please, Inspector,' she said quietly.

She had gone (she said). That was all, really. It was like suddenly deciding to write a letter or to ring the dentist or to buy some restorer for the paint brushes encrusted stiff with last year's gloss. She asked Mrs Cooper next door to baby-sit, said she'd be no longer than an hour at the very latest, and caught the 9.20 p.m. bus from the stop immediately outside the house. She got off at Cornmarket, walked quickly through Gloucester Green and reached Kempis Street by about quarter to ten. The light was shining in Baines's front window – she had never been there before – and she summoned up all her courage and knocked on the front door. There was no reply. Again she knocked – and again there was no reply. She then walked along to the lighted window and tapped upon it hesitantly and quietly with the back of her hand; but she could hear no sound and could make out no movement behind the cheap yellow curtains. She hurried back to the front door, feeling as guilty as a young schoolgirl caught out of her place in the classroom by the headmistress. But still nothing happened. She had so nearly called the whole thing off there and then; but her resolution had been wrought up to such a pitch that she made one last move. She tried the door – and found it unlocked. She opened it slightly, no more than a foot or so, and called his name.

'Mr Baines?' And then slightly louder, '*Mr Baines?*' But she received no reply. The house seemed strangely still and the sound of her own voice echoed eerily in the high entrance hall. A cold shiver of fear ran down her spine, and for a few seconds she felt sure that he was there, very near to her, watching and waiting . . . And suddenly a panic-stricken terror had seized her and she had rushed back to the lighted, friendly road, crossed over by the railway station and, with her heart pounding in her ribs, tried to get a grip on herself. In St Giles' she caught a taxi and arrived home just after ten.

That was her story, anyway. She told it in a flat, dejected voice, and she told it well and clearly. To Morse it sounded in no way like the tangled, mazy machinations of a murderer. Indeed a good deal of it he could check fairly easily: the baby-sitter, the bus conductor, the taxi driver. And Morse felt sure that all would verify the outline of her story, and confirm the approximate times she'd given. But there was no chance of checking those fateful moments when she stood outside the door of Baines's house . . . Had she gone in? And if she had, what terrible things had then occurred? The pros and cons were counterpoised in Morse's mind, with the balance tilting slightly in Mrs Phillipson's favour.

'Why did you want to see him?'

'I wanted to talk to him, that's all.'

'Yes. Go on.'

'It's difficult to explain. I don't think I knew myself what I was going to say. He was – oh, I don't know – he was everything that's *bad* in life. He was mean, he was vindictive, he was – sort of calculating. He just delighted in seeing other people squirm. I'm not thinking of anything in particular, and I don't really know all that much about him. But since Donald has been head-master he's – how shall I put it? – he's waited, hoping for things to go wrong. He was a cruel man, Inspector.'

'You hated him?'

She nodded hopelessly. 'Yes, I suppose I did.'

'It's as good a motive as any,' said Morse sombrely.

'It might seem so, yes.' But she sounded un-perturbed.

'Did your husband hate Baines, too?' He watched her carefully and saw the light flash dangerously in her eyes.

'Don't be silly, Inspector. You can't possibly think that Donald had anything to do with all this. I know I've been a fool, but you can't . . . It's impossible. He was at the theatre all night. You know that.'

'Your husband would have thought it was impossible for *you* to be knocking at Baines's door that night, wouldn't he? You were here, at home, with the children, surely?' He leaned forward and spoke more curtly again now. 'Make no mistake, Mrs Phillipson, it would have been a hell of a sight easier for him to leave the theatre than it was for you to leave here. And don't try to tell me otherwise!'

He sat back impassively in the chair. He sensed an evasion somewhere in her story, a half-truth, a curtain not yet fully drawn back; and at the same time he knew that he was almost there, and all he had to do was sit and wait. And so he sat and waited; and the world of the woman seated opposite him was slowly beginning to fall apart, and suddenly, dramatically, she buried her head in her hands and wept uncontrollably.

Morse fished around in his pockets and finally found a crumpled apology for a paper handkerchief, and pushed it gently into her right hand.

'Don't cry,' he said softly. 'It won't do either of us any good.'

After a few minutes the tears dried up, and soon the snivelling subsided. 'What *can* do us any good, Inspector?'

'It's very easy, really,' said Morse in a brisk tone. 'You tell me the truth, Mrs Phillipson. You'll find I probably know it anyway.'

But Morse was wrong – he was terribly wrong. Mrs Phillipson could do little more than reiterate her strange little story. This time, however, with a startling addition – an addition which caught Morse, as he sat there nodding sceptically, like an uppercut to the jaw. She hadn't wanted to mention it because ... because, well, it seemed so much like trying to get herself out of a mess by pushing someone else into it. But she could only tell the truth, and if that's what Morse was after she thought she'd better tell it. As she had said, she ran along to the main street after leaving Baines's house and crossed over towards the Royal Oxford Hotel; and just before she reached the hotel she saw someone she knew – knew very well – come out of the lounge door and walk across the road to Kempis Street. She hesitated and her tearful eyes looked pleadingly and pathetically at Morse.

'Do you know who it was, Inspector? It was David Acum.'

CHAPTER TWENTY-FIVE

For oily or spotty skin, first cleanse face and throat, then pat with a hot towel. Smooth on an even layer of luxurious 'Ladypak', avoiding the area immediately around the eyes.

> Directions for applying a beauty mask

AT 6.20 THE following morning Morse was on the road: it would take about five hours. He would have enjoyed the drive more with someone to talk to, especially Lewis, and he switched on the Lancia's radio for the 7.00 a.m. news. The world seemed strangely blighted: abroad there were rumours of war and famine, and at home more bankruptcies and unemployment – and a missing lord who had been dredged up from a lake in east Essex. But the morning was fresh and bright, the sky serene and cloudless, and Morse drove fast. He had left Evesham behind him and was well on the way to Kidderminster before he met any appreciable volume of traffic. The 8.00 a.m. news came and went, with no perceptible amelioration of the cosmic plight, and Morse switched over to Radio Three and listened lovingly to the Brandenburg Concerto No 5 in D. The journey was going well, and he was through Bridgnorth and driving rather too quickly round the Shrewsbury ring-road by 9.00 a.m. when he decided that a Schoenberg string quartet might be a little above his head, and switched off. He found himself vaguely pondering the lake in east Essex, and remembering the reservoir behind the Taylors' home, before switching that off, too, and concentrating with appropriate care and attention upon the perils of the busy A5. At Nesscliffe, some twelve miles north of Shrewsbury, he turned off left along the B4396 towards Bala. Wales now, and the pale green hills rose ever more steeply. He was making excellent time and he praised the gods that his journey was not being made on a dry Welsh Sunday. He was feeling thirsty already. But he was through Bala and swinging in the long left-handed loop around Llyn Tegid (reservoir again!) long before the pubs were open; and through the crowded streets of Porthmadog, festooned still with the multicoloured bunting of high summer, and past the Lloyd George Museum in Llanystumdwy, and still the hands of the fascia clock were some few minutes short of eleven. He might just as well drive on. At Four Crosses he turned right on to the Pwllheli-Caernarfon Road, and drove on into the Lleyn Peninsula, past the triple peaks of the Rivals and on to the coastal road, with the waters of Caernarfon Bay laughing and glittering in the sunshine to his left. He would stop at the next likely-looking hostelry. He had passed one in the last village, but the present tract of road afforded little for the thirsty traveller; and he was only two or three miles south of Caernarfon itself when he spotted the sign: BONT-NEWYDD. Surely the village where the Acums lived? He pulled in to the side of the road, and consulted the file in his brief-case. Yes, it was. 16 St Beuno's Road. He inquired of an ageing passer-by and learned that he was only a few 'undred yaards from St Beuno's Road, and that The Prince of Wales was just around the corner. It was five minutes past eleven.

As he sampled the local brew, he debated whether he should call at the Acums' home. Did the modern languages master come home for lunch? Morse's original plan had been to go direct to the City of Caernarfon School, preferably about lunchtime. But perhaps it would do no harm to have a little chat with Mrs Acum first? Temporarily he shelved the decision, bought another pint, and considered the forthcoming interview. Acum had lied, of course, about not leaving the conference; for Mrs Phillipson could not have had the faintest notion that Acum would be in Oxford on that Monday night. How could she? Unless ... but he dropped the fanciful line of thought. The beer was good, and at noon he was happily discussing with his host the sorry Sunday situation in the thirsty counties and the defacement of the Welsh road signs by the Nationalists. And ten minutes later, legs astraddle, he stood and contemplated the defacement of the land-lord's lavatory walls by a person or persons unknown. Several of the graffiti were unintelligible to the non-Welsh-speaker; but one that was scrawled in his native tongue caught Morse's eye, and he smiled in approbation as his bladder achingly emptied itself:

'The penis mightier than the sword.'

It was now 12.15 p.m., and if Acum were coming home to lunch, there was an obvious danger of his passing Morse in the opposite direction. Well, there was one pretty certain way of finding out. He left the Lancia at The Prince of Wales and walked.

St Beuno's Road led off right from the main road. The houses were small here, built of square, grey, granite blocks, and tiled with the purplish-blue Ffestiniog slate. The grass in the tiny front gardens was of a green two or three shades paler than the English variety, and the soil looked tired and undernourished. The front door was painted a Cambridge blue, with the black number 16 dextrously worked in the florid style of a Victorian theatre-bill. Morse knocked firmly, and after a brief interval the door opened; but opened only slightly, and then to reveal a strangely incongruous sight. A woman stood before him, her face little more than a white mask, with slits left open for the eyes and mouth, a blood-red towel swathed around the top of her head where (as, alas, with most blondes) the tell-tale roots of the hair betrayed its darker origins. It was curious to witness the lengths to which the ladies were prepared to go in order to improve upon the natural gifts their maker had endowed them with; and in the depths of Morse's mind there stirred the dim remembrance of the fair-haired woman with the spotty face in the staff photograph of the Roger Bacon Comprehensive School. He knew that this must be Mrs Acum. Yet it was not the beauty pack, smeared though it doubtless was with a practised skill, that chiefly held the inspector's rapt attention. She was holding a meagre white towel to the top of her shoulders, and as she stood half hidden by the door, it was immediately apparent that behind the towel the woman was completely naked. Morse felt as lecherous as a billy-goat. A Welsh billy-goat, perhaps. It must have been the beer.

'I've called to see your husband. Er, it is Mrs Acum, isn't it?'

The head nodded, and a hair-line fracture of the carefully assembled mask appeared at the corners of the white mouth. Was she laughing at him?

'Will he be back home for lunch?'

The head shook, and the top of the towel drooped tantalizingly to reveal the beautifully-moulded outline of her breasts.

'He's at school, I suppose?'

The head nodded, and the eyes stared blandly through the slits.

'Well, I'm sorry to have bothered you, Mrs Acum, especially at, er, such, er . . . We've spoken to each other before, you know – over the phone, if you remember. I'm Morse. Chief Inspector Morse from Oxford.'

The red towel bobbed on her head, the mask almost breaking through into a smile. They shook hands through the door, and Morse was conscious of the heady perfume on her skin. He held her hand for longer than he need have done, and the white towel dropped from her right shoulder; and for a brief and beautiful moment he stared with shameless fascination at her nakedness. The nipple was fully erect and he felt

225

an almost irresistible urge to hold it there and then between his fingers. Was she inviting him in? He looked again at the passive mask. The towel was now in place again, and she stood back a little from the door; it was fifty-fifty. But he had hesitated too long, and the chance, if chance it was, was gone already. He lacked, as always, the bogus courage of his own depravity, and he turned away from her and walked back slowly towards The Prince of Wales. At the end of the road he stopped, and looked back; but the light-blue door was closed upon him and he cursed the conscience that invariably thus doth make such spineless cowards of us all. It was perhaps something to do with status. People just didn't expect such base behaviour from a chief inspector, as if such eminent persons were somehow different from the common run of lewd humanity. How wrong they were! How wrong! Why, even the mighty had their little weaknesses. Good gracious, yes. Just think of old Lloyd George. The things they said about Lloyd George! And he was a prime minister . . .

He climbed into the Lancia. Oh God, such beautiful breasts! He sat motionless at the wheel for a short while, and then he smiled to himself. He reckoned that Constable Dickson could almost have hung his helmet there! It was an irreverent thought, but it made him feel a good deal better. He pulled carefully out of the car park and headed north on the final few miles of his journey.

CHAPTER TWENTY-SIX

> Merely corroborative detail, to add artistic verisimili-
> tude to an otherwise bald and unconvincing narrative.
>   W. S. Gilbert, *The Mikado*

A SMALL GROUP of boys was kicking a football around
at the side of a large block of classrooms which abutted
on to the wide sports field, where sets of rugby and
hockey posts demarcated the area of grass into neatly
white-lined rectangles. The rest of the school was
having lunch. The two men walked three times around
the playing fields, hands in pockets, heads slightly
forward, eyes downcast. They were about the same
build, neither man above medium height; and to the
football players they seemed unworthy of note, anonymous almost. Yet one of the two men pacing slowly over
the grass was a chief inspector of police, and the other,
one of their very own teachers, was a suspect in a
murder case.

Morse questioned Acum about himself and his
teaching career; about Valerie Taylor and Baines and
Phillipson; about the conference in Oxford, times and
places and people. And he learned nothing that seemed
of particular interest or importance. The schoolmaster
appeared pleasant enough – in a nondescript sort
of way; he answered the inspector's questions with

freedom and with what seemed a fair degree of guarded honesty. And so Morse told him, told him quietly yet quite categorically, that he was a liar; told him that he had indeed left the conference that Monday evening, at about 9.30 p.m., told him that he had walked to Kempis Street to see his former colleague, Mr Baines, and that he had been seen there; told him that, if he persisted in denying such a plain, incontrovertible statement of the truth, he, Morse, had little option but to take him back to Oxford where he would be held for questioning in connection with the murder of Mr Reginald Baines. It was as simple as that! And, in fact, it proved a good deal simpler than even Morse had dared to hope; for Acum no longer denied the plain, incontrovertible statement of the truth which the inspector had presented to him. They were on their third and final circuit of the playing fields, far away from the main school buildings, by the side of some neglected allotments, where the ramshackle sheds rusted away sadly in despairing disrepair. Here Acum stopped and nodded slowly.

'Just tell me what you did, sir, that's all.'

'I'd been sitting at the back of the hall – deliberately – and I left early. As you say, it was about half-past nine, or probably a bit earlier.'

'You went to see Baines?' Acum nodded. 'Why did you go to see him?'

'I don't know, really. I was getting a bit bored with the conference, and Baines lived fairly near. I thought I'd go and see if he was in and ask him out for a drink. It's always interesting to talk about old times, you know the sort of thing – what was going on at school, which members of staff were still there, which ones had left, what they were doing. You know what I mean.'

He spoke naturally and easily, and if he were a liar he seemed to Morse a fairly fluent one.

'Well,' continued Acum, 'I walked along there. I was in a bit of a hurry because I knew the pubs would be closed by half-past ten and time was getting on. I had a drink on the way and it must have been getting on for ten by the time I got there. I'd been there before, and thought he must be in because the light was on in the front room.'

'Were the curtains drawn?' For the first time since they had been talking together, Morse's voice grew sharper.

Acum thought for a moment. 'Yes, I'm almost certain they were.'

'Go on.'

'Well, I thought, as I say, that he must be in. So I knocked pretty loudly two or three times on the door. But he didn't answer, or at least he didn't seem to hear me. I thought he might be in the front room perhaps with the TV on, so I went to the window and knocked on it.'

'Could you hear the TV? Or see it?'

Acum shook his head; and to Morse it was all beginning to sound like a record stuck in its groove. He knew for certain what was coming next.

'It's a funny thing, Inspector, but I began to feel just a bit frightened – as if I were sort of trespassing and shouldn't really be there at all; as if he knew that I was there but didn't want to see me . . . Anyway, I went back to the door and knocked again, and then I put my head round the door and shouted his name.'

Morse stood quite still, and considered his next question with care. If he was to get his piece of information, he wanted it to come from Acum himself without too much prompting.

'You put your head round the door, you say?'

'Yes. I just felt sure he was there.'

'Why did you feel that?'

'Well, there was a light in the front room and . . .' He hesitated for a moment, and seemed to be fumbling around in his mind for some fleeting, half-forgotten impression that had given him this feeling.

'Think back carefully, sir,' said Morse. 'Just picture yourself there again, standing at the door. Take your time. Just put yourself back there. You're standing there in Kempis Street. Last Monday night . . .'

Acum shook his head slowly and frowned. He said nothing for a minute or two.

'You see, Inspector, I just had this idea that he was somewhere about. I almost *knew* he was. I thought he might just have slipped out somewhere for a few seconds because . . .' It came back to him then, and he went on quickly. 'Yes, that's it. I remember now. I remember why I thought he must be there. It wasn't just the light in the front window. There was a light on in the hall because the front door was open. Not wide open, but standing ajar as if he'd just slipped out and would be back again any second.'

'And then?'

'I left. He wasn't there. I just left, that's all.'

'Why didn't you tell me all this when I rang you, sir?'

'I was frightened, Inspector. I'd been there, hadn't I? And he was probably lying there all the time – murdered. I was frightened, I really was. Wouldn't you have been?'

Morse drove into the centre of Caernarfon, and parked his car alongside the jetty under the great walls of the first Edward's finest castle. He found a Chinese restaurant nearby, and greedily gulped down the oriental fare that was set before him. It was his first meal for twenty-four hours, and he temporarily dismissed all else from his mind. Only over his coffee did he allow his restless brain to come to grips with the case once more; and by the time he had finished his second cup of coffee he had reached the firm conclusion that, whatever improbabilities remained to be explained away, especially the reasons given for calling on Baines, both Mrs Phillipson and David Acum had told him the truth, or something approximating to the truth, at least as far as their evidence concerned itself with the visits made to the house in Kempis Street. Their accounts of what had taken place there were so clear, so mutually complementary, that he felt he should and would believe them. That bit about the door being slightly open, for example – exactly as Mrs Phillipson had left it before panicking and racing down to the lighted street. No. Acum could not have made that up. Surely not. Unless ... It was the second time that he had qualified his conclusions with that sinister word 'unless'; and it troubled him. Acum and Mrs Phillipson. Was there any link at all between that improbable pair? If link there was, it had to have been forged at some point in the past, at some point more than two years ago, at the Roger Bacon Comprehensive School. Could there have been something? It was an idea, anyway. Yet as he drove out of the castle car park, he decided on balance that it was a lousy idea. In front of the castle he passed the statue erected to commemorate the honourable member for Caernarfon (Lloyd George, no less) and as he drove out along the road to Capel Curig, his brain was as jumbled and cluttered as a magpie's nest.

He stopped briefly in the pass of Llanberis, and watched the tiny figures of the climbers, conspicuous only by their bright orange anoraks, perched at dizzying heights on the sheer mountain faces that towered massively above the road on either side. He felt profoundly thankful that whatever the difficulties of his own job he was spared the risk, at every second, and every precarious hand- and foot-hold, of a vertical plunge to a certain death upon the rocks far, far below. Yet, in his own way, Morse knew that he too was scaling a peak and knew full well the blithe exhilaration of reaching the summit. So often there was only one way forward, only one. And when one route seemed utterly impossible, one had to look for the nearly impossible alternative, to edge along the face of the cliff, to avoid the impasse, and to lever oneself painstakingly up to the next ledge, and look up again and follow the only route. On the death of Baines, Morse had considered only a small group of likely suspects. The murderer could, of course, have been someone completely unconnected with the Valerie Taylor affair; but he doubted it. There had been five of them, and he now felt that the odds against Mrs Phillipson and David Acum had lengthened considerably. That left the Taylors, the pair of them, and Phillipson himself. It was time he tried to put together the facts, many of them very odd facts, that he had gleaned about these three. It must be one of them surely; for he felt convinced now that Baines had been murdered before the visits of Mrs Phillipson and David Acum. Yes, that was the only way it could have been. He grasped the firm fact with both hands and swung himself on to a higher ledge, and discovered that from this vantage point the view seemed altogether different.

He drove to Capel Curig and there turned right on to the A5 towards Llangollen. And even as he drove he began to see the pattern. He ought to have seen it before; but with the testimony of Mrs Phillipson and Acum behind him, it became almost childishly easy now to fit the pieces into quite a different pattern. One by one they clicked into place with a simple inevitability, as on and on he drove at high speed, passing Shrewsbury and, keeping to the A5, rattling along the old Watling Street and almost missing the turning off for Daventry and Banbury. It was now nearly 8 p.m. and Morse was feeling the effects of his long day. He found his mind wandering off to that news item he had heard about the unfortunate lord in the Essex reservoir; and as he was leaving the outskirts of Banbury an oncoming car flashed its lights at him. He realized that he had been drifting dangerously over the centre of the road, and jerked himself into a startled wakefulness. He resolved not to allow his concentration to waver one centimetre, opened the side window and breathing deeply upon the cool night air, sang in a mournful baritone, over and over again, the first and only verse he could remember of 'Lead, Kindly Light'.

He drove straight home and locked up the garage. It had been a long day, he hoped he would sleep well.

CHAPTER TWENTY-SEVEN

All happy families are alike, but each unhappy family
is unhappy in its own way.

Leo Tolstoy

LEWIS WAS GETTING better. He got up for a couple
of hours just after Morse had arrived back in Oxford,
with the aid of the banister made his careful way downstairs, and joined his surprised wife on the sofa in front
of the television set. His temperature was normal now,
and though he felt weak on his legs and sapped of his
usual energy, he knew he would soon be back in har-
ness. Many of the hours in bed he had spent in thinking,
thinking about the Taylor case; and that morning he
had been suddenly struck by an idea so novel and so
exciting that he had persuaded his wife to ring the
station immediately. But Morse was out: off to Wales,
they said. It puzzled Lewis: the Principality in no way
figured in his own new-minted version of events, and he
guessed that Morse had followed one of his wayward
fancies about Acum, wasted a good many gallons of
police petrol, and advanced the investigation not one
whit. But that wasn't quite fair. In the hands of the chief
inspector things seldom stood still; they might go sideways, or even backwards, and often (Lewis agreed) they
went forwards. But they seldom stood still. Yes, Lewis

had been deeply disappointed not to catch him. Everything – well, almost everything – fitted so perfectly. It had been that item on his bedside radio at eight o'clock that had started the chain reaction; that item about some big noise being washed up in a reservoir. He knew they had dredged the reservoir behind the Taylors' home; but you could never be sure in such a wide stretch of water as that; and anyway it didn't really matter much whether it was in the reservoir or somewhere else. That was just the starting point. And then there was that old boy at the Belisha crossing, and the basket, and – oh, lots of other things. How he wished he'd caught the chief at the station! The really surprising thing was that Morse hadn't thought of it himself. He usually thought of everything – and more! But later, as the day wore on, he began to think that Morse probably *had* thought of it. After all, it was Morse himself who had suggested, right out of the blue, that she was carrying a basket.

Laboriously, during the afternoon, Lewis wrote it all down, and when he had finished the initial thrill was already waning, and he was left only with the quiet certainty that it had indeed been, for him, a remarkable brainwave, and that there was a very strong possibility that he might be right. At 9.15 p.m., he rang the station himself, but Morse had still not shown up.

'Probably gone straight home – or to a pub,' said the desk sergeant. Lewis left a message, and prayed that for the morrow the chief had planned no trip to the Western Isles.

*

Donald Phillipson and his wife sat silently watching the nine o'clock news on BBC television. They had said little all evening, and now that the children were snugly tucked up in bed, the little had dried up to nothing. Once or twice each of them had almost asked a question of the other, and it would have been the same question: is there anything you want to tell me? Or words to that effect. But neither of them had braved it, and at a quarter-past ten Mrs Phillipson brought in the coffee and announced that she was off to bed.

'You've had your fill tonight, haven't you?'

He mumbled something inaudible, and lumbered along unsteadily, trying with limited success to avoid bumping into her as they walked side by side along the narrow pavement. It was 10.45 p.m. and their home was only two short streets away from the pub.

'Have you ever tried to work out how much you spend a week on beer and fags?'

It hurt him, and it wasn't fair. Christ, it wasn't fair.

'If you want to talk about money, my gal, what about your Bingo. Every bloody night nearly.'

'You just leave my Bingo out of it. It's about the one pleasure I've got in life, and don't you forget it. And some people *win* at Bingo; you know that, don't you? Don't tell me you're so ignorant you don't know that.'

'Have you won recently?' His tone was softer and he hoped very much that she had.

'I've told you. You keep your nose out of it. I spend

my own money, thank you, not yours; and if I win that's my business, isn't it?'

'You were lashing out a bit with your money tonight, weren't you? Bit free with your favours all round, if you ask me.'

'What's that supposed to mean?' Her voice was very nasty.

'Well, you—'

'Look, if I want to treat some of my friends to a drink, that's my lookout, isn't it? It's my money, too!'

'I only meant—'

They were at the front gate now and she turned on him, her eyes flashing. 'And don't you ever dare to say anything again about my favours! Christ! You're a one to talk, aren't you – you – *bastard*!'

Their holiday together, the first for seven years, was due to begin at the weekend. The omens seemed hardly favourable.

It was half-past eleven when Morse finally laid his head upon the pillows. He shouldn't have had so much beer really, but he felt he'd deserved it. It would mean shuffling along for a pee or two before the night was out. But what the hell! He felt at peace with himself and with the world in general. Beer was probably the cheapest drug on the market, and he only wished that his GP would prescribe it for him on the National Health. Ah, this was good! He turned into the pillows. Old Lewis would be in bed, too. He would see Lewis first thing in the morning; and he was quite sure that however groggy his faithful sergeant was feeling he would sit up in his sick bed and blink with a pained, incredulous surprise. For tomorrow morning he would be able to reveal the identity of the murderer of Valerie Taylor and that of the murderer of Reginald Baines, to boot. Or, to be slightly more accurate, just the one identity; for it had been the same hand which had murdered them both, and Morse now knew whose hand it was.

CHAPTER TWENTY-EIGHT

An ill-favoured thing, sir, but mine own.
Shakespeare, *As You Like It*

'HOW'RE YOU DOING then, my old friend?'

'Much better, thanks. Should be fit again any day now.'

'Now you're not to rush things, remember that. There's nothing spoiling.'

'Isn't there, sir?' The tone of the voice caught the inspector slightly unawares, and he looked at Lewis curiously.

'What's on your mind?'

'I tried to get hold of you yesterday, sir.' He sat up in bed and reached to the bedside table. 'I thought I had a bright idea. I may be wrong, but . . . Well, here it is anyway, for what it's worth.' He handed over several sheets of notepaper, and Morse shelved his own pronouncements and sat down beside the bed. His head ached and he stared reluctantly at his sergeant's carefully written notes.

'You want me to read all this?'

'I just hope it's worth reading, that's all.'

And Morse read; and as he read a wan smile crept across his mouth, and here and there he nodded with rigorous approbation, and Lewis sank back into his pillows with the air of a pupil whose essay is receiving the alpha accolade. When he had finished, Morse took out his pen.

'Don't mind if I make one or two slight alterations, do you?' For the next ten minutes he went methodically through the draft, correcting the more heinous spelling errors, inserting an assortment of full-stops and commas, and shuffling several of the sentences into a more comprehensible sequence. 'That's better,' said Morse finally, handing back to a rueful-looking Lewis his amended masterpiece. It was an improvement, though. Anyone could see that.

To begin with, the evidence seemed to point to the fact that Valerie Taylor was alive. After all, her parents received a letter from her. But we then discovered that the letter was almost certainly not written by Valerie at all. So. Instead of assuming that she's alive, we must face the probability that she's dead, and we must ask ourselves the old question: who was the last person to see her alive? The answer is Joe Godberry, a short-sighted old fellow who ought never to have been in charge of a Belisha crossing in the first place. Could he have been wrong? He could, and in my view he was wrong: that is, he didn't see Valerie Taylor at all on the afternoon she disappeared. He says quite firmly that he did see her, but might he not have been mistaken? Might he just have seen someone who *looked* like Valerie? Well? Who looked like Valerie? Chief Inspector Morse himself thought that a photograph of Mrs Taylor was one of her daughter Valerie, and this raises an interesting possibility. Could the person seen by Godberry have been *not Valerie but Valerie's mother*? (Lewis had underlined the words thickly, and it was at this point on his first reading that Morse had nodded his approval.) If it was Valerie's mother there are two important implications. First, that the last person to see Valerie alive was none other than her own mother at lunchtime that same day. Second, that this person – Valerie's mother – had gone to a great deal of trouble to establish the fact that her daughter had left the house and returned to afternoon school. On this second point we know that mother and daughter were very similar in build and figure generally, and Mrs Taylor is still fairly slim and attractive. (It was at this point that Morse nodded again.) What was the best way of convincing anyone who might notice, the neighbours, say, or the Belisha man or the shop assistants, that Valerie had left home after lunch that day? The answer is fairly obvious. The uniform of the school which Valerie attended was quite distinctive, especially the red socks and the white blouse. Mrs Taylor could dress up in the uniform herself, run quickly down the road, keep on the far side of the crossing, and with a bit of luck there would be no trouble in persuading anyone, even the police, that her daughter had left home. We learned that on the particular Tuesday afternoon in question, Valerie would be most unlikely to be missed anyway. Games afternoon – and a real shambles. So. Let us assume that Mrs Taylor dresses up as her daughter and makes her way towards school. Chief Inspector Morse suggested early on that the person seen by Godberry was perhaps carrying a basket or some such receptacle. (Lewis had made a sorry mess of the spelling.) Now, if she had been carrying *clothes* (heavily scored by Lewis) the situation is becoming very interesting. Once Mrs Taylor has created the impression that Valerie has left for school, it is equally important that she should not create the further impression that Valerie has returned home some five or ten minutes later. Because if someone sees Valerie, or someone who looks like Valerie, returning to the Taylors' house, the careful plan is ruined. When Valerie is reported missing, the inquiries will naturally centre on the house, not on the area around the school. But she can deal with this without too much trouble. In the basket *Mrs Taylor has put her own clothes.* She goes into the ladies', just past the shopping area, and changes back into them, and then walks back, as unobtrusively as she can, probably by a roundabout route, to her own house. The real question now is this. Why all this palaver? Why should Mrs Taylor have to go to all this trouble and risk? There can only be one answer. To create the firm impression that Valerie is alive *when in fact she is dead.* If Valerie had arrived home for lunch, and if Valerie did not leave the house again, we must assume that she was killed at some time during the lunch hour in her own home. And there was, it seems, only one other person in the Taylor household during that time: Valerie's own mother.

It is difficult to believe, but the facts seem to point to the appalling probability that *Valerie was murdered by her own mother*. Why? We can only guess. There is some evidence that Valerie was pregnant. Perhaps her mother flew at her in a wild rage and struck her much harder than she intended to. We may learn the truth from Mrs Taylor herself. The next thing is – what to do? And here we have the recorded evidence of the police files. The fact is that the police were not called in until the next morning. Why so much delay? Again an answer readily presents itself. (Morse had admired his sergeant's style at this point, and the nod had signified a recognition of a literary nicety rather than any necessary concurrence with the argument.) Mrs Taylor had to get rid of the body. She waited, I think, obviously in great distress, until her husband arrived home about six; and then she told him what had happened. He has little option. He can't leave his poor wife to face the consequences of the terrible mess she's got herself into, and the two of them plan what to do. Somehow they get rid of the body, and I suspect the reservoir behind the house is the first place that occurs to them. I know that this was dragged at the time, but it's terribly easy to miss anything in so large a stretch of water. I can only suggest that it is thoroughly dragged again.

Lewis put the document back on the bedside table and Morse tapped him in congratulatory fashion upon the shoulder.

'I think it's time they made you up to inspector, my old friend.'

'You think I may be right then, sir?'

'Yes,' said Morse slowly, 'I do.'

CHAPTER TWENTY-NINE

Incest is only relatively boring.
Inscription on the lavatory
wall of an Oxford pub

LEWIS LEANED BACK into his pillows, and felt content. He would never make an inspector, he knew that, didn't even want to try. But to beat old Morse at his own game – my goodness, that was something!

'Got a drop of booze in the house?' asked Morse.

Ten minutes later he was sipping a liberal helping of whisky as Lewis dunked a chunk of bread into his Bovril.

'There are one or two things you could add to your admirable statement, you know, Lewis.' A slightly pained expression appeared on Lewis's face, but Morse quickly reassured him. 'Oh, that's pretty certainly how it happened, I'm sure of that. But there are just one or two points where we can be even more specific, I think, and one or two where we shall need a clearer picture not so much of what happened as of why it happened. Let's just go over a few of the things you say. Mrs Taylor dresses up as Valerie. I agree. You mention the school uniform and you rightly stress how distinctive this uniform is. But there's surely another small point. Mrs Taylor would not only wish in a positive way to be mistaken for her daughter, but in a negative sort of way not to be recognized facially as who she was – Valerie's mother. After all it's the face that most of us look at – not the clothes. And here I think her hair would be all-important. Their hair was the same colour, and Mrs Taylor is still too young to have more than a few odd streaks of grey. When we saw her she wore her hair on the top of her head, but I'd like to bet that when she lets it down it gives her much the same sort of look that Valerie had; and with long shoulder-length hair, doubt-less brushed forward over her face, I think the disguise would be more than adequate.'

Lewis nodded; but as the inspector said, it was only a small point.

'Now,' continued Morse, 'we surely come to the central point, and one that you gloss over rather too lightly, if I may say so.' Lewis looked stolidly at the counterpane, but made no interruption. 'It's this. What could possibly have been the motive that led Mrs Taylor to murder Valerie? Valerie! Her only daughter! You say that Valerie was pregnant, and although it isn't firmly established, I think the overwhelming probability is that she *was* pregnant; perhaps she had told her mother about it. But there's another possibility, and one that makes the whole situation far more sinister and disturb-ing. It isn't easy, I should imagine, for a daughter to hide a pregnancy from her mother for too long, and I think on balance it may well have been Mrs Taylor who accused Valerie of being pregnant – rather than Valerie who told her mother. But whichever way round it was, it surely can't add up to a sufficient motive for murdering the girl. It would be bad enough, I agree. The neighbours would gossip and everyone at school would have to know, and then there'd be the uncles and aunts and all the rest of 'em. But it's hardly a rare thing these days to have an unmarried mother in the family, is it? It could have happened as you say it did, but I get the feeling that Valerie's pregnancy had been known to Mrs Taylor for several weeks before the day she was murdered. And I think that on that Tuesday lunchtime Mrs Taylor tackled her daughter – she may have tackled her several times before – on a question which was infinitely more important to her than whether her daughter was pregnant or not. A question which was beginning to send her out of her mind; for she had her own dark and terrifying suspicions which would give her no rest, which poisoned her mind day and night, and which she had to settle one way or the other. And that question was this: *who was the father of Valerie's baby?* To begin with I automatically assumed that Valerie was a girl of pretty loose morals who would jump into bed at the slightest provocation with some of her randy boyfriends. But I think I was wrong. I ought to have seen through Maguire's sexual boastings straight away. He may have put his dirty fingers up her skirt once or twice, but I doubt that he or any of the other boys did much more. No. I should think that Valerie got an itch in her knickers as often – more often perhaps – than most young girls. But the indications all along the line were that her own particular weakness was *for older men*. Men about your age, Lewis.'

'And yours,' said Lewis. But the mood in the quiet

bedroom was sombre, and neither man seemed much amused. Morse drained his whisky and smacked his lips.

'Well, Lewis? What do you think?'

'You mean Phillipson, I suppose, sir?'

'Could have been, but I doubt it. I think he'd learned his lesson.'

Lewis thought for a moment and frowned deeply. Was it possible? Would it tie in with the other business? 'Surely you don't mean Baines, do you, sir? She must have been willing to go to bed with anyone if she let Baines . . .' He broke off. How sickening it all was!

Morse brooded a while, and stared through the bedroom window. 'I thought of it, of course. But I think you're right. At least I don't think she would have gone to bed *willingly* with Baines. And yet, you know, Lewis, it would explain a great many things if it *was* Baines.'

'I thought you had the idea that he was seeing Mrs Taylor – not Valerie.'

'I think he was,' said Morse. 'But, as I say, I don't think it was Baines.' He was speaking more slowly now, almost as if he were working through some new equation which had suddenly flashed across his mind; some new problem that challenged to some extent the validity of the case he was presenting. But reluctantly he put it aside, and resumed the main thread of his argument. 'Try again, Lewis.'

It was like backing horses. Lewis had backed the favourite, Phillipson, and lost; he'd then chosen an outsider, an outsider at least with a bit of form behind him, and lost again. There weren't many other horses in the race. 'You've got the advantage over me, sir. You went to see Acum yesterday. Don't you think you ought to tell me about it?'

'Leave Acum out of it for the minute,' said Morse flatly.

So Lewis reviewed the field again. There was only one other possibility, and he was surely a non-starter. Surely. Morse couldn't seriously . . . 'You don't mean . . . you can't mean you think it was . . . George Taylor?'

'I'm afraid I do, Lewis, and we'd both better get used to the grisly idea as quickly as we can. It's not pleasant, I know; but it's not so bad as it might be. After all, he's not her natural father, as far as we know, and so we're not fishing around in the murky waters of genuine incest or anything like that. Valerie would have known perfectly well that George wasn't her real father. They all lived together, and became as intimate as any other family. But intimate with one vital difference. Valerie grew into a young girl, and her looks and her figure developed, and *she was not his daughter*. I don't know what happened. What I do know is that we can begin to see one overwhelming motive for Mrs Taylor murdering her own daughter: the suspicion, gradually edging into a terrible certainty, that her only daughter was expecting a baby and that the father of that baby was her own husband. I think that on that Tuesday Mrs Taylor accused her daughter of precisely that.'

'It's a terrible thing,' said Lewis slowly, 'but perhaps we shouldn't be too hard on her.'

'I don't feel hard on anybody,' rejoined Morse. 'In fact, I feel some sympathy for the wretched woman.

Who wouldn't? But if all this is true, you can see what the likely train of events is. When George Taylor arrives home he's caught up in it all. Like a fly in a spider's web. His wife *knows*. It's no good him trying to wash his hands of the whole affair: he's the *cause* of it all. So, he goes along with her. What else can he do? What's more, he's in a position, the remarkably fortunate position, of being able to dispose, without suspicion and without too much trouble, of virtually anything, including a body. And I don't mean in the reservoir. George works at a place where vast volumes of rubbish and waste are piled high every day, and the same day buried without trace below the ground. And don't forget that Taylor was a man who had worked on road construction – *driving a bulldozer*. If he arrives at work half an hour early, what's to stop him using the bulldozer that's standing all ready, with the keys invitingly hung up for him on a nail in the shack? Nothing. Who would know? Who would care? No, Lewis. I don't think they put her into the reservoir. I think she lies buried out there on the rubbish dump.' Morse stopped for a second or two, and visualized the course of events anew.

'I think that Valerie must have been put into a sack or some sort of rubbish bag, and consigned for the long night to the boot of Taylor's old Morris. And in the morning he drove off early, and dumped her there, amid all the other mouldering rubbish; and he started up the bulldozer and buried her under the mounds of soil that stood ready at the sides of the tip. That's about it, Lewis. I'm very much afraid that's just about what happened. I should have been suspicious before, especially about the police not being called in until the next morning.'

'Do you think they'll find her body after all this time?'

'I should think so. It'll be a horribly messy business – but I should think so. The surveyor's department will know roughly which parts of the tip were levelled when and where, and I think we shall find her. Poor kid!'

'They put the police to a hell of a lot of trouble, didn't they?'

Morse nodded. 'It must have taken some guts to carry it through the way they did, I agree. But when you've committed a murder and got rid of the body, it might not have been so difficult as you think.'

A stray thought had been worrying Lewis as Morse had expounded his views of the way things must have happened.

'Do you think Ainley was getting near the truth?'

'I don't know,' said Morse. 'He might have had all sorts of strange ideas before he'd finished. But whether he got a scent of the truth or not doesn't really matter. What matters is that other people thought he was getting near the truth.'

'Where do you think the letter fits in, sir?'

Morse looked away. 'Yes, the letter. Remember the letter was probably posted before whoever sent it knew that Ainley was dead. I thought at the time that the whole point of it was to concentrate police attention away from the scene of the crime and on to London; and it seemed a possibility that the Taylors had cooked it up themselves because they thought Ainley was coming a bit too close for comfort.'

'But you don't think so now?'

'No. Like you, I think we've got to accept the evidence that it was almost certainly written by Baines.'

'Any idea why he wrote it?'

'I think I have, although—'

The front door bell rang in mid-sentence, and almost immediately Mrs Lewis appeared with the doctor. Morse shook hands with him and got up to go.

'There's no need for you to go. Shan't be with him long.'

'No, I'll be off,' said Morse. 'I'll call back this afternoon, Lewis.'

He let himself out and drove back to the police HQ at Kidlington. He sat in his black leather chair and looked mournfully at his in-tray. He would have to catch up with his correspondence very soon. But not today. Perhaps he had been glad of the interruption in Lewis's bedroom, for there were several small points in his reconstruction of the case which needed further cerebration. The truth was that Morse felt a little worried.

CHAPTER THIRTY

Money often costs too much.
Ralph Waldo Emerson

FOR THE NEXT hour he sat, without interruption, without a single telephone call, and thought it all through, beginning with the question that Lewis had put to him: why had Baines written the letter to the Taylors? At twelve noon, he rose from his chair, walked along the corridor and knocked at the office of Superintendent Strange.

Half an hour later, the door reopened and the two men exchanged a few final words.

'You'll have to produce one,' said Strange. 'There's no two ways about it, Morse. You can hold them for questioning, if you like, but sooner or later we want a body. In fact, we've got to have a body.'

'I suppose you're right, sir,' said Morse. 'It's a bit fanciful without a body, as you say.'

'It's a bit fanciful *with* a body,' said Strange.

Morse walked to the canteen, where the inevitable Dickson was ordering a vast plate of meat and vegetables.

'How's Sergeant Lewis, sir? Have you heard?'

254

'Much better. I saw him this morning. He'll be back any day.'

He thought of Lewis as he ordered his own lunch, and knew that he had not finally resolved the question that his sergeant had put to him. Why had Baines written that letter? He had thought of all the possible reasons that anyone ever had for writing a letter, but was still not convinced that he had a satisfactory answer. It would come, though. There was still a good deal about Baines he didn't know, but he had set inquiries in progress several days ago, and even bank managers and income tax inspectors didn't take all that long surely.

He ought to have had a closer look through his in-tray; and he would. For the moment, however, he thought that a breath of fresh air would do him good, and he walked out into the main road, turned right and found himself walking towards the pub. He didn't wish to see Mrs Taylor, and he was relieved to find that she wasn't there. He ordered a pint, left immediately he had finished it, and walked down towards the main road. Two shops he had never paid any attention to before lay off a narrow service road at the top of Hatfield Way, one a general provisions store, the other a fresh fruiterer, and Morse bought a small bunch of black grapes for the invalid. It seemed a kind thought. As he walked out, he noticed a small derelict area between the side of the provisions store and the next row of council houses. It was no more than ten square yards in extent, with two or three bicycle racks, the bric-à-brac of builders' carts from years ago – half-bricks, a flattened heap of sand; and strewing the area the inevitable empty cigarette cartons and crisps packets. Two cars stood in the small area, unobtrusive and unmolested. Morse stopped and took his bearings and realized that he was only some forty or fifty yards from the Taylors' house, a little further down towards the main road on the left. He stood quite still and gripped the bag of grapes more firmly. Mrs Taylor was in the front garden. He could see her quite clearly, her hair piled rather untidily on top of her head, her back towards him, her slim legs more those of a schoolgirl than a mother. In her right hand she held a pair of secateurs, and she was bending over the rose trees and clipping off the faded blooms. He found himself wondering if he would have been able to recognize her if she suddenly rushed out of the gate in a bright school uniform with her hair flowing down to her shoulders; and it made him uneasy, for he felt that he *would* have been able to tell at once that she was a woman and not a girl. You couldn't really disguise some things, however hard you tried; and perhaps it was very fortunate for Mrs Taylor that none of the neighbours *had* seen her that Tuesday lunchtime, and that old Joe Godberry's eyes had grown so tired and dim. And all of a sudden he saw it all plainly, and the blood tingled in his arms. He glanced around again at the small piece of waste land, shielded from the Taylors' home by the wall of the council house, looked again at the Taylors' front garden, where the wilted petals were now piled neatly at the edge of the narrow lawn, turned on his heel and walked back the long way round to Police HQ.

He had been right about his in-tray. There were detailed statements about Baines's financial position, and Morse raised his eyebrows in some surprise as he studied them, for Baines was better off than he had thought. Apart from insurance policies, Baines had over £5,000 in the Oxford Building Society, £6,000 tied up in a high-interest long-term loan with Manchester Corporation, £4,500 in his deposit account with Lloyds, as well as £150 in his current account with the same bank. It all added up to a tidy sum, and schoolmasters, even experienced second masters, weren't all that highly recompensed. The pay cheques for the previous year had all been paid directly into the deposit account, and Morse noticed with some surprise that the with-drawals on the current account had seldom amounted to more than £30 per month over that period. It seemed clear from the previous year's tax returns that Baines had no supplementary monies accruing to him from examination fees or private tuition, and although he may have risked not declaring any such further income, Morse thought that on the whole it was unlikely. The house, too, belonged to Baines: the final payment had been made some six years previously. Of course, he may well have been left a good deal of money by his parents and other relatives; but the fact remained that Baines somehow had managed to live on about seven or eight pounds a week for the last twelve months. Either he was a miser or, what seemed more likely, he was receiving a supply of ready cash fairly regularly from some quarter or quarters. And it hardly needed a mind as imaginative as Morse's to make one or two intelligent deductions on that score. There must have been several people who had shed no tears when Baines had died; indeed there had been one person who had been unable to stand it any longer and who had stuck him through with a carving knife.

CHAPTER THIRTY-ONE

> To you, Lord Governor,
> Remains the censure of this hellish villain —
> The time, the place, the torture. O enforce it!
>   Shakespeare, *Othello*, Act V

LEWIS WAS SITTING up in his dressing-gown in the front room when Morse returned at a quarter to three.

'Start next Monday, sir – Sunday if you want me – and I can't tell you how glad I am.'

'It'll all be over then with a bit of luck,' said Morse. 'Still we may have another homicidal lunatic roaming the streets before then, eh?'

'You really think this is nearly finished, sir?'

'I saw Strange this morning. We're going ahead tomorrow. Bring in both the Taylors and then start digging up all the rubbish dump – if we have to; though I think George will co-operate, even if his wife doesn't.'

'And you think it all links up with Baines's murder?'

Morse nodded. 'You were asking this morning about Baines writing that letter, and the truth is I don't quite know yet. It could have been to put the police off the scent, or to put them on – take your pick. But I feel fairly sure that one way or another it would keep his little pot boiling.'

'I don't quite follow you, sir.'

Morse told him of Baines's financial position, and Lewis whistled softly. 'He really was a blackmailer, then?'

'He was certainly getting money from somewhere, probably from more than one source.'

'Phillipson, for sure, I should think.'

'Yes. I think Phillipson had to fork out a regular monthly payment; not all that much perhaps, certainly not a ruinous sum for a man in Phillipson's position. Let's say twenty, thirty pounds a month. I don't know. But I shall know soon. There can be little doubt that Baines saw him the night he was going back home after his interview; saw him with a bit of stuff – more than likely Valerie Taylor. He could have ruined Phillipson's position straight away, of course, but that doesn't seem to have been the way that Baines's warped and devious mind would usually work. It gave him power to keep the intelligence to himself – to himself, that is, and to Phillipson.'

'He had as good a reason as anybody for killing Baines, didn't he?'

'He had, indeed. But he didn't kill Baines.'

'You sound pretty sure of yourself, sir.'

'Yes I am sure,' said Morse quietly. 'Let's just go on a bit. I think there was another member of staff Baines had been blackmailing.'

'You mean Acum?'

'Yes, Acum. It seemed odd to me from the start that he should leave a fairly promising situation in the modern languages department here at the Roger

Bacon, and take up a very similar position in a very similar school right up in the wilds of North Wales – away from his friends and family and the agreeable life of a university town like Oxford. I think that there must have been a little flurry of a minor scandal earlier in the year that Acum left. I asked him about it when I saw him yesterday, but he wouldn't have any of it. It doesn't matter much, though, and Phillipson will have to come clean anyway.'

'What do you think happened?'

'Oh, the usual thing. Somebody caught him with one of the girls with his trousers down.'

Lewis leaned his head to one side and smiled rather wearily. 'I suppose you think it may have been Valerie Taylor, sir?'

'Why not?' said Morse. 'She seems to have made most of the men put their hands on their cocks at some time, doesn't she? I should think that Phillipson got to know and Baines, too – oh yes, I'm sure Baines got to know – and they got together and agreed to hush things up if Acum would agree to leave as soon as it was practicable to do so. And I shouldn't think that Acum had any option. He'd be asked to leave whatever happened, and his wife would probably find out and – well, it would have seemed like the end of the world to a young fellow like Acum.'

'And you think Baines had the bite on Acum?'

'Pretty certain of it. I should think that Acum' (Morse chose his words carefully) ' – judging from the little I've seen of his wife – would have been a bloody fool to have ruined his career just for the sake of a brief infatuation with one of his pupils. And he didn't. He played the game and cleared out.'

'And paid up.'

'Yes. He paid up, though I shouldn't think Baines was stupid enough to expect too much from a former colleague who was probably fairly hard up anyway. Just enough, though. Just enough for Baines to relish another little show of power over one of his fellow human beings.'

'I suppose you're going to tell me next that Baines had the bite on the Taylors as well.'

'No. Just the opposite, in fact. I reckon that Baines was paying money to Mrs Taylor.'

Lewis sat up. Had he heard aright? 'You mean Mrs Taylor was blackmailing *Baines*?'

'I didn't say that, did I? Let's go back a bit. We've agreed that Baines got to know about Phillipson's little peccadillo at the Station Hotel. Now I can't imagine that Baines would merely be content with the Phillipson angle. I think that he began to grub around on the Taylor side of the fence. Now, Lewis. What did he find? You remember that George Taylor was out of work at the time, and that far from being a potential source of blackmail the Taylors were in dire need of money themselves. And especially Mrs Taylor. Baines had met them several times at parents' evenings, and I should guess that he arranged to see Mrs Taylor privately, and that he pretty soon read the temperature of the water correctly.'

'But Baines wasn't the type of man who went around doing favours.'

'Oh no. The whole thing suited Baines splendidly.'

'But he gave her money, you think?'

'Yes.'

'But she wouldn't take his money just like that, would she? I mean . . . she wouldn't expect . . .'

'Wouldn't expect to get the money for nothing? Oh no. She had something to give him in return.'

'What was that?'

'What the hell do you think it was? You weren't born yesterday, were you?'

Lewis felt abashed. 'Oh, I see,' he said quietly.

'Once a week in term time, if you want me to keep guessing, Tuesdays, likely as not, when he had the afternoon off. *Tuesday afternoons*, Lewis. Do you see what that means?'

'You mean,' stammered Lewis, 'that Baines probably . . . probably . . .'

'Probably knew more about the fate of Valerie Taylor than we thought, yes. I should think that Baines would park somewhere near the Taylors' house – not too near – and wait until Valerie had gone off back to school. Then he'd go in, get his pound of flesh, pay his stamp duty—'

'Bit dangerous, wasn't it?'

'If you're a bachelor like Baines and you're dying to spill your oats – well . . . After all, no one would *know* what was going on. Lock the door and—'

Lewis interrupted him. 'But if they'd arranged to

meet the day that Valerie disappeared, it would have been crazy for Mrs Taylor to have murdered her daughter.'

'It was crazy anyway. I don't think she would have worried too much if the police force was out the front and the fire brigade was out the back. Listen. What I think may have happened on that Tuesday is this. Baines parked pretty near the house, probably in a bit of waste land near the shops, just above the Taylors' place. He waited until afternoon school had started, and then he saw something very odd. He saw Valerie, or who he thought was Valerie, leave by the front door and run down the road. Then he went up to the house and knocked – we didn't find a key, did we? – and he got no answer. It's all a bit odd. Has his reluctant mistress – well, let's hope she was reluctant – has she slipped out for a minute? He can almost swear she hasn't, but he can't be absolutely sure. He walks back, frustrated and disappointed, and scratches his balls in the car; and something tells him to wait. And about ten minutes later he sees Mrs Taylor walking – probably walking in a great hurry – out of one of the side streets and going into the house. Has she been out over the lunchtime? Unusual, to say the least. But there's something odder still – far odder. Something that makes him sit up with a vengeance. Valerie – he would remember now – had left with a basket; and here is Valerie's mother returning *with the very same basket*. Does he guess the truth? I don't know. Does he go to the house again and knock? Probably so. And I would guess she told him she couldn't possibly see him that afternoon. So Baines walks away, and drives home, and wonders ... Wonders even harder the next day when he hears of Valerie's disappearance.'

'He guessed what had happened, you think?'

'Pretty sure he did.'

Lewis thought for a minute. 'Perhaps Mrs Taylor just couldn't face things any longer, sir, and told him that everything was finished; and he in turn might have threatened to go to the police.'

'Could be, but I should be very surprised if Baines was killed to stop him spilling the beans – or even some of them. No, Lewis. I just think that he was killed because he was detested so viciously that killing him was an act of superb and joyous revenge.'

'You think that Mrs Taylor murdered him, then?'

Morse nodded. 'You remember the first time we saw Mrs Taylor in the pub? Remember that large American-style handbag she had? It was a bit of a puzzle at first to know how anyone could ever cart such a big knife around. But the obvious way to do it is precisely the way Mrs Taylor chose. Stick it in a hand-bag. She got to Kempis Street at about a quarter-past nine, I should think, knocked on the door, told a surprised Baines some cock-and-bull story, followed him into the kitchen, agreed to his offer of a glass of something, and as he bends down to get the beer out of the fridge, she takes her knife out and – well, we know the rest.'

Lewis sat back and considered what Morse had said. It all hung loosely together, perhaps, but he was feeling hot and tired.

'Go and have a lie down,' said Morse, as if reading his thoughts. 'You've had about enough for one day.'

'I think I will, sir. I shall be much better tomorrow.'

'Don't worry about tomorrow. I shan't do anything until the afternoon.'

'It's the inquest in the morning, though, isn't it?'

'Formality. Pure formality,' said Morse. 'I shan't say much. Just get him identified and tell the coroner we've got the bloodhounds out. "Murder by person or persons unknown." I don't know why we're wasting public money on having an inquest at all.'

'It's the law, sir.'

'Mm.'

'And tomorrow afternoon, sir?'

'I'm bringing the Taylors in.'

Lewis stood up. 'I feel a bit sorry for him, sir.'

'Don't you feel a bit sorry for *her*?' There was a sharp edge on Morse's voice; and after he had gone Lewis wondered why he'd suddenly turned so sour.

At four o'clock that same afternoon, as Morse and Lewis were talking together and trying to unravel the twisted skein of the Valerie Taylor case, a tall military-looking man was dictating a letter to one of the girls from the typing pool. He had some previous experience of the young lady in question, and decided it would be sensible to make the letter even briefer than he had intended; for although it would contain no earth-shattering news, he was anxious for it to go in the evening post. He had tried to phone earlier but had declined to leave a message when he learned that the only man who could have any possible interest in the matter was out – whereabouts temporarily unknown. At four-fifteen the letter was signed and in the evening postbag.

The bombshell burst on Morse's desk at 8.45 a.m. the following morning.

CHAPTER THIRTY-TWO

When you have eliminated the impossible, whatever remains, however improbable, must be the truth.
A. Conan Doyle, *The Sign of Four*

'IT'S A MISTAKE, I tell you. It's some clown of a sergeant who's ballsed the whole thing up.' His voice was strident, exasperated. He was prepared to forgive a certain degree of inadequacy, but never incompetence of this order. The voice at the other end of the line sounded firm and assured, like a kindly parent seeking to assuage a petulant child.

'There's no mistake, I'm afraid. I've checked it myself. And for heaven's sake calm down a bit, Morse my old friend. You asked me to do something for you, and I've done it. If it comes as a bit of a shock—'

'*A bit of a shock!* Christ Almighty, it's not just a bit of a shock, believe me; it's sheer bloody lunacy!'

There was a short delay at the other end. 'Look, old boy, I think you'd better come up and see for yourself, don't you? If you still think it's a mistake – well, that's up to you.'

'Don't keep saying "if" it's a mistake. It *is* a mistake – you can put your shirt and your underpants on that, believe me!' He calmed himself down as far as he could and resumed the conversation in a tone more befitting his station. 'Trouble is I've got a damned inquest today.'

'Shouldn't let that worry you. Anybody can do that for you. Unless you've arrested somebody, of course.'

'No, no,' muttered Morse, 'nothing like that. It would have been adjourned anyway.'

'You sound a bit fed up one way or another.'

'I bloody *am* fed up,' snapped Morse, 'and who wouldn't be? I've got the case all ready for bed and you send me a scratty little note that's blown the top off the whole f— thing! How would *you* feel?'

'You didn't expect us to find anything – is that it?'

'No,' said Morse, 'I didn't. Not a load of cock like that, anyway.'

'Well, as I say, you'll be able to see for yourself. I suppose it could have been somebody else with the same name, but it's a whacking big coincidence if that's the case. Same name, same dates. No, I don't think so. You'd be pushing your luck, I reckon.'

'And I'm going on pushing it,' rejoined Morse, 'pushing it like hell, have no fear. Coincidences do happen, don't they?' It sounded more like a plea to the gods than a statement of empirical truth.

'Perhaps they do, sometimes. It's my fault, though. I should have got hold of you yesterday. I did try a couple of times in the afternoon, but . . .'

'You weren't to know. As far as you were concerned it was just one more routine inquiry.'

'And it wasn't?' said the voice softly.

'And it wasn't,' echoed Morse. 'Anyway, I'll get there as soon as I can.'

'Good. I'll get the stuff ready for you.'

*

Chief Inspector Rogers of New Scotland Yard put down the phone and wondered why the letter he had dictated and signed the previous afternoon had blown up with such obvious devastation in Morse's face. The carbon copy, he noticed, was still lying in his out-tray, and he picked it up and read it through again. It still seemed pretty harmless.

CONFIDENTIAL

For the attention of Det. Chief Inspector Morse,
Thames Valley Police HQ,
Kidlington, Oxon.

Dear Morse,

You asked for a check on the abortion clinics for the missing person, Valerie Taylor. Sorry to have taken so long about it, but it proved difficult. The trouble is all these semi-registered places where abortions still get done unofficially – no doubt for a whacking private fee. Anyway, we've traced her. She was at the East Chelsea Nursing Home on the dates you gave us. Arrived 4.15 p.m. Tuesday, under her own name, and left some time Friday a.m. by taxi. About three months pregnant. No complications. Description fits all along the line, but we could check further. She had a room-mate who might not be too difficult to trace. We await your further instructions.

Yours sincerely,

P.S. Don't forget to call when you're this way again. The beer at the Westminster is drinkable – just!

Chief Inspector Rogers shrugged his shoulders and put the carbon back in the out-tray. Morse! He always had been a funny old bird.

Morse himself sat back in his black leather chair and felt like a man who had just been authoritatively informed that the moon really was made of green cheese after all. Scotland Yard! They must have buggered it all up – must have done! But whatever they'd done, it was little use pretending he could go ahead with his intended schedule. What was the good of bringing two people in for questioning about the murder of a young girl if on the very day she was supposed to be lying dead in the boot of a car she had walked as large as life into some shabby nursing home in East Chelsea – of all places? For a few seconds Morse almost considered the possibility of taking the new information seriously. But he couldn't quite manage it. It just *couldn't* be right, and there was a fairly easy way of proving that it wasn't right. Central London lay no more than sixty miles away.

He went in to see Strange, and the superintendent, reluctantly, agreed to stand in for him at the inquest.

He rang Lewis, and told him he had to go off to London – he mentioned nothing more – and learned that Lewis would be reporting for duty again the next morning. That is, if he was needed. And Morse said, in a rather weak voice, that he thought he probably would be.

CHAPTER THIRTY-THREE

She'll be wearing silk pyjamas when she comes.
                                    Popular song

BY ANY RECKONING Yvonne Baker was a honey. She lived alone – or to be accurate she rented a single flat – in a high-rise tenement block in Bethune Road, Stoke Newington. She would have preferred a slightly more central spot and a slightly more luxurious apartment. But from Manor House tube station in Seven Sisters Road, just ten minutes' walk away, she could be in Central London in a further twenty minutes; and anyone looking around the tasteful and expensive décor of her flat would have guessed (correctly) that, whether from money honourably earned in the cosmetic department of an exclusive store in Oxford Street, or from other unspecified sources of income, Miss Baker was a young woman of not unsubstantial means.

At half-past six she lay languorously relaxed upon her costly counterpane, idly painting her long, beautifully-manicured nails with a particularly revolting shade of sickly green varnish. She wore a peach-coloured satin dressing-gown, her legs, invitingly long and slender, drawn up to her waist, her thoughts centred on the evening ahead of her. The real trouble with pyjama parties was that some of the guests hadn't quite the courage to conform to the code, and wore enough under their nightshirts or pyjamas to defeat the whole object of the simple exercise. At least *she* would show them. Some of the girls would wear a bra and panties, but she wasn't going to. Oh no. She experienced a tingle of excitement at the thought of dancing with the men, and of knowing only too clearly the effect that she would have upon them. It was a gorgeous feeling anyway, wearing so little. So sensuous, so abandoned!

She finished her left hand, held it up before her like a policeman stopping the traffic, and flexed her fingers. She then poured some removing fluid on to a wad of cotton wool and proceeded to rub off all the varnish. Her hands looked better without any nail polish, she decided. She stood up, unfastened and took off her dressing-gown, and carefully lifted out of one of the wardrobe drawers a pair of palish-green pyjamas. She had a beautiful body, and like so many of her admirers she was inordinately conscious of it. She admired herself in the long wall-mirror, fastened all but the top button of her pyjama top and began to brush her long, luxuriant, honey-coloured hair. She would be collected by car at half-past seven, and she glanced again at the alarm clock on her bedside table. Three-quarters of an hour. She walked into the living room, put a record on the turntable, and lit a cigarette of quite improbable length.

The door bell rang at ten minutes to seven, and her first thought was that the alarm clock must be slow again. Well, if it was, so much the better. She walked

gaily to the door and opened it with a beaming smile
upon her soft, full lips, a smile which slowly contracted
and finally faded away as she stared at a man she had
never seen before, who stood rather woodenly upon
the threshold. Middle-aged and rather sour.

'Hullo,' she managed.

'Miss Baker?' Miss Baker nodded. 'I'm Chief Inspector Morse. I'd like to come in and have a word with
you, if I may.'

'Of course.' A slightly worried frown puckered the
meticulously plucked eyebrows as he stood aside and
closed the door behind him.

As he explained the reason for his visit, she felt that
he was the only man within living memory upon whom
she appeared to have no visibly erotic effect. In her
pyjamas, too! He was brisk and businesslike. Two years
the previous June she had shared, had she not, a room
in the East Chelsea Nursing Home with a girl named
Valerie Taylor? He wanted to know about this girl.
Everything she could conceivably remember – every
single little thing.

The door bell rang again at twenty-five past seven
and Morse told her in an unexpectedly peremptory
tone to get rid of him, whoever he was.

'I hope you realize I'm going out to a party tonight,
Inspector.' She sounded vexed, but in reality was not so
vexed as she appeared. In an odd sort of way he was
beginning to interest her.

'So I see,' said Morse, eyeing the pyjamas. 'Just tell
him you'll be another half-hour with me – at least.' She
decided she liked his voice. 'And tell him I'll take you

myself if he can't wait.' She decided she'd rather like that.

Morse had already learned enough; and he knew – had known earlier, really – that what Rogers had written was true. There was now no doubt whatsoever that Valerie Taylor had somehow found her way into a London abortion clinic on the very same day on which she had disappeared. The doctor who ran the nursing home had been pleasantly co-operative, but had categorically refused to break what he termed the code of professional confidentiality by revealing the identity of the person or persons who had negotiated Miss Taylor's visit. It had amazed Morse that the affluent abortionist should have heard of, let alone practised, any code of professional confidentiality; but short of a forcible entry into his filing cabinets, the ambivalent doctor made it abundantly clear that further information was not forthcoming.

After explaining the situation to her pyjama-bottomed beau Miss Baker retired briefly to the bedroom, examined herself once more in the mirror, and wrapped her dressing-gown – not too tightly – around her. She was beginning to feel chilly.

'There was no need to worry too much about me,' said Morse. 'I'm pretty harmless with women, they say.' For the first time she smiled at him, fully and freely, and immediately Morse wished she hadn't.

'I'll take it off again if you'll turn the fire on, Inspector.' She purred the words at him, and the danger bells were ringing in his head.

'I shan't keep you much longer, Miss Baker.'

'Most people call me Yvonne.' She smiled again and lay back in the armchair. No one ever called Morse by his Christian name.

'I'll turn on the fire if you're not careful,' he said. But he didn't.

'You tell me she said she was from Oxford – not from Kidlington?'

'From where?'

'Kidlington. It's just outside Oxford.'

'Oh, is it? No. She said Oxford, I'm sure of that.'

Perhaps she would anyway, thought Morse. It did sound a bit more imposing. He had nearly finished. 'Just one last thing, and I want you to think very hard, Miss – er Yvonne. Did Miss Taylor mention to you at any stage who the father was? Or who she thought the father was?'

She laughed openly. 'You're so beautifully delicate, Inspector. But as a matter of fact she did, yes. She was quite a lass really, you know.'

'Who was it?'

'She said something about one of her teachers. I remember that because I was a bit surprised to learn she was still a schoolgirl. She looked much older than that. She seemed much more ... much more *knowing* somehow. She was nobody's fool, I can tell you that.'

'This teacher,' said Morse. 'Did she say anything else about him?'

'She didn't mention his name, I don't think. But she said he'd got a little beard and it tickled her every time he ... every time ... you know.'

Morse took his eyes from her and stared sadly down

at the thick-piled, dark-green carpet. It had been a crazy sort of day.

'She didn't say what he taught? What subject?'

She thought a moment. 'Do you know, I . . . I rather think she did. I think she said he was a French teacher or something.'

He drove her into the West End, tried to forget that she was off to an open-ended orgy dressed only in the pyjamas he had eyed so lovingly in her flat, and decided that life had passed him by.

He dropped her in Mayfair, where she thanked him, a little sadly, and turned towards him and kissed him fully on the lips with her soft, open mouth. And when she was gone, he looked after her, the flared pale-green bottoms of her pyjamas showing below the sleek fur coat. There had been many bad moments that day, but as he sat there in the Lancia slowly wiping the gooey, deep-orange lipstick from his mouth, he decided that this was just about the worst.

Morse drove back to Soho and parked his car on the double yellow lines immediately in front of the Penthouse Club. It was 9.00 p.m. At a glance he could see that the man seated at the receipt of custom was not Maguire, as he hoped it would be. But he was almost past caring as he walked into the foyer.

''Fraid you can't leave your car there, mate.'

'Perhaps you don't know who I am,' said Morse, with

the arrogant authority of a Julius Caesar or an Alexander walking among the troops.

'I don't care who you are, mate,' said the young man, rising to his feet, 'you just can't . . .'

'I'll tell you who I am, sonny. My name's Morse. M-O-R-S-E. Got that? And if anyone comes along and asks you whose car it is tell 'em it's mine. And if they don't believe you, just refer 'em to me, sonny boy – sharpish!' He walked past the desk and through the latticed doorway.

'But . . .' Morse heard no more. The Maltese dwarf sat dutifully at his post, and in a perverse sort of way Morse was glad to see him.

'You remember me?'

It was clear that the little man did. 'No need for ticket, sir. You go in. Ticket on me.' He smiled weakly, but Morse ignored the offer.

'I want to talk to you. My car's outside.' There was no argument, and they sat side by side in the front.

'Where's Maguire?'

'He gone. He just gone. I do' know where.'

'When did he leave?'

'Two day, three day.'

'Did he have a girlfriend here?'

'Lots of girls. Some of the girls here, some of the girls there. Who know?'

'There was a girl here recently – she wore a mask. I think her name was Valerie, perhaps.'

The little man thought he saw the light and visibly relaxed. 'Valerie? No. You mean Vera. Oh yeah. Boys oh boys!' He was beginning to feel more confident now and his dirty hands expressively traced the undulating contours of her beautiful body.

'Is she here tonight?'

'She gone, too.'

'I might have known it,' muttered Morse. 'She's buggered off with Maguire, I suppose.'

The little man smiled, revealed a mouthful of large, brilliantly white teeth, and shrugged his oversized shoulders. Morse repressed his strong desire to smash his fist into the leering face, and asked one further question.

'Did *you* ever take her out, you filthy little bastard?'

'Sometimes. Who know?' He shrugged his shoulders again and spread out his hands, palms uppermost, in a typically Mediterranean gesture.

'Get out.'

'You want to come in, mister policeman? See pretty girls, no?'

'Get out,' snarled Morse.

For a while Morse sat on silently in his car and pondered many things. Life was down to its dregs, and he had seldom felt so desolate and defeated. He recalled his first interview with Strange at the very beginning of the case, and the distaste he had felt then at the prospect of trying to find a young girl in the midst of this corrupt and corrupting city. And now, again, he had to presume that she was alive. For all his wayward unpredictability, there was at the centre of his being an inner furnace of passion for truth, for logical analysis; and inexorably now the facts, almost all the facts, were pointing to the same conclusion – that he had been wrong, wrong from the start.

A constable, young, tall, confident, tapped sharply on the car window. 'Is this your car, sir?'

Morse wound the window down and wearily identified himself.

'Sorry, sir. I just thought . . .'

'Of course you did.'

'Can I be of any assistance, sir?'

'Doubt it,' replied Morse. 'I'm looking for a young girl.'

'She live round here, sir?'

'I don't know,' said Morse. 'I don't even know if she lives in London. Not much hope for me, is there?'

'But you mean she's been seen round here recently?'

'No,' said Morse quietly. 'She's not been seen anywhere for over two years.'

'Oh, I see, sir,' said the young man, seeing nothing. 'Well, perhaps I can't help much then. Good night, sir.' He touched his helmet, and walked off, uncomprehending, past the gaudy strip clubs and the pornographic bookshops.

'No,' said Morse to himself, 'I don't think you can.'

He started the engine and drove via Shepherd's Bush and the White City towards the M40. He was back in his office just before midnight.

It did not even occur to him to go straight home. He was fully aware, even if he could give no explanation for it, of the curious fact that his mind was never more resilient, never sharper, than when apparently it was beaten. On such occasions his brain would roam restlessly around his skull like a wild and vicious tiger immured within the confines of a narrow cage, ceaselessly circumambulating, snarling savagely – and lethal. During the whole of the drive back to Oxford he had been like a chess player, defeated only after a monumental struggle, who critically reviews and analyses the moves and the motives for the moves that have led to his defeat. And already a new and strange idea was spawning in the fertile depths of his mind, and he was impatient to get back.

At three minutes to midnight he was poring over the dossiers on the Taylor case with the frenetic concentration of a hastily summoned understudy who had only a few minutes in which to memorize a lengthy speech.

At 2.30 a.m. the night sergeant, carrying a steaming cup of coffee on a tray, tapped lightly and opened the door. He saw Morse, his hands over his ears, his desk strewn with documents, and an expression of such profound intensity upon his face that he quickly and gently put down the tray, reclosed the door, and walked quickly away.

He called again at 4.30 a.m. and carefully put down a second cup of coffee beside the first, which stood where he had left it, cold, ugly-brown, untouched. Morse was fast asleep now, his head leaning back against the top of the black leather chair, the neck of his white shirt unfastened, and an expression on his face as of a young child for whom the vivid terrors of the night were past . . .

It had been Lewis who had found her. She lay supine upon the bed, fully clothed, her left arm placed across the body, the wrist slashed cruelly deep. The white coverlet was a pool of scarlet, and blood had dripped its way through the mattress. Clutched in her right hand was a knife, a wooden-handled carving knife, 'Prestige, Made in England', some 35–36 centimetres long, the cutting blade honed along its entire edge to a razor-sharp ferocity.

Chapter Thirty-Four

Things are not always what they seem;
the first appearance deceives many.

Phaedrus

LEWIS REPORTED BACK for duty at eight o'clock and found a freshly shaven Morse seated at his desk. He could scarcely hide his disappointment as Morse began to recount the previous day's events, and found himself quite unable to account for the inspector's sprightly tone. His spirits picked up, however, when Morse mentioned the crucial evidence given by Miss Baker, and after hearing the whole story, he evinced little surprise at the string of instructions that Morse proceeded to give him. There were several phone calls to make and he thought he began to understand the general tenor of the inspector's purpose.

At 9.30 he had finished, and reported back to Morse.

'Feel up to the drive then?'

'I don't mind driving one way, sir, but—'

'Settled then. I'll drive there, you drive back. Agreed?'

'When were you thinking of going, sir?'

'Now,' said Morse. 'Give the missus a ring and tell her we should be back about er . . .'

'Do you mind me mentioning something, sir?'

'What's worrying you?'

'If Valerie was in that nursing home—'

'She was,' interrupted Morse.

'—well, someone had to take her and fetch her and pay for her and everything.'

'The quack won't tell us. Not yet, anyway.'

'Isn't it fairly easy to guess, though?'

'Is it?' said Morse, with apparent interest.

'It's only a guess, sir. But if they were all in it together – you know, to cover things up . . .'

'All?'

'Phillipson, the Taylors and Acum. When you come to think of it, it would kill a lot of birds with one stone, wouldn't it?'

'How do you mean?'

'Well, if you're right about Phillipson and Valerie, he'd have a bit of a guilt complex about her and feel morally bound to help out, wouldn't he? And then there's the Taylors. It would save them any scandal and stop Valerie mucking up her life completely. And then there's Acum. It would get him out of a dickens of a mess at the school and save his marriage into the bargain. They've all got a stake in it.'

Morse nodded and Lewis felt encouraged to continue. 'They could have cooked it all up between them: fixed up the clinic, arranged the transport, paid the bill, and found a job for Valerie to go to afterwards. They probably hadn't the faintest idea that her going off like that would create such a fuss, and once they started on it, well, they just had to go through with it. So they all stuck together. And told the same story.'

'You may well be right.'

'If I am, sir, don't you think it would be a good idea to fetch Phillipson and the Taylors in? I mean, it would save us a lot of trouble.'

'Save us going all the way to Caernarfon, you mean?'

'Yes. If they spill the beans, we can get Acum brought down here.'

'What if they all stick to their story?'

'Then we'll have to go and get him.'

'I'm afraid it's not quite so easy as that,' said Morse.

'Why not?'

'I tried to get Phillipson first thing this morning. He went off to Brighton yesterday afternoon – to a headmasters' conference.'

'Oh.'

'And the Taylors left by car for Luton airport at 6.30 yesterday morning. They're spending a week on a package tour in the Channel Islands. So the neighbours say.'

'Oh.'

'And,' continued Morse, 'we're still trying to find out who killed Baines, remember?'

'That's why you've asked the Caernarfon police to pick him up?'

'Yep. And we'd better not keep him waiting too long. It's about four and a half hours – non-stop. So we'll allow five. We might want to give the car a little rest on the way.'

Outside a pub, thought Lewis, as he pulled on his overcoat. But Lewis thought wrong.

The traffic this Sunday morning was light and the

police car made its way quickly up through Brackley and thence to Towcester where it turned left on to the A5. Neither man seemed particularly anxious to sustain much conversation, and a tacit silence soon prevailed between them, as if they waited tensely for the final wicket to fall in a test match. The traffic decelerated to a paralytic crawl at road works in Wellington, and suddenly Morse switched on full headlights and the blue roof-flasher, and wailing like a dalek in distress the car swept past the stationary column of cars and soon was speeding merrily along once more out on the open road. Morse turned to Lewis and winked almost happily.

Along the Shrewsbury ring-road, Lewis ventured a conversational gambit. 'Bit of luck about this Miss Baker, wasn't it?'

'Ye-es.' Lewis looked at the inspector curiously. 'Nice bit of stuff, sir?'

'She's a prick-teaser.'

'Oh.'

They drove on through Betws-y-coed: Caernarfon 25 miles.

'The real trouble,' said Morse suddenly, 'was that I thought she was dead.'

'And now you think she's still alive?'

'I very much hope so,' said Morse, with unwonted earnestness in his voice. 'I very much hope so.'

At five minutes to three they came to the outskirts of Caernarfon, where ignoring the sign directing traffic to the city centre Morse turned left on to the main Pwllheli Road.

'You know your way around here then, sir?'

'Not too well. But we're going to pay a brief visit before we meet Acum.' He drove south to the village of Bont-Newydd, turned left off the main road and stopped outside a house with the front door painted Cambridge blue.

'Wait here a minute.'

Lewis watched him as he walked up the narrow front path and knocked on the door; and knocked again. Clearly there was no one at home. But then of course David Acum *wouldn't* be there; he was three miles away, detained for questioning on the instructions of the Thames Valley Police. Morse came back to the car and got in. His face seemed inexplicably grave.

'No one in, sir?'

Morse appeared not to hear. He kept looking around him, occasionally glancing up into the driving mirror. But the quiet street lay preternaturally still in the sunny autumn afternoon.

'Shan't we be a bit late for Acum, sir?'

'Acum?' The inspector suddenly woke from his waking dreams. 'Don't worry about Acum. He'll be all right.'

'How long do you plan to wait here?'

'How the hell do I know!' snapped Morse.

'Well, if we're going to wait, I think I'll just—' He opened the nearside door and began to unfasten his safety-belt.

'Stay where you are.' There was a note of harsh

authority in the voice, and Lewis shrugged his shoulders and closed the door again.

'If we're waiting for Mrs Acum, don't you think she may have gone with him?'

Morse shook his head. 'I don't think so.'

The time ticked on inexorably, and it was Morse who finally broke the silence. 'Go and knock again, Lewis.'

But Lewis was no more successful than Morse had been; and he returned to the car and slammed the door with some impatience. It was already half-past three.

'We'll give her another quarter of an hour,' said Morse.

'But why are we waiting for *her*, sir? What's she got to do with it all? We hardly know anything about her, do we?'

Morse turned his light-grey eyes upon his sergeant and spoke with an almost fierce simplicity. 'That's where you're wrong, Lewis. We know more about her – far more about her – than about anyone else in the whole case. You see, the woman living here with David Acum is not his real wife at all – she's the person we've been looking for from the very beginning.' He paused and let his words sink in. 'Yes, Lewis. The woman who's been living here for the past two years as Acum's wife is not his wife at all – *she's Valerie Taylor.*'

CHAPTER THIRTY-FIVE

'Now listen, you young limb,' whispered Sikes. 'Go
softly up the steps straight afore you, and along the
little hall, to the street door: unfasten it, and let us
in.'

Charles Dickens, *Oliver Twist*

LEWIS'S MOUTH GAPED in flabbergasted disbelief
as this astonishing intelligence partially percolated
through his consciousness. 'You can't mean . . .'

'But I *do* mean. I mean exactly what I say. And that's
why we're sitting here waiting, Lewis. We're waiting for
Valerie Taylor to come home at last.'

For the moment Lewis was quite incapable of any
more intelligent comment than a half-formed whistle.
'Phew!'

'Worth waiting another few minutes for, isn't she?
After all this time?'

Gradually the implications of what the inspector had
just told him began to register more significantly in
Lewis's mind. It meant . . . it meant . . . But his mental
processes seemed now to be anaesthetized, and he gave
up the unequal struggle. 'Don't you think you ought to
put me in the picture, sir?'

'Where do you want me to start?' asked Morse, in a
slightly brisker tone.

'Well, first of all you'd better tell me what's happened to the *real* Mrs Acum.'

'Listen, Lewis. In this case you've been right more often than I have. I've made some pretty stupid blunders – as you know. But at last we're getting near the truth, I think. You ask me what's happened to the real Mrs Acum. Well, I don't know for certain. But let me tell you what I think may have happened. I've hardly got a shred of evidence for it, but as I see things it must have happened something like this.

'What do we know about Mrs Acum? A bit prim and proper, perhaps. She's got a slim, boyish-looking figure, and long shoulder-length blonde hair. Not unattractive, maybe, in an unusual sort of way, but no doubt very self-conscious about the blotch of ugly spots all over her face. Then think about Valerie. She's a real honey, by all accounts. A nubile young wench, with a sort of animal sexuality about her that proves fatally attractive to the opposite sex – the men and the boys alike. Now just put yourself in Acum's place. He finds Valerie in his French class, and he begins to fancy her. He thinks she may have a bit of ability, but neither the incentive nor the inclination to make anything of it. Well, from whatever motives, he talks to her privately and suggests some extra tuition. Now let's try to imagine what might have happened. Let's say Mrs Acum has joined a Wednesday sewing class at Headington Tech. – I know, Lewis, but don't interrupt: it doesn't matter about the details. Where was I? Yes. Acum's free then on Wednesday evenings, and we'll say that he invites Valerie round to his house. But one night in March the evening class is cancelled – let's say the teacher's got flu – and Mrs Acum arrives home unexpectedly early, about a quarter to eight, and she finds them both in bed together. It's a dreadful humiliation for her, and she decides that their marriage is finished. Not that she necessarily wants to ruin Acum's career. She may feel she's to blame in some way: perhaps she doesn't enjoy sex; perhaps she can't have any children – I don't know. Anyway, as I say, it's finished between them. They continue to live together, but they sleep in different rooms and hardly speak to each other. And however hard she tries, she just can't bring herself to forgive him. So they agree to separate when the summer term is over, and Acum knows it will be better for both of them if he gets a new post. Whether he told Phillipson the truth or not, doesn't really matter. Perhaps he didn't tell him anything when he first handed in his resignation; but he may well have had to say something when Valerie tells him that she's expecting a baby and that he's almost certainly the father. So, as you yourself said this morning, Lewis, they all decide to put their heads together. Valerie, Acum, Phillipson and Mrs Taylor – I don't know about George. They arrange the clinic in London and fix up the house in North Wales here, where Valerie comes immediately after the abortion, and where Acum will join her just as soon as the school term ends. And Valerie arrives and acts the dutiful little wife, decorating the place and getting things straight and tidy; *and she's still here.* Where the real Mrs Acum is, I don't know; but we should be able to find out easily enough. If you want me to make a guess, I'd say she's living with her mother, in a little village somewhere near Exeter.'

For several minutes Lewis sat motionless within the quiet car, until aroused at length by the very silence he took a yellow duster from the glove compartment and wiped the steamy windows. Morse's imaginative reconstruction of events seemed curiously convincing, and several times during the course of it Lewis's head had nodded an almost involuntary agreement.

Morse himself suddenly looked once more at his wristwatch. 'Come on, Lewis,' he said. 'We've waited long enough.'

The side gate was locked, and Lewis clambered awkwardly over. The small top window of the back kitchen was open slightly, and by climbing on to the rain-water tub he was able to get his arm through the narrow gap and open the latch of the main window. He eased himself through on to the draining board, jumped down inside, and breathing heavily walked to the front door to let the inspector in. The house was eerily silent.

'No one here, sir. What do we do?'

'We'll have a quick look round,' said Morse. 'I'll stay down here. You try upstairs.'

The steps on the narrow flight of stairs creaked loudly as Lewis mounted aloft, and Morse stood below and watched him, his heart pounding against his ribs.

There were only two bedrooms, each of them opening almost directly off the tiny landing: one to the right, the other immediately in front. First Lewis tried the one to his right, and peered round the door. The junk room, obviously. A single bed, unmade, stood against the far wall; and the bed itself and the rest of the limited space available were strewn with the necessary and the unnecessary oddments that had yet to find for themselves a permanent place in the disposition of the Acum household: several bell-jars of home-made wine, bubbling intermittently; a vacuum cleaner, with its box of varied fitments; dusty lampshades; old curtain rails, the mounted head of an old, moth-eaten deer; and a large assortment of other semi-treasured bric-à-brac that cluttered up the little room. But nothing else. Nothing.

Lewis left the room and tried the other door. It would be the bedroom, he knew that. Tentatively he pushed open the door slightly further and became aware of something scarlet lying there upon the bed, bright scarlet – the colour of new-spilt blood. He opened the door fully now and went inside. And there, draped across the pure white coverlet, the arms neatly folded across the bodice, the waist tight-belted and slim, lay a long, red-velvet evening dress.

CHAPTER THIRTY-SIX

No one does anything from a single motive.
S. T. Coleridge, *Biographia Literaria*

THEY SAT DOWNSTAIRS in the small kitchen.

'It looks as if our little bird has flown.'

'Mm.' Morse leaned his head upon his left elbow and stared blankly through the window.

'When did you first suspect all this, sir?'

'Sometime last night, it must have been. About half-past three, I should think.'

'This morning, then.'

Morse seemed mildly surprised. It seemed a long, long time ago.

'What put you on to it, though?'

Morse sat up and leaned his back against the rickety kitchen chair. 'Once we learned that Valerie was probably still alive, it altered everything, didn't it? You see, from the start I'd assumed she was dead.'

'You must have had *some* reason.'

'I suppose it was the photograph more than anything,' replied Morse. 'The one of the genuine Mrs Acum that Mrs Phillipson showed me. It was a clear-cut, glossy photograph – not like the indistinct and out-of-date ones we've got of Valerie. Come to think of it, I doubt if either of us will recognize Valerie when we *do* see her. Anyway, I met who I *thought* was Mrs Acum when I first came up here to Caernarfon, and although she had a towel round her head I couldn't help noticing that she wasn't a natural blonde at all. The roots of her hair were dark, and for some reason' (he left it at that) 'the detail, well, just stuck with me. She'd dyed her hair, anyone could see that.'

'But we don't know that the real Mrs Acum is a natural blonde.'

'No. That's true,' admitted Morse.

'Not much to go on then, is it?'

'There was something else, Lewis.'

'What was that?'

Morse paused before replying. 'In the photograph I saw of Mrs Acum, she had a sort of, er, sort of a boyish figure, if you know what I mean.'

'Bit flat-chested you mean, sir?'

'Yes.'

'So?'

'The woman I saw here – well, she wasn't flat-chested, that's all.'

'She could have been wearing a padded bra. You just can't tell for certain, can you?'

'Can't you?' A gentle, wistful smile played momentarily about the inspector's mouth, and he enlightened the innocent Lewis no further. 'I ought to have guessed much earlier. Of course I should. They just don't have anything in common at all: Mrs Acum – and Valerie Taylor. Huh! I don't think you'd ever find anyone less like a blue-stocking than Valerie. And I've spoken to her *twice* over the phone, Lewis! More than that, I've actually *seen* her!' He shook his head in self-reproach. 'Yes. I really should have guessed the truth a long, long time ago.'

'From what you said, though, sir, you didn't see much of her, did you? You said she had this beauty-pack—'

'No, not much of her, Lewis. Not much . . .' His thoughts were very far away.

'What's all this got to do with the car-hire firms you're trying to check?' asked Lewis suddenly.

'Well, I've got to try to get *some* hard evidence against her, haven't I? I thought, funnily enough, of letting her give me the evidence herself, but . . .'

Lewis was completely lost. 'I don't quite follow you.'

'Well, I thought of ringing her up this morning first thing and tricking her into giving herself away. It would have been very easy, really.'

'It would?'

'Yes. All I had to do was to speak to her in French. You see, the real Mrs Acum is a graduate from Exeter, remember? But from what we know about poor Valerie's French, I doubt she can get very much further than *bonjour*.'

'But *you* can't speak French either can you, sir?'

'I have many hidden talents of which as yet you are quite unaware,' said Morse a trifle pompously.

'Oh.' But Lewis had a strong suspicion that Morse knew about as much (or as little) French as he did. And what's more, he'd had no answer to his question. 'Aren't you going to tell me why you'll be checking on the car-hire firms?'

'You've had enough shocks for one day.'

'I don't think one more'll make much difference,' replied Lewis.

'All right, I'll tell you. You see, we've not only found Valerie; *we've also found the murderer of Baines.*' Lewis opened and closed his mouth like a stranded goldfish, but no identifiable vocable emerged.

'You'll understand soon enough,' continued Morse. 'It's fairly obvious if you think about it. She has to get from Caernarfon to Oxford, right? Her husband's got the car. So, what does she do? Train? Bus? There aren't any services. And anyway, she's got to get there quickly, and there's only one thing she can do and that's to hire a car.'

'But we don't know yet that she *did* hire a car,' protested Lewis. 'We don't even know she can drive.'

'We shall know soon enough.'

The 'ifs' were forgotten now, and Morse spoke like a minor prophet enunciating necessary truths. And with gradually diminishing reluctance, Lewis was beginning to sense the inevitability of the course of events that Morse was sketching out for him, and the inexorable logic working through the inquiry they'd begun together. A young schoolgirl missing, and more than two years later a middle-aged schoolmaster murdered; and no satisfactory solution to either mystery. Just two insoluble problems. And suddenly, in the twinkling of an eye, there were no longer two problems – no longer even one problem; for somehow each had magically solved the other.

'You think she drove from here that day?'

'And back,' said Morse.

'And it was Valerie who . . . who killed Baines?'

'Yes. She must have got there about nine o'clock, as near as dammit.'

Lewis's mind ranged back to the night when Baines was murdered. 'So she could have been in Baines's house when Mrs Phillipson and Acum called,' he said slowly.

Morse nodded. 'Could have been, yes.'

He stood up and walked along the narrow hallway. From the window in the front room he could see two small boys, standing at a respectful distance from the police car and trying with cautious curiosity to peer inside. But for the rest, nothing. No one left and no one came along the quiet street.

'Are you worried, sir?' asked Lewis quietly, when Morse sat down again.

'We'll give her a few more minutes,' replied Morse, looking at his watch for the twentieth time.

'I've been thinking, sir. She must be a brave girl.'

'Mm.'

'And he was a nasty piece of work, wasn't he?'

'He was a shithouse,' said Morse with savage conviction. 'But I don't think that Valerie would ever have killed Baines just for her own sake.'

'What *was* her motive then?'

It was a simple question and it deserved a simple answer, but Morse began with the guarded evasiveness of a senior partner in the Circumlocution Office.

'I'm a bit sceptical about the word "motive", you know, Lewis. It makes it sound as if there's just got to be one – one big, beautiful motive. But sometimes it doesn't work like that. You get a mother slapping her child across its face because it won't stop crying. Why does she do it? You can say she just wants to stop the kid from bawling its head off, but it's not really true, is it? The motive lies much deeper than that. It's all bound up with lots of other things: she's tired, she's got a headache, she's fed up, she's just plain disillusioned with the duties of motherhood. Anything you like. When once you ask yourself what lies in the murky depths below what Aristotle called the immediate cause . . . You know anything about Aristotle, Lewis?'

'I've heard of him, sir. But you still haven't answered my question.'

'Ah, no. Well, let's just consider for a minute the position that Valerie found herself in that day. For the first time for over two years, I should think, she finds herself completely on her own. Since Acum came to join her, he's no doubt been pretty protective towards her, and for the first part of their time together here he's probably been anxious for Valerie not to be caught up in too much of a social whirl. She stays in. *And she'd bleached her hair* – probably right at the beginning. Surprising, isn't it, Lewis, how so many of us go to the trouble of making a gesture – however weak and meaningless. A sop to Cerberus, no doubt. As you know, Acum's real wife had long, blonde hair – that's the first thing anyone would notice about her; it's the first thing I noticed about her when I saw her photograph. Perhaps Acum asked her to do it; may have helped his conscience. Anyway, he must have been glad she *did* dye her hair. You remember the photograph of Valerie in the Colour Supplement? If he saw it, he must have been a very worried man. It wasn't a particularly clear photograph, I know. It had been taken over three years previously, and a young girl changes a good deal – especially between leaving school and becoming to all intents and purposes a married woman. But it still remained a photograph of Valerie and, as I say, I should think Acum was jolly glad about her hair. As far as we know, no one *did* spot the likeness.'

'Perhaps they don't read the *Sunday Times* in Caernarfon.'

For all his anti-Welsh prejudices, Morse let it go. 'She's on her own at last, then. She can do what she likes. She probably feels a wonderful sense of freedom, freedom to do something for herself – something that now, for the first time, *can* in fact be done.'

'I can see all that, sir. But *why*? That's what I want to know.'

'Lewis! Put yourself in the position Valerie and her mother and Acum and Phillipson and God knows who else must have found themselves. They've all got their individual and their collective secrets – big and little – and somebody else knows all about them. Baines knows. Somehow – well, we've got a jolly good idea how – he got to know things. Sitting all those years in that little office of his, with the telephone there and all the correspondence, he's been at the nerve-centre of a small community – the Roger Bacon School. He's second master there, and it's perfectly proper that he *should* know what's going on. All the time his ears are tuned in to the slightest rumours and suspicions. He's like a bug in the Watergate Hotel: he picks it all up and he puts it all together. And it gives to his sinister cast of character just the nourishment it craves for – the power over other people's lives. Think of Phillipson for a minute. Baines can put him out of a job any day he chooses – but he doesn't. You see, I don't think he gloried so much in the actual exercise of his power as—'

'He did actually blackmail Phillipson, though, didn't he?'

'I think so, yes. But even blackmail wouldn't be as sweet for a louse like Baines as the thought that he *could* blackmail – whenever he wanted to.'

'I see,' said the blind man.

'And Mrs Taylor. Think what he knows about her: about the arrangements for her daughter's abortion, about her elaborate lies to the police, about her heavy drinking, about her money troubles, about her anxiety that George Taylor – the only man who's ever treated her with any decency – should be kept in the dark about some of her wilder excesses.'

'But surely everybody must have known she went to Bingo most nights and had a drop of drink now and then?'

'Do you know how much she spent on Bingo and fruit machines? Even according to George it was a pound a night, and she's hardly likely to tell him the truth, is she? And she drinks like a fish – you know she does. Lunchtimes as well.'

'So do you, sir.'

'Yes, but . . . well, I only drink in moderation, you know that. Anyway, that's only the half of it. You've seen the way she dresses. Expensive clothes, shoes, accessories – the lot. And jewellery. You noticed the diamonds on her fingers? God knows what they're worth. And do you know what her husband is? He's a dustman! No, Lewis. She's been living way, way beyond her means – you must have realized that.'

'All right, sir. Perhaps that's a good enough motive for Mrs Taylor, but—'

'I know. Where does Valerie fit in? Well, I should think Mrs Taylor probably kept in touch with her daughter by phone – letters would be far too dangerous – and Valerie must have had a pretty good idea of what was going on: that her mother was getting hopelessly mixed up with Baines – that she was getting like a drug addict, loathing the whole thing in her saner moments but just not being able to do without it. Valerie must have realized that one way or another her mother's life was becoming one long misery, and she probably guessed how it was all likely to end. Perhaps her mother had hinted that she was coming to the end of her tether and couldn't face up to things much longer. I don't know.

'And then just think of Valerie herself. Baines knows all about her, too: her promiscuous background, her night with Phillipson, her affair with Acum – and all its consequences. He knows the lot. And at any time he can ruin *everything*. Above all he can ruin David Acum, because once it gets widely known that he's likely to start fiddling around with some of the girls he's supposed to be teaching, he'll have one hell of a job getting a post in *any* school, even in these permissive days. And I suspect, Lewis, that in a strange sort of way Valerie has gradually grown to love Acum more than anyone or anything she's ever wanted. I think they're happy together – or as happy as anyone could hope to be under the circumstances. Do you see what I mean, then? Not only was her mother's happiness threatened at every turn by that bastard Baines, but equally the happiness of David Acum. And one day she suddenly found herself with the opportunity of doing something about it all: at one swift, uncomplicated swoop to solve *all* the problems, and she could do that by getting rid of Baines.'

Lewis pondered a while. 'Didn't she ever think that Acum might be suspected, though? He was in Oxford, too – she knew that.'

'No, I don't suppose she gave it a thought. I mean, the chance that Acum himself would go along to Baines's place at the very same time as she did – well, it's a thousand to one against, isn't it?'

'Odd coincidence, though.'

'It's an odd coincidence, Lewis, that the 46th word from the beginning and the 46th word from the end of the 46th Psalm in the Authorized Version should spell "Shakespear".'

Aristotle, Shakespeare and the Book of Psalms. It was all a bit too much for Lewis, and he sat in silence deciding that he'd missed out somewhere along the educational line. He'd asked his questions and he'd got his answers. They hadn't been the best answers in the world, perhaps, but they just about added up. It was, one could say, satisfactory.

Morse stood up and went over to the kitchen window. The view was magnificent, and for some time he stared across at the massive peaks of the Snowdon range. 'We can't stay here for ever, I suppose,' he said at last. His hands were on the edge of the sink, and almost involuntarily he pulled open the right-hand drawer. Inside he saw a wooden-handled carving knife, new, 'Prestige, Made in England', and he was on the point of picking it up when he heard the rattle of a Yale key in the front-door lock. Swiftly he held up a finger to his mouth and drew Lewis back with him against the wall behind the kitchen door. He could see her quite clearly now, the long, blonde hair tumbling over her shoulders, as she fiddled momentarily with the inner catch, withdrew the key, and closed the door behind her.

Thinly veiled anger yet little more than mild surprise showed on her face as Morse stepped into the hallway. 'That's your car outside, I suppose.' She said it in a bleak almost contemptuous voice. 'I'd just like to know what right you think you've got to burst into my house like this!'

'You've every right to feel angry,' said Morse defencelessly, lifting up his left hand in a feeble gesture of pacification. 'I'll explain everything in a minute. I promise I will. But can I just ask you one question first? That's all I ask. Just one question. It's very important.'

She looked at him curiously, as if he were slightly mad.

'You speak French, don't you?'

'Yes.' Frowning she put down her shopping basket by the door, and stood there quite still, maintaining the distance between them. 'Yes, I do speak French. What's that—?'

Morse took the desperate plunge. '*Avez-vous appris français à l'école?*'

For a brief moment only she stared at him with blank, uncomprehending eyes, before the devastating reply slid smoothly and idiomatically from her tutored lips. '*Oui. Je l'ai étudié d'abord à l'école et après pendant trois ans à l'université. Alors je devrais parler la langue assez bien, n'est-ce pas?*'

'*Et avez-vous rencontré votre mari à Exeter?*'

'*Oui. Nous étions étudiants là-bas tous les deux. Naturelle-ment, il parle français mieux que moi. Mais il est assez évident que vous parlez français comme un anglais typique, et votre accent est abominable.*'

Morse walked back into the kitchen with the air of an educationally subnormal zombie, sat down at the table, and held his head between his hands. Why had he bothered anyway? He had known already. He had known as soon as she had closed the front door and turned her face towards him – a face still blotched with ugly spots.

'Would you both like a cup of tea?' asked Mrs Acum, as the embarrassed Lewis stepped forward sheepishly from behind the kitchen door.

CHAPTER THIRTY-SEVEN

The gaudy, blabbing and remorseful day
Is crept into the bosom of the sea.
Shakespeare, *Henry IV*, Part II

AS HE SLUMPED back in the passenger seat, Morse presented a picture of stupefied perplexity. They had left Caernarfon just after 9.00 p.m., and it would be well into the early hours before they arrived in Oxford. Each left the other to his private thoughts, thoughts that criss-crossed ceaselessly the no-man's-land of failure and futility.

The interview with Acum had been a very strange affair. Morse seemed entirely to have lost the thread of the inquiry, and his early questions had been almost embarrassingly apologetic. It had been left to Lewis to press home some of the points that Morse had earlier made, and after an initial evasiveness Acum had seemed almost glad to get it all off his chest at last. And as he did so, Lewis was left wondering where the inspector's train of thought had jumped the rails and landed in such a heap of crumpled wreckage by the track; for many of Morse's assumptions had been correct, it seemed. Almost uncannily correct.

Acum (on his own admission now) had indeed been attracted to Valerie Taylor and several times had intercourse with her; including a night in early April (not March) when his wife had returned home early one Tuesday (not Wednesday) evening from night school in Oxpens (not Headington) where she was attending art (not sewing) classes. Her teacher was down with shingles (not with flu), and the class was cancelled. It was just after eight o'clock (not a quarter to) when Mrs Acum had returned and found them lying together across the settee (not in bed), and the upshot had been veritably volcanic, with Valerie, it seemed, by far the least confounded of that troubled trio. There followed, for Acum and his wife, a succession of bleak and barren days. It was all over between them – she insisted firmly upon that; but she agreed to stay with him until their separation could be effected with a minimum of social scandal. He himself decided he must move in any case, and applied for a job in Caernarfon; and although he had been questioned by Phillipson at some length about his motives for a seemingly meaningless move to a not particularly promising post, he had told him nothing of the truth. Literally nothing. He could only pray that Valerie would keep her mouth shut, too.

Not until about three weeks before her disappearance had he spoken personally to Valerie again, when she told him that she was expecting a baby, a baby that was probably his. She appeared (or so it seemed to Acum) completely confident and unconcerned and told him everything would be all right. She begged of him one thing only: that if she were to run away he would say nothing and know nothing – that was all; and although he had pressed her about her intentions, she would only repeat that she would be all right. Did she need any money? She told him she would let him know, but, smiling slyly as she told him, she said that she was going to be all right. Everything was 'all right'. Everything was always 'all right' with Valerie. (It was at this point in Lewis's interrogation, and only at this point, that Morse had suddenly pricked up his ears and asked a few inconsequential questions.) It appeared, however, that the money side of things was not completely 'all right', for only a week or so before the day she disappeared Valerie had approached Acum and told him she would be very grateful for some money if he could manage it. She hadn't pressed her claim on him in any way, but he had been only too glad to help; and from the little enough they had managed to save – and with his wife's full knowledge – he had raised one hundred pounds. And then she had gone; and like everyone else he hadn't the faintest idea where she had gone to, and he had kept his silence ever since, as Valerie had asked him to.

Meanwhile in the Acum household the weeping wounds were at last beginning to heal; and with Valerie gone they had tried, for the first time since that dreadful night, to discuss their sorry situation with some degree of rationality and mutual understanding. He told her that he loved her, that he realized now how very much she meant to him, and how desperately he hoped that they would stay together. She had wept then, and said she knew how disappointed he must be that she could have no children of her own . . . And as the summer term drew towards its close they had decided – almost happily decided – that they would stay together, and try to patch their marriage up. In any case there had never been the slightest question of divorce: for his wife was a Roman Catholic.

So, continued Acum, they had moved together to North Wales, and life was happy enough now – or had been so until the whole thing had once more exploded in their faces with the murder of Reggie Baines, of which (he swore on his solemn honour) he was himself completely innocent. Blackmail? The whole idea was laughable. The only person who had any hold on him was Valerie Taylor, and of Valerie Taylor he had seen or heard nothing whatsoever since the day of her disappearance. Whether she were alive or whether she were dead, he had no idea – no idea at all.

There the interview had finished. Or almost finished. For it was Morse himself who had administered the *coup de grâce* which finally put his tortured and tortuous theory out of all its pain.

'Does your wife drive a car?'

Acum looked at him with mild surprise. 'No. She's never driven a yard in her life. Why?'

Lewis relived the interview as he drove on steadily through the night. And as he recalled the facts that Acum had recounted, he felt a deepening sympathy with the sour, dejected, silent figure slumped beside him, smoking (unusually) cigarette after cigarette, and feeling (if the truth be told) unconscionably angry with himself . . .

Why had he gone wrong? *Where* had he gone wrong? The questions re-echoed in Morse's mind as if repeated by some interminable interlocutor installed inside his brain. He thought back to his first analysis of the case – the one in which he had cast Mrs Taylor as the murderer not only of Reginald Baines but also of her daughter Valerie. How easy now to see why *that* was wrong! His reasoning had run aground upon the Rock Improbable and the Rock Impossible: the glaring improbability that Mrs Taylor had murdered her only daughter (mothers just didn't do that sort of thing very often, did they?); and the plain impossibility that *anyone* had murdered Valerie on the day she disappeared, since three days later, alive and well, she had climbed into the back of a taxi outside a London abortion clinic. Yes, the first analysis had been brutally smashed to pieces by the facts, and now lay sunk without a trace beneath the sea. It was as simple as that.

And what of the second analysis? *That* had seemed on the face of it to answer all the facts, or nearly all of them. What had gone wrong with that? Again his logic had foundered upon the Reef of Unreason: the glaring improbability that Valerie Taylor had either sufficient motive or adequate opportunity to murder a man who seemed to pose little more than a peripheral threat to her future happiness; and the plain impossibility that the woman living with David Acum was Valerie Taylor.

She wasn't. She was Mrs Acum. And Analysis One lay side by side with Analysis Two – irrecoverable wrecks upon the ocean floor.

Almost frenetically Morse tried to wrench his thoughts away from it all. He tried to conjure up a dream of fair women; and failing this he essayed to project upon his mind a raw, uncensored film of rank eroticism; he tried so very hard . . . But still the wretched earth-bound realities of the Taylor case crowded his brain, forbade those flights of half-forbidden fancies, and jolted him back to his inescapable mood of gloom-ridden despondency. Facts, facts, facts! Facts that one by one he once again reviewed as they marched and counter-marched across his mind. If only he'd stuck to the facts! Ainley was dead – that was a fact. Somebody had written a letter the very day after he died – that was a fact. Valerie had been alive on the days immediately following her disappearance – that was a fact. Baines was dead – that was a fact. Mrs Acum was Mrs Acum – that was a fact. But where did he go from there? He began to realize how few the facts had been; how very, very few. A lot of possible facts; a fair helping of probable facts; but few that ranked as positive facts. And once again the facts remarshalled themselves and marched across the parade ground . . . He shook his head sharply and felt he must be going mad.

Lewis, he could see, was concentrating hard upon the road. Lewis! Huh! It had been Lewis who had asked him the one question, the only question, that had completely floored him: *Why had Baines written the letter?* Why? He had never grappled satisfactorily with that question, and now it worried away at his brain again. Why? Why? Why?

It was as they swept along the old Watling Street, past Wellington, that Morse in a flash conceived a possible answer to this importunate question; an answer of astonishing and devastating simplicity. And he nursed his new little discovery like a frightened mother sheltering her only child amid the ruin of an earthquake-stricken city . . . The merry-go-round was slowing now . . . the pubs were long shut and the chips were long cold . . . his mind was getting back to normal now . . . This was better! Methodically he began to undress Miss Yvonne Baker.

Lewis had the road virtually to himself now. It was past 1.00 a.m. and the two men had not exchanged a single word. Strangely, the silence had seemed progressively to reinforce itself, and conversation now would seem as sacrilegious as a breaking of the silence before the cenotaph.

As he drove the last part of the journey his mind roved back beyond the oddly unreal events of the last few hours, and dwelt again on the early days of the Valerie Taylor case. She'd just hopped it, of course – he'd said so right at the beginning: fed up with home and school, she'd yearned for the brighter lights, the excitement and the glamour of the big city. Got shot of the unwanted baby, and finished up in a groovy, swinging set. Contented enough; even happy, perhaps. The last thing she wanted was to go back home to her moody mother and her stolid step-father. We all felt like that occasionally. We'd all like a fresh start in a new life. Like being born again ... He'd felt like running away from home when he was her age ... Concentrate, Lewis! Oxford 30 miles. He glanced at the inspector and smiled quietly to himself. The old boy was fast asleep.

They were within ten miles of Oxford when Lewis became vaguely conscious of Morse's mumbled words, muddled and indistinct; just words without coherent meaning. Yet gradually the words assumed a patterned sequence that Lewis almost understood: 'Bloody photographs – wouldn't recognize her – huh! – bloody things – huh!'

'We're here, sir.' It was the first time he had spoken for more than five hours and his voice sounded unnaturally loud.

Morse shrugged himself awake and blinked around him. 'I must have dozed off, Lewis. Not like me, is it?'

'Would you like to drop in at my place for a cup of coffee and a bite to eat?'

'No. But thanks all the same.' He eased himself out of the car like a chronic arthritic, yawned mightily, and stretched his arms. 'We'll take tomorrow off, Lewis. Agreed? We've just about deserved it, I reckon.'

Lewis said he reckoned, too. He parked the police car, backed out his own and waved a weary farewell.

Morse entered Police HQ and made his way along the dimly lit corridor to his office, where he opened his filing cabinet and riffled through the early documents in the Valerie Taylor case. He found it almost immediately, and as he lóoked down at the so familiar letter, once more his mind was sliding easily along the shining grooves. It must be. It must be!

He wondered if Lewis would ever forgive him.

CHAPTER THIRTY-EIGHT

And then there were two.
Ten Little Nigger Boys

'. . . *not generally appreciated. We all normally assume that the sex instinct is so obviously overriding, so primitively predominant that it must* . . .' Morse, newly woken and surprisingly refreshed, switched over to Radio Three; and thence to Radio Oxford. But none of the channels seemed anxious to inform him of the time of day, and he turned back to Radio Four. ' . . . *and above all, of course, by Freud. Let us assume, for example, that we have been marooned on a desert island for three days without food, and ask ourselves which of the bodily instincts most craves its instant gratification.*' With sudden interest Morse turned up the volume: the voice was donnish, slightly effeminate. '*Let us imagine that a beautiful blonde appears with a plate of succulent steak and chips* . . .' Leaning over to turn the volume higher still, Morse inadvertently nudged the tuning knob, and by the time he had recentred the station it was clear that the beautiful blonde had lost on points. ' . . . *as we tuck into the steak and* . . .' Morse switched off. 'Shert erp, you poncy twit!' he said aloud, got out of bed, pulled on his clothes, walked downstairs and dialled the speaking clock. 'At the first stroke it will be eleven – twenty-eight – and forty seconds.' She sounded nice, and Morse wondered if she were a blonde. It was over twenty-four hours since he had eaten, but for the moment steak and chips was registering a poor third on the instinct index.

Without bothering to shave he walked round to the Fletchers' Arms where he surveyed with suspicion a pile of 'freshly cut' ham sandwiches beneath their plastic cover and ordered a glass of bitter. By 12.45 p.m. he had consumed four pints, and felt a pleasing lassitude pervade his limbs. He walked slowly home and fell fully clothed into his bed. This was the life.

He felt lousy when he woke again at 5.20 p.m., and wondered if he were in the old age of youth or the youth of old age.

By 6.00 p.m. he was seated in his office, clearing up the litter from his desk. There were several messages lying there, and one by one he relegated them to an intray which never had been clear and never would be clear. There was one further message, on the telephone pad: 'Ring 01-787 24392'. Morse flicked through the telephone book and found that 787 was the STD code for Stoke Newington. He rang the number.

'Hello?' The voice was heavy with sex.

'Ah. Morse here. I got your message. Er, can I help?'

'Oh, Inspector,' purred the voice. 'It was yesterday I tried to get you, but never mind. I'm so glad you rang.' The words were slow and evenly spaced. 'I just wondered if you wanted to see me again – you know, to make a statement or something? I wondered if you'd be coming down again . . . perhaps?'

'That's very kind of you, Miss – er, Yvonne. But I think Chief Inspector Rogers will be along to see you. We shall need a statement, though – you're quite right about that.'

'Is he as nice as you are, Inspector?'

'Nowhere near,' said Morse.

'All right, whatever you say. But it would be so nice to see you again.'

'It would, indeed,' said Morse with some conviction in his voice.

'Well, I'd better say goodbye then. You didn't mind me ringing, did you?'

'No, er no, of course I didn't. It's lovely to hear your voice again.'

'Well, don't forget if you're ever this way you must call in to see me.'

'Yes, I will,' lied Morse.

'I really would love to see you again.'

'Same here.'

'You've got my address, haven't you?'

'Yes, I've got it.'

'And you'll make a note of the phone number?'

'Er, yes. Yes, I'll do that.'

'Goodbye, then, till we see each other again.' From the tone of her voice Morse guessed she must be lying there, her hands sensuously sliding along those beautiful limbs; and all he had to do was to say, yes, he'd be there! London wasn't very far away, and the night was still so young. He pictured her as she had been on the night that he had met her, the top button of the pyjama jacket already undone; and in his mind's eye his fingers gently unfastened the other buttons, one by one, and slowly drew the sides apart.

'Goodbye,' he said sadly.

He walked to the canteen and ordered black coffee.

'I thought you were taking the day off,' said a voice behind him.

'You must love this bloody place, Lewis!'

'I rang up. They said you were here.'

'Couldn't you stick it at home?'

'No. The missus says I get under her feet.'

They sat down together, and it was Lewis who put their thoughts into words. 'Where do we go from here, sir?'

Morse shook his head dubiously. 'I don't know.'

'Will you tell me one thing?'

'If I can.'

'Have you *any* idea at all about who killed Baines?'

Idly Morse stirred the strong black coffee. 'Have you?'

'The real trouble is we seem to be eliminating all the suspects. Not many left, are there?'

'We're not beaten yet,' said Morse with a sudden and unexpected lift of spirits. 'We got a bit lost in the winding mazes, and we still can't see the end of the road, but . . .' He broke off and stared through the window. In a sudden gust of wind a shower of leaves rained down from the thinning trees.

'But what, sir?'

'Somebody once said that the end is the beginning, Lewis.'

'Not a particularly helpful thing to say, was it?'

'Ah, but I think it was. You see, we know what the beginning was.'

'Do we?'

'Oh yes. We know that Phillipson met Valerie Taylor one night, and we know that when he was appointed headmaster he discovered that she was one of his own pupils. That was where it all began, and that's where we've got to look now. There's nowhere else to look.'

'You mean . . . Phillipson?'

'Or Mrs Phillipson.'

'You don't think—'

'I don't think it matters much which of them you go for. They had the same motive; they had the same opportunity.'

'How do we set about it?'

'How do *you* set about it, you mean. I'm leaving it to you, Lewis.'

'Oh.'

'Want a bit of advice?' Morse smiled weakly. 'Bit of a cheek, isn't it, me giving you advice?'

'Of course I want your advice,' said Lewis quietly. 'We both know that.'

'All right. Here's a riddle for you. You look for a leaf in the forest, and you look for a corpse on the battle-field. Right? Where do you look for a knife?'

'An ironmonger's shop?'

'No, not a *new* knife. A knife that's been used – used continuously; used so much that the blade is wearing away.'

'A butcher's shop?'

'Warmer. But we haven't got a butcher in the case, have we?'

'A kitchen?'

'Ah! Which kitchen?'

'Phillipson's kitchen?'

'They'd only have one knife. It would be missed, wouldn't it?'

'Perhaps it *was* missed.'

'I don't think so, somehow, though you'll have to check. No, we need to find a place where knives are in daily use; a lot of knives; a place where no one would notice the loss of a single knife; a place at the very heart of the case. Come on, Lewis! Lots of people cutting up spuds and carrots and meat and everything . . .'

'The canteen at the Roger Bacon School,' said Lewis slowly.

Morse nodded. 'It's an idea, isn't it?'

'Ye-es.' Lewis pondered for a while and nodded his agreement. 'But you say you want *me* to look into all this? What about you?'

'I'm going to look into the only other angle we've got left.'

'What's that?'

'I've told you. The secret of this case is locked away in the beginning: Phillipson and Valerie Taylor. You've got one half; I've got the other.'

'You mean . . .?' Lewis had no idea what he meant.

Morse stood up. 'Yep. You have a go at the Phillipsons. I shall have to find Valerie.' He looked down at Lewis and grinned disarmingly. 'Where do you suggest I ought to start looking?'

Lewis stood up, too. 'I've always thought she was in London, sir. You know that. I think she just . . .'

But Morse was no longer listening. He felt the icy fingers running along his spine, and there was a sudden wild elation in the pale-grey eyes. 'Why not, Lewis? Why not?'

He walked back to his office, and dialled the number immediately. After all, she *had* invited him, hadn't she?

CHAPTER THIRTY-NINE

The only way of catching a train I ever discovered is
to miss the one before.

G. K. Chesterton

'MUMMY?' ALISON MANAGED a very important frown
upon her pretty little face as her mother tucked her
early into bed at 8 p.m.

'Yes, darling?'

'Will the policemen be coming to see Daddy again
when he gets back?'

'I don't think so, darling. Don't start worrying your
little head about that.'

'He's not gone away to prison or anything like that,
has he?'

'Of course he hasn't, you silly little thing! He'll be
back tonight, you know that, and I'll tell him to come
in and give you a big kiss – I promise.'

Alison was silent for a few moments. 'Mummy, he's
not done anything wrong, has he?'

'No, you silly little thing. Of course he hasn't.'

Alison frowned again as she looked up into her
mother's eyes. 'Even if he *did* do something wrong,
he'd still be my daddy, wouldn't he?'

'Yes. He'd still be your daddy, whatever happened.'

'And we'd forgive him, wouldn't we?'

'Yes, my darling . . . And you'd forgive Mummy, too, wouldn't you, if she did something wrong? Especially if . . .'

'Don't worry, Mummy. God forgives everybody, doesn't he? And my teacher says that we must all try to be like him.'

Mrs Phillipson walked slowly down the stairs, and her eyes were glazed with tears.

Morse left the Lancia at home and walked down from North Oxford to the railway station. It took him almost an hour and he wasn't at all sure why he'd decided to do it; but his head felt clear now and the unaccustomed exercise had done him good. At twenty past eight he stood outside the station buffet and looked around him. It was dark, but just across the way the street lights shone on the first few houses in Kempis Street. So close! He hadn't quite realized just how close to the railway station it was. A hundred yards? No more, certainly. Get off the train on Platform 2, cross over by the subway, hand your ticket in . . . For a second or two he stood stock-still and felt the old familiar thrill that coursed along his nerves. He was catching the 8.35 train – the same train that Phillipson could have caught that fateful night so long ago . . . Paddington about 9.40. Taxi. Let's see . . . Yes, with a bit of luck he'd be there about 10.15.

He bought a first-class ticket and walked past the barrier on to Platform No 1, and almost immediately the loudspeaker intoned from somewhere in the station roof above: 'The train now arriving at Platform I, is for Reading and Paddington only. Passengers for ...' But Morse wasn't listening.

He sat back comfortably and closed his eyes. Idiot! Idiot! It was all so simple really. Lewis had found the pile of books in the store-room and had sworn there'd been no dust upon the top one; and all Morse had done had been to shout his faithful sergeant's head off. Of course there had been no dust on the top book! Someone had taken a book from the top of the selfsame pile – a book that was doubtless thick with dust by then. Taken it recently, too. So very recently in fact that the book at the top of the remaining pile was virtually free from dust when Lewis had picked it up. Someone. Yes, a someone called Baines who had taken it home and studied it very hard. *But not because he'd wished to forge a letter in Valerie Taylor's hand.* That had been one of Morse's biggest mistakes. There was, as he had guessed the night before, a blindingly obvious answer to the question of why Baines had written the letter to Valerie's parents. *The answer was that he hadn't.* Mr and Mrs Taylor had received the letter on the Wednesday morning and had been in two minds about taking it to the police – George Taylor himself had told Morse exactly that. Why? Obviously because they couldn't decide whether it had come from Valerie or not: it might just have been a hoax. It must surely have been Mrs Taylor who had taken it to Baines; and Baines had very sensibly taken an exercise book from the store-room and written out his own parallel version of the brief message, copying as accurately as he could the style and shape of

Valerie's own lettering as he found it in the Applied Science book. And then he'd compared the letter from Valerie with his own painstaking effort, and pronounced to Mrs Taylor that at least in his opinion the letter seemed completely genuine. That was how things must have happened. And there was something else, too. The logical corollary of all this was that Mr and Mrs Taylor had no idea at all about where Valerie was. For more than two years they had heard nothing whatsoever from her. And if both of them were genuinely puzzled about the letter, there seemed one further inescapable conclusion: *the Taylors were completely in the clear.* Go on, Morse! Keep going! With a smooth inevitability the pieces were falling into place. Keep going!

Well, if this hypothesis were correct, the overwhelming probability was that Valerie was alive and that she had written the letter herself. It was just as Peters said it was; just as Lewis said it was; just as Morse himself had said it *wasn't.* Moreover, as he had learned the previous evening, there was a very interesting and suggestive piece of corroborative evidence. Acum had given it to him: Valerie was always using the expression 'all right', he'd said. And on his return Morse had checked the letter once again:

Just to let you know I'm alright so don't worry.
Sorry I've not written before but I'm alright.

And Ainley (poor old Ainley!) had not only known that she was still alive; he'd actually found her – Morse felt sure of that now. Or, at the very least, he'd discovered where she could be found. Stolid, painstaking old Ainley! A bloody sight better cop than he himself would ever be. (Hadn't Strange said the same thing – right at the beginning?) Valerie could never have guessed the full extent of the hullabaloo that her disappearance had caused. After all, hundreds of young girls went missing every year. Hundreds. But had she suddenly learned of it, so long after the event? Had Ainley actually met her and told her? It seemed entirely probable now, since the very next day she had sat down and written to her parents for the very first time. That was all. Just a brief scratty little letter! And that prize clown Morse had been called in. Big stuff. Christ! What a mess, what a terribly unholy mess he'd made of everything!

They were well into the outskirts of London now, and Morse walked out to the corridor and lit a cigarette. Only one thing worried him now: the thought that had flashed across his mind as he stood outside the station buffet and looked across at Kempis Street. But he'd know soon enough now; so very soon he'd know it all.

CHAPTER FORTY

For she and I were long acquainted
And I knew all her ways.
A. E. Housman, *Last Poems*

IT WAS JUST after ten-thirty when he paid and tipped the taxi driver: it cost him more than the return first-class fare to London. At the bottom of the building he found, as before, the lift for the even-numbered floors on his left and that for the odd on his right. He remembered the floor. Of course he did.

She was radiant. That was the best epithet for her, although there were many others. She wore a thin black sweater in which her full and bra-less breasts bobbed irresistibly; and a long black skirt, slit high along her leg and leaving a sublime uncertainty of what she wore below. Her mouth, just as he had seen it last, was stickily seductive, the lips moist and slightly parted, the teeth so gleaming white. O Lord, have mercy on our souls!

'What would you like to drink, Inspector? Whisky? Gin?'

'Whisky, please. Lovely.'

She disappeared into the kitchen, and Morse moved quickly over to a small shelf of books beside the deeply-leathered divan. Rapidly he flicked open the front covers of the books there, and as rapidly replaced them.

Only one of them held his attention and that only for a few seconds, when the grey eyes momentarily flashed with a glint of satisfaction, if not surprise.

He was seated on the divan when she returned with a large whisky in a cut-glass tumbler and sat down beside him.

'Aren't *you* drinking?'

Her eyes met his and held them. 'In a minute,' she whispered, linking her arm through his, the tips of her fingers gently tracing slow designs along his wrist.

Softly he took her hand in his, and for a short sweet second the thrill was that of a sharp electric shock that shot along his veins, and a zig-zag current that sparked across his temples. He looked down at her delicately-fingered left hand, and saw across the bottom of the index finger the faint white line of an old scar – like the scar that was mentioned in the medical report on Valerie Taylor, when she had cut herself with a carving knife – in Kidlington, when she was a pupil at the Roger Bacon School.

'What shall I call you?' she asked suddenly. 'I can't go on calling you "Inspector" all night, can I?'

'It's a funny thing,' said Morse. 'But no one ever calls me by my Christian name.'

Lightly she touched his cheek with her lips, and her hand moved slowly along his leg. 'Never mind. If you don't like your name, you can always change it, you know. There's no law against that.'

'No, there isn't. I could always change it if I wanted to, I suppose. Just like you changed yours.'

Her body stiffened and she took her hand away. 'And what on earth is *that* supposed to mean?'

'You told me your name was Yvonne the last time I saw you. But that isn't your real name, is it? Is it, Valerie?'

'*Valerie?* You can't possibly . . .' But she was unable to articulate her thoughts beyond that point, and a look of profound perplexity appeared to cross her beautiful face. She stood up.

'Look, Inspector, or whatever your name is, my name's Yvonne Baker – you'd better get that straight before we go any further. If you don't believe me you can ring the couple on the floor below. I was at school in Seven Sisters Road with Joyce—'

'Go ahead,' said Morse blandly. 'Ring up your old school pal if you want to. Why not tell her to come up to see us?'

A look of anger flashed across her face and momentarily made it less than beautiful. She hesitated; then walked over to the phone and dialled a number.

Morse leaned back and sipped his whisky contentedly. Even from across the room he could hear the muted, metallic purrs with perfect clarity; he found himself mentally counting them . . . Finally she put down the phone and came back to sit beside him once more. He reached to the book-shelf, abstracted a small hardbound copy of *Jane Eyre*, and opened the front cover. Inside was the label of the Roger Bacon Comprehensive School, on which Valerie's own name appeared, appended to those of her literary predecessors:

Angela Lowe	5C
Mary Ann Baldwin	5B
Valerie Taylor	5C

He passed it across to her. 'Well?'

She shook her head in exasperation. 'Well what?'

'Is it yours?'

'Of course it isn't mine. It's Valerie's – you can see that. She gave it me to read in the clinic. It was one of her O-level set books, and she thought I'd enjoy reading it. But I never got round to it and I . . . I just forgot to give it her back, that's all.'

'And that's your story?'

'It isn't a *story*. It's the *truth*. I don't know—'

'What went wrong at home, Valerie? Did you—'

'Oh *God*! What the hell are you on about? I'm not *Valerie*. It's . . . I . . . I . . . I just don't know where to start. Look, my parents live in Uxbridge – can you understand that? I can ring them. *You* can ring them. I—'

'I know your parents, Valerie. You got so fed up with them that you left them. Left them without a word of explanation – at least until Ainley found you. And then at long last you *did* write home—'

'What are you *talking* about? *Ainley*? Who's he? I've . . . Oh, what's the good!' Her voice had grown shrill and harsh, but suddenly she subsided almost helplessly against the back of the divan. 'All right, Inspector! Have it your way. You tell *me* what happened.'

'You wrote home then,' continued Morse. 'You hadn't realized what a terrible fuss you'd caused until

Inspector Ainley saw you. But Ainley was killed. He was killed in a road accident on his way back to Oxford on the very same day he saw you.'

'I'm sorry to interrupt, Inspector. But I thought I was Yvonne Baker. When did I suddenly change to Valerie Taylor?' Her voice was quite calm now.

'You met Yvonne in the abortion clinic. You were fed up with home, fed up with school; and Yvonne . . . well, probably, she put the idea into your head. For argument's sake, let's say she was a girl with lots of money, rich parents – probably going off to Switzerland or somewhere for a year's holiday after it was all over. Why not take her name? Start a new life? You've nothing to lose, have you? You'd decided not to go back home, whatever happened. You hardly saw your mother anyway, except at lunchtimes, and her only real interests in life were booze and Bingo – and men, of course. And then there's your step-father: not very bright, perhaps, but likeable enough, in an odd sort of way. That is until he started getting a bit too fond of his beautiful step-daughter. And your mother got to know about that, I think, and when you got yourself pregnant, she suspected a terrible thing. She suspected that he might well be the father, didn't she? And she flew into an almighty rage about it, and for you this was the last straw. You just had to go; and you *did* go. But fortunately you had someone to help you; your headmaster. There's no need to go into all that – but *you* know all about it as well as I do. You could count on him – always. He fixed up the clinic, and he gave you some money. You'd probably packed a case the night before

331

and arranged to meet him somewhere to stow it away safely in the boot of his car. And then on the Tuesday he picked you up just after school had started for the afternoon and took you to the railway station. You only had a bag with you – no doubt with your clothes in it – and you changed on the train and arrived at the clinic. Shall I go on?'

'Yes please. It's quite fascinating!'

'You just interrupt me if I go wrong, that's all.'

'But . . .' She gave it up and sat there silently shaking her head.

'I'm guessing now,' continued Morse, 'but I should think Yvonne put you on to a job – let's say a job in a West End store. The school-leavers hadn't crowded the market yet, and it was fairly easy for you. You'd need a testimonial or a reference, I realize that. But you rang Phillipson and told him the position, and he took care of that. It was your first job. No bother. No employment cards, or stamps or anything. So that was that.'

Morse turned and looked again at the chic, sophisticated creature beside him. They wouldn't recognize her back in Kidlington now, would they? They'd remember only the young schoolgirl in her red socks and her white blouse. They would always attract the men, these two – mother and daughter alike. Somehow they shared the same intangible yet pervasive sensuality, and the Lord had fashioned them so very fair.

'Is that the finish?' she asked quietly.

Morse's reply was brusque. 'No, it's not. Where were you last Monday night?'

'Last Monday night? What's that got to do with you?'

'What train did you catch the night that Baines was killed?'

She looked at him in utter astonishment now. 'What train are you talking about? I haven't—'

'Didn't you go there that night?'

'Go *where*?'

'You know where. You probably caught the 8.15 from Paddington and arrived in Oxford at about 9.30.'

'You must be *mad*! I was in Hammersmith last Monday night.'

'Were you?'

'Yes, I *was*. I always go to Hammersmith on Monday nights.'

'Go on.'

'You really want to know?' Her eyes grew softer again, and she shook her head sadly. 'If you must know there's a sort of . . . sort of party we have there every Monday.'

'What time?'

'Starts about nine.'

'And you were there last Monday?'

She nodded, almost fiercely.

'You go every Monday, you say?'

'Yes.'

'Why aren't you there tonight?'

'I . . . well, I just thought . . . when you rang . . .' She looked at him with doleful eyes. 'I didn't think it was going to be like this.'

'What time do these parties finish?'

'They don't.'

'You stay all night, you mean.'

She nodded.

'Sex parties?'

'In a way.'

'What the hell's that supposed to mean?'

'You know. The usual sort of thing: films to start with . . .'

'Blue films?'

Again she nodded.

'And then?'

'Oh God! Come off it. Are you trying to torture yourself, or something?'

She was far too near the truth, and Morse felt miserably embarrassed. He got to his feet and looked round fecklessly for his coat. 'You'll have to give me the address, you realize that.'

'But I can't. I'd—'

'Don't worry,' said Morse wearily. 'I shan't pry any more than I have to.'

He looked once more around the expensive flat. She must earn a lot of money, somehow; and he wondered if it was all much compensation for the heartache and the jealousy that she must know as well as he. Or perhaps we weren't all the same. Perhaps it wasn't possible to live as she had done and keep alive the finer, tenderer compassions.

He looked across at her as she sat at a small bureau, writing something down: doubtless the address of the bawdy house in Hammersmith. He had to have that, whatever happened. But did it matter all that much? He knew instinctively that she was there that night, among the wealthy, lecherous old men who gloated over pornographic films, and pawed and fondled the figures of the high-class prostitutes who sat upon their knees unfastening their flies. So what? He was a lecherous old man too, wasn't he? Very nearly, anyway. Just a sediment of sensitivity still. Just a little. Just a little.

She came over to him, and for a moment she was very beautiful again. 'I've been very patient with you, Inspector, don't you think?'

'I suppose so, yes. Patient, if not particularly co-operative.'

'Can I ask *you* a question?'

'Of course.'

'Do you want to sleep with me tonight?'

The back of Morse's throat felt suddenly very dry. 'No.'

'You really mean that?'

'Yes.'

'All right.' Her voice was brisker now. 'Let me be "co-operative" then, as you call it.' She handed him a sheet of notepaper on which she had written two telephone numbers.

'The first one's my father's. You may have to drag him out of bed, but he's almost certainly home by now. The other one's the Wilsons, downstairs. As I told you, I was at school with Joyce. I'd like you to ring them both, please.'

Morse took the paper and said nothing.

'Then there's this.' She handed him a passport. 'I know it's out of date, but I've only been abroad once. To Switzerland, three years ago last June.'

With a puzzled frown Morse opened the passport

and the unmistakable face of Miss Yvonne Baker smiled up at him in gentle mockery from a Woolworth polyfoto. Three years last June . . . whilst Valerie Taylor was still at school in Kidlington. Well before she . . . before . . .

Morse took off his coat and sat down once again on the divan. 'Will you ring your friends below, Yvonne? And if you're feeling very kind, can I please ask you to pour me another whisky? A stiff one.'

At Paddington he was informed that the last train to Oxford had departed half an hour earlier. He walked into the cheerless waiting room, put his feet up on the bench, and soon fell fast asleep.

At 3.30 a.m. a firm hand shook him by the shoulder, and he looked up into the face of a bearded constable.

'You can't sleep here, sir. I shall have to ask you to move on, I'm afraid.'

'You surely don't begrudge a man a bit of kip, do you, officer?'

'I'm afraid I shall have to ask you to move on, sir.'

Morse almost told him who he was. But simultaneously the other sleepers were being roused and he wondered why he should be treated any differently from his fellow men.

'All right, officer.' Huh! 'All right': that's what Valerie would have said. But he put the thought aside and walked wearily out of the station. Perhaps he'd have more luck at Marylebone. He needed a bit of luck somewhere.

CHAPTER FORTY-ONE

Pilate saith unto him, What is truth?
                              John, xviii

DONALD PHILLIPSON WAS a very worried man. The
sergeant had been very proper, of course, and very
polite: 'routine inquiries', that was all. But the police
were getting uncomfortably close. A knife that might
be missing from the school canteen – that was perfectly
understandable: but from his own kitchen! And it was
no great surprise that he himself should be suspected
of murder: but Sheila! He couldn't talk to Sheila, and
he wouldn't let her talk to him: the subject of Valerie
Taylor and, later, the murder of Baines lay between
them like a no-man's-land, isolated and defined, upon
which neither dared to venture. How much did Sheila
know? Had she learned that Baines was blackmailing
him? Had she learned or half-guessed the shameful
reason? Baines himself may have hinted at the truth to
her. Baines! God rot his soul! But whatever Sheila had
done or intended to do on the night that Baines was
killed was utterly unimportant, and he wished to know
nothing of it. Whichever way you looked at it, it was he,
Donald Phillipson, who was guilty of murdering Baines.

The walls of the small study seemed gradually to be
closing in around him. The cumulative pressures of the

last three years had now become too strong, and the tangled web of falsehood and deceit had enmeshed his very soul. If he were to retain his sanity he had to do *something*; something to bring a period of peace to a conscience tortured to its breaking-point; something to atone for all the folly and the sin. Again he thought of Sheila and the children and he knew that he could hardly face them for much longer. And interminably his thoughts went dancing round and round his head and always settled to the same conclusion. Whichever way you looked at it, it was he and only he who was guilty of murdering Baines.

Morning school was almost over, and Mrs Webb was tidying up her desk as he walked through.

'I shan't be in this afternoon, Mrs Webb.'

'No. I realize that, sir. You never are on Tuesdays.'

'Er, no. Tuesday afternoon, of course. I'd, er . . . I'd forgotten for the minute.'

It was like hearing the phone in a television play: he knew there was no need to answer it himself. He still felt wretchedly tired and he buried his head again in the pillows. Having found no more peace at Marylebone than at Paddington, he had finally arrived back in Oxford at 8.05 a.m., and had taken a taxi home. One way or another it had been an expensive débâcle.

An hour later the phone rang again. Shrill, peremptory, now, registering at a higher level of his consciousness; and shaking his head awake, he reached for the receiver on the bedside table. He yawned an almighty 'Yeah?' into the mouthpiece and levered himself up to a semi-vertical position.

'Lewis? What the hell do you want?'

'I've been trying to get you since two o'clock, sir. It's—'

'What? What time is it now?'

'Nearly three o'clock, sir. I'm sorry to disturb you but I've got a bit of a surprise for you.'

'Huh, I doubt it.'

'I think you ought to come, though. We're at the station.'

'Who do you mean by "we"?'

'If I told you that, sir, it wouldn't be a surprise, would it?'

'Give me half an hour,' said Morse.

He sat down at the table in Interview Room One. In front of him lay a document, neatly typed but as yet unsigned, and he picked it up and read it:

'I have come forward voluntarily to the police to make this statement, and I trust that to some extent this may weigh in my favour. I wish to plead guilty to the murder of Mr Reginald Baines, late second master of the Roger Bacon Comprehensive School, Kidlington, Oxon. The reasons I had for killing him are not, in my view, strictly relevant to the criminal procedings, that will be brought against me, and there are certain things which everyone should have the right to hold sacrosanct. About the details of the crime, too, I wish for the present to say nothing. I am aware that the question of deliberate malice and premeditation may be of great importance, and for this reason I wish to notify my lawyer and to take the benefit of his advice.

I hereby certify that this statement was made by me in the presence of Sergeant Lewis, CID, Thames Valley Police, on the day and at the time subscribed. Your obedient servant,'

Morse looked up from the sheet of typing and turned his light-grey eyes across the table.

'You can't spell "proceedings",' he said.

'Your typist, Inspector. Not me.' Morse reached for his cigarettes and offered them across. 'No thank you, I don't smoke.'

Without dropping his eyes, Morse lit a cigarette and drew upon it deeply. His expression was a mixture of vague distaste and tacit scepticism. He pointed to the statement. 'You want this to go forward?'

'Yes.'

'As you wish.'

They sat silently, as if neither had anything further to say to the other. Morse looked across to the window, and outside on to the concrete yard. He'd made so many stupid blunders in the case; and no one was likely to thank him overmuch for making yet another. It was the only sensible solution, perhaps. Or *almost* the only sensible solution. Did it matter? Perhaps not. But still upon his face remained the look of dark displeasure.

'You don't like me much, do you, Inspector?'

'I wouldn't say that,' replied Morse defensively. 'It's

just . . . It's just that you've never got into the habit of telling me the truth, have you?'

'I've made up for it now, I hope.'

'*Have you?*' Morse's eyes were hard and piercing, but to his question there was no reply.

'Shall I sign it now?'

Morse remained silent for a while. 'You think it's better this way?' he asked very quietly. But again there was no reply, and Morse passed across the statement and stood up. 'You've got a pen?'

Sheila Phillipson nodded, and opened her long, expensive leather hand-bag.

'Do you believe her, sir?'

'No,' said Morse simply.

'What do we do, then?'

'Ah, let her cool her heels in a cell for a night. I dare say she's got a good idea what happened, but I just don't think she killed Baines, that's all.'

'She's covering up for Phillipson, you think?'

'Could be. I don't know.' Morse stood up. 'And I'll tell you something else, Lewis: I don't bloody well care! I think whoever killed Baines deserves a life peerage – not a life sentence.'

'But it's still our job to find out who did, sir.'

'Not for much longer, it isn't. I've had a bellyful of this lot – and I've failed. I'm going to see Strange in the morning and ask him to take me off the case.'

'He won't be very happy about that.'

'He's never very happy about anything.'

'It doesn't sound like you, though, sir.'

Morse grinned almost boyishly. 'I've disappointed you, haven't I, Lewis?'

'Well, yes, in a way – if you're going to pack it all in now.'

'Well, I am.'

'I see.'

'Life's full of disappointments, Lewis. I should have thought you'd learned that by now.'

Alone Morse walked back to his office. If the truth could be told he felt more than a little hurt by what Lewis had just said. Lewis was right, of course, and had spoken with such quiet integrity: *but it's still our job to find out who did it.* Yes, he knew that; but he'd tried and tried and *hadn't* found out who did it. Come to think of it, he hadn't even found out if Valerie Taylor were alive or dead ... Just now he'd tried to believe Sheila Phillipson; but the plain fact was that he couldn't. Anyway, if what she said were true, it was much better for someone else to finish off the formalities. Much better. And if she were just shielding her husband ... He let it go. He had sent Lewis round to see Phillipson, but the headmaster was neither at home nor at school, and for the time being the neighbours were looking after the children.

Whatever happened, this Tuesday afternoon was now the end, and he thought back to that first Tuesday afternoon in Phillipson's study ... What, if anything, had he missed in the case? What small, apparently insignificant detail that might have set him on the proper tracks? He sat for half an hour and thought and thought, and thought himself nowhere. It was no good: his mind was stale and the wells of imagination and inspiration were dry as the Sahara sands. Yes, he *would* see Strange in the morning and hand it all over. He could still make a decision when he wanted to, whatever Lewis might think.

He walked over to the filing cabinet and for the last time took out the mass of documents on the case. They now filled two bulging box-files, and pulling back the spring clips Morse tipped the contents of each haphazardly on to his desk. At least he ought to put the stuff into some sort of order. It wouldn't take all that long, and his mind positively welcomed the prospect of an hour or two of fourth-grade clerical work. Neatly and methodically he began stapling odd notes and sheets to their respective documents, and ordering the documents themselves into a chronological sequence. He remembered the last time he had tipped the contents (not so bulky then) on to his desk, when Lewis had noticed that odd business about the lollipop man. A red herring, that, as it turned out. Yet it *could* have been a vitally important point, and he himself had missed it. Had he missed anything else, amidst this formidable bumf? Ah, forget it! It was too late now, and he continued with his task. Valerie's reports next. They'd better go into some sort of order, too, and he shuffled them into their sequence. Three reports a year: autumn term; spring term; summer term. No reports at all for the first year in the school, but all the others were there

– except one: the report for the summer term of the fourth year. Why was that? He hadn't noticed that before ... The brain was whirring into life once more – but no! Morse snapped off the current impatiently. It was nothing. The report was just lost; lots of things got lost. Nothing at all sinister about that ... Yet in spite of himself he stopped what he was doing and sat back again in the black leather chair, his fingertips together on his lower lip, his eyes resting casually on the school reports that lay before him. He'd read them all before, of course, and knew their contents well. Valerie had been one of those many could-do-better-if-she-tried pupils. Like all of us ... In fact, the staff at the Roger Bacon School could quite easily have dispensed with terminal reports in Valerie's case: they were all very much the same, and one would have done quite as well as another. Any one. The last one, for example – the report on her spring term's progress (or rather lack of it) in the year in which she'd disappeared. Idly Morse looked down at it again. Acum's signature was there beside the French: 'Could do so well if only she tried. Her accent is surprisingly good, but her vocabulary and grammar are still very weak.' Same old comment. In fact there was only one subject in which Valerie had apparently not hidden her light beneath the bushel of her casual indifference; and oddly enough that was Applied Science and Technology. Funny, really, girls tackling subjects like that. But the curriculum had undergone mysterious developments since his own school days. He picked up the earlier reports and read some of the comments of the science staff: 'Good with her hands'; 'A good term's work'; 'Has good mechanical sense'. He got up from his chair and went over to the shelf where earlier he'd stacked Valerie's old exercise books. It was there: Applied Science and Technology. Morse flicked through the pages. Yes, the work was good, he could see that – surprisingly good . . . *Hold it a minute!* He looked through the book again, more carefully now, and read the headings of the syllabus: Work; Energy; Power; Velocity Ratio; Efficiency of Machines; Simple Machines; Levers; Pulleys; Simple Power-transmission Systems; Car Engines; Clutches . . .

He walked back to his desk slowly, like a man in a dreamlike daze, and read the last spring term report once more: French, and Applied Science and Technology . . .

Suddenly the hair on his flesh stood erect. He felt a curious constriction in his throat, and a long shiver passed icily down his spine. He reached for the phone and his hand shook as he dialled the number.

CHAPTER FORTY-TWO

I came fairly to kill him honestly.
Beaumont and Fletcher, *The Little*
French Lawyer

VALERIE TAYLOR UNSCREWED the latest tube of skin-lotion – her sixth prescription. The last time she'd been to the doctor he'd asked rather pointedly if she were worried about anything; and perhaps she was. But not to *that* extent. She'd never worried overmuch about anything, really: just wanted to live in the present and enjoy herself ... Carefully she smeared some of the white cream over the ugly spots. How she prayed they would go! Over a month now – and still they persisted, horribly. She'd tried almost everything, including those face-mask things: in fact she had been wearing one of them when Chief Inspector Morse had called. Mm. She thought of Morse. Bit old, perhaps, but then she'd always felt attracted to the older men. Not that David was old. Quite young, really, and he'd been awfully nice to her, but ...

Morse's face, when she'd answered him in French! She smiled at the recollection. Phew! What a bit of luck that had been! Just as well she'd been with David on those two trips to France with his sixth-formers, although she'd probably have been all right anyway. It had taken a fair bit of cajoling on David's part, but as it turned out she'd really enjoyed her two years in the French Conversation Class at Caernarfon Tech. At the very least it was a chance to get out once a week, and it got so boring being on her own in the house all day. Nothing to do; nothing much to do if she *did* get out more. Not that she blamed David, but . . .

Bloody spots! She wiped off the lotion and applied a new layer. It might be better to leave them alone – let the sun get at them. But the sky this Tuesday evening was a sullen grey, and the weather would soon be getting cold again; far colder than it would be in the south. Like last winter. Brrh! She didn't intend to face another winter like that . . . The washing-up was done and David sat downstairs in the living room marking exercise books. He was always marking exercise books. He would be awfully upset, of course, but . . .

She stepped over to the wardrobe and took out the long red-velvet dress she'd taken to the cleaners last week. Inclining her head slightly, she held it against her body and stood before the mirror. Dinner-plates, parties, dancing . . . It had been such a long time since she'd been out – been out *properly*, that is . . . The dark roots of her hair had now grown almost half an inch into the pseudo-blonde, and it all began to look so *obvious*. She would buy another bottle of 'Poly-bleach' tomorrow. Or would she bother? After all, she'd got to Oxford and back pretty easily . . . Not that she would hire a car again. Couldn't afford it, for a start. Much easier to get a bus into Bangor, and then hitch-hike down the A5. A lot of men still drove the roads and hoped that every mile they'd see a lone, attractive girl. Yes, that would be much easier, and the A5 went all the way to London . . .

It was a good job she'd mentioned the car to David. That really *had* worried her – whether they'd check up on the car-hire firms. She'd not told David the truth, of course; just said she'd gone to see her mother. Yes, she'd admitted how silly and dangerous it was, and had promised David never to think of doing it again. But it had been a very sensible precaution that – warning him to tell them that she couldn't drive. If they ever asked, that was. And Morse had asked, it seemed. Clever man, Morse . . . She'd been a fraction naughty – hadn't she? – the first time he had called. Yes. And the second time – phew! That had perhaps been the very worst moment of all, when she'd opened the door and found him looking through her kitchen drawer. She'd bought a new one, naturally, but it had been *exactly* the same sort of knife, brand new . . . Funny, really; he hadn't even mentioned it . . .

Valerie looked at herself once more in the mirror. The spots looked better now, and she closed the bedroom door behind her . . . Morse! She smiled to herself as she walked down the creaking stairs. His face! *Oui. Je l'ai étudié d'abord à l'école et après . . .*

The phone rang in Caernarfon Police HQ and the switchboard put the call through to the duty inspector.

'All right. Put him on.' He clamped his hand firmly over the mouthpiece and mumbled a few hurried words *sotto voce* to the sergeant sitting opposite. 'It's Morse again.'

'Morse, sir?'

'Yes, you remember. That fellow from Oxford who buggered us all about at the weekend. I wonder what . . . Hello. Can I help you?'

EPILOGUE

There are tears of things and mortal matters touch
the heart.

Virgil, *Aeneid I*

IT WAS NOT until Saturday morning that a somewhat
disgruntled Lewis was at last summoned into Morse's
office to hear something of the final developments.

The Caernarfon police had felt (with some justification, admitted Morse) that they had insufficient
evidence on which to hold Valerie Taylor – even if they
accepted Morse's vehement protestations that the
woman living as Mrs Acum *was* Valerie Taylor. And
when Morse himself had arrived on Wednesday morning, it had been too late: the driver of the 9.50 a.m. bus
from Bont-Newydd to Bangor had remembered her
clearly; and a petrol-pump attendant had noticed her
('So would you have done, officer!') as she stood beside
the forecourt waiting to thumb a lift down the A5.

Lewis had listened carefully, but one or two things
still puzzled him. 'So it must have been Baines who
wrote the letter?'

'Oh yes. It couldn't have been Valerie.'

'I wouldn't be *too* sure, sir. She's a pretty clever girl.'

And I'm a clown, thought Morse. The car, the
French, and the spots: a combination of circumstance

and coincidence which had proved too much even for *him* to accept; a triple-oxer over which he would normally have leaped with the blithest assurance, but at which, in this instance, he had so strangely refused. After all, it would have been very odd if a mechanically minded girl like Valerie hadn't even bothered to take a driving test; and she wasn't too bad at *spoken* French – even at school. Those reports! If only—

'Big coincidence, wasn't it – about the spots, I mean?'

'No, not really, Lewis. Don't forget that both of them were sleeping with Acum; and Acum's got a beard.'

It was something else that Lewis hadn't considered, and he let it go. 'She's gone to London, I suppose, sir?'

Morse nodded wearily, a wry smile upon his lips. 'Back to square one, aren't we?'

'You think we'll find her?'

'I don't know. I suppose so – in the end.'

On Saturday afternoon the Phillipson family motored to the White Horse Hill at Uffington. For Andrew and Alison it was a rare treat, and Mrs Phillipson watched them lovingly as they gambolled with gay abandon about the Downs. So much had passed between her and Donald these last few days. On Tuesday evening their very lives together had seemed to be hanging by the slenderest of threads. But now, this bright and chilly afternoon, the future stretched out before them, open and free as the broad landscape around them. She would write, she decided, a long, long letter to Morse, and try to thank him from the bottom of her heart. For on that terrible evening it had been Morse who had found Donald and brought him to her; it had been Morse who had seemed to know and to understand all things about them both . . .

On Saturday evening Mrs Grace Taylor sat staring blankly through the window on to the darkened street. They had returned from their holiday in mid-afternoon, and things seemed very much the same as she had left them. At a quarter-past eight, by the light of the street lamp, she saw Morse walking slowly, head down, towards the pub. She gave him no second thought.

Earlier in the evening she had gone out into the front garden and clipped off the heads of a few last fading roses. But there had been one late scarlet bloom that was still in perfect flower. She had cut that off too, and it now stood on the mantelshelf, in a cheap glass vase that Valerie had won on a shooting stall at St Giles's Fair, beneath the ducks that winged their way towards the ceiling in the empty room behind her.

Some of them never did come home . . . never.

LAST BUS TO WOODSTOCK

PRELUDE

'LET'S WAIT just a *bit* longer, please,' said the girl in dark-blue trousers and the light summer coat. 'I'm sure there's one due pretty soon.'

She wasn't quite sure though, and for the third time she turned to study the time-table affixed in its rect-angular frame to Fare Stage 5. But her mind had never journeyed with any confidence in the world of columns and figures, and the finger tracing its tentatively hori-zontal course from the left of the frame had little chance of meeting, at the correct coordinate, the finger descending in a vaguely vertical line from the top. The girl standing beside her transferred her weight impatiently from one foot to the other and said, 'I don' know abou' you.'

'Just a minute. *Just a minute.*' She focused yet again on the relevant columns: 4, 4A (not after 18.00 hours), 4E, 4X (Saturdays only). Today was Wednesday. That meant . . . If 2 o'clock was 14.00 hours, that meant . . .

'Look, sweethear', you please yourself bu' I'm going to hitch i'.' Sylvia's habit of omitting all final 't's seemed irritatingly slack. 'It' in Sylvia's diction was little more than the most indeterminate of vowel sounds, articu-lated without the slightest hint of a consonantal finale.

1

If they ever became better friends, it was something that ought to be mentioned.

What time was it now? 6.45 p.m. That would be 18.45. Yes. She was getting somewhere at last.

'Come on. We'll get a lif' in no time, you see. Tha's wha' half these fellas are looking for – a bi' of skir'.'

And, in truth, there appeared no reason whatsoever to question Sylvia's brisk optimism. No accommodating motorist could fail to be impressed by her minimal skirting and the lovely invitation of the legs below.

For a brief while the two girls stood silently, in uneasy, static truce.

A middle-aged woman was strolling towards them, occasionally stopping and turning her head to gaze down the darkening length of the road that led to the heart of Oxford. She came to a halt a few yards away from the girls and put down her shopping bag.

'Excuse me,' said the first girl. 'Do you know when the next bus is?'

'There should be one in a few minutes, love.' She peered again into the grey distance.

'Does it go to Woodstock?'

'No, I don't think so – it's just for Yarnton. It goes to the village, and then turns round and comes back.'

'Oh.' She stepped out towards the middle of the road, craned her neck, and stepped back as a little convoy of cars approached. Already, as the evening shaded into dusk, a few drivers had switched on their side-lights. No bus was in sight, and she felt anxious.

'We'll be all *righ*',' said Sylvia, a note of impatience

in her voice. 'You see. We'll be 'avin' a giggle abou' i' in the morning.'

Another car. And another. Then again the stillness of the warm autumn evening.

'Well, you can stay if you like – I'm off.' Her companion watched as Sylvia made her way towards the Woodstock roundabout, some two hundred yards up the road. It wasn't a bad spot for the hitch-hiker, for there the cars slowed down before negotiating the busy ring-road junction.

And then she decided. 'Sylvia, wait!'; and holding one gloved hand to the collar of her lightweight summer coat, she ran with awkward, splay-footed gait in pursuit.

The middle-aged woman kept her watch at Fare Stage 5. She thought how many things had changed since she was young.

But Mrs Mabel Jarman was not to wait for long. Vaguely her mind toyed with a few idle, random thoughts – nothing of any moment. Soon she would be home. As she was to remember later on, she could describe Sylvia fairly well: her long, blonde hair, her careless and provocative sensuality. Of the other girl she could recall little: a light coat, dark slacks – what colour, though? Hair – lightish brown? 'Please try as hard you can, Mrs Jarman. It's absolutely vital for us that you remember as much as you can . . .' She noticed a few cars, and a heavy, bouncing articulated lorry, burdened with an improbably large number of wheel-less car-bodies. Men? Men with no other passengers? She would try so hard to recall. Yes, there had been men, she was sure of that. Several had passed her by.

At ten minutes to seven an oblong pinkish blur gradually assumed its firmer delineation. She picked up her bag as the red Corporation bus slowly threaded its way along the stops in the grey mid-distance. Soon she could almost read the bold white lettering above the driver's cab. What was it? She squinted to see it more clearly: WOODSTOCK. Oh dear! She had been wrong then, when that nicely spoken young girl had asked about the next bus. Still, never mind! They hadn't gone far. They would either get a lift or see the bus and manage to get to the next stop, or even the stop after that. 'How long had they been gone, Mrs Jarman?'

She stood back a little from the bus stop, and the Woodstock driver gratefully passed her by. Almost as soon as the bus was out of sight, she saw another, only a few hundred yards behind. This must be hers. The double-decker drew into the stop as Mrs Jarman raised her hand. At two minutes past seven she was home.

Though a widow now, with her two children grown up and married, her pride-and-poverty semi-detached was still her real home, and her loneliness was not without its compensations. She cooked herself a generous supper, washed up, and turned on the television. She could never understand why there was so much criticism of the programmes. She herself enjoyed virtually

everything and often wished she could view two channels simultaneously. At 10 o'clock she watched the
main items on the News, switched off, and went to bed.
At 10.30 she was sound asleep.

It was at 10.30 p.m., too, that a young girl was found
lying in a Woodstock courtyard. She had been brutally
murdered.

PART ONE

Search for a girl

CHAPTER ONE

Wednesday, 29 September

FROM ST GILES' in the centre of Oxford two parallel roads run due north, like the prongs of a tuning fork. On the northern perimeter of Oxford, each must first cross the busy northern ring-road, along which streams of frenetic motorists speed by, gladly avoiding the delights of the old university city. The eastern branch eventually leads to the town of Banbury, and thence continues its rather unremarkable course towards the heart of the industrial midlands; the western branch soon brings the motorist to the small town of Woodstock, some eight miles north of Oxford, and thence to Stratford-upon-Avon.

The journey from Oxford to Woodstock is quietly attractive. Broad grass verges afford a pleasing sense of spaciousness, and at the village of Yarnton, after only a couple of miles, a dual carriageway, with a tree-lined central reservation, finally sweeps the accelerating traffic past the airport and away from its earlier paralysis. For half a mile immediately before Woodstock, on the left-hand side, a grey stone wall marks the eastern boundary of the extensive and beautiful grounds of Blenheim Palace, the mighty mansion built by good Queen Anne for her brilliant general, John Churchill,

1st Duke of Marlborough. High and imposing wrought-iron gates mark the main entrance to the Palace drive, and hither flock the tourists in the summer season to walk amidst the dignified splendour of the great rooms, to stand before the vast Flemish tapestries of Malplaquet and Oudenarde, and to see the room in which was born that later scion of the Churchill line, the great Sir Winston himself, now lying in the once-peaceful churchyard of nearby Bladon village.

Today Blenheim dominates the old town. Yet it was not always so. The strong grey houses which line the main street have witnessed older times and could tell their older tales, though now the majority are sprucely converted into gift, antique and souvenir shops – and inns. There was always, it appears, a goodly choice of hostelries, and several of the hotels and inns now clustered snugly along the streets can boast not only an ancient lineage but also a cluster of black AA stars on their bright yellow signs.

The Black Prince is situated half-way down a broad-side-street to the left as one is journeying north. Amidst the Woodstock peerage it can claim no ancient pedigree, and it seems highly improbable, alas, that the warrior son of King Edward III had ever laughed or cried or tippled or wenched in any of its precincts. Truth to tell, a director of the London company which bought the old house, stable-yards and all, some ten years since, had noticed in some dubiously authenticated guidebook that somewhere thereabouts the Prince was born. The director had been warmly congratulated by his Board for this felicitous piece of research, and not less for his subsequent discovery that the noble Prince did not as yet figure in the Woodstock telephone directory. The Black Prince it was then. The gifted daughter of the first manager had copied out from a children's encyclopaedia, in suitably antique script, a brief, if somewhat romantic, biography of the warrior Prince, and put the finished opus into her mother's oven for half an hour at 450°. The resultant manuscript, reverently brown with age, was neatly, if cheaply, framed and now occupied a suitable position of honour on the wall of the cocktail lounge. Together with the shields of the Oxford colleges nailed neatly along the low stained beams, it added tone and class.

For the last two and a half years Gaye had been the resident 'hostess' of the Black Prince – 'barmaid', thought the manager, was a trifle *infra dignitatem*. And he had a point. 'A pint of your best bitter, luv,' was a request Gaye seldom had to meet and she now associated it with the proletariat; here it was more often vodka and lime for the bright young things, Manhattan cocktails for the American tourists, and gin and French – with a splash of Italian – for the Oxford dons. Such admixtures she dispensed with practised confidence from the silvery glitter and sparkle of bottles ranged invitingly behind the bar.

The lounge itself, deeply carpeted, with chairs and wall-seats covered in a pleasing orange shade, was gently bathed in half light, giving a chiaroscuro effect reminiscent, it was hoped, of a Rembrandt nativity scene. Gaye herself was an attractive, auburn-haired girl and tonight, Wednesday, she was immaculately dressed in a black trouser-suit and white-frilled blouse. A flash of gems on the second and third fingers of her left hand, betokened gentle warning to the mawkish amateur playboy, and perhaps – as some maintained – a calculated invitation to the wealthy professional philanderer. She was, in fact, married and divorced, and now lived with one young son and a mother who was not unduly chagrined at the mildly promiscuous habits of a precious daughter who had been unfortunate enough to marry such 'a lousy swine'. Gaye enjoyed her divorced status as much as she enjoyed her job, and she meant to keep them both.

Wednesday, as usual, had been a fairly busy evening, and it was with some relief when, at 10.25 p.m., she politely, but firmly, called for last drinks. A young man, seated on a high stool at the inner corner of the bar, pushed his whisky glass forward.

'Same again.'

Gaye glanced quizzically into unsteady eyes, but said nothing. She pushed her customer's glass under a priority whisky bottle and placed it on the counter, holding out her right hand and mechanically registering the tariff with her left. The young man was obviously drunk. He fumbled slowly and ineffectually through his pockets before finding the correct money, and after one mouthful of his drink he eased himself gingerly off his seat, measured the door with an uncertain eye, and made a line as decently straight as could in the circumstances be expected.

The old courtyard where once the horses had clattered over the cobbled stones had access from the street through a narrow archway, and had proved an invaluable asset to the Black Prince. A rash of fines for trespassing on the single and double yellow lines which bordered even the most inhospitable and inaccessible stretches of road was breeding a reluctant respect for the law; and any establishment offering 'PATRONS ONLY, cars left at owners' risk' was quite definitely in business. Tonight, as usual, the courtyard was tightly packed with the inevitable Volvos and Rovers. A light over the archway threw a patch of inadequate illumination over the entrance to the yard; the rest lay in dark shadow. It was to the far corner of this courtyard, that the young man stumbled his way; and almost there he dimly saw something behind the furthest car. He looked and groped silently. Then horror crept up to the nape of his neck and against a padlocked stable door he was suddenly and violently sick.

CHAPTER TWO

Wednesday, 29 September

THE MANAGER OF the Black Prince, Mr Stephen Westbrook, contacted the police immediately after the body was found, and his call was acted upon with commendable promptitude. Sergeant Lewis of the Thames Valley Police gave him quick and clear instructions. A police car would be at the Black Prince within ten minutes; Westbrook was to ensure that no one left the premises and that no one entered the courtyard; if anyone insisted on leaving, he was to take the full name and address of the person concerned; he should be honest if asked what all the trouble was about.

The evening's merriness wilted like a sad balloon and voices gradually hushed as the whispered rumour spread: there had been a murder. None seemed anxious to leave; two or three asked if they could phone. All felt suddenly sober, including a pale-faced young man who stood in the manager's office and whose scarcely touched whisky still stood on the counter of the cocktail lounge.

With the arrival of Sergeant Lewis and two uniformed constables, a small knot of people gathered curiously on the pavement opposite. It did not escape their notice that the police car had parked immediately across the access to the courtyard, effectively sealing the exit. Five minutes later a second police car arrived, and eyes turned to the lightly built, dark-haired man who alighted. He conversed briefly with the constable who stood guard outside, nodded his head approvingly several times and walked into the Black Prince.

He knew Sergeant Lewis only slightly, but soon found himself pleasurably impressed by the man's level-headed competence. The two men conferred in brisk tones and very quickly a preliminary procedure was agreed. Lewis, with the help of the second constable, was to list the names, home addresses and car registrations of all persons on the premises, and to take brief statements of their evening's whereabouts, and immediate destinations. There were over fifty people to see, and Morse realized that it would take some time.

'Shall I try to get you some more help, Sergeant?'

'I think the two of us can manage, sir.'

'Good. Let's get started.'

A door, forming the side entrance to the Black Prince, led out into the courtyard and from here Morse stepped gingerly out and looked around. He counted thirteen cars jammed tight into the limited space, but he could have missed one or two, for the cars furthest away were little more than dark hulks against the high back wall, and he wondered by what feats of advanced-motoring skill and precision their inebriated owners could ever negotiate the vehicles unscathed through the narrow exit from the yard. Carefully he shone his torch around and slowly perambulated the yard. The driver of the last car parked on the left-hand side of the yard had presciently backed into the narrow lot and left himself a yard or so of room between his nearside and the wall; and stretched along this space was the sprawling figure of a young girl. She lay on her right side, her head almost up against the corner of the walls, her long blonde hair now cruelly streaked with blood. It was immediately clear that she had been killed by a heavy blow across the back of the skull, and behind the body lay a flat heavy tyre-spanner, about one and a half inches across and some eighteen inches in length – the type of spanner with its undulating ends so common in the days before the inauguration of instant tyre repairs. Morse stood for a few minutes, gazing down at the ugly scene at his feet. The murdered girl wore a minimum of clothing – a pair of wedge-heeled shoes, a very brief dark-blue mini-skirt and a white blouse. Nothing else. Morse shone his torch on the upper part of the body. The left-hand side of the blouse was ripped across; the top two buttons were unfastened and the third had been wrenched away, leaving the full breasts almost totally exposed. Morse flashed his torch around and immediately spotted the missing button – a small, white, mother-of-pearl disc winking up at him from the cobbled ground. How he hated sex murders! He shouted to the constable standing at the entrance to the yard.

'Yes, sir?'

'We need some arc-lamps.'

'It would help, I suppose, sir.'

'Get some.'

'Me, sir?'

'Yes, you!'

'Where shall I get . . .?'

'How the hell do I know,' bellowed Morse.

By a quarter to midnight Lewis had finished his task and he reported to Morse, who was sitting with *The Times* in the manager's office, drinking what looked very much like whisky.

'Ah Lewis.' He thrust the paper across. 'Have a look at 14 down. Appropriate eh?' Lewis looked at 14 down. *Take in bachelor? It could do.* (3). He saw what Morse had written into the completed diagram: BRA. What was he supposed to say? He had never worked with Morse before.

'Good clue, don't you think?'

Lewis, who had occasionally managed the *Daily Mirror* coffee-time crossword was out of his depth, and felt much puzzled.

'I'm afraid I'm not very hot on crosswords, sir.'

'"Bachelor" – that's BA and "take" is the letter "r", *recipe* in Latin. Did you never do any Latin?'

'No, sir.'

'Do you think I'm wasting your time, Lewis?'

Lewis was nobody's fool and was a man of some honesty and integrity. 'Yes, sir.'

An engaging smile crept across Morse's mouth. He thought they would get on well together.

'Lewis, I want you to work with me on this case.' The sergeant looked straight at Morse and into the hard, grey eyes. He heard himself say he would be delighted.

'This calls for a celebration,' said Morse. 'Landlord!'

Westbrook had been hovering outside and came in smartly. 'A double whisky.' Morse pushed his glass forward.

'Would *you* like a drink, sir?' The manager turned hesitantly to Lewis.

'Sergeant Lewis is on duty, Mr Westbrook.'

When the manager returned, Morse asked him to assemble everyone on the premises, including staff, in the largest room available, and drinking his whisky in complete silence, skimmed through the remaining pages of the newspaper.

'Do you read *The Times*, Lewis?'

'No, sir; we take the *Mirror*.' It seemed a rather sad admission.

'So do I sometimes,' said Morse.

At a quarter past midnight Morse came into the restaurant-room where everyone was now gathered. Gaye's eyes met and held his briefly as he entered, and she felt a strong compulsion about the man. It was not so much that he seemed mentally to be undressing her, as most of the men she knew, but as if he had already done so. She listened to him with interest as he spoke.

He thanked them all for their patience and co-operation. It was getting very late and he didn't intend to keep them there any longer. They would now know why the police were there. There had been a murder in the courtyard – a young girl with blonde hair. They would appreciate that all the cars in the courtyard must stay where they were until the morning. He knew this meant that some of them would have difficulty getting

18

home, but taxis had been ordered. If anyone wished to report to him or to Sergeant Lewis anything at all which might be of interest or value to the inquiry, however unimportant it might seem, would such a person please stay behind. The rest could go.

To Gaye it seemed an uninspired performance. Happening to be on the scene of a murder ought surely to be a bit more exciting than this? She would go home now, where her mother and her young son would be fast asleep. And even if they weren't, she couldn't tell them much, could she? Already the police had been there over an hour and a half. It wasn't exactly what she'd come to expect from her reading of Holmes or Poirot, who by this time would doubtless have interviewed the chief suspects, and made some startling deductions from the most trivial phenomena.

The murmuring which followed the end of Morse's brief address died away as most of the customers collected their coats and moved off. Gaye rose, too. Had she seen anything of interest or value? She thought back on the evening. There was, of course, the young man who had found the girl ... She had seen him before, but she couldn't quite remember who it was he'd been with, or when. And then she had it – blonde hair! She'd been in the lounge with him only last week. But a lot of girls these days peroxided their hair. Perhaps it was worth mentioning? She decided it was and walked up to Morse.

'You said the girl who has been murdered had blonde hair.' Morse looked at her and slowly nodded.

'I think she was here last week – she was with the man who found her body tonight. I saw them here. I work in the lounge.'

'That's very interesting, Miss – er?'

'Mrs. Mrs McFee.'

'Please forgive me, Mrs McFee. I thought you might have been wearing all those rings to frighten off the boys who come to drool at you over the counter.'

Gaye felt very angry. He was a hateful man. 'Look, Inspector whatever your name is, I came to tell you something I thought might be helpful. If you're going . . .'

'Mrs McFee,' broke in Morse gently, looking at her with an open nakedness in his eyes, 'if I lived anywhere near, I'd come in myself and drool over you every night of the week.'

At just after 1.00 a.m. a primitive, if reasonably effective, relay of arc-lamps was fixed around the courtyard. Morse had instructed Lewis to detain the young man who had found the murdered girl until they had taken the opportunity of investigating the courtyard more closely. The two men now surveyed the scene before them. There was a great deal of blood, and as Sergeant Lewis looked down on her, he felt a deep revulsion against the violence and senselessness of murder. Morse appeared more interested in the starry heavens above.

'Do you study the stars, Lewis?'

'I read the horoscopes sometimes, sir.'

Morse appeared not to hear. 'I once heard of a

group of schoolchildren, Lewis, who tried to collect a million matchsticks. After they'd filled the whole of the school premises, they decided they'd have to pack it up.' Lewis thought it his duty to say something, but all appropriate comment eluded him.

After a while, Morse reverted his attention to more terrestrial things, and the two of them looked down again at the murdered girl. The spanner and the solitary white button lay where Morse had seen them earlier. There was nothing much else to see but for the trail of dried blood that led almost from one end of the back wall to the other.

The young man sat in the manager's office. His mother, though expecting him to be late, would be getting worried; and so was he. Morse finally came in at 1.30 a.m. whilst the police surgeon, the photographers and the fingerprint men busied themselves about the courtyard.

'Name?' he asked.

'Sanders, John Sanders.'

'You found the body?'

'Yes, sir.'

'Tell me about it.'

'There's not much to tell really.'

Morse smiled. 'Then we needn't keep you long, need we, Mr Sanders?'

The young man fidgeted. Morse sat opposite him, looked him hard in the eye and waited.

'Well, I just walked into the courtyard and there she

21

was. I didn't touch her, but I knew she was dead. I came straight back in to tell the manager.'

Morse nodded. 'Anything else?'

'Don't think so.'

'When were you sick, Mr Sanders?'

'Oh yes. I was sick.'

'Was it after or before you saw the girl?'

'After. It must have upset me seeing her there – sort of shock, I suppose.'

'Why don't you tell me the truth?'

'What do you mean?'

Morse sighed. 'You haven't got your car here have you?'

'I haven't got a car.'

'Do you usually have a stroll round the courtyard before you go home?' Sanders said nothing. 'How much drink did you have tonight?'

'A few whiskies – I wasn't drunk.'

'Mr Sanders, do you want me to find out from someone else?' It was clear from Sanders's manner that he hardly welcomed an inquiry along such lines. 'What time did you come here?' continued Morse.

'About half past seven?'

'And you got drunk and went out to be sick.' Reluctantly Sanders agreed. 'Do you usually drink on your own?'

'Not usually.'

'Who were you waiting for?' Sanders did not reply. 'She didn't show up?'

'No,' he said flatly.

'But she did come, didn't she?'

'No, I told you. I was on my own all the time.'

'But she did come, didn't she?' repeated Morse quietly. Sanders looked beaten. 'She came,' continued Morse in the same quiet voice. 'She came and you saw her. You saw her in the courtyard, and she was dead.'

The young man nodded.

'We'd better have a little chat, you and me,' said Morse ungrammatically.

CHAPTER THREE

Thursday, 30 September

As HE STOOD alone in the bedroom of Sylvia Kaye, Morse felt measurably relieved. The grim duties of the night were over, and he switched on the natural defence mechanism of his weary mind. He wished to forget the awakening of Mrs Dorothy Kaye, and the summoning of her husband from his night-shift in the welding division of the Cowley car plant; the fatuous, coarse recriminations and the overwhelming hurt of their bitter, empty misery. Sylvia's mother was now under sedation, postponing the day and the reckoning; whilst Sergeant Lewis sat at headquarters learning what he could from Sylvia's father. He took many pages of careful notes but doubted if it all amounted to much. He was to join Morse in half an hour.

The bedroom was small, one of three in a neat semi-detached house in Jackdaw Court, a quiet crescent with rotting wooden fences, a few minutes' walk off the Woodstock Road. Morse sat down on the narrow bed and looked around him. He wondered if the neatness of the bed was mum's doing, for the remainder of the room betrayed the slack and untidy living of the murdered girl. A vast coloured portrait of a pop artist was pinned rather precariously above the gas fire in the chimney breast, and Morse reminded himself that he might understand young people rather better if he had a teenage family of his own; as it was, the identity of the handsome youth was cloaked in anonymity and whatever pretentions he may have had would for Morse be for ever unknown. Several items of underwear draped the table and chair which, with a whitewood wardrobe, substantively comprised the only other furniture. Morse gingerly picked up a flimsy black bra lying on the chair. His mind flashed back to that first glimpse of Sylvia Kaye, rested there a few seconds and slowly returned through the tortuous byways of the last unpleasant hours. A pile of women's magazines was awkwardly stacked on the window-sill, and Morse cursorily flicked his way through make-up hints, personal problems and horoscopes. Not even a paragraph of pornography. He opened the wardrobe door and with perceptibly deeper interest examined the array of skirts, blouses, slacks and dresses. Clean and untidy. Mounds of shoes, ultra-modern, wedged, ugly: she wasn't short of money. On the table Morse saw a travel brochure for package trips to Greece, Yugoslavia and Cyprus, white hotels, azure seas and small print about insurance liability and small-pox regulations; a letter from Sylvia's employer explaining the complexities of VAT, and a diary, the latter revealing nothing but a single entry for 2 January: 'Cold. Went to see *Ryan's Daughter.*'

Lewis tapped on the bedroom door and entered. 'Find anything, sir?' Morse looked at his cheerful sergeant distastefully, and said nothing. 'Can I?' asked Lewis his hand hovering above the diary.

'Go ahead,' said Morse.

Lewis examined the diary, turning carefully through the days of September. Finding nothing, he worked meticulously through every page. 'Only one day filled in, sir.'

'I don't even get that far,' said Morse.

'Do you think "cold" means it was a cold day or she had a cold?'

'How do I know,' snapped Morse, 'and what the hell does it matter?'

'We could find out where *Ryan's Daughter* was on in the first week of January,' suggested Lewis.

'Yes, we could. And how much the diary cost and who gave it to her and where she buys her biros from. Sergeant! We're running a murder enquiry not a stationery shop!'

'Sorry.'

'You may be right though,' added Morse.

'I'm afraid Mr Kaye hadn't got much to tell me, either, sir. Did you want to see him?'

'No. Leave the poor fellow alone.'

'We're not making very rapid progress then.'

'Oh, I don't know,' said Morse. 'Miss Kaye was wearing a white blouse, wasn't she?'

'Yes.'

'What colour bra would your wife wear under a white blouse?'

'A lightish-coloured one, I suppose.'

'She wouldn't wear a black one?'

'It would show through.'

'Mm. By the way, Lewis, do you know when lighting-up time was yesterday evening?'

''Fraid I don't, off hand,' replied Lewis, 'but I can soon find out for you.'

'No need for that,' said Morse. 'According to the diary you just inspected, yesterday, 29 September, was St Michael and All Angels' day and lighting-up time was 6.40 p.m.'

Lewis followed his superior officer down the narrow stairs, and wondered what was coming next. Before they reached the front door, Morse half turned his head: 'What do you think of Women's Lib, Lewis?'

At 11.00 a.m. Sergeant Lewis interviewed the manager of the Town and Gown Assurance Company, situated on the second and third storeys above a flourishing tobacconist's shop in the High. Sylvia had worked there – her first job – for just over a year. She was a copy-typist, having failed to satisfy the secretarial college at which she had studied for two years after leaving school that the ungainly and frequently undecipherable scrawls in her shorthand note-book bore sufficient relationship to the missives originally dictated. But her typing was reasonably accurate and clean, and the company, the manager assured Lewis, had no complaints about its late employee. She had been punctual and unobtrusive.

'Attractive?'

'Well – er, yes. I suppose she was,' replied the

manager. Lewis made a note and wished Morse were there; but the Inspector said he felt thirsty and had gone into the Minster across the way.

'She worked, you say, with two other girls,' said Lewis. 'I think I'd better have a word with them if I can.'

'Certainly, officer.' The manager, Mr Palmer, seemed a fraction relieved.

Lewis questioned the two young ladies at considerable length. Neither was 'a particklar friend' of Sylvia. She had, as far as they knew, no regular beau. Yes, she had boasted occasionally of her sexual exploits – but so did most of the girls. She was friendly enough, but not really 'one of the girls'.

Lewis looked through her desk. The usual bric-à-brac. A bit of a broken mirror, a comb with a few blonde hairs in it, yesterday's *Sun*, pencils galore, rubbers, typewriter ribbons, carbons. On the wall behind Sylvia's desk was pinned a photograph of Omar Sharif, flanked by a typewritten holiday rota. Lewis saw that Sylvia had been on a fortnight's holiday in the latter half of July, and he asked the two girls where she'd been to.

'Stayed at home, I think,' replied the elder of the two girls, a quiet, serious-looking girl in her early twenties.

Lewis sighed. 'You don't seem to know much about her, do you?' The girls said nothing. Lewis tried his best to elicit a little more co-operation, but met with little success. He left the office just before midday, and strolled over to the Minster.

'Poor Sylvia,' said the younger girl after he had gone.

'Yes, poor Sylvia,' replied Jennifer Coleby.

Lewis eventually, and somewhat to his surprise, discovered Morse in the 'gentlemen only' bar at the back of the Minster.

'Ah, Lewis.' He rose and placed his empty glass on the bar, 'What's it to be?' Lewis asked for a pint of bitter. 'Two pints of your best bitter,' said Morse cheerfully to the man behind the bar, 'and have one yourself.'

It became clear to Lewis that the topic of conversation before his arrival had been horse racing. Morse picked up a copy of *Sporting Life* and walked over to the corner with his assistant.

'You a betting man, Lewis?'

'I sometimes put a few bob on the Derby and the National, sir, but I'm not a regular gambler.'

'You keep it that way,' said Morse, with a note of seriousness in his voice. 'But look here, what do you think of that?' He unfolded the racing paper and pointed to one of the runners in the 3.15 at Chepstow: The Black Prince. 'Worth a quid, would you say, sergeant?'

'Certainly an odd coincidence.'

'10 to 1,' said Morse, drinking deeply on his beer.

'Are you going to back it, sir?'

'I already have,' said Morse, glancing up at the old barman.

'Isn't that illegal, sir?'

'I never studied that side of the law.' Doesn't he want to solve this murder, thought Lewis, and as if Morse read his unspoken words he was promptly asked for a report on the deceased's position with Town and Gown. Lewis did his best, and Morse did not interrupt. He seemed rather more interested in his pint of beer. When he finished, Morse told him to get back to headquarters, type his reports, then get home and have some sleep. Lewis didn't argue. He felt dog-tired, and sleep was fast becoming a barely remembered luxury.

'Nothing else, sir?'

'Not until tomorrow when you'll report to me at 7.30 a.m. sharp – unless you want to put a few bob on The Black Prince.' Lewis felt in his pocket and pulled out 50p.

'Each way, do you think?'

'You'll kick yourself if it wins,' said Morse.

'All right. 50p to win.'

Morse took the 50p, and as Lewis left he saw the barman pocket the coin, and pull a further pint for the enigmatic Chief Inspector.

CHAPTER FOUR

Friday, 1 October

PROMPT AT 7.30 next morning, Lewis tapped on the inspector's door. Receiving no answer, he cautiously tried the knob and peered round the door. No sign of life. He walked back to the front vestibule and asked the desk-sergeant if Inspector Morse was in yet.

'Not seen 'im.'

'He said he'd be here at half-seven.'

'Well, you know the Inspector.'

I wish I did, thought Lewis. He walked along to pick up the reports he had wearily typed out the previous afternoon, and read them through carefully. He'd done his best, but there was little to go on. He walked on to the canteen and ordered a cup of coffee. Constable Dickson, an officer whom Lewis knew fairly well, was enthusiastically assaulting a plate of bacon and tomatoes.

'How's the murder job going, Sarge?'

'Early days yet.'

'Old Morse in charge, eh?'

'Yep.'

'Funny bugger, isn't he?' Lewis didn't disagree. 'I know one thing,' said Dickson. 'He was here till way gone midnight. Got virtually everyone in the building jumping about for him. I reckon every phone on the premises was red hot. God, he can work, that chap, when he wants to.'

Lewis felt a little shame-faced. He himself had slept sweetly and soundly from six the previous evening until six that morning. He reckoned that Morse deserved his sleep, and sat down to drink a cup of coffee.

Ten minutes later a freshly shaven Morse walked brightly into the canteen. 'Ah, there you are Lewis. Sorry to be late.' He ordered a coffee and sat opposite. 'Bad news for you, I'm afraid.' Lewis looked up sharply. 'You lost your money. The constipated camel came in second.'

Lewis smiled. 'Never mind, sir. I just hope you didn't lose too much yourself.'

Morse shook his head. 'Oh no, I didn't lose anything; in fact I made a few quid. I backed it each way.'

'But . . .' began Lewis.

'C'mon,' said Morse. 'Drink up. We've got work to do.'

For the next four hours the two of them were busy sorting the reports flowing in from the wide-flung inquiries Morse had initiated the previous day. At twelve noon, Lewis felt he knew more about Sylvia Kaye than he did about his wife. He read each report with great care – Morse's orders – and felt that many of the facts were beginning to fix themselves firmly in his mind. Morse, he noticed, devoured the reports with an amazing rapidity, reminiscent of someone skipping through a tedious novel; yet occasionally he would re-read the odd report with a fascinated concentration.

'Well?' said Morse finally.

'I think I've got most things pretty straight, sir.'

'Good.'

'You seemed to find one or two of the reports very interesting, sir.'

'Did I?' Morse sounded surprised.

'You spent about ten minutes on that one from the secretarial college, and it's only half a page.'

'You're very observant, Lewis, but I'm sorry to disappoint you. It was the most ill-written report I've seen in years, with twelve – no less – grammatical monstrosities in ten lines! What's the force coming to?'

Lewis didn't know what the force was coming to and hadn't the courage to inquire into the Inspector's statistical findings on his own erratic style. He asked instead, 'Do you think we're getting anywhere, sir?'

'Doubt it,' replied Morse.

Lewis wasn't so sure. Sylvia's movements on the previous Wednesday seemed established. She had left the office in the High at 5.00 p.m., and almost certainly walked the hundred yards or so to the No 2 bus stop outside University College. She had arrived home at 5.35 p.m. and had a good meal. She told her mother she might be late home, left the house at roughly 6.30 p.m. wearing – as far as could be established – the clothes in which she was found. Somehow she had got to Woodstock. It all seemed to Lewis a promising enough starting-point for a few preliminary inquiries.

'Would you like me to get on to the bus company, sir, and see the drivers on the Woodstock run?'

'Done it,' said Morse.

'No good?' Disappointment showed in the sergeant's voice.

'I don't think she went by bus.'

'Taxi, sir?'

'Improbable wouldn't you think?'

'I don't know, sir. It might not be all that expensive.'

'Perhaps not, but it seems most improbable to me. If she'd wanted a taxi, she'd have rung up from home – there's a phone there.'

'She may have done just that, sir.'

'She didn't. No phone call was made by any member of the Kaye household yesterday.'

Lewis was experiencing a dangerous failure of confidence. 'I don't seem to be much help,' he said. But Morse ignored the comment.

'Lewis, how would you go from Oxford to Woodstock?'

'By car, sir.'

'She hadn't got a car.'

'Get a lift with one of her friends?'

'You wrote the report. She doesn't seem to have had many girl friends.'

'A boy friend, you think, sir?'

'Do you?'

Lewis thought a minute. 'Bit odd if she was going with a boy friend. Why didn't he pick her up at her house?'

'Why not, indeed?'

'She wasn't picked up at home?'

'No. Her mother saw her walking away.'

'You've interviewed her mother then, sir.'

'Yes. I spoke to her last night.'

'Is she very upset?'

'She's got broad shoulders, Lewis, and I rather like her. Of course she's terribly upset and shocked. But not quite so heart-broken as I thought she'd be. In fact I got the idea her beautiful daughter was something of a trial to her.'

Morse walked over to a large mirror, took out a comb and began to groom his thinning hair. He carefully drew a few strands across a broad area of nakedness at the back of his skull, returned the comb to his pocket and asked a perplexed Sergeant Lewis what he thought of the effect.

'You see, Lewis, if Sylvia didn't go by bus, taxi or boy friend, how on earth did she ever get to Woodstock? And remember that get to Woodstock somehow she assuredly did.'

'She must have hitched it, sir.'

Morse was still surveying himself in the mirror. 'Yes, Lewis, I think she did. And that is why,' he took out the comb again and made some further passes at his straggling hair, 'that is why I think I must put in a little TV appearance tonight.' He picked up the phone and put through a call to the Chief Superintendent. 'Go and get some lunch, Lewis, I'll see you later.'

'Can I order anything for you, sir?'

'No. I've got to watch my figure,' said Morse.

The death of Sylvia Kaye had figured dramatically in Thursday afternoon's edition of the *Oxford Mail*, and prominently in the national press on Friday morning. On Friday evening the news bulletins on both BBC and ITV carried an interview with Chief Inspector Morse, who appealed for help from anyone who had been on the Woodstock Road between 6.40 p.m. and 7.15 p.m. on the evening of Wednesday, 29 September. Morse informed the nation that the police were looking for a very dangerous man who might attack again at any time; for the killer of Sylvia Kaye, when brought to justice, would face not only the charge of wilful murder, but also the charge of sexual assault and rape.

Lewis had stood in the background as Morse faced the camera crews and joined him after his performance was over.

'That damned wind!' said Morse, his hair blown into a tufted wilderness.

'Do you really think he might kill someone else, sir?'

'Doubt it very much,' said Morse.

CHAPTER FIVE

Friday, 1 October

EACH EVENING OF the week, with rare exceptions, Mr Bernard Crowther left his small detached house in Southdown Road, North Oxford, at approximately 9.40 p.m. Each evening his route was identical. Methodically closing behind him the white gate which enclosed a small, patchy strip of lawn, he would turn right, walk to the end of the road, turn right again, and make his way, with perceptible purposefulness in his stride, towards the lounge bar of the Fletcher's Arms. Though an articulate man, indeed an English don at Lonsdale College, he found it difficult to explain either to his disapproving wife or indeed to himself exactly what it was that attracted him to this unexceptionable pub, with its ill-assorted, yet regular and amiable clientele.

On the night of Friday, 1 October, however, Crowther would have been observed to remain quite still for several seconds after closing the garden gate behind him, his eyes downcast and disturbed as if he were pondering deep and troublous thoughts; and then to turn, against his habit and his inclination, to his left. He walked slowly to the end of the road, where, on the left beside a row of dilapidated garages, stood a public telephone-box. Impatient at the best of times, and this was not the best of times, he waited restlessly and awkwardly, pacing to and fro, consulting his watch and throwing wicked glances at the portly woman inside the kiosk who appeared ill-equipped to face the triangular threat of the gadgeted apparatus before her, an uncooperative telephone exchange and her own one-handed negotiations with the assorted coinage in her purse. But she was fighting on and Crowther, in a generous moment, wondered if one of her children had been taken suddenly and seriously ill with dad on the night-shift and no one else to help. But he doubted whether her call was as important as the one he was about to make. News bulletins had always gripped his attention, however trivial the items reported; and the item he had watched on the BBC news at 9.00 p.m. had been far from trivial. He could remember verbatim the words the police inspector had used: 'We shall be very glad if any motorist . . .' Yes, he could tell them something, for he had played his part in the terrifying and tragic train of events. But what was he going to say? He couldn't tell them the truth. Nor even half the truth. His fragile resolution began to crumble. He'd give that wretched woman another minute – one minute and no longer.

At 9.50 p.m. that same evening an excited Sergeant Lewis put through a call to Chief Inspector Morse. 'A break, sir. I think we've got a break.'

'Oh?'

'Yes. A witness, sir. A Mrs Mabel Jarman. She saw the murdered girl . . .'

'You mean,' interrupted Morse, 'she saw the girl who was later murdered, I suppose.'

'That's it. We can get a full statement as soon as we like.'

'You mean you haven't got one yet?'

'She only rang five minutes ago, sir. I'm going over straight away. She's local. I wondered if you wanted to come.'

'No,' said Morse.

'All right, sir. I'll have the whole thing typed up and ready for you in the morning.'

'Good.'

'Bit of luck, though, isn't it? We'll soon get on to this other girl.'

'What other girl?' said Morse quietly.

'Well, you see, sir . . .'

'What's Mrs Jarman's address?' Morse reluctantly took off his bedroom slippers, and reached for his shoes.

'Bit late on parade tonight, Bernard. What's it to be?'

Bernard was well liked at the Fletcher's Arms, always ready to fork out for his round – and more. All the regulars knew him for a man of some academic distinction; but he was a good listener, laughed as heartily as the next at the latest jokes, and himself occasionally waxed eloquent on the stupidity of the government and the incompetence of Oxford United. But tonight he spoke of neither. By 10.25 p.m. he had drunk three pints of best bitter with his usual practised fluency and got up to go.

''Nother one before you go, Bernard?'

'Thanks, no. I've had just about enough of that horse piss for one night.'

'You in the dog house again.'

'I'm always in the bloody dog house.'

He walked back slowly. He knew that if the bedroom light was on, his wife, Margaret, would be reading in bed, waiting only for her errant husband to return. If there was no light, she would probably be watching TV. He came to a decision as foolish as the ones he had made as a boy when he would race a car to the nearest lamppost. If she was in bed, he would go straight in, if she was still up, he would ring the police. He turned into the road, and saw immediately that the bedroom light was on.

Mrs Jarman gave her testimony in a brisk, if excited, fashion. Her memory proved surprisingly clear, and Sergeant Lewis's notes grew fat with factual data. Morse left things to him. He wondered if Lewis had been right in thinking this was the big break, and considered, on reflection, that he was. He himself felt impatient and bored with the trained and thorough pedanticism with which his sergeant probed and queried the chronology of the bus stop encounter. But he knew it had to be done and he knew that Lewis was doing it well. For three-quarters of an hour he left them to it.

'Well, I want to thank you very much, Mrs Jarman.' Lewis closed his note-book and looked, in a mildly satisfied manner, towards his chief.

'Perhaps,' said Morse, 'I could ask you to come to see us in the morning? Sergeant Lewis will have your statement typed out, and we'd like you to have a look through it to see that he's got it all right – just a formality, you know.'

Lewis stood up to go, but Morse's veiled glance told him to sit down again.

'I wonder, Mrs Jarman,' he said, 'if you could do us one last favour. I'd just love a cup of tea. I know it's late but . . .'

'Why, of course, Inspector. I wish you'd said so before.' She hurried off and the policemen heard a spurt of water and a clatter of cups.

'Well, Sergeant, you've done a good job.'

'Thank you, sir.'

'Now listen. That bus. Get on to it as soon as you can.'

'But you said you'd checked the buses, sir.'

'Well check 'em again.'

'All right.'

'And,' said Morse, 'there's that articulated lorry. With a bit of luck we can trace that.'

'You think we can?'

'You've got a definite time – what else do you want, man?'

'Anything else, sir?' said Lewis in a subdued voice.

'Yes. Stay and make a few more notes. I won't be long.'

41

The kitchen door opened and Mrs Jarman reappeared. 'I was just wondering whether you gentlemen would like a little drop of whisky, instead of tea. I've had a bottle since Christmas – I don't usually drink myself.'

'Now, now,' said Morse, 'you are a very resourceful woman, Mrs Jarman.' Lewis smiled wanly. He knew what was coming. *Déjà vu.*

'I think a little drop of Scotch would do me the power of good. Perhaps you'll have a drop yourself?'

'Oh no, sir, I'll have a cuppa, if you don't mind.' She opened a drawer in the cupboard and brought out two glass tumblers.

'Just the one glass then, Mrs Jarman,' said Morse. 'It's a pity, I know, but Sergeant Lewis here is on duty and you will appreciate that a policeman is not allowed to consume any alcoholic drink whilst on duty. You wouldn't want him to break the law, would you?'

Lewis muttered to himself.

Morse smiled into his liberal dose of whisky whilst his assistant soberly stirred a diminutive cup of wickedly dark brown tea.

'Mrs Jarman I just want to ask you one or two more questions about what you've said to Sergeant Lewis. I hope you don't feel too tired?'

'Oh no.'

'Do you remember how this "other girl" seemed? Was she a bit cross? A bit nervous?'

'I don't think she was – well, I don't know. Perhaps she was a bit nervous.'

'A bit frightened?'

42

'Oh no. Not that. A bit sort of, er, excited. Yes, that's it, a bit excited.'

'Excited and impatient.'

'I think so.'

'Now, I want you to think back. Just close your eyes if you like, and picture yourself at the bus stop again. Can you recall anything, anything at all, that she said. She asked you if the next bus went to Woodstock. You've told us that. Anything else?'

'I can't remember. I just can't seem to remember.'

'Now, Mrs Jarman, don't rush yourself. Just relax and picture it all again. Take your time.'

Mrs Jarman closed her eyes and Morse watched her with keen anticipation. She said nothing. Morse at last broke the embarrassing silence. 'What about the girl who was murdered? Did she say anything else? She wanted to hitch-hike, you said.'

'Yes, she kept saying something like "Come on".'

'"It'll be all right"?' added Morse.

'Yes. It'll be all right. We'll have a giggle about it in the morning.'

Morse's blood froze. He remained utterly motionless. But Mrs Jarman's memory had dredged its last.

Morse relaxed. 'We've kept you up late, but you've been wonderful. And this must be a real priority brand of Scotch?'

'Oh, would you like a little drop more, sir?'

'Well, I think I wouldn't perhaps say no, Mrs Jarman. Yes, a drop of the finest Scotch I've tasted in years.'

As Mrs Jarman turned her back to refill his glass, Morse sternly motioned Lewis to stay where he was, and for the next half hour he tried with every subtlety he knew to jog the good lady's recollection of her chance encounter with the murdered girl and her companion. But to no avail.

'Just one more thing, Mrs Jarman. When you come to see us in the morning, we shall be holding an identity parade. It won't take more than a minute or two.'

'You mean you want me to . . . Oh dear!'

At 11.45 p.m. Morse and Lewis took their leave of Mrs Jarman. They were standing by their cars when the door of the house suddenly opened again and Mrs Jarman came hurriedly towards Morse.

'There's just one more thing, sir. I've just remembered. When you said close your eyes and just picture things. I've thought of something. The other girl, sir. When she ran, she ran with a sort of splay-footed run – do you know what I mean, sir?'

'Yes I do,' said Morse.

The two men returned to HQ. After enquiring whether any further calls had come through and learning there were none, Morse called Lewis to his office.

'Well, my friend?' Morse looked pleased with himself.

'You told her we're going to have an identity parade?' asked a puzzled Lewis.

'We are. Now tell me this. What would you say was the most vital fact we learned from Mrs Jarman?'

'We learned quite a few pieces of valuable information.'

'Yes, we did. But only one fact that really made your hair stand on end, eh?' Lewis tried to look intelligent.

'We learned, did we not,' said Morse, 'that the girls would have a bit of a giggle about it all in the morning?'

'Oh, I see,' said Lewis, not seeing.

'You see what it means? They would be meeting in the morning – Thursday morning, and we know that Sylvia Kaye was in employment and we know where, do we not?'

'So the other girl works there, too.'

'The evidence would seem to point very much that way, Lewis.'

'But I was there, sir, and none of them said a word.'

'Don't you find that very interesting?'

'I don't seem to have done a very good job, do I?' Lewis looked disconsolately down at the Chief Inspector's carpet.

'But don't you see,' continued Morse, 'we now know that one of the girls – how many were there?'

'Fourteen.'

'That one of those girls is at the very least withholding vital evidence and at the best telling us a heap of lies.'

'I didn't talk to them all, sir.'

'Good God, man! They knew what you were there for, didn't they? One of their colleagues is murdered. A sergeant of the murder squad comes to their office. What the hell did they think you'd gone for? Service the bloody typewriters? No, you did well, Lewis. You didn't force our little girl to weave her tangled web for us. She thinks she's OK and that's how I want it.' Morse got up. 'I want you to get some sleep, Lewis. You've got work to do in the morning. But just before you go, find me the private address of Mr Palmer. I think a little visit is called for.'

'You're not thinking of knocking him up now, are you, sir?'

'Not only am I going to knock him up as you put it, Lewis, I am going to ask him, very nicely of course, to open up his offices for me and I am going to look through the private drawers of fourteen young ladies. It should be an exciting business.'

'Won't you need a search warrant, sir?'

'I never did understand the legal situation over search warrants,' complained Morse.

'I think you ought to have one, sir.'

'And perhaps you'll let me know where the hell I find anyone to sign a warrant at this time of the night – or morning, whatever it is.'

'But if Mr Palmer insists on his legal rights . . .' began Lewis.

'I shall tell him we're trying to find out who raped and murdered one of his girls,' snapped Morse, 'not looking for dirty postcards from Pwllheli!'

'Wouldn't you like me to come with you, sir?'

'No. Do as I say and go to bed.'

'Well, good luck, sir.'

'I shan't need it,' said Morse. 'I know you'd never believe it, but I can be an officious bastard when I want to be. Mr Palmer will be out of bed as if he'd got a flea in his pyjama bottoms.'

*

But the manager of the Town and Gown Assurance Co., though condescending to get out of bed, flatly refused to get out of his pyjamas – top or bottom. He asked Morse for his authority to search his offices, and once having established that Morse had none, he proved adamant to all the cajolings and threats that Morse could muster. The Inspector reflected that he had badly underestimated the little manager. After prolonged negotiation, however, a policy was finally agreed. All the staff of the Town and Gown would be assembled in the manager's office at 8.45 a.m. the following morning, where they would all be asked if they had any objections to the police opening any incoming private correspondence. If there were no objection (Palmer assured Morse), the Inspector could open all correspondence, and, if need be, make confidential copies of any letter which might be of value. Furthermore all the female employees would be asked to attend an identity parade at the Thames Valley HQ some time later the same morning. Palmer would need some time to arrange a skeleton servicing of the telephone exchange and other vital matters. It was a good job it was Saturday; the office closed at midday.

Perhaps, thought Morse in retrospect, things hadn't worked out too badly. He wearily drove to HQ and wondered why, with all his experience, he had rushed so wildly into such an ill-considered and probably futile scheme as he had contemplated. Yet, for all that, he thought that he had in some strange way been right. He felt in his bones that there was an urgency about this stage of the investigation. He felt he was poised for a big breakthrough, though he did not at this stage realize how many breaks-through would be required before the case was solved. Nor did he realize that in an oddly perverse way Palmer's refusal to allow him unauthorized entry to his premises had presented him with one gigantic piece of luck. For a letter, addressed to one of the young ladies in Palmer's employ, was already on its way, and no power on earth, except the inefficiency of some unsuspecting sorting clerk, could – or indeed did – prevent its prompt delivery.

Morse returned to HQ and spent the next hour at his desk. He finished at 4.15 a.m. and sat back in his black leather chair. Little point in going home now. He pondered the case, at first with a slow, methodical analysis of the facts known hitherto and then with what, if he had been wider awake, he would wish to have called a series of swift, intuitive leaps, all of which landed him in areas of twilight and darkness. But he knew that whatever had taken place on Wednesday evening had its causation in the activities of certain persons, and that these persons had been motivated by the ordinary passions of love and hate and greed and jealousy. That wasn't the puzzle at all. It was the interlocking of the jigsaw pieces, those pieces that would now be coming into his hands. He dozed off. He fitfully dreamed of an attractive red-headed barmaid and a blonde beauty with blood all over her hair. He always seemed to dream of women. He sometimes wondered what he would dream about if he got himself married. Women probably, he thought.

CHAPTER SIX

Saturday 2 October, a.m.

'WHAT *NEXT*?' SAID Judith, Mr Palmer's confidential secretary. 'Opening our letters, he said!'

'You could have said no,' replied Sandra, an amiable, feckless girl, who had, on merit, made no advance either in status or in salary since joining the office three years ago.

'I almost did,' chimed in Ruth, a flutter-lashed girl with the brains of a butterfly. 'If Bob sent me one of his real passionate ones, coo!' She giggled nervously.

Most of the girls were young and unmarried and lived with their parents, and because of late morning postal deliveries and a fear that parents might pry into matters not concerning them, several of them had invited their correspondents to address mail to the office. Indeed, so many incoming letters were marked 'Private and Confidential', 'Personal' and the like, that an unsuspecting observer might have surmised that the Town and Gown was the headquarters of a classified intelligence department. But Palmer countenanced such mild abuse of his establishment with philosophic quietude, whilst at the same time keeping a hawk-like eye on the office telephone accounts. It seemed to him a fair arrangement.

Each girl in her own way had been a little overawed by Morse, and his quietly spoken requests were conceded with no audible murmur of dissent. Of course they all wanted to help. In any case he was only going to get copies of the mail and everything would be treated with the utmost confidentiality. Nevertheless Ruth had given an audible sigh of relief on discovering that this was a morning when Bob had temporarily exhausted his supply of lecherous suggestions. However broadminded they were, well . . .

'I think we all ought to help them find out about poor old Sylvia,' said Sandra. For all her low-geared intellect she was a girl of ready sensitivity and had been deeply saddened, and a little frightened, by Sylvia's death. She wished in her own innocent way that she could contribute something to the inquiry, and she sensed disappointment, though little surprise, that no one had written to her.

There were seven personal letters and two postcards for Morse to study, and as he cursorily cast his eye over each before placing it in the copying machine, he felt it was all rather foolish. Still, there was the identity parade, of which he had high hopes, although here again in the sobering light of the morning the expectancy index had already fallen several points.

'Have you been on an identity parade before?' said Sandra.

'Of course not,' replied Judith. 'People don't get involved in murders every week, do they?'

'Just wondered.'

'What do we *do*?' asked Ruth.

'We do what we're told.' Judith believed passionately in the virtues of authority, and she sometimes wished that Mr Palmer, though he was very nice of course, would be just a little firmer and not quite so friendly with one or two of his employees.

'I saw one once at the pictures,' said Sandra.

'I saw one on the telly,' said Ruth. 'Will it be like that?'

Afterwards they decided it was like that. Disappointing really. A nondescript woman walked along and looked at each of them as they spoke the words, 'Do you know when the next bus is?' You couldn't really be frightened of her. Wouldn't it have been awful, though, if she'd put her hand on your shoulder? But she didn't. She'd walked past all the girls and then walked back and then walked off. That Inspector – he'd been hoping, hadn't he? And that was a bit funny at the end, wasn't it? Running to the door at the far end of the yard. What was that all about?

'They got the crook in the picture,' said Sandra.

'And on the telly,' said Ruth.

'You shouldn't believe all you see,' said Judith.

Morse was sitting in his office at midday, when Lewis came in. 'Well, sir? Any good?'

Morse shook his head.

'No good at all?'

'She thought two or three of them might be her.'

'Well, that narrows it down a bit, sir.'

'Not really. I've heard defending counsels make

powdered mincemeat out of witnesses who swore on their grandfathers' graves that they were absolutely *positive* about an identification. No, Lewis. It doesn't help us much, I'm afraid.'

'What about your other idea, sir? You know, the girl had a funny splayed sort of run.'

'Oh, we got them to run all right.'

Lewis sensed he had landed on a sore point. 'No good, sir.' It was a statement, not a question.

'That's right, Lewis. No good. And it might have occurred, it might just have occurred, Lewis, to members of the crime squad, to me, Lewis, and to you, that all girls run in the *same ham-footed bloody way*.' He blasted the last few words at his sergeant, who waited for the hurricane to subside.

'You could do with a pint of beer, sir.'

Morse looked a little happier. 'You may be right.'

'I've got a bit of news, sir.'

'Let's have it.'

'Well, the bus – that's out. I got the driver and conductor of the 6.30 p.m. 4E from Carfax. There were only a dozen or so on the bus anyway, most of them regulars. Our two girls pretty certainly didn't get to Woodstock by bus.'

'We don't know for certain that both of them got to Woodstock anyway,' said Morse.

'But Sylvia got there, didn't she, sir, and the other girl asked for the bus there?'

'I'm beginning to wonder if Mrs Jarman is such a helpful witness, after all.'

'I think she is, because that's only the bad news.'

'You've got some *good* news?' Morse tried to sound a bit more cheerful.

'Well, it's that lorry the old girl told us about. Quite easy really to trace it. You see at Cowley there's this system with car-bodies. When they . . .'

'Yes, I know. You did a sharp job, Lewis. But cut the trimmings.'

'He remembers them. A Mr George Baker – lives in Oxford. And listen to this, sir. He saw the two girls getting into a car. A *red* car – he was sure of that. Chap driving – not a woman. He remembered because he often picks up hitchers, especially if they're girls; and he saw these two just beyond the roundabout – about fifty yards ahead. He would have given them a lift, he said, but this other car pulls up, and he has to pull out to get past. He saw the blonde all right.'

'We're a despicable lot, aren't we?' said Morse. 'Would you have picked them up?'

'I don't usually, sir. Only if they're in uniform. I was glad of a few lifts myself when I was in the Forces.'

Morse reflected carefully on the new evidence. Things were certainly moving.

'What did you say about a pint?'

They sat silently in the White Horse at Kidlington and Morse decided that the beer was drinkable. Finally he broke the silence. 'A red car, eh?'

'Yes, sir.'

'Interesting piece of research for you. How many men in Oxford own red cars?'

'Quite a few, sir.'

'You mean a few thousand.'

'I suppose so.

'But we could find out?'

'I suppose so.'

'Such a problem would not be beyond the wit of our efficient force?'

'I suppose not, sir.'

'But what if he doesn't live in Oxford?'

'Well, yes. There is that.'

'Lewis, I think the beer is dulling your brain.'

But if alcohol was dimming Lewis's intellectual acumen, it had the opposite effect on Morse. His mind began to function with an easy clarity. He ordered Lewis to take the weekend off, to get some sleep, to forget Sylvia Kaye, and to take his wife shopping; and Lewis was happy to do so.

Morse, not an addictive smoker, bought twenty king sized cigarettes and smoked and drank continuously until 2.00 p.m. What had really happened last Wednesday evening? He was tormented by the thought that a sequence of events, not in themselves extraordinary, had taken place; that each event was the logical successor of the one before it; that he knew what one or two of these events had been; that if only his mind could project itself into a series of naturally causal relationships, he would have it all. It needed no startling, visionary leap from ignorance to enlightenment. Just a series of logical progressions. But each progression landed him at a dead end, like the drawings in children's annuals where one thread leads to the treasure

54

and all the others lead to the edge of the page. Start again.

'I'm afraid I shall have to ask you to drink up,' said the landlord.

CHAPTER SEVEN

Saturday, 2 October, p.m.

MORSE SPENT THE afternoon of Saturday, 2 October, sitting mildly drunk in his office. He had smoked his packet of cigarettes by 4.30 p.m. and rang for more. His mind grew clearer and clearer. He thought he saw the vaguest pattern in the events of the evening of Wednesday, 29 September. No names – no idea of names, yet – but a pattern.

He looked through the letters he had copied from the Town and Gown: they seemed a sorry little package. Some he dismissed immediately: not even a deranged psychiatrist could have built the flimsiest hypotheses on five of the nine pieces of evidence. One of the postcards read: 'Dear Ruth, Weather good, went swimming twice yesterday. Saw a dead jellyfish on the beach. Love, T.' How very sad to be a jellyfish, thought Morse. Only three of the communications held Morse's attention; then two; then one. It was a typewritten note addressed to Miss Jennifer Coleby and it read:

Dear Madam,
    After asessing the mny applications we have received, we must regretfully inform you that our application has been unsuccessful. At the begining of

November however, further posts will become
available, and I should, in all honesty, be sorry to loose
the opportunity of reconsidering your position then.

We have now alloted the September quota of
posts in the Psycology Department; yet it is probable
that a reliably qualified assistant may be required to
deal with the routnie duties for the Principal's office.
Yours faithfully,

It was subscribed by someone who did not appear
particularly anxious that his name be shouted from the
house-tops. An initial 'G' was clear enough, but the
surname to which it was floridly appended would have
remained an enigma to the great Champollion himself.

So Miss Jennifer Coleby is after a new job, said Morse
to himself. So what? Hundreds of people applied for
new jobs every day. He sometimes thought of doing so
himself. He wondered why he'd thought the letter
worth a second thought. Typically badly written –
unforgivable misprints. And misspellings. No one in the
schools cared much these days about the bread-and-
butter mechanisms of English usage. He'd been
brought up in the hard school: errors of spelling,
punctuation and construction of sentences had been
savagely penalized by outraged pedagogues, and this
had made its mark on him. He had become pedantic
and fussy and thought back on the ill-written travesty of
a report he had read from one of his own staff only two
days before, when he had mentally totted up the
mistakes like an examiner assessing a candidate's work.
'Asessing.' Yes, that was wrong in this letter – among

other things. The country was becoming increasingly illiterate – for all the fancy notions of the progressive educationalists. But if his own secretary had produced such rubbish, she would be out on her neck – today! But she was exceptional. Julie's initials at the bottom of any letter were the sure imprimatur of a clean and flawless sheet of typing. Just a minute though . . . Morse looked again at the letter before him. No reference at all. Had G. Thingamajig typed it himself? If he had – what was he? A senior administrator of some university department? If he had . . . Morse grew more and more puzzled. Why was there no letter heading? Was he worrying his head over nothing?

Well, there was one way of deciding the issue. He looked at his watch. Already 5.30 p.m. Miss Coleby would probably be at home now, he thought. Where did she live? He looked at Lewis's careful details of the address in North Oxford. An interesting thought? Morse began to realize how many avenues he had not even started to explore. He put on his greatcoat and went out to his car. As he drove the two miles down into Oxford, he resolved that he would rid himself as far as he could of all prejudice against Miss Jennifer Coleby. But it was not an easy thing to do; for, if Mrs Jarman's memory could be trusted, the ambitious Miss Coleby was one of the three girls who may have made the journey to Woodstock that night with the late Miss Sylvia Kaye.

Jennifer Coleby rented, with two other working girls, a semi-detached property in Charlton Road where each paid a weekly rent of £8.25, inclusive of electricity and gas. It meant a fat rake-off of almost £25 a week for the provident landlord who had snapped up two such properties for what now seemed a meagre £6,500 some six years since. But it was also a blessing for three enterprising girls who, for such a manageable outlay, were reasonably happy to share the narrow bathroom and the even narrower lavatory. Each girl had a bed-room (one downstairs), the kitchen was adequate for their evening meals, and all of them used the lounge in which to sit around, to chat and watch TV when they were in. These arrangements, apart from the bathroom, worked surprisingly well. Seldom were the girls in together during the day, and so far they had avoided any major confrontation. The landlord had forbidden men-friends in the bedrooms and the girls had accepted this Diktat without contention. There had, of course, been a few infractions of the ban, but the household had never degenerated into overt promis-cuity. One rule the girls imposed upon themselves – no record players; and for this, at least, their elderly neighbours were profoundly grateful. The house was kept tidy and clean, as Morse immediately saw as the door was opened by a sad girl eating a tomato sandwich.

'I've called to see Miss Coleby, if I may. Is she in?'

Dark, languorous eyes looked at him carefully, and Morse found himself tempted to wink at her.

'Just a minute.' She walked leisurely away, but sud-denly turned her head to ask, 'Who shall I say?'

'Er, Morse. Chief Inspector Morse.'

'Oh.'

A cool, clean-looking Jennifer, dressed in blouse and jeans, came out to greet Morse, without apparent enthusiasm.

'Can I help you, Inspector?'

'I wonder if we could have a few words together? Is it convenient?'

'It will have to be, I suppose. You'd better come in.'

Morse was shown into the lounge, where Miss Dark-eyes sat pretending to be deeply engrossed in a report on the Arsenal v. Tottenham match.

'Sue, this is Inspector Morse. Do you mind if we speak here?'

Sue stood up, and a little too theatrically, thought Morse, switched off the set. He observed her slow, graceful movements and smiled to himself, approvingly. 'I'll be upstairs, Jen.' She glanced at Morse before she left, saw the incipient smile at the corners of his mouth and afterwards swore to Jennifer that he had winked at her.

Jennifer motioned Morse to sit on the settee, and sat opposite him in an armchair.

'How can I help, Inspector?'

Morse noticed a copy of Charlotte Brontë's *Villette* balancing like a circumflex accent over the arm of her chair.

'I'm having – purely routine, of course – to check the movements of all the er . . . persons . . .'

'Suspects?'

'No, no. Those who worked with Sylvia. You understand that this sort of thing has to be done.'

'Of course. I'm surprised you haven't done it before.' Morse was a little taken aback. Indeed, why *hadn't* he done it before? Jennifer continued. 'Last Wednesday evening, I got home a bit later than usual – I went round Blackwells to spend a book token. It was my birthday last week. I got home about six, I should think. You know what the traffic's like in the rush hour.' Morse nodded. 'Well, I had a bit to eat – the other girls were here – and went out about, let's see, about half past six I should think. I got back about eight – perhaps a bit later.'

'Can you tell me where you went?'

'I went to the Summertown library.'

'What time does the library close?'

'Seven-thirty.'

'You spent about an hour there.'

'That seems to be a reasonable conclusion, Inspector.'

'It seems a long time. I usually spend about two minutes.'

'Perhaps you're not very fussy what you read.'

That's a point, thought Morse. Jennifer spoke with an easy, clear diction. A good education, he thought. But there was more than that. There was a disciplined independence about the girl, and he wondered how she got on with men. He thought it would be difficult to make much headway with this young lady – unless, of course, *she* wanted to. She could, he suspected, be very nice indeed.

'Are you reading that?'

She laid a delicately manicured hand lightly upon *Villette*. 'Yes. Have you read it?'

''Fraid not,' confessed Morse.

'You should do.'

'I'll try to remember,' muttered Morse. Who was

supposed to be conducting this interview? 'Er, you stayed an hour?'

'I've told you that.'

'Did anyone see you there?'

'They'd have a job not to, wouldn't they?'

'Yes, I suppose they would.' Morse felt he was losing his way. 'Did you get anything else out?' He suddenly felt a bit better.

'You'll be interested to know that I got that as well.' She pointed to a large volume, also lying open, on the carpet in front of the TV set. 'Mary's started to read it.' Morse picked it up and looked at the title. *Who was Jack the Ripper?*

'Mm.'

'I'm sure you've read that.'

Morse's morale began to sag again. 'I don't think I've read that particular account, no.'

Jennifer suddenly smiled. 'I'm sorry, Inspector. I'm very much of a bookworm myself, and I have far more spare time than you, I'm sure.'

'Coming back to Wednesday a minute, Miss Coleby. You say you were back about eight.'

'Yes, about then. It could have been quarter past, even half past, I suppose.'

'Was anyone in when you got back?'

'Yes. Sue was in. But Mary had gone off to the pictures. *Day of the Jackal* I think it was; she didn't get back until eleven.'

'I see.'

'Shall I ask Sue to come down?'

'No. No need to bother.' Morse realized he was

probably wasting his time, but he stuck it out. 'How long does it take to walk to the library?'

'About ten minutes.'

'But it took you almost an hour, perhaps, if you didn't get back until eight-thirty?'

Again the pleasant smile, the regular white teeth, a hint of gentle mockery around the lips. 'Inspector, I think we'd better ask Sue if she remembers the time, don't you?'

'Perhaps we should,' said Morse.

When Jennifer left the room Morse was looking around with sombre, weary eyes, when suddenly a thought flashed through his mind. He was deadly quick as he picked up *Villette*, turned to the inside of the cover and deftly replaced it over the arm of the chair. Sue came in, and quickly confirmed that as far as she could remember Jennifer had been back in the house at some time after eight. She couldn't be more precise. Morse got up to take his leave. He hadn't mentioned the very thing he had come to discuss, and he wasn't going to. That could come later.

He sat for a few minutes in the driving seat of his car and his blood ran hot and cold. He had not quite been able to believe his eyes. But he'd seen it in black and white, or rather dark blue on white.

Morse knew the Oxford library routine only too well, for he rarely returned his own irregular borrowings without having to pay a late fine. The library worked in weeks, not days, for books borrowed, and the day that every 'week' began was Wednesday. If a book was borrowed on a Wednesday, the date for return was exactly

14 days later – that Wednesday fortnight. If a book was borrowed on Thursday, the date for return was a fortnight after the following Wednesday, 20 days later. The date-stamp was changed each Thursday morning. This working from Wednesday to Wednesday simplified matters considerably for the library assistants and was warmly welcomed by those borrowers who found seven or eight hundred pages an excessive assignment inside just fourteen days. Morse would have to check, of course, but he felt certain that only those who borrowed books on Wednesday had to return books within the strict 14-day limit. Anyone taking out a book *on any other day* would have a few extra days' grace. If Jennifer Coleby had taken *Villette* from the library on Wednesday last, the date-stamp for return would have read Wednesday, 13 October. But it didn't. *It read Wednesday, 20 October.* Morse knew beyond any reasonable doubt that Jennifer had lied to him about her movements on the night of the murder. And why? To that vital question there seemed one very simple answer.

Morse sat still in his car outside the house. From the corner of his eye he saw the lounge curtain twitch slightly, but he could see no one. Whoever it was, he decided to let things stew a while longer. He could do with a breath of fresh air, anyway. He locked the car doors and sauntered gently down the road, turned left into the Banbury Road and walked more briskly now towards the library. He timed himself carefully: nine and a half minutes. Interesting. He walked up to the library door marked PUSH. But it didn't push. The library had closed its doors two hours ago.

CHAPTER EIGHT

Saturday, 2 October

BERNARD CROWTHER'S WIFE, Margaret, disliked the weekends, and effected her household management in such a way that neither her husband nor her twelve-year-old daughter nor her ten-year-old son enjoyed them very much either. Margaret had a part-time job in the School of Oriental Studies, and suspected that throughout the week she put in more hours of solid work than her gentle, bookish husband and her idle, selfish offspring put together. The weekend, *they* all assumed, was a time of well-earned relaxation; but they didn't think of her. 'What's for breakfast, mum?' 'Isn't dinner ready yet?' Besides which, she did her week's wash on Saturday afternoons and tried her best to clean the house on Sundays. She sometimes thought that she was going mad.

At 5.30 on the afternoon of Saturday, 2 October, she stood at the sink with bitter thoughts. She had cooked poached eggs for tea ('What, again?') and was now washing up the sticky yellow plates. The children were glued to the television and wouldn't be bored again for an hour or so yet. Bernard (she ought to be thankful for small mercies) was cutting the privet hedge at the back of the house. She knew how he hated gardening, but that was one thing she was *not* going to do. She wished he would get a move on. The meticulous care he devoted to each square foot of the wretched hedge exasperated her. He'd be in soon to say his arms were aching. She looked at him. He was balding now and getting stout, but he was still, she supposed, an attractive man to some women. Until recently she had never regretted that she had married him fifteen years ago. Did she regret the children? She wasn't sure. From the time they were in arms she had been worried by her inability to gossip in easy, cosy terms with other mums about the precious little darlings. She had read a book on Mothercraft and came to the worrying conclusion that much of motherhood was distasteful to her – even nauseating. Her maternal instincts, she decided, were sadly underdeveloped. As the children grew into toddlers, she had enjoyed them more, and on occasion she had only little difficulty in convincing herself that she loved them both dearly. But now they seemed to be getting older and worse. Thoughtless, selfish and cheeky. Perhaps it was all her fault – or Bernard's. She looked out again as she stacked the last of the plates upright on the draining rack.

It was already getting dusk after another glorious day. She wondered, like the bees, if these warm days would never cease ... Bernard had managed to advance the neatly clipped and rounded hedge by half a foot in the last five minutes. She wondered what he was thinking about, but she knew that she couldn't ask him.

The truth was, and Margaret had descried it dimly

for several years now, that they were drifting apart. Was that her fault, too? Did Bernard realize it? She thought he did. She wished she could leave him, leaving everything and go off somewhere and start a new life. But of course she couldn't. She would have to stick it out. Unless something tragic happened – or was it *until* something tragic happened? And then she knew she would stand by him – in spite of everything.

Margaret wiped the formica tops around the sink, lit a cigarette and went to sit in the dining-room. She just could not face the petty arguments and the noise in the lounge. She picked up the book Bernard had been reading that afternoon, *The Collected Works of Ernest Dowson*. The name was vaguely familiar to her from her school-certificate days and she turned slowly through the poems until she found the lines her class had been made to learn. She was surprised how well she could recall them:

> I cried for madder music and for stronger wine,
> But when the feast is finish'd and the lamps expire,
> Then falls thy shadow, Cynara! the night is thine;
> And I am desolate and sick of an old passion,
>   Yea, hungry for the lips of my desire:
> I have been faithful to thee, Cynara! in my fashion.

She read them again and for the first time seemed to catch the rhythm of their magical sound. But what did they *mean*? Forbidden fruits, a sort of languorous, illicit, painful delight. Of course, Bernard could tell her all about it. He spent his life exploring and expounding the beautiful world of poetry. But he wouldn't tell her because she couldn't ask.

It must have been an awful strain for Bernard meeting another woman once a week. How long had she known? Well, for certain, no more than a month or so. But in a strangely intuitive way, much longer than that. Six months? A year? Perhaps more. Not with that particular girl, but there may have been others. Her head was aching. But she'd taken so many codeine recently. Oh, let it ache! What a mess! Her mind was going round and round. Privet hedge, poached eggs, Ernest Dowson, Bernard, the tension and deceit of the past four days. My God! What was she going to do? It couldn't go on like this.

Bernard came in. 'My poor arms don't half ache!'

'Finished the hedge?'

'I'll finish it off in the morning. It's those abhorrèd shears. I shouldn't think they've been sharpened since we moved here.'

'You could always take them in.'

'And get 'em back in about six months.'

'You exaggerate.'

'I'll get it finished in the morning.'

'It'll probably be raining.'

'Well, we could do with a drop of rain. Have you seen the lawn? It's like the plains of Abyssinia.'

'You're never been to Abyssinia.'

The conversation dropped. Bernard went to his desk and took out some papers. 'I thought you'd be watching the telly.'

'I can't stick being with the children.'

Bernard looked at her sharply. She was near to tears. 'No,' he said. 'I know what you mean.' He looked soberly and almost tenderly at Margaret. Margaret, his wife! Sometimes he treated her so thoughtlessly, so very thoughtlessly. He walked across and laid a hand on her shoulder.

'They're pretty insufferable, aren't they? But don't worry about it. All kids are the same. I'll tell you what . . .'

'Oh, don't bother! You've made all those promises before. I don't care. I don't care, I tell you. As far as I'm concerned they can go to hell – and you with them!'

She began to sob convulsively and ran from the room. He heard her go into their bedroom above, and listened as the sobs continued. He put his head in his hands. He would have to do something, and he would have to do it very soon. He was in real danger now of losing everything. He might even have lost it already . . . Could he tell Margaret everything? She would never, never forgive him. What about the police? He'd almost told them, or, at least, he'd almost told them part of it. He looked down at Dowson's works and saw where the page was open. He knew that Margaret had been reading it and his eyes fell upon the same poem:

Surely the kisses of her bought red mouth were sweet;
But I was desolate and sick of an old passion,
    When I awoke and found the dawn was gray:
I have been faithful to thee, Cynara, in my fashion.

Yes, it had been sweet enough, it would be dishonest to pretend otherwise; but how sour it tasted now. It would have been a huge relief to have ended it all long ago, above all to have broken free from the web of lies and deceit he had spun around himself. Yet how beguiling had been the prospect of those extra-marital delights. Conscience. Damned conscience. Nurtured in a sensitive school. Fatal.

Though not a believer himself, Bernard conceded the empirical truth of the Pauline assertion that the wages of sin is death. He wanted desperately to be rid of the guilt and the remorse, and remembered vaguely from his school days in the bible-class how lustily they had all given voice to many a chorus on sin:

> Though your sins be as scarlet, scarlet, scarlet,
> They shall be whiter, yea whiter than snow.

But he couldn't pray these days – his spirit was parched and desolate. His primitive, eager religiosity was dulled now and overlaid with a deep and hard veneer of learning, culture and cynicism. He was well rehearsed in all the theological paradoxes, and the fizz of academic controversy was no longer a delight. Whiter than snow, indeed! More like the driven slush.

He walked over to the window which looked out on to the quiet road. Lights shone in most of the windows. A few people walked past; a neighbour was taking his dog to foul some other pavement. An L-driver was struggling to turn her car around, and was painfully succeeding, though the line of symmetry through MAC's Self-drive Zodiac rarely progressed more than seven or eight degrees at any one manoeuvre. More like a thirty-three point turn, he thought. The instructor must be a patient chap. He had tried to teach Margaret to drive once ... Still, he had made up for that. She had her own Mini now. He watched for several minutes. A man walked by, but though he thought he seemed familiar, Bernard didn't recognize him. He wondered who he was and where he was going, and kept him in sight until he turned right into Charlton Road.

As Morse had walked past, he too was wondering what to do. Best have it out with Jennifer now? He didn't know, but he thought on the whole it was. Conscious that he had not covered himself with glory at the earlier interview, he decided mentally to rehearse his new approach.

'You want to ask me some more questions?'

'Yes.' Tight-lipped and masterly.

'Won't you come in?'

'Yes.'

'Well?'

'Thus far you've told me nothing but a pack of lies. I suggest we start again.'

'I don't know what you're talking about ...' Slowly and pointedly he would get up from the chair and walk towards the door. He would utter not one further word.

But as he opened the door, Jennifer would say, 'All right, Inspector.' And he would listen. He thought he had a good idea of what she would tell him.

That he would have been wrong, he was not to learn for some time yet; for he discovered that Jennifer had gone out. The languid Sue, her long legs bronzed and bare, had no idea where she had gone. 'Won't you come in and wait, Inspector?' The full lips parted and quivered slightly. Morse both looked and felt alarmingly vulnerable. He consulted his wrist-watch for moral support. 'You're very kind but . . . perhaps I'd better not.'

CHAPTER NINE

Sunday, 3 October

MORSE SLEPT SOUNDLY for almost twelve hours, and
awoke at 8.30 a.m. He had returned home immediately
after his second call to Charlton Road with a splitting
headache and a harassed mind. Now, as he blinked
awake, he could scarcely believe how fresh he felt.

The last book Morse himself had taken from the
library and which now lay, three weeks overdue, on his
writing desk, was Edward de Bono's *A Five-Day Course in
Lateral Thinking.* He had followed the course conscien-
tiously, refused to look at any of the answers in advance,
and reluctantly concluded that even the most sympa-
thetic assessment of his lateral potential was gamma
minus minus. But he had enjoyed it. Moreover he had
learned that a logical, progressive, 'vertical' assault
upon a sticky problem might not always be the best. He
had not really understood some of the jargon too well,
but he had grasped the substantial points. 'How can
one drive a car up a dark alley if the headlights are not
working?' It didn't matter what the answer was. The
thing to do was to suggest *anything* a driver might
conceivably do: blow the horn, take the roof rack off,
lift the bonnet up. It didn't matter. The mere contemplation of futile solutions was itself a potent force in

reaching the right conclusion: for sooner or later one would turn on a blinker and, hey presto!, the light would dawn. In an amateurish way Morse had tried out this technique and had surprised himself. If a name was on the tip of his tongue, he stopped thinking directly about it, and merely repeated anything he knew – the state capitals of the USA – anything; and it seemed to work.

As he lay awake he decided temporarily to shelve the murder of Sylvia Kaye. He was making progress – he knew that. But his mind lacked incision; it was going a bit stale. With a rest today (and he'd deserved one) he'd be back on mental tip-toe in the morning.

He got up, dressed and shaved, cooked himself a succulent looking mixture of bacon, tomatoes and mushrooms, and felt good. He ran a leisurely eye through the Sunday papers, checked his pools, wondered if he was the only man in England who had picked in his 'any eight from sixteen' permutation not a single score-draw, and lit a cigarette. He would sit and idle the time away until noon, have a couple of pints and get lunch out somewhere. It seemed a civilized prospect. But he was never happy without something to do, and before long was mentally debating whether to put some Wagner on the record player or do a crossword. Crosswords were a passion with Morse, although since the death of the great Ximenes he had found few composers to please his taste. On the whole he enjoyed the *Listener* puzzles as much as any, and for this purpose took the periodical each week. On the other hand he delighted in Wagnerian opera and had the complete cycle of *The Ring*. He decided to do both, and to the opening bars of the richly scored Prelude to *Das Rheingold*, he sat back and turned to the penultimate page of the *Listener*. This was the life. The Rhinemaidens swam gracefully to and fro and it was a few minutes before Morse felt willing to let the music drift away to the periphery of his attention. He read the preamble to the crossword:

'Each of the across clues contains, in the definition, a deliberate misprint. Each of the down clues is normal, although the words to be entered in the diagram will contain a misprint of a single letter. Working from 1 across to 28 down the misprinted letters form a well-known quotation which solvers . . .'

Morse read no more. He leapt to his feet. A solo horn expired with a dying groan as he switched off the record player and snatched his car keys from the mantelpiece.

His in-tray was high with reports, but he ignored them. He unlocked his cabinet, took out the file on the Sylvia Kaye murder, and extracted the letter addressed to Jennifer Coleby. He knew there had been something wrong with the whole thing. His mouth was dry and his hand trembled slightly, like a schoolboy opening his O-level results:

Dear Madam,
    After asessing the mny applications we have received, we must regretfully inform you that our

application has been unsuccessful. At the begining of
November however, further posts will become
available, and I should, in all honesty, be sorry to
loose the opportunity of reconsidering your position
then.

   We have now alloted the September quota of
posts in the Psycology Department; yet it is probable
that a reliably qualified assistant may be required to
deal with the routnie duties for the Principal's office.
Yours faithfully,

How wrong-headed he had been! Instead of thinking,
as he had done, with such supercilious arrogance, of
the illiteracy and incompetence of some poor block-
head of a typist, *he should have been thinking exactly the
opposite.* He'd been a fool. The clues were there. The
whole thing was phoney – why hadn't he spotted that
before? When you boiled it down it was a nonsense
letter. He had first made the mistake of concentrating
upon individual mistakes and not even bothering to see
the letter as a synoptic whole. But not only that. He had
compounded his mistake. For if he had read the letter
as a letter, he might have considered the mistakes as
mistakes – *deliberate mistakes.* He took a sheet of paper
and started: 'asessing' – 's' omitted; 'mny' – 'a' omitted;
'begining' – 'n' omitted; 'loose' – 'o' inserted; 'Psycology' – 'h' omitted. SANOH – whatever that signified.
Look again. 'our' – shouldn't it be 'your'? 'y' omitted;
'routnie' – 'n' and 'i' transposed. What did that give
him? SAYNOHNI. Hardly promising. Try once more,
'alloted' – surely two 't's? 't' omitted. And there it was

staring him in the face. The 'G' of course from the signature, the only recognizable letter therein: SAY NOTHING. Someone had been desperately anxious for Jennifer not to say a word – and Jennifer, it seemed, had got the message.

It had taken Morse two minutes, and he was glad that Jennifer had been out the previous evening. He felt sure that faced with her lies about the visit to the library, she would have said how sorry she was and that she must have got it wrong. It must have been Thursday, she supposed; it was so difficult to think back to events of even the day before, wasn't it? She honestly couldn't remember; but she would try very hard to. Perhaps she had gone for a walk – on her own, of course.

But she would find things more awkward now. Strangely Morse felt little sense of elation. He had experienced an odd liking for Jennifer when they had met, and in retrospect he understood how difficult it must have been for her. But he must look the fact squarely in the face. She was lying. She was shielding someone – that someone who in all probability had raped and murdered Sylvia. It was not a pretty thought. Every piece of evidence now pointed unequivocally to the fact that it was Jennifer Coleby who had stood at Fare Stage 5 with Sylvia on the night of the 29th; that it was she who had been given a lift by a person or persons unknown (pretty certainly the former) as far as Woodstock; that there she had witnessed something about which she had been warned to keep her silence. In short that Jennifer Coleby *knew the identity of the man who had murdered Sylvia Kaye.* Morse suddenly wondered if she was in danger, and it was this fear which prompted his immediate decision to have Jennifer held on suspicion of being an accessory to the crime of murder. He would need Lewis in.

He reached for his outside phone and rang his sergeant's home number.

'Lewis?'

'Speaking.'

'Morse here. I'm sorry to ruin your weekend, but I want you here.'

'Straight away, sir?'

'If you can.'

'I'm on my way.'

Morse looked through his in-tray. Reports, reports, reports. He crossed through his own initials immediately, barely glancing at such uncongenial titles as *The Drug Problem in Britain*, *The Police and the Public*, and *The Statistics for Crimes of Violence in Oxfordshire* (second quarter). At the minute he was interested only in one statistic which would doubtless, in time, appear in the statistics of violent crime in Oxfordshire (third quarter). He'd no time for reports. He suspected that about 95% of the written word was never read by anyone anyway. But there were two items which held his attention. A report from the forensic lab on the murder weapon, and a supplementary report from the pathology department on Sylvia Kaye. Neither did more than confirm what he already knew or at any rate suspected. The tyre-lever proved to be a singularly unromantic specimen. Morse read all about its shape, size, weight . . . But why bother? There was no mystery about the lever at all. The landlord of the Black Prince had spent the afternoons of Tuesday, 28th and Wednesday, 29th tinkering with an ancient Sunbeam, and had unwittingly left his tool kit outside the garage on the right at the back of the courtyard where he kept the car. There were no recognizable prints – just the ugly evidence, at one of the lever's curving ends, that it had crashed with considerable force into the bone of a human skull. There followed a gory analysis, which Morse was glad to skip.

It was only a few minutes before Lewis knocked and entered.

'Ah, Lewis. The gods, methinks, have smiled weakly on our inquiries.' He outlined the developments in the case. 'I want Miss Jennifer Coleby brought in for questioning. Be careful. Take Policewoman Fuller with you if you like. Just held for questioning, you understand? There's no question at all of any formal arrest. If she prefers to ring up her legal advisers, tell her it's Sunday and they're all playing golf. But I don't think you'll have much trouble.' On the latter point, at least, Morse guessed correctly.

Jennifer was sitting in interrogation room 3 by 3.45 p.m. On Morse's instructions, Lewis spent an hour with her, making no mention whatever of the information he had been given earlier in the afternoon. Lewis mentioned quietly that, in spite of all their inquiries, they had not been able to trace the young lady, seen by two independent witnesses, who had been with Sylvia Kaye an hour or so before she was murdered.

'You must be patient, Sergeant.'

Lewis smiled weakly, like the gods. 'Oh, we're patient enough, miss, and I think with a little co-operation we shall get there.'

'Aren't you getting any co-operation?'

'Would you like a cup of tea, miss?'

'I'd prefer coffee.'

Policewoman Fuller hurried off; Jennifer moistened her lips and swallowed; Lewis brooded quietly. In the tug-of-war silence which ensued it was Lewis who finally won.

'You think I'm not co-operating, Sergeant?'

'Are you?'

'Look, I've told the Inspector what I know. Didn't he believe me?'

'Just what did you tell the Inspector, miss?'

'You want me to go over all that again?' Jennifer's face showed all the impatience of a schoolgirl asked to rewrite a tedious exercise.

'We shall have to have a signed statement in any case.'

Jennifer sighed. 'All right. You want me to account for my movements – I think that's the phrase, isn't it? – on Wednesday night.'

'That's right, miss.'

'On Wednesday night . . .' Laboriously Lewis began to write. 'Shall I write it out for you?' asked Jennifer.

'I think I ought to get it down myself, miss, if you don't mind. I haven't got a degree in English, but I'll do my best.' A quick flash of caution gleamed in Jennifer's eyes. It was gone immediately, but it had been there and Lewis had seen it.

Half an hour later, Jennifer's statement was ready. She read it, asked if she could make one or two amendments – 'only spelling, Sergeant' – and agreed that she could sign it.

'I'll just get it typed out, miss.'

'How long will that take?'

'Oh, only ten minutes.'

'Would you like me to do it? It'll only take me about two.'

'I think we ought to do it ourselves, miss, if you don't mind. We have our regulations, you know.'

'Just thought I might be able to help.' Jennifer felt more relaxed.

'Shall I get you another cup of coffee, miss?'

'That would be nice.' Lewis got up and left.

Policewoman Fuller seemed singularly uncommunicative, and for more than ten minutes Jennifer sat in silence. When the door finally opened it was Morse who entered carrying a neatly typed sheet of foolscap.

'Good afternoon, Miss Coleby.'

'Good afternoon.'

'We've met before.' The tide of relaxation which had reached high watermark with Lewis's departure quickly ebbed and exposed the grating shingle of her nerves. 'I walked down to the library after I left you yesterday,' continued Morse.

'You must enjoy walking.'

'They tell me walking is the secret of perpetual middle age.'

With an effort, Jennifer smiled. 'It's a pleasant walk, isn't it?'

'It depends which way you go,' said Morse.

Jennifer looked sharply at him and Morse, as Lewis earlier, noted the unexpected reaction. 'Well, I would like to stay and talk to you, but I hope you will let me sign that statement and get back home. There are several things I have to do before tomorrow.'

'I hope Sergeant Lewis mentioned that we have no authority to keep you against your will?'

'Oh yes. The sergeant told me.'

'But I shall be very grateful if you can agree to stay a little longer.'

The back of Jennifer's throat was dry. 'What for?' Her voice was suddenly a little harsher.

'Because,' said Morse quietly, 'I hope you will not be foolish enough to sign a statement which you know to be false' – Morse raised his voice – 'and which I know to be false.' He gave her no chance to reply. 'This afternoon I gave instructions for you to be held for questioning since I suspected, and still suspect, that you are withholding information which may be of very great value in discovering the identity of Miss Kaye's murderer. That is a most serious offence, as you know. It now seems that you are foolish enough to compound such stupidity with the equally criminal and serious offence of supplying the police with information which is not only inaccurate but demonstrably false.' Morse's voice had risen in crescendo and he ended with a mighty thump with his fist upon the table between them.

Jennifer, however, did not appear quite so abashed as he had expected.

'You don't believe what I told you?'

'No.'

'Am I allowed to ask why not?' Morse was more than a little surprised. It was clear to him that the girl had recovered whatever nerve she may have lost. He clearly and patiently told her that she could not possibly have taken out her library books on Wednesday evening, and that this could be proved without any reasonable doubt. 'I see.' Morse waited for her to speak again. If he had been mildly surprised at her previous question, he was flabbergasted by her next. 'What were *you* doing at the time of the murder last Wednesday evening, Inspector?'

What was he doing? He wasn't quite sure, but any such admission would hardly advance his present cause. He lied. 'I was listening to some Wagner.'

'Which Wagner?'

'*Das Rheingold.*'

'Is there anyone who could back up your story? Did anyone see you?'

Morse surrendered. 'No.' In spite of himself, he had to admire the girl. 'No,' he repeated, 'I live on my own. I seldom have the pleasure of visitors – of either sex.'

'How very sad.'

Morse nodded. 'Yes. But you see, Miss Coleby, I am not as yet suspected of dressing up in women's clothes and standing at the top of the Woodstock Road hitching a lift with Sylvia Kaye.'

'And *I* am?'

'And you are.'

'But presumably I'm not suspected of raping and murdering Sylvia?'

'I hope you will allow me a modicum of intelligence.'

'You don't understand.'

'What's that supposed to mean?'

'Hasn't it occurred to you that Sylvia probably enjoyed being raped?' There was bitterness in her tone, and her cheeks were flushed.

'That seems to assume that she was raped *before* she died, doesn't it?' said Morse quietly.

'I'm sorry – that was a horrid thing to say.'

Morse followed up his advantage. 'My job is to discover what happened from the moment Sylvia and her friend – *and I believe that was you* – got into a red car on the other side of the Woodstock roundabout. For some reason this other girl has not come forward, and I don't think the reason's very hard to find. *She knew the driver of the car,* and she's protecting him. She's probably frightened stiff. But so was Sylvia Kaye frightened stiff, Miss Coleby. More than that. She was so savagely struck on the back of the head that her skull was broken in several places and lumps of bone were found in her brain. Do you like the sound of that? It's an ugly, horrible sight is murder and the trouble with murder is that it usually tends to wipe out the only good witness of the crime – the victim. That means we've got to rely on other witnesses, normal ordinary people most of them, who accidentally get caught up at some point in the wretched business. They get scared; OK. They'd rather not get mixed up in it; OK. They think it's none of their business, OK – but we've got to rely on some of them having enough guts and decency to come forward and tell us what they know. And that's why you're here, Miss Coleby. I've got to know the truth.'

He took the statement that Jennifer had made and tore it into pieces. But he could not read her mind. As he had been speaking she had been gazing through the window of the little office into the outside yard, where the day before she had stood with her office colleagues.

'Well?'

'I'm sorry, Inspector. I must have caused you a lot of trouble. It was on Thursday that I went to the library.'

'And on Wednesday?'

'I did go out. And I did go on the road to Woodstock – but I didn't get as far as Woodstock. I stopped at the Golden Rose at Begbroke – that's what, about two miles this side of Woodstock. I went into the lounge and bought a drink – a lager and lime. I drank it out in the garden and then went home.'

Morse looked at her impatiently. 'In the dark, I suppose.'

'Yes. About half past seven.'

'Well – go on.'

'What do you mean – "go on"? That was all.'

'Do you want me to . . .' began Morse, his voice fuming. 'Fetch Lewis!' he barked. Policewoman Fuller read the gale warning and hurried out.

Jennifer appeared untroubled, and Morse's anger subsided.

It was Jennifer who broke the silence. 'You mustn't be too angry with me, Inspector.' Her voice had become little more than a whisper. Her hand went to her forehead and for a while she closed her eyes. Morse looked at her closely for the first time. He had not noticed before how attractive she could be. She wore a light-blue summer coat over a black jumper, with gloves in matching black. Her cheek bones were high and there was animation in her face, her mouth slightly open revealing the clean lines of her white teeth. Morse wondered if he could ever fall for her, and decided, as usual, that he could.

'I've been so flustered, and so frightened.'

He had to lean forward slightly to catch her words. He noticed that Lewis had come in and motioned him silently to a chair.

'Everything will be all right, you see.' Morse looked at Lewis and nodded as the sergeant prepared to take down the second draft of the evidence of Miss Jennifer Coleby.

'Why were you frightened?' asked Morse gently.

'Well, it's all been so strange – I don't seem to be able to wake up properly since . . . I don't seem to know what's real and what's not. So many funny things seem to be happening.' She was still sitting with her head in her hand, looking blankly at the top of the table. Morse glanced at Lewis. Things were almost ready.

'What do you mean – "funny things"?'

'Just everything really. I'm beginning to wonder if I know what I *am* doing. What am I doing *here*? I thought I'd told you the truth about Wednesday – and now I realize I didn't. And there was another funny thing.' Morse watched her keenly. 'I had a letter on Saturday morning telling me I'd not been chosen for a job – *and I don't even remember applying for it*. Do you think I'm going mad?'

So that was going to be her story! Morse experienced the agony of a bridge player whose ace has just been covered by the deuce of trumps. The two policemen looked at each other, and both were conscious that Jennifer's eyes were on them.

'Well, now.' Morse hid his disappointment and disbelief as well as he was able. 'Let's just get back to Wednesday night, shall we? Can you repeat what you just told me? I want Sergeant Lewis to get it down.' His voice sounded exasperated.

Jennifer repeated her brief statement and Lewis, like the Inspector before him, looked temporarily bewildered.

'You mean,' said Morse, 'that Miss Kaye went on to Woodstock, but that you only went as far as Begbroke?'

'Yes, that's exactly what I mean.'

'You asked this man to drop you at Begbroke?'

'What man are you talking about?'

'The man who gave you a lift.'

'But I didn't get a lift to Begbroke.'

'You *what?*' shrieked Morse.

'I said I didn't get a lift. I would never hitch-hike anyway. I think you ought to know something, Inspector. *I've got a car.*'

While Lewis was getting the second statement typed, Morse retreated to his office. Had he been wrong all along? If what Jennifer now claimed was true, it would certainly account for several things. On the same road, on the same night and one of her own office friends murdered? Of course she would feel frightened. But was that enough to account for her repeated evasions? He reached for the phone and rang the Golden Rose at Begbroke. The jovial-sounding landlord was anxious to help. His wife had been on duty in the lounge on Wednesday. Could she possibly come down to Kidlington Police HQ? Yes. The landlord would drive her himself. Good. Quarter of an hour, then.

'Do you remember a young lady coming in to the lounge last Wednesday? On her own? About half past seven time?'

The richly ringed and amply bosomed lady wasn't sure.

'But you don't often get women coming in alone, do you?'

'Not often, no. But it's not all *that* unusual these days, Inspector. You'd be surprised.'

Morse felt that little would surprise him any more. 'Would you recognize someone like that? Someone who just dropped in one night?'

'I think so, yes.'

Morse rang Lewis, who was still waiting with Jennifer in the interview room.

'Take her home, Lewis.'

The landlady of the Golden Rose stood beside Morse at the inquiry desk as Jennifer walked past with Lewis.

'That her?' he asked. It was his penultimate question.

'Yes. I think it is.'

'I'm most grateful to you,' lied Morse.

'I'm glad I could help, Inspector.'

Morse showed her to the door. 'I don't suppose you happen to remember what she ordered, do you?'

'Well, as a matter of fact, I think I do, Inspector. It was lager and lime, I think. Yes, lager and lime.'

It was half an hour before Lewis returned. 'Did you believe her, sir?'

'No,' said Morse. He felt more frustrated than depressed. He realized that he had already landed himself in a good deal of muddle and mess by his own inadequacies. He had refused the offer of the auxiliary personnel available to him, and this meant that few of the many possible leads had yet been checked and documented. Sanders, for example – surely to any trained officer the most obvious target for immediate and thorough investigation – he had thus far almost totally ignored. Indeed, even a superficial scrutiny of his conduct of the case thus far would reveal a haphazardness in his approach almost bordering upon negligence. Only the previous month he had himself given a lecture to fellow detectives on the paramount importance in any criminal investigation of the strictest and most disciplined thoroughness in every respect of the inquiry *from the very beginning*.

And yet, for all this, he sensed in some intuitive way (a procedure not mentioned in his lecture) that he was vaguely on the right track still; that he had been right in allowing Jennifer to go; that although his latest shot had been kicked off the line, sooner or later the goal would come.

For the next hour the two officers exchanged notes on the afternoon's interrogation, with Morse impatiently probing Lewis's reaction to the girl's evasions, glances, and gestures.

'Do you think she's lying, Lewis?'

'I'm not so sure now.'

'Come off it, man. When you're as old as I am you'll recognize a liar a mile off!'

Lewis remained doubtful: he was by several years the older man anyway. Silence fell between them.

'Where do we go from here, then?' said Lewis at last.

'I think we attack down the other flank.'

'We do?'

'Yes. She's shielding a man. Why? Why? That's what we've been asking ourselves so far. And you know where we've got with that line of inquiry? Nowhere. She's lying, I know that; but we haven't broken her – not yet. She's such a good liar she'd get any damned fool to believe her.'

Lewis saw the implication. 'You could be wrong, sir.'

Morse blustered on, wondering if he was. 'No, no, no. We've just been tackling the case from the wrong angle. They tell me, Lewis, that you can climb up the Eiger in your carpet slippers if you go the easy way.'

'You mean we've been trying to solve this the hard way?'

'No. I mean just the opposite. We've been trying to solve it the easy way. Now we've got to try the hard way.'

'How do we do that, sir?'

'We've been trying to find out who the other girl was, because we thought she could lead us to the man we want.'

'But according to you we *have* found her.'

'Yes. But she's too clever for us – and too loyal. She's been warned to keep her mouth shut – not that she needed much telling, if I'm any judge. But we're up against a brick wall for the time being, and there's only one alternative. The girl won't lead us to the man? All right. We find the man.'

'How do we start on that?'

'I think we shall need a bit of Aristotelian logic, don't you?'

'If you say so, sir.'

'I'll tell you all about it in the morning,' said Morse.

Lewis paused as he reached the door. 'That identification of Miss Coleby, sir. Did you think it was satisfactory – just to take the landlady's word for it?'

'Why not?'

'Well, it was all a bit casual, wasn't it? I mean, it wasn't exactly going by the book.'

'What book?' said Morse.

Lewis decided that his mind had got itself into a quite sufficient muddle for one day, and he left.

Morse's mind, too, was hardly functioning with crystalline lucidity; yet already emerging from the mazed confusion was the germ of a new idea. He had suspected from the start that Jennifer Coleby was lying; would have staked his professional reputation upon it. But he could have been wrong, at least in one respect. He had tried to break Jennifer's story, but had he been trying to break it *at the wrong point?*

What if all she had told him was perfectly true? ... The same revolving pro's and con's passed up and down before his eyes like undulating hobby-horses at a fairground, until his own mind, too, was a dizzying whirl and he knew that it was time to give it all a rest.

CHAPTER TEN

Wednesday, 6 October

THE COCKTAIL LOUNGE of the Black Prince was seldom busy for the hour after opening time at 11.00 a.m., and the morning of Wednesday, 6 October, was to prove no exception. The shockwave of the murder was now receding and the Black Prince was quickly returning to normality.

It was amazing how quickly things sank into the background, thought Mrs Gaye McFee as she polished another martini glass and stacked it neatly among its fellows. But not really; only that morning an incoming air-liner had crashed at Heathrow with the loss of seventy-nine lives. And every day on the roads . . .

'What'll it be, boys?' The speaker was a distinguished-looking man, about sixty years old, thick set, with silvery-grey hair and a ruddy complexion. Gaye had served him many times before and knew him to be Professor Tompsett (Felix to his friends, who were rumoured not to be legion) – emeritus Professor of Elizabethan Literature at Oxford University, and the recently retired Vice-Principal of Lonsdale College. His two companions, one a gaunt, bearded man in his late twenties, the other a gentle-looking bespectacled man of about forty-five, each ordered gin and tonic.

'Three gin and tonics.' Tompsett had an incisive, imperative voice, and Gaye wondered if he got his college scout to stir his morning coffee.

'Hope you're going to enjoy life with us, young Melhuish!' Tompsett laid a broad hand on his bearded companion's shoulder, and was soon engrossed in matters which Gaye was no longer able to follow. A group of American servicemen had come in and were losing no time in quizzing her about the brands of lager, the menu, the recent murder, and her home address. But she enjoyed Americans, and was soon laughing good-naturedly with them. As usual, the lager-pump was producing more froth than liquid substance and Gaye noticed, waiting patiently at the other end of the bar, the bespectacled member of the Oxford triumvirate.

'Shan't be a second, sir.'

'Don't worry. I'm in no great rush.' He smiled quietly at her, and she saw the glimmer of a twinkle in his dark eyes, and she hurriedly squared the account with the neighbourly Americans.

'Now, sir.'

'We'd all like the same again, please. Three gins and tonics.' Gaye looked at him with interest. The landlord had once told her that if anyone ordered 'gins and tonics' instead of the almost universal 'gin and tonics' – he really *was* a don. She wished he would speak again, for she liked the sound of his voice with its sarft Glarcestershire accent. But he didn't. Nevertheless, she stayed at his end of the bar and lightly repolished the martini glasses.

'Whatawe done to you, honeybunch?' and similar endearing invitations emanated regularly from her other clients, but Gaye quietly and tactfully declined their ploys; she watched instead the man from Gloucestershire. Tompsett was in full flow.

'He didn't even go to my inaugural when he was up. What do you think of that, Peter, old boy.'

'Don't blame him really,' said Peter. 'We all sit and salivate over our own prose, Melhuish, and we kid ourselves it's bloody marvellous.'

The Professor of Elizabethan Literature laughed good-humouredly and half-drained his glass. 'Been here before, Melhuish?'

'No, I haven't. Rather nice, isn't it?'

'Bit notorious now, you know. Murder here last week.'

'Yes, I read about it.'

'Young blonde. Raped and murdered, right in the yard out there. Pretty young thing – if the newspapers are anything to go by.'

Melhuish, newly appointed junior fellow at Lonsdale, very bright and very anxious, was beginning to feel a little more at home with his senior colleagues.

'Raped, too, was she?'

Tompsett drained his glass. 'So they say. But I've always been a bit dubious myself about this rape business.'

'Confucius, he say girl with skirt up, she run faster than man with trousers down, eh?'

The two older men smiled politely at the tired old joke, but Melhuish wished he hadn't repeated it: off-key, over-familiar. Gaye heard the clear voice of Tompsett rescuing the conversation. He was no fool, she thought.

'Yes, I agree with you, Melhuish. We mustn't get too serious about rape. God, no. Happens every day. I remember a couple of years back there was a young gal here – you'd remember her, Peter – quick, clear mind, good worker, marvellous kid. She was taking Finals and had eight three-hour papers. She'd done her seventh paper on the Thursday morning – no it was the Friday, or was it . . . but that's beside the point. She took her last but one paper in the morning with just one more fence to jump in the afternoon. Well, she went off to her digs out at Headington for lunch and – begger me! – she got raped on her way back. Just think of the shock for the poor lass. You remember, Peter? Anyway, she insisted on taking the last paper and do you know, Melhuish – she did better on the last paper than she'd done on all the others!'

Melhuish laughed heartily and took the empty glasses.

'You make it up as you go along,' muttered Peter.

'Well, it was a good story, wasn't it?' said Tompsett.

Gaye lost the thread of their talk for a few minutes, and when she picked it up again, it was clear that the conversation had taken a slightly more serious turn. They always said that gin was a depressant.

'. . . not necessarily raped *before* being murdered, you know.'

'Oh, shut up, Felix.'

'Bit revolting, I know. But we all read the Christie business, didn't we? Wicked old bugger, he was!'

'Do they think that's what happened here?' asked Melhuish.

'Do you know, I might have been able to tell you that,' said Tompsett. 'Old Morse – good chap! – he's in charge of the case, and we've had him at the college guest-evenings. He was invited tonight, but he had to cry off. Had a minor accident.' Tompsett laughed. 'Fell off a ladder! Christ, who'd ever believe it? Here's a chap in charge of a murder inquiry and he falls off a bloody ladder!' Tompsett was highly amused.

The Americans had renounced all hope and the bar had emptied now. The three men walked across to the table by the window.

'Well, we'd better see what they can offer us for lunch,' said Peter. 'I'll get the menu.'

Gaye held out a large expensive-looking folder and presented it, already opened, like a neophyte offering the collect for the day to an awesome priest.

Peter looked through quickly, a gentle cynicism showing on his face. He looked up at Gaye and found her watching him. 'Do you recommend "Don's Delight" or "Proctor's Pleasure"?' He asked it in an undertone.

'I shouldn't have the steak if I were you,' her voice as quiet as his.

'Are you free this afternoon?'

She weighed up the situation for several seconds before nodding her head, almost imperceptibly.

'What time shall I pick you up?'

'Three o'clock?'

'Where?'

'I'll be just outside.'

At four o'clock the two lay side by side in the ample double-bed in Peter's rooms in Lonsdale College. His left arm was around her neck, his right hand gently caressing her breasts.

'Do you believe a young girl can get raped?' he asked.

Gaye considered the problem. Contented in mind and in body, she lay for a while contemplating the ornate ceiling. 'It must be jolly difficult for the man.'

'Mm.'

'Have you ever raped a woman?'

'I could rape you, any day of the week.'

'But I wouldn't let you. I wouldn't put up any resistance.'

He kissed her full lips again, she turned eagerly towards him.

'Peter,' she whispered in his ear, 'rape me again!'

The phone blared suddenly, shrill and urgent in the quiet room. Blast!

'Oh, hullo Bernard. What? No. Sitting idling, you know. What? Oh, tonight. Yes. Well, about seven, I think. Why not call in for me? We can have a quick drink together. Yes. Felix? Oh, he's well tanked-up already. Yes. Yes. Well, look forward to it. Yes. Bye.'

'Who's Bernard?'

'Oh, he's an English don here. Good chap. Pretty bad sense of timing, though.'

'Does he have a set of rooms like this?'

'No, no. He's a family man is Bernard. Lives up in North Oxford. Quiet chap.'

'*He* doesn't rape young girls then?'

'What, Bernard? Good lord, no. Well, I don't think so . . .'

'You're a quiet man, Peter.'

'Me?' She fondled him lovingly, and abruptly terminated all further discussion of Mr Bernard Crowther, quiet family man of North Oxford.

PART TWO

Search for a man

CHAPTER ELEVEN

Wednesday, 6 October

BEGINNING ITS LIFE under a low (Head Room 12 ft) railway bridge, and proceeding its cramped and narrow way for several hundred yards past shabby rows of terraced houses that line the thoroughfare in tight and mean confinement, the Botley Road gradually broadens into a spacious stretch of dual carriageway that carries all west-bound traffic towards Faringdon, Swindon and the sundry hamlets in between. Here the houses no longer shoulder their neighbours in such grudging proximity, and hither several of the Oxford businessmen have brought their premises.

Chalkley and Sons is a sprawling, two-storeyed building, specializing in household fittings, tiling, wallpaper, paint and furniture. It is a well-established store, patronized by many of the carpenters (discount), the interior decorators (discount), and almost all the do-it-yourselfers from Oxford. At the furthest end of the ground floor show rooms there is a notice informing the few customers who have not yet discovered the fact that the Formica Shop is outside, over the yard, second on the left.

In this shop a young man is laying a large sheet of formica upon a wooden table, a table which has a deep, square groove cut longitudinally through its centre. He pulls towards him, along its smoothly running gliders, a small automatic saw, and carefully lines up its wickedly polished teeth against his pencilled mark. Deftly he flicks out a steel ruler and checks his measurement. He appears content with a rapid mental calculation, snaps a switch and, amid a grating whirr, slices through the tough fabric with a clean and deadly swiftness. He enjoys that swiftness! Several times he repeats the process: lengthways, sideways, narrowly, broadly, and stacks the measured strips neatly against the wall. He looks at his watch; it is almost 12.45 p.m. An hour and a quarter. He locks the sliding doors behind him, repairs to the staff wash-room, soaps his hands, combs his hair and, with little regret, temporarily turns his back upon the premises of Mr Chalkley and his sons. He pats a little package which bulges slightly in the right-hand pocket of his overcoat. Still there.

Although his immediate destination is no more than ten minutes' walk away, he decides to take a bus. He crosses the road and traverses in the process as many lines, continuous, broken, broad, narrow, yellow, white, as one may find in the key to an Ordnance Survey map; for the Oxford City Council has escalated its long war of attrition against the private motorist and has instituted a system of bus lanes along the Botley Road. A bus arrives almost immediately, and the dour Pakistani one-man crew silently discharges his manifold duties. The young man always hopes that the bus is fairly full so that he may sit beside one of the mini-skirted, knee-booted young girls returning to the city; but today it is almost empty. He sits down and looks mechanically around him.

He alights at the stop before the railway bridge (where the bus must make a right-hand detour to avoid a scalping from the iron girders), threads his way to a dingy street behind the shabby rows of houses, and enters a small shop. The legend above the door of Mr Baines's grimy, peeling shop-front reads 'Newsagent and Tobacconist'. But such is the nature of Mr Baines's establishment that he employs no cohorts of cheeky boys and girls to deliver his morning and evening newspapers, nor does his stock of tobacco run to more than half a dozen of the more popular brands of cigarettes. He sells neither birthday cards nor ice-cream nor confectionery. Mr Baines – yes, he is a shrewd man – calculates that he can make as much profit from one swift, uncomplicated transaction as from the proceeds of one day's paper rounds, or from the sale of a thousand cigarettes. For Mr Baines is a dealer in hard pornography.

Several customers are standing along the right-hand side of the narrow shop. They flick their way through a bewildering variety of gaudy, glossy girlie magazines, with names that ring with silken ecstasies: *Skin* and *Skirt* and *Lush* and *Lust* and *Flesh* and *Frills*. Although the figures of the scantily clad models which adorn the covers of these works are fully and lewdly provocative, the browsers appear to riffle the pages with a careless, casual boredom. But this is the appearance only. A notice, in Mr Baines's own hand, warns every potential purveyor of these exotic fruits that 'the books are to be bought'; and Mrs Baines sits on her hard stool behind the counter and keeps her hard eyes upon each of her committed clients. The young man throws no more than a passing glance at the gallery of thrusting naked-ness upon his right and walks directly to the counter. He asks, audibly, for a packet of twenty Embassy and slides his package across to Mrs Baines; which lady, in her turn, reaches beneath the counter and passes forward a similar brown-paper parcel to the young man. How Mr Baines himself would approve! It is a single, swift, uncomplicated transaction.

The young man stops at the Bookbinder's Arms across the road and orders bread and cheese and a pint of Guinness. He feels his usual nagging impatience, but gloats inwardly in expectation. Five o'clock will soon be here and the journey to Woodstock is infinitely quicker now, with the opening of the new stretch of the ring-road complex. His mother will have his cooked meal ready, and then he will be alone. In his own perverted way he has grown almost to enjoy the anticipation of it all, for over the last few months it has become a weekly ritual. Expensive, of course, but the arrangement is not unsatisfactory, with half-price back on everything returned. He drains his Guinness.

Sometimes he still feels guilty (a little) – though not so much as he did. He realizes well enough that his dedication to pornography is coarsening whatever sens-ibilities he may once have possessed; that his craving is settling like some cancerous, malignant growth upon his mind, a mind crying out with ever-increasing desperation for its instant, morbid gratification. But he can do nothing about it.

Prompt at 2.00 p.m on Wednesday, 6 October, Mr John Sanders is back in the formica shop, and once more the gyrating saw, whining in agony, can be heard behind the sliding doors.

On Wednesday evenings during term-time the Crowther household was usually deserted from 7.00 p.m to 9.00 p.m. Mrs Margaret Crowther joined a small group of earnest middle-aged culture-vultures in a WEA evening class on Classical Civilization; weekly the children, James and Caroline, swelled the oversubscribed membership of the Wednesday disco at the nearby Community Centre; Mr Bernard Crowther disliked both pop and Pericles.

On the night of Wednesday, 6 October, Margaret left the house at her usual time of 6.30 p.m. Her classes were held about three miles away in the Further Education premises on Headington Hill, and she was anxious to secure a safe and central parking-lot for the proudly sparkling Mini 1000 which Bernard had bought for her the previous August. Diffidently she backed out of the garage (Bernard had agreed to leave his own 1100 to face the winter's elements in the drive) and turned into the quiet road. Although still nervous about her skills, especially in the dark, she relished the little drive. There was the freedom and independence of it all – it was her car, she could go wherever *she* wanted. On the by-pass she took her usual deep breath and concentrated inordinately hard. Car after car swished by her on the outside lane, and she fought back her instinctive reaction to raise her right foot from its gentle pressure on the accelerator and to cover the brake pedal. She was conscious of the headlights of all the oncoming cars, their drivers, she was sure, brashly confident and secure. She fiddled with her safety belt and daringly glanced at the dashboard to ensure that her lights were dipped. Not that she ever had them on full anyway, for fear that in the sudden panic of dipping them she would press the switch the wrong way and turn them off altogether. At the Headington roundabout she negotiated the lanes competently, and uneventfully covered the remainder of her journey.

When she had first considered committing suicide, the car had seemed a very real possibility. But she now knew that she could never do it that way. Driving brought out all her primitive instincts for safety and self-preservation. And anyway, she couldn't smash up her lovely new Mini. There were other ways . . .

She parked carefully, getting in and out of the car several times before she was perfectly happy that it was as safely ensconced and as equidistanced from its neighbours as she could manage, and entered the large, four-storeyed, glass-fronted building that ministered to the needs of the city's maturer students. She saw Mrs Palmer, one of her classmates, starting up the stairs to Room C26.

'Hullo, Mrs Crowther! We all missed you last week. Were you poorly?'

'What's wrong with those two?' asked James.

A quarter of an hour after Margaret's departure, Bernard Crowther had caught the bus down to Lonsdale College, where he dined one or two nights a week. The children were alone.

'Not unusual, is it?' said Caroline.

'They hardly talk to one another.'

'I 'spect all married people get like that.'

'Didn't used to be like that.'

'*You* don't help much.'

'Nor do you.'

'Wha' do you mean?'

'Ah – shut up!'

'You misery.'

'F – off!'

These days their conversation seldom lasted longer. With a few minor permutations and, in the presence of mum and dad, a few concessions to conventional middle-class morality, their parents had heard it many times. It worried Margaret deeply and infuriated Bernard, and each wondered secretly if all children were as vicious, ill-tempered and uncooperative as their own. Not that James and Caroline were uppermost in either parent's mind this Wednesday evening.

*

As one of the senior fellows of his college, Bernard had naturally been invited to the memorial jamboree for the ex-vice-principal who had retired the previous summer. The dinner was to begin at 7.30 p.m., and Bernard arrived in Peter's room with half an hour to spare. He poured himself a gin and vermouth and sat back in a faded armchair. He thought he liked Felix Tompsett – the old sod! Certainly he ate too much, and drank too much and, if many-tongued rumour could be believed (why not?), he had done a lot of other things too much. But he was a good 'college man'; it was on his advice that the college had bought up a lot of property in the early sixties and his understanding of interest rates and investment loans was legendary. Odd really, thought Bernard. He finished his gin and shrugged into his gown. Preprandial sherry would be flowing in the Senior Common Room, and the two friends made their way thither.

'Well, Bernard! How are you, old boy?' Felix's smile beamed a genuine welcome to his old colleague.

'Can't grumble,' replied Bernard lamely.

'And how's that lovely wife of yours?'

Bernard grabbed a sherry. 'Oh fine, fine.'

'Lovely woman.' Felix mused on. He had obviously begun to celebrate his own commemoration with pre-meditated gusto, but Bernard couldn't match his bonhomie. He thought of Margaret as the conversation burbled around him ... He tuned in again just in time to laugh convincingly at Felix's discovery of a recent inscription on the wall of the gents in the Minster bar.

'Bloody good, what?' gaffawed Felix.

The party moved next door and sat down to the evening's feast. Bernard always felt that they had far too much to eat, and tonight they had far, far too much to eat. As he struggled his way through the grapefruit cocktail, the turtle soup, the smoked salmon, the tournedos Rossini, the gateau, the cheese and the fruit, he thought of the millions in the world who had not eaten adequately for weeks or even months, and saw in his mind the harrowing pictures of the famine victims of Asia and Africa . . .

'You're quiet tonight,' said the chaplain, passing Bernard the claret.

'Sorry,' said Bernard. 'It must be all this food and drink.'

'You must learn to take the gifts the good Lord showers upon us, my boy. You know, as I get older I must confess to the greater appreciation of two things in life – natural beauty and the delights of the belly.'

He leaned back and poured half a glass of vintage claret towards his vast stomach. Bernard knew that some men were naturally fat – all to do with the metabolic rate, or something. But there were no fat men in Belsen . . .

But whatever other confessions the good chaplain may have been about to divulge were cut short by the toast to Her Majesty and the clearing of the Principal's throat as he rose to his feet to begin his encomium of Felix Tompsett. They had all heard it all before. A few necessary alterations in the hackneyed, hallowed phrases – but basically the same old stuff. Felix would be leaving holes in so many aspects of college life; it would be difficult to fill the holes . . . Bernard thought of Margaret. Why not leave the bloody holes unfilled . . . One of the foremost scholars of his generation . . . Bernard looked at his watch. 9.15 p.m. He couldn't go yet. Anecdotes and laughter . . . Bernard felt pretty sure they would all be reminded of that incident when a disgruntled undergraduate had pissed all over Felix's carpet two years ago . . . Back to the academic stuff. Top-of-the-head. Phoney . . . His work on the Elizabethan lyric poets . . . why, the old bastard had spent most of his time doing first-hand research on the historic inns of Oxfordshire. Or with the women . . . For the first time Bernard wondered if Felix had made any overtures to Margaret. He'd better not . . .

Felix spoke well. Slightly drunk, amiable, civilized . . . quite moving really. Come on! 9.45 p.m. The presentation was made and the company broke up by 10.00 p.m. Bernard rushed out of college and ran through the Broad to St Giles', where he found a taxi immediately. But even before the taxi stopped, he saw some movement outside the darkened house. His heart raced in panic-stricken despair. James and Caroline stood beside the front door.

'You might have . . .' began Caroline.

Bernard hardly heard. 'Where's your mother?' His voice was hard and urgent.

'Don't know. We thought she must have been with you.'

'How long have you been waiting?' He spoke with a clipped authority the children had seldom heard.

''Bout half an hour. Mum's always been here before . . .'

Bernard opened the front door. 'Ring up the tech. at Headington. Ask if they've finished.'

'You do it, Caroline.'

Bernard brought his right hand with vicious force across James's face. 'Do it!' he hissed.

He went to the gate. No one. He prayed for the sound of a car, any car. Car! A cold sweat formed on his forehead as he darted to the garage. The door was locked. He found the key. His hand shook convulsively. He opened the door.

'What on earth are you doing?'

Bernard started, and in his heart blessed all the gods that were and are and are to be. 'Where the hell have you been?' In a fraction of a second his terrible, agonized fear had flashed to anger – relieved, fierce, beautiful anger.

'As a matter of fact the starter-motor's gone on the Mini. I couldn't get anyone to fix it and in the end I had to catch a bus.'

'You could have let me know.'

'Oh yes, of course. You want me to ring round all the garages, then you, and then presumably the kids.' Margaret herself was becoming very angry. 'What's all the fuss about? Just because *I'm* late for a change!'

'The children have been waiting no end of time.'

'So what!' Margaret stormed into the house, and

113

Bernard heard the high-pitched voices within. He closed the front gate and then the garage. He locked and bolted the front door. He felt happy, happier than he had felt for many days and many hours.

CHAPTER TWELVE

Wednesday, Thursday; 6, 7 October

MORSE DID NOT know what had persuaded him, after seven months of promises and prevarications, to fill in the ragged gaping hole above the kitchen door where the electrician had led in the wires for a new power-point. Everything had been wrong from the start anyway. The Polyfilla powder, purchased some two years previously, had hardened into a solid block of semi-concrete within its packet; the spatula he used for cracking eggs and filling cracks had mysteriously vanished from the face of the earth; and the primitive household steps never had stood four-square on their rickety legs. Perhaps he had taken inspiration from Mr Edward de Bono and his recipe for lateral thought. But whatever the motive for his sudden urge to see the wretched hole filled in, Morse had taken a vertical plunge, like some free-fall parachutist, from the top of the steps, when the cord restraining the uprights to a functional 30° angle suddenly snapped and the whole apparatus collapsed into a straight line beneath him. Like Hephaestus, thrown o'er the crystal battlements, he landed with an agonizing jolt upon his right foot, lay with a feeling of nausea for two or three minutes, wiping the cold sweat which formed upon his brow, and finally limped his way to the front room and lay breathing heavily on the settee. After a while the foot was a little easier and he felt somewhat reassured; but half an hour later the swelling began and a fitful, sharp pain nagged away at his instep. He wondered if he could drive, but knew it would be foolish to try. It was 8.30 p.m. on Tuesday, 5 October. Only one thing for it. He hobbled and hopped across to the telephone and rang Lewis, and within the half hour he was sitting disconsolately in the accident room of the Radcliffe Infirmary, waiting for the result of the X-ray. A young boy sitting on the bench next to Morse was wringing his left hand in some agony (car door) and two men badly injured in a road accident were wheeled by for priority treatment. He felt a little less depressed.

He was finally seen by an almost unintelligible Chinese doctor who held up his X-ray pictures to the light with the disinterestedness of a bored guest having a casual glance at one of the holiday slides of his host. 'Nobrocken. Creepancrushes.' From the competent nurse into whose hands he was now delivered, Morse gathered that no bones were broken and that the treatment prescribed was crêpe bandage and hospital crutches.

He expressed his thanks to nurse and doctor as he swung along diffidently towards the waiting Lewis. 'You,' shouted the doctor after him. 'You, Mr Morse. Nowork twodays. You rest. OK?'

'I think I shall be all right, thanks,' said Morse.

'You, Mr Morse. Youwangebetter, eh? Nowork. Two days. Rest. OK?'

'OK.' Oh God!

Morse hardly slept through Tuesday night; he had a vicious toothache in each of the toes on his foot. He swallowed Disprin after Disprin and finally towards dawn dozed off from sheer exhaustion. Lewis called several times during the prolonged agonies of Wednesday and watched the Inspector fall into a blessedly deep sleep at about 9.00 p.m.

When Lewis greeted him the next morning, Morse felt better; and because he felt better, his mind reverted to the murder of Sylvia Kaye, and because his mind was not now wholly preoccupied with the tribulations of his right foot, he felt a great depression grow upon him. He felt like a quiz contestant who had almost got some of the answers right, had others on the tip of his tongue, but had finished up with nothing. One always longed to start again . . .

He lay with these troubled thoughts on his mind. Lewis was fussing around. Good old Lewis. They'd all be having a good laugh at the station, he thought. Humiliating, falling off a ladder. Well he hadn't fallen *off* a ladder. He'd fallen *through* one.

'Lewis! You told everybody what happened, I suppose?'

'Yes, sir.'

'Well?'

'They think you're making it up. They think you've got gout really. You know – too much port.'

Morse groaned. He could picture himself limping round with every other person stopping him to enquire into the circumstances of the disaster. He'd write it all out, have it photocopied, and distribute the literature around the station.

'Still painful, sir?'

'Of course it bloody well is. You've got millions of nerve endings all over your bloody toes. You know that, don't you?'

'I had an uncle, sir, who had a beer barrel run over his toes.'

'Shut up,' winced Morse. The thought of anything, let alone a beer barrel, being within three feet of his injured foot was quite unbearable. Beer barrel, though. Morse was getting better.

'Are the pubs open yet?'

'Fancy a drink, sir?' Lewis looked pleased with himself.

'Wouldn't mind a jar.'

'As a matter of fact I brought a few cans in last night, sir.'

'Well?'

Lewis found some glasses, and positioning a chair a goodly distance from 'the foot', poured out the beer.

'Nothing new?' asked Morse.

'Not yet.'

'Mm.'

The two men drank in silence. Some of the answers almost right ... others on the tip of his tongue ... What, wondered Morse, if he had been right, or almost right? If only he could start again ... Suddenly he sat up, forgot his incapacity, yelped 'Oh, me foot!' and leaned back again into his nest of pillows. He *could* start again, couldn't he? 'Lewis, I want you to do me one or two favours. Get me some writing paper – it's in the writing-desk downstairs; and what about some fish and chips for lunch?'

Lewis nodded. As he went off for the writing paper Morse interrupted him.

'Three favours. Open a few of those cans.'

A thought had been floating around in Morse's mind for several days, elusive as a bar of soap in a slippery bath. In the beginning was the thought, and the thought became word and Morse unwrapped the text carefully and read the message. *Im Anfang war die Hypothese.* In the beginning was the hypothesis. But before formulating any hypothesis, even of the most modest order, Morse decided that he would feel sharper in body, mind and spirit with a good wash and a shave. Slowly and painfully he got out of bed, tacked crabwise around the walls and ended up by hopping over the last few feet of the bathroom floor. It took him almost an hour to complete his toilet, but he felt a new man. He retraced his irregular progress and gently heaved his right foot into a comfortable niche alongside a spare pillow stuffed down at the bottom of the bed. He felt exhausted but wonderfully refreshed. He closed his eyes and fell fast asleep.

Lewis wondered if he should wake him, but the pungent smell of fried batter and vinegar saved him the trouble.

'What's the time, Lewis? I've been asleep.'

'Quarter past one, sir. Do you want the fish and

chips on a plate? Me and the wife always eat 'em off the paper – seems to taste better somehow.'

'They say it's the newsprint sticking to the chips,' replied Morse, taking the oily package from his sergeant and tucking in with relish. 'You know, Lewis, perhaps we've been going about this case in the wrong way.'

'We have, sir?'

'We've been trying to solve the case in order to find the murderer, right?'

'I suppose that's the general idea, isn't it?'

'Ah, but we might get better results the other way round.'

'You mean . . .' But though Morse waited it was clear that Lewis had no idea whatsoever what he meant.

'I mean we ought to find the murderer in order to solve the case.'

'I see,' said Lewis, unseeing.

'I'm glad you do,' said Morse. 'It's as clear as daylight – and open some of these bloody curtains, will you?'

Lewis complied.

'If,' continued Morse, 'if I told you who the murderer was and where he lived, you could go along and you could arrest him, couldn't you?' Lewis nodded vaguely and wondered if his superior officer had caught his skull on the kitchen sink before landing on his precious right foot. 'You could, couldn't you? You could bring him here to see me, you could keep him at a safe distance from my grievous injury – and he could tell us all about it, eh? He could do all our work for us, couldn't he?'

Morse jabbered on, his mouth stuffed with fish and chips, and with genuine concern Lewis began to doubt the Inspector's sanity. Shock was a funny thing; he'd seen it many times in road accidents. Sometimes two or three days afterwards some of the parties would go completely gaga. They'd recover of course . . . Or had Morse been drinking? Not the beer. The opened cans were still unpoured. A heavy responsibility suddenly seemed to descend on Lewis's shoulders. He was sweating slightly. The room was hot, the autumn sun bright upon the glass of the bedroom window.

'Can I get you anything, sir?'

'Yep. Flannel and soap and towel. By Jove, your wife's right, Lewis. I'll never eat 'em off a plate again.'

A quarter of an hour later a bewildered sergeant let himself out of the front door of Morse's flat. He felt a little worried and would have felt even more so if he had been back in the bedroom at that moment to hear Morse talking to himself, and nodding occasionally whenever he particularly approved of what he heard coming from his own lips.

'Now my first hypothesis, ladies and gentlemen, and as I see things the most vital hypothesis of all – I shall make many, oh yes, I shall make many – is this: that the murderer is living in North Oxford. You will say this is a bold hypothesis, and so it is. Why should the murderer not live in Didcot or Sidcup or even Southampton? Why should he live in North Oxford? Why not, coming nearer home, why not just in Oxford? I can only repeat to you that I am formulating a hypothesis, that is, a supposition, a proposition, however wild, assumed for the sake of argument; a theory to be proved (or disproved – yes, we must concede that) by reference to facts, and it is with facts and not with airy-fairy fancies that I shall endeavour to bolster my hypothesis. *Im Anfang war die Hypothese,* as Goethe might have put it. And please let it not be forgotten that I am Morse of the Detective, as Dickens would have said. Oh yes, a detective. A detective has a sensibility towards crime – he feels it; he must feel it before he can detect it. There are indications which point to North Oxford. We need not review them all here, but the *ambience* is right in North Oxford. And if I am wrong, why, no harm is done to our investigation. We are propounding a hypothesis, that is, a supposition, a proposition, however wild ... I've said all that before, though. Where was I, now? Oh yes. I wish you to accept, provisionally, dubiously, hopelessly if needs be, my premier hypothesis. The murderer is a resident of North Oxford. Now I mentioned facts, and I shall not disappoint you. Aristotle classified the animals, I believe, by subdividing them, and subdivision will be our method of procedure. Aristotle, that great man, divided and subdivided – species, subspecies, genera (Morse was getting lost) genera, species, subspecies and so on until he reached – what did he reach? – *the individual specimen of the species.'* (That sounded better.) 'I, too, will divide. In North Oxford there are, let us say, "*x*" number of people. Now we further hypothesize that our murderer is a male. Why can we be confident of this fact? Because, ladies and gentlemen, the murdered girl was *raped.* This is a *fact,* and we shall bring forward at the trial the

evidence of eminent medical personnel to . . .' Morse
was tiring a little, and fortified himself with another can
of beer. 'As I was saying, our murderer is male. We can
therefore divide our number x by, let us say, er, four –
leaving the women and children out of our reckoning.
Now can we subdivide again, you will ask? Indeed,
we can. Let us guess at the age of our murderer. I
put him – I am diffident, and you will accuse me of
formulating sub-hypotheses – between 35 and 50. Yes,
there are reasons . . .' But Morse decided to skip them.
They weren't all that convincing, perhaps, but he
had reasons, and he wished to sustain the impetus of
his hypothesis. 'We may then further subdivide our
number x by two. That seems most reasonable, does it
not? Let us continue. What else can we reasonably
hypothesize? I believe – for reasons which I realize may
not be fully acceptable to you all – that our suspect is a
married man.' Morse was feeling his way with an
increasing lack of confidence. But the road ahead was
already clearing; the fog was lifting and dissipating in
the sun, and he resumed with his earlier briskness.
'Now this means yet a further diminution in the power
of x. Our x is becoming a manageable unit, is it not?
But not yet is the focus of our *camera hypothetica* fixed
with any clear delineation upon our unsuspecting
quarry. But wait! Our man is a regular drinker, is he
not? It is surely one of our more reasonable claims, and
gives to our procedure not only the merits of hypothet-
ical plausibility, but also of extreme probability. Our
case is centred upon the Black Prince, and one does
not visit the Black Prince in order to consult the tax

inspector.' Morse was wilting again. His foot was throbbing again with rhythmic pain, and his mind wandered off for a few minutes. Must be those Disprin. He closed his eyes and continued his forensic monologue within his brain.

He must, too, surely he must, figure in at least the top 5% of the IQ range? Jennifer wouldn't fall for an ignorant buffoon, would she? That letter. Clever chap, well schooled. *If* he wrote it. If, if, if. Carry on. Where's our *x* now? Go on. He must be attractive to women. Yet who can say what attracts those lovely creatures? But yes. Say yes. Subdivide. Cars! God, he'd forgotton cars. Not everyone has a car. About what proportion? Never mind, subdivide. Just a minute – *red* car. He felt slightly delirious. Just a fraction longer . . . That really would be a significant subdivision. The *x* was floating slowly away, and now was gone. The pain was less vicious. Comfortable . . . almost . . . comfortable . . .

He was woken at 4.00 p.m. by Lewis's inability to manage the front door without a disturbing clatter. And when Lewis anxiously put his head round the bedroom door, he saw Morse scribbling as furiously as Coleridge must have scribbled when he woke up to find, full grown within his mind, the whole of *Kubla Khan*.

'Sit down, Lewis. Glad to see you.' He continued to write with furious rapidity for two or three minutes. Finally he looked up. 'Lewis, I'm going to ask you some questions. Think carefully – don't rush! – and give me some intelligent answers. You'll have to guess, I know, but do your best.'

Oh hell, thought Lewis.

'How many people live in North Oxford?'

'What do you call "North Oxford", sir?'

'I'm asking the questions, you're answering 'em. Just think generally what *you* think North Oxford is; let's say Summertown and above. Now come on!'

'I could find out, sir.'

'Have a bloody guess, man, can't you?'

Lewis felt uncomfortable. At least he could see that only three of the beer cans were empty. He decided to plunge in. 'Ten thousand.' He said it with the assurance and unequivocal finality of a man asked to find the sum of two and two.

Morse took another sheet of paper and wrote down the number 10,000. 'What proportion of them are men?'

Lewis leaned back and eyed the ceiling with the confidence of a statistical consultant. 'About a quarter.'

Morse wrote down his second entry neatly and carefully beneath the first: 2,500. 'How many of those men are between 35 and 50?'

Quite a lot of retired people in North Oxford, thought Lewis, and quite a lot of young men on the estates. 'About half, no more.'

The third figure was entered: 1,250. 'How many of them are married, would you say?'

Lewis considered. Most of them, surely? 'Four out of five, sir.'

Morse formed the figures of his latest calculation with great precision: 1,000.

'How many of them regularly go out for a drink – you know what I mean – pubs, clubs, that sort of thing?'

Lewis thought of his own street. Not so many as some people thought. The neighbours on either side of him didn't – mean lot! He thought of the street as a whole. Tricky this one. 'About half.'

Morse revised his figure and went on to his next question. 'You remember the letter we had, Lewis. The letter Jennifer Coleby said she knew nothing about?' Lewis nodded. 'If we were right in thinking what we did, or what I did, would you say we were dealing with a man of high intelligence?'

'That's a big if, isn't it, sir?'

'Look, Lewis. That letter was written by our man – just get that into your head. It was the big mistake he made. It's the best clue we've got. What the hell do they pay us for. We've got to follow the clues, haven't we?' Morse didn't sound very convinced, but Lewis assured him that they had to follow the clues. 'Well?'

'Well what, sir?'

'Was he an intelligent man?'

'Very much so, I should think.'

'Would you think of writing a letter like that?'

'Me? No, sir.'

'And you're pretty bright, aren't you Sergeant?'

Lewis squared his shoulders, took a deep breath and decided not to minimize his intellectual capacity. 'I'd say I was in the top 15%, sir.'

'Good for you! And our unknown friend? You

remember he not only knows how to spell all the tricky words, he knows how to misspell them, too!'

'Top 5%, sir.'

Morse wrote down the calculation.

'What proportion of middle-aged men are attractive to women?' Silly question! Morse noticed the derision in Lewis's face. 'You know what I mean. Some men are positively repulsive to women!' Lewis seemed unconvinced. 'I know all about these middle-aged Romeos. We're all middle-aged Romeos. But some men are more attractive to women than others, aren't they?'

'I don't get many falling for me, sir.'

'That's not what I'm asking you. Say something, for God's sake!'

Lewis plunged again. 'Half? No, more than that. Three out of five.'

'You're sure you mean that?'

Of course he wasn't sure. 'Yes.'

Another figure. 'How many men of this age group have cars?'

'Two out of three.' What the hell did it matter?

Morse wrote down his penultimate figure. 'One more question. How many people own red cars?'

Lewis went to the window and watched the traffic going by. He counted. Two black, one beige, one dark blue, two white, one green, one yellow, one black. 'One in ten, sir.'

Morse had shown a growing excitement in his manner for the last few minutes. 'Phew! Who'd have believed it? Lewis, you're a genius!'

Lewis thanked him for the compliment and asked

wherein his genius lay. 'I think, Lewis, that we're looking for a male person, resident in North Oxford, married – probably a family, too; he goes out for a drink fairly regularly, sometimes to Woodstock; he's a well-educated man, may even be a university man; he's about 35 to 45, as I see him, with a certain amount of charm – certainly, I think a man some of the young ladies could fall for; finally he drives a car – to be precise a red car.'

'He'd be as good as anyone, I suppose.'

'Well, even if we're a bit out here and there, I'd bet my bottom dollar he's pretty likely to fit into most of those categories. And, do you know, Lewis, *I don't think there are many who fall into that category.* Look here.' He passed over to Lewis the sheet of paper containing the figures.

North Oxford	10,000
Men?	2,500
35–50?	1,250
Married?	1,000
Drinker?	500
Top 5%?	25
Charm?	15
Car?	10
Red Car?	1

Lewis felt a guilty sense of responsibility for the remarkable outcome of these computations. He stood by the window in the fading light of afternoon, and saw two red cars go by one after the other. How many people *did* live in North Oxford? Was he really in the top 15%? 25% more likely. 'I'm sure, sir, that we could check a lot of these figures.' Lewis felt constrained to voice his suspicions. 'I don't think you can just fiddle about with figures like that, anyway. You'd need to ...' He had a dim recollection of the need for some statistical laws operating on data; the categories had to be ordered and reduced in logical sequence; he couldn't quite remember. But it was all little more than an elaborate game to amuse a fevered brain. Morse would be up in a day or so. Better look after him and humour him as best he could. But was there any logic in it? Was it all *that* stupid? He looked again at the paper of figures and another red car went by. There were nine 'ifs'. He stared gloomily out of the window and mechanically counted the next ten cars. Only one red one! North Oxford was, of course, the biggest gamble. But the fellow had to live somewhere, didn't he? Perhaps the old boy was not so cuckoo as he'd thought. He looked at the sheet yet again ... The other big thing was that letter. *If* the murderer had written it.

'What do you think then, Lewis?'

'Might be worth a go.'

'How many men do you want?'

'We'd need to do a bit of thinking first, wouldn't we?'

'What do you mean?'

'The local authorities could help a good deal. First we'd need some up-to-date lists of residents.'

'Yes. You're right. We need to think it through before we do anything.'

'That's what I thought, sir.'

'Well?'

'We could get straight on to it in the morning, sir, if you felt up to it.'

'Or we could get straight on to it now if *you* felt up to it?'

'I suppose we could.'

Lewis rang his long-suffering spouse, and conferred with Morse for the next two hours. After he had left, Morse reached for a bedside phone and was lucky to find the Chief Superintendent still in his office. And half an hour later Morse was still talking, and ruefully cursing himself for having forgotten to reverse the charges.

CHAPTER THIRTEEN

Saturday, 9 October

ON THE MORNING of Saturday, 9 October Bernard Crowther sat at his desk in his front room reading Milton, but not with his usual thrilled enjoyment. He was lecturing on *Paradise Lost* this term and in spite of his thorough and scholarly mastery of the work he felt he should do a little more homework. Margaret had caught the bus to Summertown to do her shopping and his car was ready outside to pick her up at midday. The children were out. Goodness knew where . . .

He was surprised to hear the front door bell ring, for they had few callers. Butcher perhaps. He opened the door.

'Why, Peter! What a surprise! Come in, come in.' Peter Newlove and Bernard had been firm friends for years. They had arrived at Lonsdale College the same term and since then had enjoyed a warm and genuine relationship. 'What brings you here? Not very often we have the pleasure of seeing you in North Oxford. I thought you played golf on Saturday mornings, anyway.'

'I couldn't face it this morning. Bit chilly round the fairways, you know.' The weather had turned much colder the last two days, and the autumn had suddenly grown old. The day seemed bleak and sour. Peter sat down. 'Working on Saturday morning, Bernard?'

'Just getting ready for next week.'

Peter looked across at the desk. 'Ah. *Paradise Lost*, Book I. I remember that. We did it for higher certificate.'

'You've read it since, of course.'

'*From morn to noon he fell, from noon to dewy eve, a summer's day.* What about that?'

'Very fine.' Bernard looked out of the window and saw the white hoar-frost still unmelted on his narrow lawn.

'Is everything all right, Bernard?' The man from Gloucestershire spoke with an abrupt kindliness.

'Course everything's all right. Why did you say that?' It was clear to Peter that everything was far from right.

'Oh, I don't know. You just seemed a bit on edge on Wednesday night. Scuttled away like a startled hare after the dinner.'

'I'd forgotten that Margaret would be late, and I knew the kids would be waiting outside.'

'I see.'

'Was it that obvious?'

'No, not really. I was watching you, that's all. You didn't seem your old self when we had a drink together, and I thought you might be a bit under the weather.' Bernard said nothing. 'Everything OK with you and, er, Margaret?'

'Oh, yes. Fine. I've got to collect her, by the way, at twelve. What's the time now?'

'Half past eleven.' Peter rose to his feet.

'No, don't go! We've got time for a quick drink. What'll you have?'

'Are you going to have one?'

'Of course I am. Whisky?'

'Fine.'

Bernard withdrew to the kitchen to get the glasses, and Peter stood in front of the window, looking out into the narrow street. A car, white and pale blue, with a light (not flashing) on the roof and POLICE marked in bold black lettering across its side, was parked across the way, two or three doors to the left. It had not been there when Peter arrived. As he watched, a police constable, with a black and white chequered band around his flat, peaked hat, was coming out of a front gate. A middle-aged woman walked with him and the two were talking freely, pointing between them to every point of the compass. More talk and further pointing arms. Was she pointing here? The constable had a list in his hand and he was clearly checking some names. The woman stood with her apron around her, clutching her arms about her middle to keep warm and chattering interminably on.

Bernard came in, the glasses clattering a little on the tray. 'Say when!'

'I see you've got a few criminals in the road, Bernard.'

'What did you say?' Bernard looked up sharply.

'Is the law always prowling around here like this?' Peter got no further. The door bell rang twice; shrill, peremptory. Bernard opened the door and stood face to face with the young constable.

'Can I help you, officer?'

'Yes, I think so, sir, if you will. Won't take more'n a minute. Is this your car, sir?' He pointed to the red 1100 outside.

'Yes, it is.'

'Just checking, sir. We've had a lot of cars stolen recently. Just checking.' He made a note in his book. 'Can you remember the registration number, sir?'

Mechanically Bernard recited the number.

'That's yours all right then, sir. Have you got your log-book handy, sir?'

'Is it necessary?'

'Well, it is rather important, if you don't mind, sir. We're checking as thoroughly as we can.'

Peter heard the conversation through the open door and felt strangely worried. Bernard came in and poked about haphazardly in his desk. 'Where the hell's Margaret . . . They're checking on stolen cars, Peter. Shan't be a minute.' He looked ashen, and could find nothing. 'I'm sorry, officer,' he called. 'Come in a minute, will you?'

'Thank you, sir. Don't worry if you can't put your hand on the log-book, sir. You can give me the information yourself quite easily.'

'What do you want to know?'

'Full name, sir?'

'Bernard Michael Crowther.'

'Age, sir?'

'Forty-one.'

'Married, sir?'

'Yes.'

'Children?'

'Two.'

'Occupation?'

'University lecturer.'

'That's about all, sir.' He closed his book. 'Oh, just one more thing. Have you left your car unlocked recently? You know what I mean. Is it locked now, for example?'

'No, I don't think so.'

'No, it isn't, sir. I tried all the doors before I called. It's an open invitation to car thieves, you know.'

'Yes, I'm sure you're right. I'll try to remember.'

'Do you use your car much, sir?'

'Not a great deal. Running around a bit in Oxford. Not much really.'

'You don't take it out when you go for a drink, for example?'

Peter thought he saw the daylight. Bernard had been drinking and driving, had he?

'No, not very often,' answered Bernard. 'I usually go round to the Fletcher's. It's not far; I always walk there.'

'Would you take the car if you went drinking outside Oxford, sir?'

'I'm afraid I would,' said Bernard slowly, in a helpless sort of way.

'Well, don't drink too much, sir, if you're driving. But I'm sure you know all about that.' The constable glanced quickly round the room and looked drily at the two large tumblers of whisky; but he said nothing more until he reached the door. 'You don't know anyone else in the road who's got a red car, do you, sir? I've got to make a few more inquiries.'

Bernard thought, but his mind was swimming. He couldn't think of anybody. He closed his eyes and put his left hand on his forehead. Every day in term time he walked to the far end of the road. Red car? Red car? His was the only one, he was pretty sure of that.

'Well don't worry, sir. I'll just make one or two more, er ... Anyway, thank you for your help, sir.' He was gone. But not, Peter noticed, to make any more inquiries in that particular road. He walked straight to the police car (left unlocked) and immediately accelerated away.

Some ten minutes later as he drove along to Woodstock, Peter Newlove was glad he'd never married. The same woman – thirty, forty, fifty years! Not for him. He couldn't imagine poor old Bernard jumping into bed that afternoon for a riotous half-hour romp with Margaret. Whereas ... He thought of Gaye undressing, and his right foot pressed hard upon the accelerator.

An immensely excited Constable McPherson rushed across the forecourt of the Thames Valley HQ where earlier the same morning he had seen poor old Morse staggering painfully along, his arms encircling the shoulders of two of his burly mates. Wow! McPherson felt like a man with eight draws up on the treble-chance pool. As he had driven the few miles from North Oxford to Kidlington, he sensed a feeling of unprecedented elation. For the last four years his uniformed career had been uniformly undistinguished; he had apprehended no significant villain; he had witnessed no memorable breach of either the civil or the criminal code. But blessed indeed he was today! As he had neared the Banbury Road roundabout he had switched on the wailing siren and the winking blue light, and had delighted in the deference accorded to him by his fellow motorists. He felt mightily important. Why not? He *was* mightily important – for today, at least.

Inside the station, McPherson debated for a second or two. Should he report to Lewis? Or should he report his intelligence direct to the Inspector? The latter course seemed on reflection the more appropriate, and he made his way along the corridors to Morse's door, knocked and just caught the muffled 'come in' from the other side.

'And what can I do for you, Constable?'

McPherson made his report with an accuracy and incisiveness that was impressive, and Morse congratulated him upon the prompt and efficient discharge of his duty. McPherson, though mightily gratified with the compliment, was a little surprised that Morse himself seemed not immediately anxious to summon the cohorts of the law. But he'd done his own job – done it well.

'Excuse me if I don't stand up – gout, you know – but . . .' He shook McPherson's hand warmly. 'It won't go unnoticed, believe me.'

After McPherson's departure, Morse sat silently and thoughtfully for a few minutes. But so he had been sitting when the constable had entered. It would have been so disappointing for McPherson to have known, and anyway McPherson had been the immediate cause. No, he could never have had the heart to confess that Mr Bernard Crowther had telephoned in at 11.45 a.m. wishing, he said, to make a statement.

Crowther had insisted that he should present himself, that on no account were the police to collect him, that he expected the authorities at least to allow to a witness, coming forward voluntarily with what might be valuable information, the normal courtesy of not being picked up like a common felon. Morse had agreed, and Bernard promised to be with him at 2.30 p.m.

Morse found himself apologizing for his immobility and his first impression of Crowther was surprisingly agreeable. The man was nervous – that was plain for all to see; but there was an odd charm and dignity about the fellow; that sort of middle-aged schoolmaster-type that some of the girls might have a crush on.

'Look, Inspector – you are a Chief Inspector, I think – I have never in my life been inside a police station until this moment. I am not conversant with normal police practice and procedure. So I have taken the precaution of writing out, very rushed, I'm afraid, the statement I wish to make.'

Chapter Fourteen

Saturday, 9 October

On the evening of Wednesday, September 29th, I left my house in Southdown Road at 6.45 p.m. I drove my car to the roundabout at the north end of the Banbury Road, where I turned left and travelled for four hundred yards or so along Sutherland Avenue to the roundabout at the northern end of the Woodstock Road. Here I turned off the A40 and took the road north to Woodstock. Night was already drawing in and I switched the side-lights on, in common, I noticed, with the majority of the other motorists. Yet although it was that awkward half light in which it is most difficult to drive, it was not dark enough for full head-lights; it was certainly not dark enough for me to miss two young girls standing a little way beyond the roundabout on the grass verge alongside the self-service filling-station. The girl nearer to the road I saw clearly. She was an attractive girl with long fair hair, white blouse, short skirt and a coat over her arm. The other girl had walked on a few yards and had her back towards me; she seemed to be quite happy to leave the business of getting a lift to her companion. But she had darkish hair, I think, and if I remember correctly was a few inches taller than her friend.

I must now try to be completely honest with you. I have often been guilty of romantic day-dreams, even vaguely erotic day-dreams, about picking up some wildly attractive woman and finding her a rare and disturbing combination of brains and beauty. In my silly imaginings the preliminary and diffident skirmishing would lead gradually but inevitably to the most wanton delights. But this, remember, has always been a day-dream and I mention it simply to excuse myself for having stopped at all. I shouldn't feel guilty and apologetic about such things; yet in all honesty I do feel so, and have always felt so.

But that is by the way. I leaned over and opened the nearside front door and said that I was going to Woodstock, if that would help. The blonde girl said something like 'Oh, super'. She turned round to her companion and said (I think), 'What did I tell you?' and got into the front seat beside me. The other girl opened the rear door and got in also. What conversation there was was desultory and disappointing. The girl beside me reiterated at intervals that this was 'a real bi' of luck' (she had a typical Oxford manner of speech) because she had missed the bus; I think the girl sitting in the back spoke only once and that was to ask the time. I mentioned as we passed the gates of Blenheim Palace that this was about it, and I understood that it would do them fine. I dropped them as soon as we reached the main street, but I didn't notice where they went. It was natural for me to believe, as I did, that they were going to meet their boy friends.

There is little more to say. What I have written above is a true record of the events which, as I now realize, later in the evening led up to the murder of one of the girls I had driven.

I have just reread what I have written and am conscious that it perhaps says little which can help your investigation. I am also aware that my statement will give rise to two questions: first, why was I myself going to Woodstock on the night of 29 September, and second, why did I not come forward earlier with my evidence? The two questions are really one, and I shall feel a great weight off my shoulders to be able to answer it; nevertheless, it is my earnest hope that what I have to say can be treated by the police with the strictest confidentiality, since other people, themselves completely innocent, would be hurt beyond telling if it were to become generally known.

For the last six months or so I have been having an affair with another woman. We have been able to meet regularly once a week, almost always on Wednesday evenings, when my wife and children are away from home and when no awkward questions are likely to arise. On Wednesday, 29th, I was on my way to meet this woman by the side gates of Blenheim Palace at 7.15 p.m. I parked my car outside the Bear Hotel and walked there. She was waiting. We walked into Blenheim gardens, beside the lake, and through the trees – it is a most beautiful spot. It was, of course, dangerous for us, since so many people from Oxford go out for a meal in Woodstock. But we were always careful, and the element of risk was itself perhaps part of the excitement.

I need say no more. I read the account of the murder and later watched Detective Chief Inspector Morse make his appeal on television. I wish you to know that I almost telephoned there and then; in fact I waited outside a telephone box in Southdown Road for several minutes that same evening with a firm resolve to come forward immediately. But this is making excuses, and I have none to offer. I fully understand, as you will, that I have not, even at this late stage, come forward of my own volition. When a police constable called at my home this morning, I realized that you were on to me, and thought it best to offer this statement straight away. I perpetuated to my wife the rigmarole which the constable had given me about stolen cars, and I told her that I would be coming here. I would do anything in the world to avoid hurting her (yet, it is probable, I know, that I have hurt her already), and I should be most grateful if any part of my statement not relevant to the strict terms of the inquiries you are conducting can be kept secret.

That I am genuinely sorry for the inconvenience and needless extra work which I have caused, will, I trust, be obvious from what I have said here. If it is not, let me hasten to state now my profound apologies for my selfish and cowardly course of action. I am,

   Your humble servant,
      Bernard Michael Crowther.

Morse read the statement slowly. When he had finished he looked across the table at Crowther, then looked down again at the statement and re-read it with even greater concentration. When he had finished, he leaned back in his black leather chair, carefully picked up his injured right foot, put it across his left knee and rubbed it lovingly.

'I've hurt my foot, Mr Crowther.'

'Have you? I'm sorry to hear that. My medical friends say that feet and hands are about the worst things to knock about – something to do with the multiplicity of nerve endings.'

He had a pleasant voice and manner. Morse looked him fully in the eyes. For several seconds neither man flinched, and Morse thought he saw a basic honesty in the man. But he could not conceal from himself a draining sense of disappointment and anticlimax; like Constable McPherson he had thought of a big pools win, only to find that instead of 'telegrams required' the forecast was very low. 'Yes.' He picked up the conversation. 'I shan't be walking round Blenheim Park tonight, sir.'

'Nor shall I,' said Bernard.

'Very romantic, I should think, having a bit on the side like that.'

'You make it sound very crude.'

'Wasn't it?'

'Perhaps so.'

'Are you still seeing her?'

'No. My philandering days are over now, I hope.'

'Have you seen her since that night?'

'No. It's all off. It seemed better.'

'Does she know that you picked the two girls up?'

'Yes.'

'Is she upset – that it's all over, I mean?'

'I suppose so, a bit.'

'What about you?'

'To be truthful, it's a great relief. I'm not a very accomplished Casanova and I hated all the lying.'

'You realize, of course, that it would help a great deal if this young lady – is she young, by the way?'

For the first time Bernard hesitated. 'Fairly young.'

'If this young lady,' continued Morse, 'would come forward and corroborate your evidence?'

'Yes. I know it would.'

'But you don't want that.'

'I'd rather you disbelieved my story than dragged her into it.'

'You're not going to tell me who she is? I can promise you that I will handle the business myself.'

Bernard shook his head. 'I'm sorry. I can't do that.'

'I could try to find her, you know,' said Morse.

'I couldn't stop that.'

'No, you couldn't.' Morse moved his foot carefully back to the cushion strategically placed under his desk. 'You could be withholding vital evidence, Mr Crowther.' Bernard said nothing. 'Is she married?' persisted Morse.

'I'm not going to talk about her,' he said quietly, and Morse sensed a steely resolve in the man.

'Do you think I could find her?' His foot shot with

pain, and he picked it up again. Oh, what the hell, he thought; if this bit of stuff likes him to tickle her tits under the trees, what's that got to do with me? Bernard had not answered and Morse changed his tack. 'You realize, I'm sure, that this other girl, the one who sat in the back seat, she's the one who might be able to give us a line?' Crowther nodded. 'Why do you think we haven't heard from her?'

'I don't know.'

'Can't you think of any reason?'

Bernard could, that was clear, but he did not put his thoughts into words.

'You can, can't you, Mr Crowther? Because it could be exactly the same reason which accounted for your reluctance to come forward.' Bernard nodded again. 'She could tell us, perhaps, who Sylvia Kaye's boy friend was, where she was going to meet him, what they were going to do – she might be able to tell us such a lot, don't you think?'

'I didn't get the idea they knew each other very well.'

'Why do you say that?' asked Morse sharply.

'Well, they didn't chatter much together. You know how young girls do: pop music, dances, discos, boy friends – they just didn't talk much – that's all.'

'You didn't catch her name?'

'No.'

'Have you tried to think if Sylvia used her name?'

'I've tried to tell you all I can remember. I can't do any more.'

'Betty, Carole, Diana, Evelyn ... no?' Bernard

remained impassive. 'Gaye, Heather, Iris, Jennifer . . .' Morse could not make out the mildest flicker of response in Bernard's eyes. 'Had she got nice legs?'

'Not so nice as the other's, I don't think.'

'You noticed those?'

'What do you think? She was sitting next to me.'

'Any erotic day-dreams?'

'Yes,' said Crowther, with a fierce burst of honesty.

'It's a good job it's not a criminal offence,' sighed Morse, 'otherwise we'd all be inside.' He noticed a light smile play for a brief second on Crowther's worried face. I can see him being attractive to some women, thought Morse. 'What time did you get home that night?'

'About a quarter to nine.'

'Was that the usual time, you know, because of, er, your, er, wife and so on?'

'Yes.'

'An hour a week, was that it?'

'Not much longer.'

'Was it worth it?'

'It seemed so – at the time.'

'You didn't call at the Black Prince that evening?'

'I've never been in the Black Prince.' It sounded very definite. Morse looked down at the statement again and noticed the beautifully formed handwriting; it seemed a pity to type it out. He questioned Crowther for a further half an hour, and gave it up soon after 4.00 p.m.

'We shall have to keep your car here a while, I'm afraid.'

'You will?' Crowther sounded disappointed.

'Yes, we might just find something, you know – hair, that sort of thing. They can do wonderful things these days, our forensic boys.' He got up from his chair and asked Crowther for his crutches. 'I'll promise you one thing,' said Morse. 'We'll keep your wife out of it. I'm sure you can make up something to tell her. After all, you're used to that sort of thing, aren't you, sir?'

Morse limped out behind Crowther and ordered the desk sergeant to get some transport. 'Leave your car keys with me please, sir,' said Morse. 'You should have the car back early next week.' The two men shook hands and Crowther was to wait only a few minutes before he was ushered into a police car. Morse watched him go with mixed feelings. He felt he'd handled things satisfactorily. He needed to think now, not to talk. Funny, though, that about the other girl's legs; Mrs Jarman said she was wearing slacks . . .

He summoned assistance and was helped across to Crowther's car. The doors were opened. He struggled his way into the nearside front seat and sat back, manoeuvring his foot as carefully as he could, and stretching his legs as far as possible in front of him. He closed his eyes and pictured the legs of Sylvia Kaye, long, tanned, finely formed, rising up to her brief skirt. He thought she might have leaned back, too. 'Hot pants!' he said, almost to himself.

'Pardon, sir?' said the sergeant who had helped him into the car.

*

By an odd coincidence (or was it?) Studio 2 in Walton Street was presenting a double sexploitation bill whose titles were calculated to titillate even the most jaded appetite. The first, 2.00–3.05 p.m., was *Danish Blue* (not, judging from the mounds of female flesh that burst their bounds in the stills outside, a film about the manufacturing of cheese) and from 3.20–5.00 p.m. the main attraction of the week, entitled *Hot Pants*.

At 5.00 p.m. the earlier addicts were leaving, and a small group of men stood inside the foyer waiting for admission. One of these would normally have joined the early brigade, for this was for him a weekly occurrence. But he had been needed by Messrs Chalkley and Sons for two hours' overtime in the formica shop. He would not, this week, be able to stay round and see the programme twice; but the films seldom met his inflated expectations or the infinite promise of the coming-shortly trailers. On these occasions he seldom looked about him, and it was just as well in the late afternoon of Saturday, 9 October, that once again he averted his eyes from his fellow voyeurs. For standing no more than four feet away from him, ostensibly checking the times of the next programme, but keeping himself carefully and unobtrusively out of the limelight, was the sergeant seconded to Detective Chief Inspector Morse for the inquiry into the murder of Sylvia Kaye. Lewis thought that this was one of Morse's more rewarding assignments, and he suspected that, but for his accident, his chief might well have undertaken it himself.

Chapter Fifteen

Monday, 11 October

THE WEEKEND DRIFTED by, and the leaves continued to fall. Morse was feeling more cheerful; he could now put a good deal of weight on to his foot, and on Monday morning, deciding that he could exchange his crutches for a pair of sticks, he arranged for McPherson to drive him down to the Radcliffe Infirmary Outpatients' (Accident) Department.

He questioned McPherson closely as they drove. What impression had he formed of Crowther? What had been Crowther's immediate reaction? What was he like at home did he think? What had he been doing when McPherson called? Morse found the young constable surprisingly intelligent and observant, and told him so. Furthermore he found a good deal in the information he had been given that interested him and aroused his curiosity.

'What had he been reading – did you manage to see?'

'No, sir. But books on literature, I think. You know, poetry.' Morse let it pass.

'He had a writing-desk, you say?'

'Yes, sir. You know, papers all over it.'

Morse mentally resolved not to count up the 'you

knows' he'd had so far and the 'you knows' he was surely going to get. 'Was there a typewriter there?' He said it casually enough.

'Yes. You know, one of those portable things.'

Morse said no more. Waved through the narrow yards of the Infirmary, that seemed in conspiracy to prevent too many injured citizens from gaining immediate access to the Outpatients' Department, the police car parked itself, with no objections from porters, orderlies or traffic wardens, on a broad stretch of concrete marked 'Ambulances Only'. A policeman's parking lot was sometimes not an unhappy one. Morse had foreseen the swopping of crutches for sticks as a straightforward transaction; but it was not to be. There appeared to be an unbreached egalitarianism in the world of all injured brothers, and Morse was constrained to take his proper place and wait his proper time whilst the proper formalities were completed. He sat on the same bench, skipped through the same old edition of *Punch*, and felt the same impatience; he heard the same Chinese doctor, his sang-froid seemingly disturbed by the inability of a little boy to sit still: 'Youwannagetbetter, li'l boy, youbetter sidstill.'

Morse stared gloomily at the floor and found himself watching the nurses' legs go by. Not much to make the blood boil really. Except one pair – beautiful! Morse would like to have seen the rest of the delicious damsel, but she had walked swiftly past. Fat, so-so, thin, so-so – and then those legs again and this time they stopped miraculously in front of him.

'I hope you're being looked after all right, Inspector Morse?'

The Inspector was visibly stunned. He looked up slowly, straight and deep into the sad, come-hither face of darling Dark-eyes, co-resident of the cool Miss Jennifer Coleby. 'You remember me?' said Morse; a little illogically, thought the girl standing directly above him.

'Don't you remember *me*?' she asked.

'How could I forget you?' said the Inspector, slipping at last into a smooth forward gear. How lovely she was! 'You work here?'

'If I may say so, Inspector, you must have asked a great many more intelligent questions in your time.' She wore her uniform becomingly – and Morse always thought a nurse's uniform did more for a girl than all the fine feathers of the fashion houses.

'No, not very bright, was it?' he confessed. She smiled – delightfully.

'Have a seat,' said Morse, 'I'd like to have a chat with you. We didn't say much before, did we?'

'I'm sorry, Inspector. I can't do that. I'm on duty.'

'Oh.' He was disappointed.

'Well . . .'

'Just stay a minute,' said Morse. 'You know, I really would like to see you, some time. Can I see you when you come off duty?'

'I'm on duty until six.'

'Well, I could meet . . .'

'At six I shall go home and have a quick meal, and then at seven . . .'

'You've got a date.'

'Well, let's say I'm busy.'

'Lucky bugger,' mumbled Morse. 'Tomorrow?'

'Not tomorrow.'

'Wednesday?' Morse wondered mournfully if the progression through the remaining days of the week was anything more than a hollow formality; but she surprised him.

'I could see you on Wednesday evening, if you like.'

'Could you?' Morse sounded like an eager schoolboy. They arranged to meet in the 'Bird and Baby' in St Giles' at 7.30 p.m. Morse tried to sound more casual: 'I can take you home, of course, but perhaps it would be better not to pick you up. You can get a bus all right?'

'I'm not a child, Inspector.'

'Good. See you then.' She turned away. 'Oh, just a minute,' called Morse. She walked back to him. 'I don't know your name yet, Miss . . .'

'Miss Widdowson. But you can call me Sue.'

'Is that just for special friends?'

'No,' said Miss Widdowson. 'Everyone calls me Sue.'

For the first week of the case Morse had felt confident in his own abilities, like a schoolboy with a tricky problem in mathematics to work out who had the answer book secretly beside him. From the very beginning of the case he thought he had glimpsed a Grand Design – he would have to juggle about a bit with the pieces of evidence that came to hand, but he knew the pattern of the puzzle. For this reason he had not, he realized,

considered the evidence *qua* evidence, but only in rela-
tion to his own prejudiced reconstruction of events. And
having failed to work out an answer to his problem
which bore the faintest similarity to the agreed solution
in the answer book, he was now beginning seriously to
wonder if, after all, the answer book was wrong. Sometimes on the eve of a big horse-race he had read through
the list of runners and riders, closed his eyes and tried
to visualize the headlines on the sports page of the
following morning's newspaper. He'd had little success
with that, either. Yet he still thought he was on the right
track. He was, as he saw himself, a persevering man,
although he was wide awake to the possibility that to
Lewis (sitting across the table now) his perseverance
might well be considered stubbornness, and to his
superiors sheer pig-headedness.

In fact Lewis was not at that moment considering the
stubbornness of his chief at all; he was contemplating
with great distaste the orders he had just received.

'But do you think it's proper to do it this way, sir?'

'I doubt it,' said Morse.

'But it's not legal, surely?'

'Probably not.'

'But you want me to do it.' Morse ignored the non-
question. 'When?'

'You'd have to make sure he was out first.'

'How do you suggest . . .'

Morse interrupted him. 'Christ man, you're not in
apron strings. Use your nous!'

Lewis felt angry as he walked across to the canteen
and ordered a cup of coffee.

'What's the matter, Sarge?' Constable Dickson was eating again.

'That bloody man Morse – that's what's the matter,' muttered Lewis, setting down his cup with such vigour that half the contents slopped messily into the saucer.

'I see you like your coffee half and half, Sarge,' said Dickson. 'Half in the cup and half in the saucer.' He was highly amused.

McPherson walked in and ordered coffee. 'Solved the murder yet, Sergeant?'

'No we bloody haven't,' snapped Lewis. He got up and left the grey-looking apology untouched – half in the cup and half in the saucer.

'What's eating him?' asked McPherson. 'God, he don't know how lucky he is. Damn good chap, Inspector Morse. I tell you, if he don't get to the bottom of that Woodstock business, nobody will.'

It was a nice compliment and Morse could have done with it. After Lewis had left, he sat for a long time, his hands together in front of his face, fingertips to fingertips, eyes closed, as if praying to some benign divinity for light along the darkening path. But Morse had long ago, albeit unwillingly, discounted the existence of any supernatural agency. He was fishing patiently in the troubled waters of his mind.

He got his bite about 4.30 p.m., and limped across to the file on the Woodstock murder. Yes, they were both there. He took them out and read them again –

for the umpteenth time, it seemed. He must be right. He had to be. But still he wondered if he was.

The first thing (but it was a minnow, not a shark) that arrested his attention was that in both the letter from the (pretty certainly) bogus employer, and in the statement made by Crowther, the writer had used the form 'I should'. Morse, not as conversant as he should have been with some of the niceties of English grammar, more often than not – almost always now he thought of it – used the form 'would'. He could hear himself dictating: 'Dear Sir, I would be very glad to . . .' Ought he to have said 'I should?' He reached for Fowler's *Modern English Usage.* There it was: 'The verbs *like, prefer, care, be glad, be inclined,* etc., are very common in first-person conditional statements (*I should like to know* etc.). In these *should,* not *would,* is the correct form in the English idiom.' Well, thought Morse, we learn something new every day. But somebody knew all about it already. So he should, though; he was an English don, wasn't he? What about Mr G – undecipherable who had something to do with a misspelt Psychology Department? (Blast – he'd not even checked that yet). But Mr G was a university man, too, wasn't he? said a still small voice at the back of Morse's mind. A very little minnow! Interesting though.

He read the documents yet again. Just a minute. Hold on. Yes. This wasn't a minnow. Surely not! 'Yet it is not improbable . . .' The phrase appeared in each document. A mannered phrase. 'Yet' standing at the beginning of its clause; not the commonest of syntactical structures. And what about 'not improbable'. That was a figure of speech Morse had learned at school. 'St Paul was a citizen of no mean city.' He consulted Fowler again. That was it. *Litotes*. Parallel expressions raced through his mind. 'Yet it is probable ...'; 'But it is probable/likely ...'; 'But it may be ...'; 'Maybe ...'; 'I think ...'; 'But I think ...' Odd. Very odd. A very mannered phrase.

And there was another coincidence. The phrase 'in all honesty' also appeared in each letter. What would he himself have written? 'Frankly', 'honestly', 'to be frank', 'truthfully'? Come to think of it, it didn't mean very much at all. Three little weasel words. The letter really was most odd. Had his first appraisal of its significance been over-sophisticated, too clever-clever? But people *did* do that sort of thing. Wives and husbands did it in war-time, communicating to each other a wealth of factual data unsuspected by the army censors. 'I'm sorry to hear little Archie's got the croup. Will write again soon,' might well have concealed the military intelligence that Trooper Smith was to be posted from Aldershot to Cairo next Saturday. Fanciful? No! Morse believed that he had been right.

The evening shadows fell across his desk, and he replaced the Woodstock file and locked the cabinet. The answer was slowly coming, and it seemed to be the answer in the answer book.

CHAPTER SIXTEEN

Tuesday, 12 October

ON TUESDAY MORNING at 11.00 a.m., half an hour after Crowther had boarded a bus to the city centre, a small business van, bearing the legend 'Kimmons Typewriters' drew up outside the Crowther residence in Southdown Road. A man, wearing a lightweight grey jacket with 'Kimmons' embroidered across the pocket, alighted from the van and walked through the white gate, past the scraggy lawn, and knocked. Margaret Crowther, wiping her hands on her apron, opened the door.

'Yes?'

'Mr Crowther live here, please?'

'Yes.'

'Is he in?'

'No, not at the minute.'

'Oh. You Mrs Crowther?'

'Yes.'

'Your husband rang to ask us to look at his typewriter. He said the carriage was getting stuck.'

'Oh, I see. Come in, will you?'

The typewriter man rather ostentatiously took from his pocket a small box, containing, one must have supposed, the requisite tools of the trade, stepped with an obvious diffidence into the narrow hallway and was ushered into the room off the right-hand side of the hall where Bernard Crowther spent so much of his time considering the glories of the English literary heritage. He spotted the typewriter immediately.

'Do you need me?' Mrs Crowther seemed anxious to resume her culinary duties.

'No, no. Shan't be more than a few minutes – unless it's really wonky.' His voice sounded strained.

'Well, call me when you've finished. I'm only in the kitchen.'

He looked carefully around, made a few perfunctory tappings on the typewriter, slid the carriage tinkling to and fro several times, and listened carefully. He could hear the clink of plates and saucers; he felt fairly safe and very nervous. Quickly he slid open the top drawer on the right of the small desk: paper-clips, biros, rubbers, elastic bands – nothing very suspicious. Systematically he tried the two lower drawers, and then the three on the left. All pretty much the same. Wadges of notes clipped together, bulky agendas for college meetings, file-cases, writing paper, more writing paper and yet more – ruled, plain, headed, foolscap, folio, quarto. He repeated his pathetic little pantomime and heard, in welcome counter-point, an answering clatter of crockery. He took one sheet from each of the piles of writing paper, folded them carefully and put them into his inside pocket. Finally taking one sheet of quarto he stood it in the typewriter, twiddled the carriage and quickly typed two lines of writing:

After asessing the mny applications we have received,
we must regretfully inform you that our application.

Mrs Crowther showed him to the door. 'Well, that
should be all right now, Mrs Crowther. Dust in the
carriage-bearings, that's all.' Lewis hoped it sounded all
right.

'Do you want me to pay you?'

'No. Don't bother about that now.' He was gone.

At twelve noon Lewis knocked on Bernard Crowther's
door in the second court of Lonsdale College and
found him finishing a tutorial with a young, bespectacled, long-haired undergraduate.

'No rush, sir,' said Lewis. 'I can wait perfectly happily
until you've finished.'

But Crowther had finished. He had met Lewis the
previous Saturday, and was anxious to hear whatever
must be heard. The youth was forthwith dismissed with
the formidable injunction to produce an essay for the
following tutorial on 'Symbolism in *Cymbeline*', and
Crowther shut the door. 'Well, Sergeant Lewis?'

Lewis told him exactly what had occurred that morning; he made no bones about it and confessed that he
had not enjoyed the subterfuge. Crowther showed little
surprise and seemed anxious only about his wife.

'Now, sir,' said Lewis. 'If you say you expected a man
from Kimmons to come and look at your typewriter, no
harm's been done. I want to assure you of that.'

'Couldn't you have asked me?'

'Well, yes, sir, we could. But I know that Inspector Morse wanted to make as little fuss as possible.'

'Yes, I'm sure.' Crowther said it with an edge of bitterness in his voice. Lewis got up to go. 'But why? What did you expect to find?'

'We wanted to find out, sir, if we could, on what machine a certain, er, a certain communication was written.'

'And you thought I was involved?'

'We have to make inquiries, sir.'

'Well?'

'Well what, sir?'

'Did you find out what you wanted?'

Lewis looked uneasy. 'Yes, sir.'

'And?'

'Shall we say, sir, that we didn't find anything at all, er – at all incriminating. That's about the position, sir.'

'You mean that you thought I'd written something on the typewriter and now you think I didn't.'

'Er, you'd have to ask Inspector Morse about that, sir.'

'But you just said that the letter wasn't written on . . .'

'I didn't say it was a letter, sir.'

'But people do write letters on typewriters don't they, Sergeant?'

'They do, sir.'

'You know, Sergeant, you're beginning to make me feel guilty.'

'I'm sorry, sir. I didn't mean to do that. But in a job like ours you've got to suspect everybody really. I've told you all I can, sir. Whatever typewriter we're looking for wasn't the one in your house. But there's more than one typewriter in the world, isn't there, sir?'

Crowther did not contest the truth of the assertion. A large bay window gave a glorious view on to the silky grass of the second court, smooth and green as a billiard table. Before the window stood a large mahogany desk, littered with papers and letters and essays and books. And in the centre of this literary clutter there sat, four-square upon the desk, a large, ancient, battered typewriter.

On his way back to Kidlington Lewis drove through the broad tree-lined sweep of St Giles' and took the right fork to follow the Banbury Road up through North Oxford. As he passed the large engineering block on his right, he saw a tallish woman in dark slacks and a long heavy coat walking along, every few steps sticking out a thumb in what seemed a particularly demoralized and pessimistic way. She had long blonde hair, natural by the look of it, reaching half-way down her back. Lewis thought of Sylvia Kaye. Poor kid. He passed the blonde just as she turned her head, and he blinked hard. What a world we live in! For the lovely blonde had a lovely beard and side-whiskers down to his chin. Interesting thought . . .

Morse had been unable to conceal his exasperation when Lewis had reported to him earlier and when, with ridiculous rapid certitude, he had established that the letter on which he had pinned his faith had neither been written on Crowther's personal typewriter nor on any of the brands of writing paper so carefully filched from Crowther's personal store. His one worry then had been to paper over the cracks of irregularity in police procedure, and it was for this reason that he had immediately dispatched Lewis to talk to Crowther. To the report of this interview he listened with care, if without enthusiasm, when Lewis returned at 1.00 p.m.

'Not the happiest of mornings then, Sergeant.'

'No. I'd rather not do that sort of thing again, sir.'

Morse sympathized. 'I don't think we've done any harm though, have we, Lewis? I'm not worried so much about Crowther – he's hardly been above-board with us, has he? But Mrs Crowther ... could have been tricky. Thanks, anyway.' He spoke with genuine feeling.

'Never mind, sir. At least we tried.' Lewis felt much better.

'What about a drink?' said Morse. The two men went off in lighter spirits.

It had occurred to neither of the policemen that women of the intelligence and experience of Mrs Margaret Crowther would do anything but automatically and unquestioningly accept the *bona fides* of any Tom, Dick and Harry of a tradesman. Furthermore, Mrs Crowther had herself been a confidential secretary before she married Bernard; in fact the typewriter was hers and that very morning she herself had typed out two letters on the same machine, one addressed to her husband and one addressed to Inspector Morse, c/o Thames Valley Police HQ, Kidlington. The typewriter was in perfect order, she knew that; and she had seen the nervous man from Kimmons Typewriters as he had slid open the drawers of Bernard's desk. She wondered what he was looking for, but she didn't really care. In a gaunt, weary way she had even smiled as she closed the door behind him. She would fairly soon be ready to post the two letters. But she wanted to be sure.

Morse worked at his desk through most of the afternoon. The report on Crowther's car had come in, but appeared to signify little. One long blonde hair, heavily peroxided, was found on the floor behind the nearside driving seat, but that was about it. No physical traces whatsoever of the second girl. Several other reports, but again nothing that appeared to advance the progress of the investigation. He turned his attention to other matters. He had to appear the next morning in the Magistrates' Court: there were briefs and memorandums to read. His mind was grateful to have, for a change, some tangible data to assimilate and he worked through the material quite oblivious to the passage of time. When he looked at his watch at 5.00 p.m. he was surprised how swiftly the afternoon had gone by. Another day over – almost. New day tomorrow. For some reason he felt contented and he wondered to himself if that reason had anything to do with Wednesday and Sue Widdowson.

He rang Lewis, who was about to go home. Yes, of course he could come along. Perhaps he could just ring his long-suffering wife? She'd probably just got the chips in the pan. 'You say, Lewis, that Crowther has got another typewriter in his rooms in college. I think we ought to check. Well?'

'Anything you say, sir.'

'But you'd like to do it straight this time, wouldn't you?'

'I think that would be best, sir.'

'Anything you say, Lewis.'

Morse knew the Principal of Lonsdale College fairly well and he rang him up there and then. Lewis was a little surprised at Morse's request. The chief really was doing it properly this time. He listened to the monologue. 'How many typewriters would there be? Yes. Yes. Including those . . . Yes. As many as that? But it could be done? Well that would be an enormous help, of course . . . You'd rather it that way? No, doesn't matter to me . . . By the end of the week? Good. Most grateful. Now listen carefully . . .'

Morse gave his instructions, iterated his thanks at inordinate length, and beamed at his sergeant when he finally cradled the phone. 'Co-operative chap that, Lewis.'

'Not much option, had he?'

'Perhaps not. But it will save us a lot of time and trouble.'

'You mean save *me* a lot of time and trouble.'

'Lewis, my friend, we're a team you and me, are we not?' Lewis nodded a grudging assent. 'By the end of the week we shall have evidence from every typewriter in Lonsdale College. What about that?'

'Including Crowther's?'

'Of course.'

'Wouldn't it have been a bit easier . . .'

'To fire straight at the bull's-eye? It would. But you said you wanted to do this in accordance with the great unprejudiced principles of English law, did you not? We haven't got a thing on Crowther. He's probably as innocent as my Aunt Freda.'

Since Lewis had never seen or heard of the said Aunt Freda he refrained from direct comment. 'Do you think Crowther's our man, sir?'

Morse stuck his thumb in the corner of his mouth. 'I don't know, Lewis. I just don't know.'

'I had a bit of an idea today, sir,' said Lewis after a pause. 'I saw what I thought was a girl and when I got close and she turned round she wasn't a she, she was a he.'

'You explain yourself very succinctly, Sergeant.'

'But you know what I mean.'

'Yes, I do. When we were boys we tried to look like boys; if you looked like a girl you were a cissy. Nowadays you've got young fellows with eye make-up and handbags. Makes you wonder.'

But Morse hadn't quite seen his point and Lewis filled in the picture. He was no ideas man, he'd always realized that, and felt great diffidence in putting his notion forward. 'You see, sir, I was just thinking. We know Mrs Jarman saw the two girls' (he needn't have gone on, but Morse held his peace) 'at the bus stop.

She must have been right, surely. She actually spoke to one of them and the other one was Sylvia Kaye. All right. The next thing is that the lorry driver, Baker, saw the girls being picked up at the other side of the roundabout by a man in a red car. But it was getting dark. He said they were two girls. *But he might have been wrong.* I could have sworn I saw a girl this morning – but I was wrong. Everybody has been dazzled by Sylvia – all the eyes were on her and no wonder. But what if the lorry driver had seen Sylvia and another person, and what if this other person looked like a girl but wasn't. *The other person could have been a man.* Remember, sir, the other girl Mrs Jarman saw was wearing slacks, and the descriptions we had from Baker fitted so well we thought they must be the same two people. But what if the other girl decided in the end not to hitch-hike to Woodstock. What if she caught up with Sylvia, told her she wasn't going to bother to go to Woodstock after all, and what if Sylvia met up with some man, probably someone she knew anyway, who'd been waiting for a lift before she got there, and the two of them hitched together. I know you've probably thought of this anyway, sir' (Morse gave no indication either way – he hadn't) 'but I thought I ought to mention it. We've been trying to find the man who did this and I just thought he might have been in the car with Sylvia all along.'

'We've got Crowther's evidence you know, Sergeant,' said Morse slowly.

'I know, sir. I'd like to see that again if I could. As I

remember it he didn't have *much* to say about his second passenger, did he?'

'No, that's true,' admitted Morse. 'And I can't help thinking he knows more than he's told us anyway.' He walked over to the filing cabinet, took from his files the statement of Bernard Crowther, read the first sheet, passed it over to Lewis, and read the second. When both men had finished, they looked at each over the table.

'Well, sir?'

Morse read it out: '"The girl nearer to the road I saw clearly. She was an attractive girl with long fair hair, white blouse, short skirt and a coat over her arm. The other girl had walked on a few yards and had her back towards me; she seemed to be quite happy to leave the business of getting a lift to her companion. But she had darkish hair, I think, and if I remember correctly was a few inches taller than her friend . . ." What do you think?'

'Not very definite is it, sir?'

Morse searched for the other relevant passage: '"I think the girl sitting in the back spoke only once and that was to ask the time . . ." You may have got something, you know,' said Morse.

Lewis warmed to his theory. 'I've often heard, sir, that when a couple are hitching the girl shows a leg, as it were, and the man keeps out of the way. You know, suddenly shows himself when the car stops and it's too late for the driver to say no.'

'That didn't happen here though, Sergeant.'

'No. I know that, sir. But it fits a bit doesn't it: "seemed quite happy to leave the business of getting a lift to her companion."' Lewis felt he should quote his evidence, too.

'Mm. But if you're right, what happened to the other girl?'

'She could have gone home, sir. Could have gone anywhere.'

'But she wanted to go to Woodstock very badly, didn't she, according to Mrs Jarman.'

'She could have got to the bus stop.'

'The conductor doesn't remember her.'

'But when we asked him we were thinking of two girls, not one.'

'Mm. Might be worth checking again.'

'And another thing, sir.' The tide was coming in inexorably and was lapping already at the sand-castles of Morse's Grand Design.

'Yes?'

'I hope you don't mind me mentioning it, sir, but Crowther says that the other girl was a few inches taller than Sylvia.' Morse groaned, but Lewis continued, remorseless as the tide. 'Now Sylvia Kaye was 5′ 9″, if I remember it right. If the other girl was Jennifer Coleby she must have been wearing stilts, sir. She's only about 5′ 6″, isn't she—'

'But don't you see, Lewis? That's the sort of thing he *would* lie about. He's trying to put us off. He wants to protect this other girl.'

'I'm only trying to go on the evidence we've got, sir.'

Morse nodded. He thought seriously that he should

take up schoolteaching – primary school would be about his level; spelling, he thought, the safest bet. Why hadn't he thought about that height business before? But he knew why. In the Grand Design it was Crowther who had been the guilty man.

And now the waves were curling perilously close to the last of the sand-castles; had already filled the moat and breached the rampart. It was 6.00 p.m., and Lewis's second batch of chips was getting cold.

Morse limped out of the building with Lewis, and the two stood talking by the sergeant's car for several minutes. Lewis felt rather like a pupil in Morse's putative primary school who had caught his master out in the spelling of a simple word, and he hesitated to mention a little thing that had been on his mind for several days. Should he keep it for tomorrow? But he knew that Morse had a busy day in front of him at the courts. He plunged in.

'You know the letter, sir, addressed to Jennifer Coleby?'

Morse knew it by heart. 'What about it?'

'Could there have been some fingerprints on the original copy?'

Morse heard the question and stared blankly into the middle distance. At last he shook his head sadly. 'Too late now.'

The primary school became a distinctly firmer prospect as the minutes ticked by. The sand-castle lurched forward and prepared to topple headlong. It was time someone else took over; he would see the Commissioner.

A police car stopped a few yards from him. 'Want some help, sir?'

'I'm all right, thanks.' Morse shook off his gloom. 'I'll be back in training next week. You'll see me in the first-team squad for the next home game.'

The constable laughed. 'Bit of a nuisance, though. Especially when you can't drive.'

Morse had almost forgotten his car. It had been locked up for over a week now. 'Constable, jump in the front with me, will you? It's high time I had a try.' He climbed into the driving seat, waggled his right foot over the brake and accelerator, pushed the foot with firmness on the brake-pedal, and decided he could cope. He started the engine, drove off round the yard, tested his ability to do the right things, came to a stop, got out and beamed like an orphan handed a teddy bear.

'Not bad, eh?' The constable helped Morse into the building and along to his office.

'You'll be able to use your car again tomorrow, won't you, sir?'

'I think I shall,' said Morse.

He sat down and thought of tomorrow. The Commissioner. In the afternoon would be best, perhaps. He rang the Commissioner's number, but there was no reply. He was seeing someone else, too, in the evening. He was looking forward to seeing Sue Widdowson – it was little use pretending he wasn't. But what a mess he'd made of it. The 'Bird and Baby' indeed! Why on earth hadn't he invited her to the Elizabeth or the Sorbonne or the Sheridan. And why hadn't he arranged to pick her up, like any civilized man would have done? Hang Jennifer Coleby! It wasn't too late, though, was it? She would be home by now. He looked at his watch: 6.30 p.m., the *Oxford Mail* lay on his desk and he scanned the entertainments page. *Hot Pants* and *Danish Blue*, he noticed, had been retained for a second week 'by public demand'. He could have taken her to the pictures, of course. Perhaps not to Studio 2, though. Restaurants. Not much there. Then he spotted it. '*Sheridan Dinner Dance*: double ticket – £6. 7.30–11.30 p.m. Bar. Dress informal.' He rang the Sheridan. Yes, a few double tickets still available, but he would have to collect them tonight. Could he ring back in a quarter of an hour or so? Yes. They would keep a double ticket for him.

Jennifer Coleby's telephone number was somewhere in the file and he soon found it. He thought over what he was to say. 'Miss Widdowson – that would be best. He hoped that Sue would answer.

Brr. Brr. He felt excited. Fool.

'Yes?' A young girl's voice, but whose? The line crackled.

'Is that Oxford 54385?

'Yes, it is. Can I help you?' Morse's heart sank. It was unmistakably the cool, clear voice of Jennifer Coleby. Morse tried in some inchoate way to speak as if he wasn't Morse. 'I want to speak to Miss Widdowson if she's there, please.'

'Yes, she is. Who shall I say is calling?'

'Oh tell her it's one of her old school friends,' replied the unMorselike voice.

'I'll get her straight away, Inspector Morse.'

'Sue! Su-ue!' he heard her shouting. 'One of your old school friends on the line!'

'Hello. Sue Widdowson here.'

'Hello.' Morse didn't know what to call himself. 'Morse here. I just wondered if you'd like to make it the Sheridan tomorrow night instead of going for a drink. There's a dinner-dance on and I've got tickets. What do you say?'

'That'd be lovely.' Morse thought he liked her voice. 'Absolutely lovely. Several of my friends are going. Should be great fun.'

Oh no! thought Morse. 'Not too many, I hope. I don't want to have to share you with a lot of others, you know.' He said it lightly with a heavy heart.

'Well, quite a few,' admitted Sue.

'Let's make it some other place, shall we? Do you know anywhere?'

'Oh, we can't do that. You've got the tickets anyway. We'll enjoy it – you'll see.'

Morse wondered if he would ever learn to tell the truth. 'All right. Now I can pick you up, if you like. Would that suit you?'

'Oh, yes please. Jenny was going to run me down in her car – but if you . . .'

'All right. I'll pick you up at 7.15.'

'7.15 it is then. Is it long dresses?' Morse didn't know. 'Never mind – I can easily find out.'

From one of your many friends, doubtless, thought Morse. 'Good. Looking forward to it.'

'Me, too.' She put down the receiver and Morse's own endearing adieu was left unspoken. Was he really looking forward to it? They were usually a bit of an anticlimax, these things. Still it would do him good. Or serve him right. He didn't much care. He'd have a decent meal anyway, and it would be good to hold a young girl in his arms again, tripping the light fantastic ... Oh hell! He'd forgotten all about that. He was going out of his mind, the stupid, senseless fool that he was. He could no more invite the fair Miss Widdowson to share the delights of a dreamy waltz than invite a rabbi to a plate of pork. He hobbled to the enquiry desk. 'Get me a car, Sergeant.'

'There'll be one in a few minutes, sir. We've got to ...'

'Get me a car now, Sergeant. And I mean *now*.' The last word resounded harshly through the open hall and several heads turned round. The desk Sergeant reached for the phone. 'I'll be waiting outside.'

'Want some help, sir?' The desk sergeant was a kindly man, and had known the Inspector for several years. Morse waited by the desk. He was angry with himself and he had many reasons for feeling so. But why he should think he had a right to take things out on one of his old friends he could not imagine. He cursed his own selfishness and discourtesy.

'Yes, Sergeant, I could do with some help.' It had not been Morse's day.

CHAPTER SEVENTEEN

Wednesday, 13 October, a.m.

A FREAK STORM struck the Oxford area in the early hours of Wednesday morning, demolishing chimneys, blowing down television aerials and lifting roof-tiles in its path. The 7.00 a.m. News reported a trail of devastation in Kidlington, Oxon, where a Mrs Winifred Fisher had a narrow escape when the roof of a garage broke its moorings and crashed through an upstairs window. 'I just can't describe it,' she said. 'Terrifying.' The portable radio stood on the bedside table along with a telephone and an alarm clock which, at 6.50 a.m., had wakened Morse from a long, untroubled sleep.

He got out of bed when the news had finished and peered through the curtains. At least his own garage seemed intact. Funny, though, that the storm had not awakened him. Gradually the memory of yesterday's events filtered through his consciousness and settled like a heavy sediment at the bottom of his mind. Gone were the flights of angels that had guarded him in sleep and he sat on the edge of his bed fingering the rough stubble on his chin and wondering what this day would bring. Increasingly, as the case progressed, the graph of his moods was resembling a jagged mountain range, peaks and valleys, troughs and elations.

At a quarter to eight he was shaved, washed and dressed, and feeling fresh and confident. He swilled out the dregs from his late-night cup of Horlicks, rinsed his late-night whisky glass, filled the kettle and turned his attention to a major problem.

For the last few days he had worn, around his wounded foot, an outsize white plimsoll, loosely laced, and slit down the heel. It was time to get back to something normal. He was loath to appear in the court in such eccentric footwear and he could hardly believe that Miss Widdowson would be overjoyed with a semi-plimsolled escort at the dance. He had two pairs of shoes only and a dangerously low supply of suitable socks; and with such limited permutations of possibilities, the prospect of being presentably shod that day was somewhat remote. He slipped his faithful battered plimsoll back on, and decided to buy a large pair of shoes from M and S, his favourite store. It was going to be an expensive day. He drank a cup of tea, and looked out of the window. His dustbin lid was leaning against the front gate, with litter everywhere. He must remember to have a look at the roof-tiles . . .

In retrospect he thought he had got yesterday's events out of all perspective; he had been standing too close to the trees, and now he thought he saw again the same familiar wood, labyrinthine, certainly, as before – but still the same. He was feeling his old resilient self, or almost so. But the drastic course of action he had contemplated – what about that? He would have to consider things again; he had a more immediate problem on his mind. Where were his pen, his comb and his wallet? Amazingly, and with deep relief, he found them all in the same heap on the bedroom mantelpiece.

The faithful old Lancia was still there. It had been a good buy. Powerful, reliable, and 300 miles on a full tank. He had often thought of changing it but never had the heart. He eased himself into the narrow gap between the door of the driver's seat and the white-washed wall of the garage. It was always a tricky manoeuvre and he was getting no thinner. But it felt good to sit at the wheel again. He gave the old girl a bit more choke than usual – after all she had been standing idle for a week – and pressed the starter. Chutter ... chutter ... chutter ... chutter. No. Bit more choke? But he mustn't flood her. Again. Chutter ... chutter ... chutter ... chutter ... chutter ... Odd. He'd never had much difficulty before. Third time lucky, though. Chutter ... chutter ... chutter. Battery must be getting a bit low. Oh dear. Give her a minute or two's rest. Let her get her breath back. This time, then! Chutter ... chutter ... Bugger! Once more. Chutt ... 'Just my bloody luck,' he said to himself. 'How the hell am I supposed to get about without...' He stopped and shivered involuntarily. A grey dawn was breaking in his mind and the purple mysteries of the morning were shot with the rays of the rising sun. 'Bliss was it in that dawn to be alive.' Wordsworth, wasn't it? It had been in *The Times* crossword last week. The waves were at last receding from the beach. The white crests of the breakers rolled ceaselessly and tirelessly towards the shore, but their strength was gone. He saw the Grand

Design before him and the last little sand-castle had survived the mighty sea.

The manager of Barker's garage in Oxford was so impressed by Inspector Morse's courteous call upon his services that a new battery was on its way in ten minutes, and installed in fifteen. The clouds were high and white and the sun shone brightly. Open weather, as Jane Austen would have called it. Morse retrieved the dustbin lid, and meticulously gathered up all the litter from his garden.

The university city of Oxford was busy this morning, the third full day of the Michaelmas term. First-year undergraduates, with spankingly new college scarves tossed over their shoulders, eagerly explored the bookshops of the Broad, and a trifle self-consciously strode down the High into the crowded Cornmarket, into Woolworths and Marks and Spencer and thence, according to taste, into the nearest pubs and the coffee shops. At 1.00 p.m. Morse was sitting on a chair in the self-service men's shoe department in the basement of M and S. He normally took size 8, but was now experimenting with patience and determination. Size 9 seemed of little use, and after considerable trafficking in stockinged feet between the show counter and his chosen chair, he plumped for size-10 black leather slip-ons. They seemed huge and were, of course, potentially useless in the long run. But who cared? He could wear two pairs of socks on his left foot. Which reminded him. He paid for the shoes, adjusted his plimsoll, much to the bewilderment of a large, morose-looking cashier, who looked as if she might wear size 10 herself, and proceeded to the hosiery counter where he purchased half a dozen gaudy pairs of lightweight socks. If he had been able, he would have walked out into Cornmarket with a light step. The car was functioning, the courts were finished, the case was flourishing.

Others, too, were making their purchases. Trade was thriving this morning, and not only in the large stores in the main streets in Oxford city centre. At about the same time that Morse, the megapode, tucked his purchases beneath his arm, one further swift, uncomplicated transaction was being effected in the rundown back street behind the Botley Road, and it could be argued that this time, at least, John Sanders had struck the better bargain.

CHAPTER EIGHTEEN

Wednesday, 13 October, p.m.

AT LONSDALE COLLEGE Wednesday, 13th was the first full guest-night of the Michaelmas term and Bernard Crowther left home a little earlier than usual. At 6.15 p.m. he knocked on Peter Newlove's rooms and walked in, not waiting for a reply.

'That you, Bernard?'

'It's me.'

'Pour yourself a drink. Shan't be a minute.'

Bernard had passed the Lodge as he came in and had picked up three letters from his pigeon-hole. Two he opened raggedly and relegated cursorily to his jacket pocket. The third was marked 'confidential', and contained a card 'From the Principal':

'The police, in the course of their investigations into the recent murder at Woodstock, are anxious to trace the provenance of a typed letter which has come into their possession and which they think may be material evidence in their inquiries. I have been asked by the police to see that every typewriter in the college is checked and I am asking all my colleagues to comply with this request. The Bursar has agreed to undertake this duty and it is my view, and also that of the Vice-Principal, that we must readily accede to this proper request. I have therefore informed Chief Inspector Morse, who is heading the murder inquiries, that we as a collegiate body are most anxious to co-operate in any way possible. The Bursar has an inventory of all college typewriters; but there may be private typewriters in the rooms of several fellows, and I ask that information concerning them should be given to the Bursar immediately. Thank you for your help.'

'What's up, Bernard? Don't you want a drink?' Peter had come in from the bathroom and stood combing his thinning hair with a thinning comb.

'Have you had one of these?'

'I have indeed received a communication from our revered and reverend Principal, if that's what you mean.'

'What's it all about?'

'Don't know, dear boy. Mysterious though, isn't it?'

'When's the great investigation due?'

'Due? It's done. At least mine is. Little girl came in this afternoon – with the Bursar, of course. Typed out some cryptic message and then she was gone. Pity really. Lovely little thing. I must try to spend a bit more time in the Bursary.'

'I shan't be able to help much myself, I'm afraid. That bloody thing of mine was manufactured in the Middle Ages and hasn't had a ribbon in it for six months. I think it's what they call "seized-up", anyway.'

'Well, that's one suspect less, Bernard. Now are you going to have a drink or not?'

'Don't you think we shall have enough booze tonight?'

'No, dear boy, I don't.' Peter sat down and pulled on an expensive pair of heavy, brown brogues: size 10s, but not purchased from the self-service shoe department at Marks and Spencer.

'We've just got time for a quick one, I think.' It was almost 7.30 p.m. 'What would you like?'

'Dry sherry for me, please. I shan't be a minute. Must powder my nose.' She went off to the cloakroom. There were only a few people in the lounge bar and Morse, served without delay, took the drinks over to the corner of the room and sat down.

The Sheridan was the most fashionable of the Oxford hotels and most visiting stars of stage, screen, sport and television found themselves booked in at this well-appointed, large, stone building just off the bottom of St Giles'. A striped canopy stretched out over the pavement and a flunkey stood his station beside the gleaming name-plate on the shallow steps leading down to the street from the revolving doors. Morse suspected that the management kept a red carpet rolled up somewhere on the premises. Not that it had been rolled out this evening; in fact he had been unable to find any parking space at all in the hotel's narrow yard and had been forced to park his car along St Giles'. It wasn't perhaps the best of starts, and they had said little to each other.

He watched her as she came back. She had parted with her coat and walked with enviable elegance towards him, her long deep-red velvet dress gently affirming the lines of her graceful body. And suddenly, sweetly his heart beat stronger, and their eyes met and she smiled. She sat beside him and he was aware again, as he had been as she sat beside him in the car, of the strange and subtle promise of her perfume.

'Cheers, Sue.'

'Cheers, Inspector.'

He didn't know what to do about this name trouble. He felt like an ageing schoolmaster meeting one of his old pupils and being rather embarrassed by the 'sirs' in every other sentence, and yet feeling it phoney to have it otherwise. He let the 'Inspectors' pass. Things could change, of course. Morse offered her a cigarette but she declined. As she sipped her sherry Morse noticed the long and delicately manicured fingers: no rings, no nail-polish. He asked her about her day's work and she told him. It was all a little strained. They finished their drinks and walked out of the lounge and up the stairs to the Evans Room, Sue lifting her dress slightly as she negotiated the stairs, and Morse trying to forget the tightness in his right shoe and frenziedly arching the left foot to prevent the shoe from falling off completely.

The room was arranged with subdued and delicate decorum: around a small, well-polished dance-floor tables were set at regular intervals, the silver cutlery gleaming on the white tablecloths and a red candle lit on each table, the blue and yellow flames tapering into a slimness, almost as exquisite, thought Morse, as Sue Widdowson herself. Several couples were already seated and it was sadly clear to Morse that some of her wretched friends were among them. A small band played some languorous melody that lingered in the mind and as they were shown to their table a young couple took the floor, blithely and obliviously, feeding deep upon each other's eyes.

'You've been here before?'

Sue nodded, and Morse followed the young couple with his eyes and decided not to give too free a rein to his imagination. A waiter came to them with the menu, and Morse welcomed the diversion.

'Do they throw in the wine?'

'We get a bottle between us.'

'Is that all?'

'Isn't that enough?'

'Well, it's a special occasion, isn't it?' Sue was non-committal. 'What about a bottle of champagne?'

'You've got to drive me home, remember?'

'We could get a taxi.'

'What about your car?'

'Perhaps the police will pick it up.' Sue laughed and Morse saw her white teeth and the fullness of her lips. 'What do you say?'

'I'm in your hands, Inspector.' Would you were, he thought.

Several other couples were now dancing and Sue was watching them. 'You enjoy dancing?' Sue kept her eyes on the dancers and nodded. A young Adonis waved a hand in their direction.

'Lo Sue. All right?' Sue raised a hand in greeting.

'Who's that?' asked Morse aggressively.

'Doctor Eyres. He's one of the housemen at the Radcliffe.' She seemed almost hypnotized by the scene.

But she turned back into Morse's orbit with the arrival of the champagne, and after a while the conversation took a freer course. Morse chattered as amiably and interestingly as he could and Sue seemed pleasantly relaxed. They ordered their meal, and Morse poured another glass of champagne. The band stopped; the couples on the floor clapped half-heartedly for a few seconds and retired to the perimeter tables. Dr Eyres and his heavily mascaraed young brunette made their way towards Morse's table, and Sue seemed glad to see them.

'Doctor Eyres this is Inspector Morse.' The two men shook hands. 'And this is Sandra. Sandra this is Inspector Morse.' The leaden-eyed Sandra, it transpired, was also a nurse and worked with Sue at the Radcliffe Infirmary. The band resumed its plangent strains.

'Mind if I had this dance with Sue, Inspector?'

'Of course not,' smiled Morse. You lousy, lecherous medico. Sandra sat down and looked at Morse with obvious interest in her eyes.

'I'm awfully sorry not to be able to ask you to dance,' he said, 'but I've had an accident with my foot. Nearly better, though.'

Sandra was sympathy itself. 'Oh dear. How did that happen?'

For the fiftieth time in the last seven days Morse repeated the attendant circumstances of his escapade. But his mind was all on Sue. As she escorted the houseman to the floor he thought of Coleridge:

> The bride hath paced into the hall,
> Red as a rose is she.

He watched them dance; he saw Sue's arms closely round her partner's neck, her body close to his; and then his cheek was brushing her hair, her head happily resting on his shoulder. Morse felt sick of a jealous dread. He turned his eyes away from the smooching couples. 'Do you know, I reckon I could just about cope with this dance myself,' he said. 'May I?' He took her hand, led her to the floor and, firmly placing his right arm round her waist, drew her towards him. Rapidly, however, he realized the extent of his own stupidity. His injured foot was working like a dream, but lacking the confidence to lift his other foot more than a centimetre off the dance-floor he was soon kicking his partner's toes with monotonous and ill-received regularity. Mercifully the dance was quickly over, and mumbling profuse apologies about his ill-educated feet Morse slopped his way back to the haven of his table. Sue was still talking in an animated way to Doctor Eyres, and after Sandra had rejoined them, the trio erupted into peals of laughter.

Ten minutes earlier Morse had anticipated that even the most succulent steak would taste tonight as dry as the Dead Sea apples, but he tucked into his meal with a will. At least he could eat. Even if he couldn't dance, even if he'd forgotten how middle-aged he'd now become, even if Sue was yearning for someone else, he could still eat. And jolly good it was. They said little and when something was said, as they drank their coffees, it came as a big surprise.

'Why did you ask me out, Inspector?'

Morse looked at her, the hair light-brown and lifted

softly from her face, her face itself all freshness and delight, the cheeks now faintly flushed with wine; and above all the magic of those wide and doleful eyes. Had he asked her with any firm purpose? He wasn't sure. He put his elbows on the table, rested his chin on his clasped hands. 'Because I find you so very beautiful and I wanted to be with you.'

Sue looked at him for several seconds, her eyes unblinking and gentle. 'Do you mean that?' she asked quietly.

'I don't know if I meant it when I asked you. But I mean it now – I think you know I do.' He spoke simply and calmly and he held her eyes with his own as he spoke. He saw two splendid tears forming on her lower lids and she reached across and laid her hand upon his arm.

'Come and dance with me,' she whispered.

The floor was crowded and they did little more than sway slowly to the sweet, low rhythm of the band. Sue leaned her head lightly against his cheek and Morse felt with a wonderful joy the moisture of her eyes. He wished the world would stop and that this heavenly moment could be launched on the eternal seas. He kissed her ear and said some awkward, loving things, and Sue nuzzled deeper and deeper into his arms and pulled him even more closely to her. They stood together as the music ended, and Sue looked up at him. 'Can we go now, please. Somewhere on our own?'

Morse remembered little of the next few minutes. He had waited in a dream-like state beside the revolving doors and arm-in-arm the two had slowly walked along St Giles' towards the car.

'I want to talk to you,' said Sue when they were sitting in the car.

'I'm listening.'

'You know when you said that you might not have meant ... might not have meant what you said. Oh, I'm getting all muddled. What I mean is – you did want to ask me something, didn't you?'

'Did I?' asked Morse.

'You know you did. About Jennifer. That's where we both came in, wasn't it? You thought she'd got something to do with the Woodstock murder...' Morse nodded. 'And you wanted to ask me about her boy friends and that sort of thing.'

Morse sat silently in the darkness of his car. 'I'm not going to ask you now, Sue. Don't worry.' He put his arm around her and drew her towards him and tenderly kissed the softest, heavenliest lips that ever the Almighty made. 'When can we meet again, Sue?' As soon as he had spoken he knew that something was wrong. He felt her body tauten; she moved away from him, felt for her handkerchief and blew her nose. She was on the verge of tears. 'No,' she said, 'we can't.'

Morse felt a hurt that he had never known before, and his voice was strained and unbelieving. 'But why? Why? Of course we can meet again, Sue.'

'We can't.' Her voice for the moment seemed matter-of-fact and final. 'We can't meet again, Inspector, because ... because I'm engaged to be married.'

She just managed to blurt out the last word before burying her head on Morse's shoulder and bursting into anguished tears. Morse kept his arm tightly around her and listened with unfathomable sadness to her convulsive sobs. The front window had steamed over with their breath and Morse perfunctorily wiped away the moisture with the back of his right hand. Outside he saw the massive outer wall of St John's College. It was only 10.00 p.m. and a group of undergraduates were laughing gaily outside the Porter's Lodge. Morse knew it well. He'd been an undergraduate there himself; but that was twenty years ago and life since then had somehow passed him by.

They drove in silence up to North Oxford and Morse pulled up the Lancia directly in front of Sue's front door. As he did so the door opened and Jennifer Coleby came out with her car-keys in her hand, and walked towards them.

'Hello, Sue. You're home early, aren't you?'

Sue wound the window down. 'We didn't want to get stopped for drinking and driving.'

'Are you coming in for a coffee?' asked Jennifer. The question was directed obliquely through the car window to Morse.

'No. I think I'd better get home.'

'See you in a minute then,' said Jennifer to Sue. 'Just going to put the car away.' She climbed into a smart little Fiat and drove smoothly off to her rented garage in the next street.

'Good little cars, Fiats,' said Morse.

'No better than English cars, are they?' asked Sue. She was bravely trying not to make a fool of herself again.

'Very reliable, I'm told. And even if something does go wrong, there's a good agent pretty near, isn't there?' Morse hoped he sounded casual enough, but he didn't really care.

'Yes, right on the doorstep, really.'

'I've always found Barkers pretty good myself.'

'She does, too,' said Sue.

'Well, I suppose I'd better go.'

'Are you sure you won't come in for some coffee?'

'Yes. I'm quite sure.'

Sue took his hand and held it lightly in her own. 'You know I shall cry myself to sleep, don't you?'

'Don't say that.' He didn't want to be hurt any more.

'I wish you were going to sleep with me,' she whispered.

'I wish you were going to sleep with me for ever, Sue.'

They said no more. Sue got out of the car, waved as the Lancia slowly moved off, and turned towards the front door, her face blinded with tears.

Morse drove to Kidlington with a heavy heart. He thought of the first time he had seen Miss Dark-eyes and now he thought of the last. Would things had been otherwise! He thought of the saddest line of poetry he had ever read:

Not a line of her writing have I, not a thread of her hair

and felt no better for the thought. He didn't want to go home; he had never realized before how lonely he had become. He stopped at the White Horse, ordered a double whisky and sat down in an empty corner. She hadn't even asked his name ... He thought of Doctor Eyres and his dark-eyed Sandra and supposed, without a hint of envy, that they were probably getting into bed by now. He thought of Bernard Crowther and doubted if his illicit liaisons with his girl in Blenheim Park were tinged with half the sadness that he himself now felt. He thought of Sue and her fiancé and hoped he was a good fellow. He bought another double whisky and, maudlin and fuddled, left soon after the landlord shouted time.

He put away the car with exaggerated care and heard the phone ringing before he could open the door. His heart raced. He rushed into the hall just as the phone stopped. Was it her? Was it Sue? He could always ring back. What was the number? He didn't know. It was in his files at Police HQ. He could ring there. He picked up the phone – and put it down. It wouldn't be Sue. If it was, she could ring back. She'd probably been ringing all the time he'd been sitting in the White Horse. Blast it. Ring again, Sue. Just to let me hear you speak. Ring again, Sue. But the telephone rang no more that night.

CHAPTER NINETEEN

Thursday, 14 October

BERNARD CROWTHER HAD a hangover on Thursday morning. He would be lecturing in the Schools at 11.00 a.m. and he contemplated his notes on 'Influences on Milton's Poetical Style' with a growing sense of apprehension. Margaret had brought him a cup of hot black coffee at a quarter to nine; she always knew – and usually said so. She had been up since half-past six, cooked the children's breakfast, washed some shirts and blouses, made the beds, hoovered the bedrooms and she was now putting on her coat in the hall. She put her head round the door. 'You all right?' How Bernard hated the reminder!

'Fine.'

'Do you want anything from town – Milk of Magnesia tablets?' They seemed perpetually in a state of eruptive belligerence, staring at each other over a long-disputed frontier. Margaret! Margaret! He wished he could talk to her.

'No. No thanks. Look, Margaret, I've got to go down myself pretty soon. Can you wait a few minutes?'

'No. Must be off. You home for lunch?'

What was the point? 'No. I'll have a bite to eat in college.' He heard the front door bang and watched as she walked quickly to the end of the road and round the corner and out of sight. He went to the kitchen, filled a glass with cold water and dropped in two tablets of soluble Disprin.

Morse and Lewis conferred from nine to ten that morning. There were several loose ends to tie up and several interesting trails to follow. At least, that's how Morse explained things to Lewis. After Lewis had left him, he had a call from a young reporter on the *Oxford Mail*, as a result of which a brief paragraph would appear in the evening edition. Routine answers. He couldn't tell anyone much, but he tried to sound as confident as he could. It was good for morale.

He got the Kaye file and spent the next hour rereading the documents in the case. At 11.00 a.m. he put the file away, reached for the Oxford and District telephone directory, looked under the Cs for the number he wanted, and rang the manager of Chalkley and Sons, Botley Road. He was unlucky. John Sanders had not come in that morning; his mother had phoned – bad cold or something.

'What's your opinion of him?' asked Morse.

'He's all right. Quiet, little bit surly, perhaps. But most of them are these days. Works well enough, I think.'

'Well, I'm sorry to have bothered you. I wanted a quick word with him, that's all.'

'About this murder at Woodstock?'

'Yes. He found the girl, you know.'

'Yes. I read about it and of course everyone tried to talk to him about it.'

'Did he have much to say?'

'Not really. Didn't seem to want to talk. Understandable, I suppose.'

'Yes. Well, thanks once again.'

'You're very welcome. Do you want his home address?'

'No thanks. I've got it here.'

Lewis was rather more fortunate. Mrs Jarman was at home, dusting the stairs.

'But I don't understand, Sergeant. I'm *sure* they were both girls.'

Lewis nodded. 'Just checking up on one or two things.'

'But I spoke to one of them, as you know, and the other poor girl – well, you know ... And I thought they were *about* the same height; but it's ever so difficult to remember you know ...' Yes, Lewis knew. He left her to dust the stairs.

He found the bus conductor drinking coffee in the canteen at Gloucester Green.

'*One* girl getting on the bus? But you said *two* before.'

'Yes, I know. But we've got an idea that perhaps only one got on.'

'Sorry. I can't remember. I am sorry, honest – but it's a long time ago now.'

'Yes. Don't worry. As I said – just an idea. If you do happen to think of anything ...'

'Of course.'

George Baker was digging his garden. ''Allo mate. I seen you before.'

'Sergeant Lewis Thames Valley Police.'

'Ah. Course, Wha' can a do forya?'

Lewis explained his visit but George's answer was only marginally less discouraging than those of the others.

'We-ell, I s'pose it *could* a been a fella, bu' swipe me mate, I could a swore as both of 'em was women.'

Memories were fading and the case was growing stale. Lewis went home for lunch.

At 2.00 p.m. he was ushered into the office of the car service manager of Barkers Garage on the Banbury Road, where he spent more than an hour working his way methodically through hundreds of carbon copies of work-sheets, customers' invoices, booking-ledgers and other sundry records of car repairs for the weeks beginning September 22 and 27. He found nothing. He spent a further hour going back to the beginning of September, increasingly conscious that his task was futile. Miss Jennifer Coleby, although she had an account with Barkers, had not brought in her car for any repairs or service since July. She had bought the car new from the garage over three years ago; HP nearly finished; no trouble with payments; no serious mechanical faults. 6,000 service on 14 July, with a few oddments put right. £13.55. Bill paid July 30.

Lewis was disappointed if not surprised. Morse seemed to have a bee in his bonnet about this Coleby woman. Perhaps this would put him off for good? But he doubted it. He walked over the road to the news-agents and bought the evening newspaper. A caption near the botton right-hand corner of the front page caught his eye:

WOODSTOCK KILLING
BREAKTHROUGH NEAR

'Following intensive activity, police are quietly confident that the killer of Sylvia Kaye, found raped and murdered at the Black Prince, Wood-stock, on the night of 29 September will soon be found. Chief Inspector Morse of the Thames Valley HQ, who is heading the murder inquiry, said today that several key witnesses had already come forward and he considered that it would only be a matter of time before the guilty party was brought to justice.'

Lewis thought it must be a hoax.

The confident head of the murder inquiry, if ever invited to take his eight discs to a desert island, would have answered 'Committees' to the inevitable question about what he would be most glad to have got away from. The meeting called for this Thursday afternoon to consider pensions, promotions and appointments stretched on and on like an arid desert. His only contribution throughout was a word of commendation for Constable McPherson. It seemed a justifiable excuse for contravening his customary and caustic taciturnity. The meeting finally broke up at five minutes past five, when he yawned his way back to his office and found

Lewis reading the prospects for Oxford United's visit to Blackpool the following Saturday.

'Seen this, sir?' Lewis handed him the newspaper and pointed to the caption portending judgement day for the Woodstock killer.

Morse read the item with weary composure. 'They do twist things a bit, these reporters, don't they?'

Sue Widdowson's day, too, dragged drearily by. She'd wanted desperately to talk to Morse again last night. Who knows what she might have said? Was his phone out of order? But in the cold light of morning she had realized how foolish it would have been. David was coming on Saturday for the weekend, and she would be meeting him at the station at the usual time. Dear David. She had received another letter that morning. He was so nice and she liked him so very much. But . . . No! She had just *got* to stop thinking of Morse. It had been almost impossible. Sandra had been full of questions and Doctor Eyres had patted her bottom far too intimately, and she was lousily, hopelessly miserable.

Mrs Amy Sanders was worried about her son. He had seemed listless and off-colour for a week or so now. In the past he had taken the odd day or two off work, and more than once she had had to lay it on a bit thick in describing to Messrs Chalkley the symptoms of some fictitious malady which had temporarily stricken her dear boy. But today she was genuinely concerned. John had been sick twice during the night and was lying shivering and sweating when she had called him at 7.00 a.m. He had eaten nothing all day and, against her son's wishes, she had rung the doctor's surgery at 5.00 p.m. No, she had not thought it urgent, but would be most grateful if the doctor could call some time.

The bell rang at 7.30 p.m. and Mrs Sanders opened the front door to find a man she had never seen before. Still, the doctors these days were always changing around.

'Does Mr John Sanders live here?'

'Yes. Come in, doctor. I'm ever so glad you could call.'

'I'm not a doctor, I'm afraid. I'm a Police Inspector.'

The landlord of the Bell at Chipping Norton took the booking himself at 8.30 p.m. He consulted the register and picked up the phone again.

'For tomorrow night and Saturday night, you said?'

'Yes.'

'I think we can do that all right, sir. Double room. Do you want a private bathroom?'

'That would be nice. And a double bed if you've got one. We never seem to sleep well in these twin beds.'

'Yes. We can do that.'

'I'm afraid I shan't have time to confirm it in writing.'

'Oh don't worry about that, sir. If you could just let me have your name and address.'

'Mr and Mrs John Brown, Hill Top, Eaglesfield (all one word), Bristol.'

'I've got that.'

'Good. My wife and I look forward to seeing you. We should be there about five.'

'We hope you'll enjoy your stay, sir.'

The landlord put down the phone and wrote the names of Mr and Mrs J. Brown in the booking register. His wife had once added up the number of John Browns booked into the Bell: in one month alone there were seven. But it wasn't his job to worry too much about that. Anyway, the man had sounded most polite and well educated. Nice voice, too: West Countryish – rather like his own. And there must be one or two quite genuine John Browns somewhere.

CHAPTER TWENTY

Friday, 15 October, a.m.

MORSE WOKE UP late on Friday morning. *The Times* was already on the floor in the hall and one letter was protruding precariously through the letter box. It was a bill from Barkers – £9.25. He stuck it, with several of its fellows, behind the clock on the mantelpiece.

The car purred into life at the first gentle touch. He had the sticks in the back of the car and decided to run down to the Radcliffe Infirmary before going to the office. As he joined the patiently crawling, never-ending line of traffic in the Woodstock Road, he debated his course of action. He could see her quite by chance, of course – as he had last time; or he could ask for her. But would she want that? He longed just to *see* her again and, dammit!, she would be there. What could be more natural? He had dreamed about Sue the previous night, but in a vague, elusive sort of way which had left her standing in the forecourt of his mind. *Had* it been her on the phone on Wednesday night?

He turned off, across the traffic, into the yard of the Radcliffe, stopped on double yellow lines, collared the nearest porter, gave him the sticks and the promissory note of the bearer to return the same, and told him to see to it. Police!

The road was clear as he left Oxford and he cursed himself savagely every other minute. He should have gone in – stupid fool. He knew deep down he wasn't a stupid fool, but it didn't help much.

Lewis was waiting for him. 'Well, what's the programme, sir?'

'I thought we'd take a gentle bus ride a little later, Lewis.' Ah well. His not to reason why. 'Yes. I thought we'd go to Woodstock on the bus together. What about that?'

'Has the car conked out again?'

'No. Going like a dream. So it should. Had a bill for the bloody battery this morning. Guess how much.'

'Six, seven pounds.'

'Nine pounds twenty-five!'

Lewis screwed up his nose. 'Cheaper if you'd gone to the tyre and battery people up in Headington. They don't charge for any labour. I've always found them very good.'

'You sound as if you're always having car trouble.'

'Not really. Had a few punctures lately, though.'

'Can't you change a tyre yourself?'

'Well yes. Course I can. I'm not an old woman you know, but you've got to have a spare.'

Morse wasn't listening. He felt the familiar tingle of the blood freezing in his arms. 'You're a genius, Sergeant. Pass me the telephone directory. Consult the yellow pages. Here we are – only two numbers. Which shall we try first?'

'What about the first one, sir?'

A few seconds later Morse was speaking to Cowley

Tyre and Battery Services. 'I want to speak to the boss of the place. It's urgent. Police here.' He winked at Lewis. 'Ah, hullo. Chief Inspector Morse here. Thames Valley ... No, no. Nothing like that ... Now, I want you to look up your records for the week beginning 27 September ... Yes. I want to know if you supplied a battery or mended a puncture for a Miss Jennifer Coleby. C-O-L-E-B-Y. Yes. It might have been any day – probably Tuesday or Wednesday. You'll ring me back? Get on with it straight away, please. It's most urgent. Good. You've got my number? Good. Cheers.' He rang the second number and repeated the patter. Lewis was turning over the Sylvia Kaye file that lay open on Morse's desk. He studied the photographs – large, glossy, black and white photographs with amazingly clear delineation. He looked again at the shots of Sylvia Kaye as she lay that night in the yard of the Black Prince. She'd been really something, he thought. The white blouse had been torn sharply on the left-hand side, and only the bottom of the four buttons remained fastened. The left breast was fully revealed and Lewis was strongly reminded of the provocative poses of the models in the girlie magazines. It could almost have been an erotic experience – looking through those pictures; but Lewis remembered the back of the blonde head and the cruelly shattered skull. He thought of his own darling daughter – thirteen now; she was getting a nice little figure ... God, what a world to bring up children in. He hoped and prayed that she would be all right, and he felt a deep and burning need to find the man who did all that to Sylvia Kaye.

Morse had finished.

'Can you put me in the picture, sir?' asked Lewis.

Morse sat back and thought for a few minutes. 'I suppose I ought to have told you before, Lewis. But I couldn't be sure – well, can't be sure now – about one or two things. Pretty well from the beginning I thought I had a good idea of the general picture. I thought it was like this. Two girls want a lift to Woodstock and we've got some fairly substantial evidence that they *were* picked up – *both* of them.' Lewis nodded. 'Now neither the driver nor the other girl came forward. The question I asked myself was "why?". Why were both these people anxious to keep quiet? There were pretty obvious reasons why *one* of them should keep his mouth shut. But why both? It seemed most improbable to me that the pair of them could be partners in crime. So. What are we left with? One very strong possibility, as I saw it, was that they knew each other. But that didn't seem quite good enough, somehow. Most people don't withhold evidence, certainly don't tell complicated lies, just because they know each other. But what if they have, between them, some guilty reason for wanting to keep things very quiet indeed? And what if such a guilty reason is the fact that they know each other rather *too* well? What if they are – not to put too fine a point on things – having an affair with each other? The situation's not so good for them, is it? With a murder in the background – not so good at all.' Lewis wished he'd get on with it. 'But let's go back a bit. On the face of it our evidence suggested from the word go that the encounter between the two girls and the driver of the car was pure chance: Mrs Jarman's evidence is perfectly clear on that point. Now we have discovered, after a good deal of unnecessary trouble, who the driver of the red car was: Crowther. In his evidence he admits that he is having an affair with another woman and that the venue for these extramarital excursions is Blenheim Park. Furthermore, again on his own evidence, he was going to see his lady-love on the night of Wednesday, 29 September. Now at this point I took a leap in the dark. What if the lady-love was one of the girls he picked up?'

'But . . .' began Lewis.

'Don't interrupt, Lewis. Now, was the lady-love Sylvia Kaye? I don't think so. We know that Mr John Sanders had a date, however vague, with Sylvia on the 29th. It doesn't prove things one way or the other, but Sylvia is the less likely choice of the two. So. We're left with our other passenger – Miss, or Mrs X. It is clear from Mrs Jarman's evidence that Miss X seemed anxious and excited, and I think no one gets too anxious and excited about going to Woodstock unless that person has a date, and an important date at that, and not very much time to spare. Crowther said an hour or so at the most, remember?'

'But . . .' He thought better of it.

'We also learned from what Mrs Jarman said that Sylvia knew the other girl. There was that business of having a giggle about it in the morning. So, we try the place where Sylvia works and we find an extraordinary, quite inexplicable letter written to Miss Jennifer Coleby, who has become my odds-on favourite for the Miss X title. I agree that the evidence of the letter is not conclusive; worth following up though. She's a clever girl, our Jennifer. She has two spanners to throw in the works. First, she seems to have been at a pub this side of Woodstock instead of in Blenheim Park; second – and this really worried me and still does – why does she have to bus to Woodstock, or hitch-hike, if she's got a car? Which, as we know, she has. It seemed a fatal objection. But is it? *My* car wouldn't start on Wednesday morning because the battery was flat. You said that *you* had a few punctures recently and you said you could mend them. You said you were not an old woman. Now Jennifer Coleby is not an old woman – but *she's a woman*. What if she discovered that her car wouldn't start? What would she do? Ring up her garage. That was pretty obvious and hence your visit to Barkers, where you drew a blank. I thought I saw the light, though, this morning. I had a bill for my car-battery and you mentioned the tyre and battery people. The real question then is *when* did Jennifer discover her car was out of order? Surely not before she got back from work, at about 5.30 p.m. Now not many garages these days are going to do much at that time; the staff has all gone. But your little tyre and battery men don't work, methinks, to union hours, and they are worth trying. I must assume that Jennifer could get no one to see to her car that night – not because they couldn't do it, but because they *couldn't do it in time*. She may not have discovered the trouble until about 6.15 or 6.30 p.m. But I think she tried to get something done – and failed. Well, what's she to do? Naturally, she can get a bus. She's never had to bus before, but she's seen the Woodstock buses often enough and that's why I believe it was Jennifer who was seen at Fare Stage 5 on the night Sylvia was murdered. She meets an impatient fellow-traveller, Sylvia, and the two of them decide to hitchhike. They walk past the roundabout and a car stops: Crowther's car. It's hardly a coincidence, is it? He's got to get to Woodstock, too, and he's bound to be going there at roughly the same time as Jennifer. Whether he knew it was her – it was getting fairly dark – I just don't know. I suspect he did.' Morse stopped.

'And what happened then, do you think, sir?'

'Crowther has told us what happened for the next few miles.'

'Do you believe him?'

Morse sat thoughtfully and didn't answer immediately. The phone rang. 'No,' said Morse, 'I don't believe him.' Lewis watched the Inspector. He could not hear what was being said on the other end of the line. Morse listened impassively.

'Thank you very much,' he said finally. 'What time would be convenient? All right. Thank you.' He put down the phone, and Lewis looked at him expectantly.

'Well, sir?'

'I told you Lewis. You're a genius.'

'Her car *was* out of order?'

Morse nodded. 'Miss Jennifer Coleby rang the Cowley Tyre and Battery Co. at 6.15 p.m. on the evening of Wednesday, 29 September. She said it was urgent – a very flat front tyre. They couldn't get there until sevenish and she said that was too late.'

'We're making headway, sir.'

'We are, indeed. Now what about our bus ride?'

The two men caught the 11.35 4A to Woodstock. It was half empty and they sat in the front seat on the upper deck. Morse was silent and Lewis mulled over the strange developments in the case. The bus made good speed and stopped only four times before reaching Woodstock. At the third of these stops Morse gave his sergeant a dig in the ribs and Lewis looked out to see where they were. The bus had pulled into a shallow lay-by just outside Begbroke, at a large, thatched house with its garden crowded with tables and chairs set under brightly striped umbrellas; he bent his head down to the bottom of the side window to see the name of the public house and read the two words Golden Rose.

'Interesting?' said Morse.

'Very,' replied Lewis. He thought he might as well say something.

They alighted at Woodstock and Morse led the way. 'Ready for a pint, Sergeant?'

They walked into the cocktail bar of the Black Prince. 'Good morning, Mrs McFee. You won't remember me, I suppose?'

'I remember you very well, Inspector.'

'What a memory,' said Morse.

'What can I get for you, gentlemen?' She was clearly not amused.

'Two pints of best bitter, please.'

'Official business?' Her dislike of Morse's manner was not quite enough to stifle her natural curiosity.

'No. No. Just a friendly visit to look at you again.' He's in good spirits this morning, thought Lewis.

'I see from the paper that you're hoping ...' she fumbled for the words.

'We're making progress, aren't we, Sergeant?'

'Oh yes,' said Lewis. After all, he was the other half of those intensive inquiries.

'Don't they ever give you a few hours off?' asked Morse.

'Oh, they're very good really.' She was softening a little towards him; it was always nice to be reminded how hard she worked. 'As a matter of fact I've got tonight and all of Saturday and Sunday off.'

'Where shall we go?' asked Morse.

The hostess smiled professionally. 'Where do you suggest, Inspector?' Good for you, my girl, thought Lewis.

Morse asked for the menu and studied it in some detail.

'What's the food like here?' asked Morse.

'Why don't you try it?'

Morse appeared to consider the possibility but asked instead if there was a good fish-and-chip shop near by. There wasn't. Several customers had come in and the policemen left by the side entrance and walked into the yard. To their right, a car was sitting up on its haunches, with each of the front wheels off. Underneath the car, suitably protected from the grease and oil, and wielding a formidable wrench, lay the landlord of the Black Prince, and by his side the folding tool-box which had so recently housed a long and heavy tyre-spanner.

Unnoticed by Morse and Lewis as they left the premises, a young man had entered the cocktail bar and ordered a tonic water. Mr John Sanders had apparently made a sufficient recovery from his bouts of shivery fever to join once more in the social life of Woodstock, if not to resume his duties with Messrs Chalkley and Sons.

On the bus journey back Morse was deeply engrossed in a Midland Counties bus time-table and a map of North Oxford. Occasionally he looked at his watch and made a brief entry in a note-book. Lewis felt hungry. It had been a pity about the fish-and-chip shop.

Chapter Twenty-One

Friday, 15 October, p.m.

A BULKY ENVELOPE marked 'confidential' arrived on Morse's desk at 3.30 that afternoon – 'from the Principal'. He had done a very careful and thorough job – that was quite clear. There were ninety-three typewriters, it appeared, in Lonsdale College. Most of them belonged to the college and had found their various ways into the rooms of the fellows; over twenty were the personal property of members of the college. Ninety-three sheets of paper, each numbered, were neatly arranged beneath a bull-dog clip. Two further sheets, stapled together, provided the key to the typewritten specimens, and, appropriately enough, the Principal's typewriter was given the no. 1 designation. Morse riffled the sheets. It was going to be a bigger job than he'd thought, and he rang the laboratory boys. He learned it would take an hour or so.

Lewis had spent most of the afternoon typing his reports and did not return to Morse's office until 4.15 p.m.

'You hoping to have the weekend off, Lewis?'

'Not if there's something you want me for, sir.'

'I'm afraid we have rather a lot to do. I think it's time we had a little confrontation, don't you?'

'Confrontation?'

'Yes. A gentle little confrontation between a certain Miss Coleby and a certain Mr Crowther. What do you think?'

'Might clear the air a bit.'

'Ye-es. Do you think the old establishment could run to four clean cups of coffee in the morning?'

'You want me to join you?'

'We're a team, Lewis, my boy. I've told you that before.' Morse rang Town and Gown and asked for Mr Palmer.

'Hew shell I see is calling?' It was the prim little Judith.

'Mister Plod,' said Morse.

'Howld on, please, Mr Plod . . . you're threw.'

'I didn't quite catch your name, sir? Palmer here.'

'Morse. Inspector Morse.'

'Oh, hullo, Inspector.' Stupid girl!

'I want to have a word with Miss Coleby. Confidential. I wonder if . . .'

Palmer interrupted him. 'I'm awfully sorry, Inspector. She's not here this afternoon. She wanted to spend a long weekend in London and, well . . . we do occasionally show a little er flexibility, you know. It sometimes helps the er the smooth running . . .'

'London, you say?'

'Yes. She said she was going to spend the weekend with some friends. She caught the lunch-time train.'

'Did she leave an address?'

'I'm sorry. I don't think she did. I could try to er . . .'

'No. Don't bother.'

'Can I take a message?'

'No. I'll get in touch with her when she comes back.' Perhaps he could see Sue again . . . 'When will she be back, by the way?'

'I don't really know. Sunday evening I should think.'

'All right. Well, thank you.'

'Sorry I couldn't be . . .'

'Not your fault.' Morse put down the phone with less than average courtesy.

'One of our birds has flown, Lewis.' He turned his attention to Bernard Crowther and decided to try the college first.

'Porter's Lodge.'

'Can you put me through to Mr Crowther's rooms, please?'

'Just a minute, sir.' Morse drummed the table with the fingers of his left hand. Come on!

'Are you there, sir?'

'Yes. I'm still here.'

'No reply, I'm afraid, sir.'

'Is he in college this afternoon?'

'I saw him this morning, sir. Just a minute.' Three minutes later Morse was wondering if the wretched porter had taken a gentle stroll around the quad.

'Are you there, sir?'

'Yes, I'm still here.'

'He's away somewhere, sir, for the weekend. It's a conference of some sort.'

'Do you know when he's due back?'

'Sorry, sir. Shall I put you through to the college office?'

'No, don't bother. I'll ring again later.'

'Thank you, sir.'

Morse held the phone in his hands for a few seconds and finally put it down with the greatest circumspection. 'I wonder. I wonder . . .' He was lost in thought.

'It seems *both* of our birds have flown, sir.'

'I wonder if the conference is being held in London.'

'You don't think . . .?'

'I don't know what to think,' said Morse.

Nor was he sure what to think when half an hour later the findings of the laboratory were phoned through. Lewis watched the Inspector's curious reactions.

'Are you sure . . .? You're quite sure . . .? Yes. Well, many thanks. You'll bring them over? Good. Thank you.'

'Well, Lewis, you're in for a surprise.'

'About the note?'

'Yes. About the note – the note someone wrote to the young lady who is now visiting "some friends" in London. They say they know whose typewriter it was.'

'And whose was it?'

'That's what's puzzling me. We've never heard of him before! He's a Mr Peter Newlove.'

'And who's Mr Peter Newlove?'

'It's time we found out.' He rang Lonsdale College for the second time that afternoon and found the same slow-motion porter presiding over the Lodge.

'Mr Newlove, sir? No, I'm afraid he's not in college. Just let me check in the book . . . No, sir. He's away till Monday. Can I take a message? No? All right. Goodbye, sir.'

'Well, that's that,' said Morse. '*All* our birds have flown. And I don't see much point in staying here, do you?' Lewis didn't.

'Let's just tidy up all this mess,' said Morse.

Lewis gathered together the papers on his side of the table – the photographs of Sylvia Kaye and the carefully drawn diagrams of the yard at the Black Prince, annotated in thin, spidery writing with details of everything found therein. He looked again at the close-ups of the murdered girl lying there, and felt a paternally protective urge to cover the harsh nakedness of her beautiful body.

'I'd like to get the bastard who did this,' he muttered.

'What's that?' Morse took the photographs from him.

'He must be a sex maniac, don't you think, sir? Tearing off her clothes like that and leaving her for anyone and everyone to see. God, I wish I knew who he was!'

'Oh, I don't think there's much difficulty about that,' said Morse.

Lewis looked at him incredulously. 'You mean you *know*?'

Morse nodded slowly, and locked away the file on Sylvia Kaye.

PART THREE

Search for a killer

Chapter Twenty-Two

Sunday, 17 October

SUE SAW DAVID off on the Birmingham train at 7.13 on Sunday evening. She told him what a marvellous weekend it had been – and so it had. On Saturday they had gone to the cinema, had a delicious Chinese meal and generally luxuriated in being together. Most of Sunday they had spent in Headington at the home of David's parents, pleasant, warm-hearted people, sensible enough to leave the two young love-birds alone for the greater part of the day. They hoped to marry some time next autumn, after David had finished his postgraduate year of research in metallurgy at the University of Warwick. He was hopeful (for he had taken a 'first') of getting a lectureship somewhere, and Sue encouraged him: she would rather be married to a lecturer than to an industrial chemist, or whatever metallurgists became. She thought that was the only thing about David of which she couldn't wholeheartedly approve – his choice of metallurgy. It had something to do with her own schooldays and the distaste she'd always felt amid the smells and silver slivers of the metalwork shop. There was something, too, about the *hands* of people who worked with metal: a sort of ingrained griminess, however patiently they were scrubbed.

The train lingered at Oxford station for several minutes and Sue kissed David fully and freely as he leaned from the window of an empty carriage.

'It's been lovely seeing you again, darling,' said David.

'Super.'

'You enjoyed it, didn't you?'

'Of course I did.' She laughed gaily. 'Why on earth did you ask that?'

David smiled. 'It's just nice to know, that's all.' They kissed again, and Sue walked along with him for a few yards as the train pulled out.

'See you in a fortnight. Don't forget to write.'

'I won't,' said Sue. 'Bye.' She waved until the train had left the platform and she watched it curving its way towards the north, the red light on the rear coach bobbing and winking in the gathering darkness.

She walked slowly back down the platform, along the subway and up to the barrier on the other side. She gave in her platform ticket and made her way to Carfax. Here she had to wait for half an hour before a number 2 bus came along, and it was eight o'clock before she got off in North Oxford. She crossed the road and with her head down walked along Charlton Road and thought about the last two days. She could never have told David about Wednesday night. There was nothing to tell anyway, was there? Just a minor peccadillo. She supposed most people had their foolish moments – even engaged people – and there were some things that just could not be told. Not that David would have been jealous; he wasn't that sort, at all – mild, equable, balanced David. Perhaps she wouldn't mind if he were a bit jealous. But she knew, or thought she knew, that he wasn't; she could spot jealousy a mile off. She thought of Morse. She really had been very naughty at the Sheridan with Doctor Eyres, and Morse had been jealous – rabidly, furiously jealous. She'd secretly enjoyed making him jealous until . . . Well, she wasn't going to think of him any more . . . But she'd never cried over David . . . She wondered if Morse believed her when she said she would be crying herself to sleep on Wednesday night. She hoped he had, for it was true. There she went again, starting with David and finishing with *him*. He'd probably not given her another thought . . . David! He was her man. Married to David she would be happy at last. Marriage. A big step, they all said. But she was twenty-three now . . . She hoped Morse *had* given her another thought . . . Forget him!

But she was not to be allowed to forget him. As she reached the house she saw the Lancia outside. Her heart pounded against her ribs and a wave of involuntary joy coursed through her blood. She let herself in and went straight to the living-room. There he was, sitting talking to Mary. He stood up as she came in.

'Hullo.'

'Hullo,' she said weakly.

'I really called to see Miss Coleby, but I gather she may not be back yet for a while. So I've been having a delightful little chat with Mary here.'

Mary indeed! Dumpy, freckled, little man-eater! Why don't you go, Mary? Mary, why don't you leave us alone – just for a few minutes? Please! She felt viciously jealous. But Mary seemed very taken with the charming Inspector and showed no signs of imminent surrender. Sue, still wearing her summer coat, sat on the arm of a chair, trying to resist the wave of desperation that threatened to engulf her.

She heard herself say: 'She'll catch the 8.15 from Paddington, I should think. Probably get here about ten.'

That was two hours. Two whole hours. If only Mary would go! He might ask her out for a drink and they could talk. But the wave swept her over, and she left the room and rushed upstairs. Morse got up as she left and thanked Mary for her hospitality. As he opened the front door he turned to Mary. Would she ask Sue to come down for a second? He would like to have a quick word with her. Mary, too, disappeared upstairs and blessedly faded from the scene. Morse stepped out into the concrete drive and Sue appeared, framed in the doorway. She stopped there.

'You wanted a word with me, Inspector?'

'Which room do you sleep in, Sue?' She stepped out and stood next to him. Her arm brushed his as she pointed to the window immediately above the front door, and Morse felt a jagged ache between his temples. He wasn't a tall man and she was almost his own height in the very high wedge-heeled shoes she wore. She dropped her arm and their hands met in an accidental, beautiful way. Leave your hand there, Sue. Leave it there, my darling. He felt the electric thrill of the contact and gently, softly he ran his finger tips along her wrist.

'Why do you want to know that?' Her voice sounded hoarse and breathless.

'I don't know. I suppose if I drive past and see a light on in your window I shall know it's you in there.'

Sue could bear it no longer. She took her hand from his and turned away. 'You came to see Jennifer, then?'

'Yes.'

'I'll tell her, of course – when she comes in.' Morse nodded.

'You think she's got something to do with the Woodstock business, don't you?'

'Something, perhaps.'

They stood in silence for a minute. Sue was wearing a sleeveless dress and she was trying not to shiver.

'Well, I'd better be off.'

'Goodnight, then.'

'Goodnight.' He turned towards the gate and had almost reached it when he turned round. 'Sue?' She stood in the doorway.

'Yes?'

He walked back. 'Sue, would you like to come out with me for a little while?'

'Oh . . .' Sue got no further. She flung her arms around him and cried joyfully on his shoulder, and neither heard the front gate open.

'If you'll excuse me, please?' said a cool, well-spoken voice, and Jennifer Coleby edged past them into the house.

*

The other wanderers, too, were just returning. Bernard Crowther had returned from London on the same train as Jennifer Coleby; but they had travelled in separate parts of the train, and no one watching them alight at platform number 2 could have formed the slightest suspicion that either was aware of the other's existence.

About this time, too, Peter Newlove was taking his leave of a red-headed, radiant girl in Church Street, Woodstock. They kissed again with eagerness and seeming insatiability.

'I'll be in touch, Gaye.'

'Make sure you do – and thanks again.'

It had been an expensive weekend; very expensive, in fact. But it was, in Peter's view, worth almost every penny.

CHAPTER TWENTY-THREE

Monday, 18 October

ON MONDAY MORNING, Morse decided that however embarrassing it would be he had his job to do. How he dreaded it, though! Here was the big moment, the dénouement of the case (of that he felt quite confident) and yet he felt as if he himself were the guilty party. Lewis collected Jennifer Coleby in his own car; Morse felt he could just about spare her the official trappings. Bernard Crowther said he would make his own way, if that was all right. It was. Morse had tried to think out the likeliest approaches, but his concentration had been lapsing sadly. He decided to let things take their course.

At 10.25 a.m. Crowther arrived, five minutes early, and Morse poured him coffee and asked him a few casual questions about the 'conference'.

'Oh. The usual thing, you know. One long yawn,' said Crowther.

'What was it about exactly?'

'University admissions. Arguing the toss about A-level requirements. We've not very popular with the Schools Council, you know. They think Oxford is the last bastion of academic élitism. Still, I suppose it is really . . .' He had no chance to develop his theme.

Lewis came in with Jennifer Coleby, and Crowther got to his feet.

'You two know each other?' asked Morse. There was not a hint of cynicism in his voice. Strangely, or so it seemed to Morse, Jennifer and Crowther shook hands. 'Good mornings' were exchanged, and Morse, a trifle nonplussed, poured two more coffees.

'You *do* know each other?' He sounded rather unsure of himself.

'We live fairly near each other, don't we, Mr Crowther?'

'We do, yes. I've often seen you on the bus. It's Miss Coleby, I think, isn't it? You come round for the SPCC.'

Jennifer nodded.

Morse got up and passed the sugar basin round. He felt he couldn't sit still.

During the next few minutes Lewis was forced to wonder if the Inspector had lost his grip completely. He um'd and ah'd and said 'to be honest with you' and 'we have some reason to suppose' and finally managed to suggest to his pair of prime suspects, almost apologetically, that they might be having an affair with each other.

Jennifer laughed almost aloud and Bernard smiled shyly. It was Bernard who spoke first. 'I'm sure I feel very flattered, Inspector, and I very much wish perhaps that I *was* having some secret affair with Miss Coleby. But I'm afraid the answer's no. What else can I say?'

'Miss Coleby?'

'I think I have spoken to Mr Crowther twice in my

life – to ask him for a donation to the SPCC. I sometimes see him on the bus going into town – we get on and off at the same stops. But I think he always goes upstairs and I never do. I hate the smell of cigarettes.'

Morse, who was smoking his third cigarette, felt once more that he was getting the worst of things with Jennifer Coleby. He turned to Crowther.

'I must ask you this, sir. Please think very carefully before you answer, and remember that you are here in connection with a murder, the murder of the girl who was travelling in your car.' Morse saw a look of surprise on Jennifer's face. 'Was Miss Coleby here the other passenger you picked up that night?'

Bernard replied with an immediacy and conviction that sorely troubled Morse. 'No, Inspector, she wasn't. Of that you can be completely assured.'

'And you, Miss Coleby. Do you deny that you were the other passenger in Mr Crowther's car?'

'Yes. I do deny. Absolutely.'

Morse drained his coffee.

'Do you want us to sign anything, Inspector?' There was a deep cynicism in Jennifer's face.

Morse shook his head. 'No. Sergeant Lewis has made notes on what you've both said. One more question though, Miss Coleby, if you don't mind. Can you give me the address of the friends you stayed with in London this weekend?'

Jennifer took a plain envelope from her handbag and wrote down an address in Lancaster Gardens. As an afterthought she added the telephone number, and handed the envelope to Morse.

'They're lying – both of 'em,' said Morse when they had gone.

Crowther had to get to the centre of Oxford and had gallantly offered a lift to his fellow-suspect. Morse wondered what they would be talking about. Lewis had said nothing.

'Did you hear me?' Morse was angry.

'Yes, sir.'

'I said they're a pair of prize liars. LIARS.' Lewis remained silent. He thought the Inspector was wrong, terribly wrong. He himself was no stranger to interviewing liars and he had the firm conviction that both Crowther and Coleby were telling the plain truth.

Morse looked hard at his sergeant. 'Come on! Out with it!'

'What do you mean, sir?'

'What do I mean? You know what I mean. You think I'm up the bloody pole, don't you? You think I'm going bonkers. You're willing to believe what everyone else says, but you don't believe *me*. Come on. Tell me! I want to know.'

Lewis was upset. He didn't know what to say, and Morse was losing the last remnants of his self-control, his eyes blazing and his voice growing vicious and deadly. 'Come on. You tell me. You heard what I said. I want to know!'

Lewis looked at him and saw the bitter failure in the Inspector's eyes. He wished he could put things right, but he couldn't. It had been the quality in him that from the start had endeared him to Morse. It was his basic honesty and integrity.

'I think you're wrong, sir.' It took a lot of saying, but he said it, and he deserved better than Morse's cruel rejoinder.

'You think I'm wrong? Well let me tell you some- thing, Lewis. If anyone's wrong here, it's not me – it's *you*. Do you understand that? YOU – not me. If you've not got the nous to see that those two slimy toads are *lying*, lying to save their own necks, you shouldn't be on this case. Do you hear me? *You shouldn't be on this case.*'

Lewis felt a deep hurt; but not for himself. 'Perhaps you ought to have someone else with you, sir. On the case, I mean.'

'You may be right.' Morse was calming down a little and Lewis sensed it.

'There's this man Newlove, sir. Shouldn't we . . .'

'Newlove? Who the hell's he?' Lewis had said the wrong thing, and Morse's latent anger and frustration rose to fever pitch again. 'Newlove? We've never heard of the bloody man before. All right – he's got a typewriter. That's not a sin, is it? He didn't write that letter. CROWTHER DID! And if you don't see that you must be blind as a bloody bat!'

'But don't you think . . .'

'Oh, bugger off, Lewis. You're boring me.'

'Does that mean I'm off the case, sir?'

'I don't know. I don't care. Just bugger off and leave me alone.' Lewis went out and left him alone.

The phone rang a few minutes later. Morse picked the receiver up and closed his mind to everything. 'I'm not here,' he snapped, 'I've gone home.' He slammed down the receiver and sat brooding savagely within himself. He even forgot Sue. The last castle had finally collapsed. Having stood the flood so long, it was now a flattened heap of formless sand. But even as it fell a curious clarification was dawning across his mind. He got up from his leather chair, opened the cabinet and took out the file on Sylvia Kaye. He opened it at the beginning and was still reading it late into the afternoon, when the shadows crept across the room and he found it difficult to read, and a new and horrifying thought was taking birth in the depths of his tortured mind.

The dramatic news broke at a quarter-past seven. Margaret Crowther had committed suicide.

CHAPTER TWENTY-FOUR

Monday, 18 October

BERNARD CROWTHER, AFTER dropping Jennifer Coleby in the High, had been lucky in finding a parking space in Bear Lane. Not even the dons were permitted to park outside the college now. He had lunched in the Senior Common Room and spent the afternoon and early evening working. Both the children were away for a week on a school camping holiday in nearby Whitham Woods. On such ventures it was customary for the parents to visit their children on one evening during the week, but the young Crowthers had told their parents not to bother; and that was that. At least it would be a chance for Bernard and Margaret to have a few decent meals, instead of the inevitable chips and tomato sauce with everything.

Bernard left college at about twenty-past six. The roads were getting free again by now and he had an easy journey home. He let himself in with his Yale key and hung up his coat. Funny smell. Gas?

'Margaret?' He put his brief-case in the front room. 'Margaret?' He walked to the kitchen and found the door locked. 'Margaret!' He rattled the knob of the kitchen door, but it was firmly locked on the other side. He banged on the door. 'Margaret! Margaret! Are you there?' He could smell the gas more strongly now. His mouth went completely dry and there was wild panic in his voice. 'MARGARET!' He rushed back to the front door, through the side gate, and tried the back door. It was locked. He whimpered like a child. He looked into the kitchen through the large window above the sink. The electric light was on and for a fraction of a second a last ember of hope flared up, and glowed, and then was gone. The surrealistic sight that met his eyes was so strangely improbable that it registered itself blankly as a meaningless picture on the retina of his eyes – a sight without significance – a waxwork model, bright-eyed and brightly hued, with a fixed, staring smile. What was she doing sitting on the floor like that? Cleaning the oven?

He picked up a house-brick lying by the side of the wall, smashed a pane in the window, and cut his fingers badly as he reached for the catch and opened the window from the inside. The nauseating smell of gas hit him with an almost physical impact, and it was some seconds before, holding his handkerchief to his face, he climbed awkwardly in through the window and turned off the gas. Margaret's head was just inside the oven, resting on a soft red cushion. In a numbed, irrational way he thought he should put the cushion back where it came from; it was from the settee in the lounge. He looked down with shocked, zombie-like eyes at the jagged cuts on his hand and mechanically dabbed them with his handkerchief. He saw the sticky brown paper lining the gaps by the door-jambs and the window, and noticed that Margaret had cut the ends as neatly as she always did when she wrapped the children's birthday presents. The children! Thank God they were away! He saw the scissors on the formica top over the washing machine, and like an automaton he picked them up and put them in the drawer. The smell was infinitely sickly still, and he felt the vomit rising in his gorge. And now the horror of it all was gradually seeping into his mind, like a pool of ink into blotting paper. He knew that she was dead.

He unlocked the kitchen door, picked up the phone in the hall and in a dazed, uncomprehending voice he asked for the police. A letter addressed to him was lying beside the telephone directory. He picked it up and put it in his breast pocket and returned to the kitchen.

Ten minutes later the police found him there, sitting on the floor beside his wife, his hand on her hair, his eyes bleak and glazed. He had been deaf to the strident ringing of the front door bell.

Morse arrived only a few minutes after the police car and the ambulance. It was Inspector Bell of the Oxford City Police who had called Morse; Crowther had insisted on it. The two Inspectors had met several times before and stood in the hallway talking together in muted voices. Bernard had been led unresistingly from the kitchen by a police doctor and was now sitting in the lounge, his head sunk into his hands. He appeared unaware of what was going on or what was being said, but when Morse came into the lounge he seemed to come to life again.

'Hullo, Inspector.' Morse put his hand on Crowther's shoulder, but could think of nothing to say that might help. Nothing could help. 'She left this, Inspector.' Bernard reached into his breast pocket and pulled out the sealed envelope.

'It's for you, you know, sir; it's addressed to you – not to me,' said Morse quietly.

'I know. But you read it. I can't.' He put his head in his hands again, and sobbed quietly.

Morse looked enquiringly at his fellow-Inspector. Bell nodded and Morse carefully opened the letter.

Dear Bernard,

When you read this I shall be dead. I know what this will mean to you and the children and it's only this that has kept me from doing it before – but I just can't cope with life any longer. I am finding it so difficult to know what to say – but I want you to know that it's not your fault. I have not been all that a wife should be to you and I have been a miserable failure with the children, and everything has built up and I long for rest and peace away from it all. I just can't go on any longer. I realize how selfish I am and I know that I'm just running away from everything. But I shall go mad if I don't run away. I must run away – I haven't the courage to stand up to things any longer.

On your desk you will find all the accounts. All the bills are paid except Mr Anderson's for pruning the apple trees. We owe him £5 but I couldn't find his address.

I am thinking of the earlier times when we were so

happy. Nothing can take them from us. Look after the
children. It's my fault – not theirs. I pray that you
won't think too badly of me and that you can forgive
me.
Margaret.

It wasn't going to be much comfort, but Crowther had
got to face it some time.

'Please read it, sir.'

Bernard read it, but he showed no emotion. His
despair could plumb no lower depths. 'What about the
children?' he said at last.

'Don't worry yourself about that, sir. We'll look after
everything.' The police doctor's voice was brisk. He was
no stranger to such situations, and he knew the procedure from this point on. It wasn't much that he could
do – but it was something.

'Look, sir, I want you to take . . .'

'What about the children?' He was a shattered,
broken man, and Morse left him to the ministrations of
the doctor. He retired with Bell to the front room, and
noticed the list of the accounts, insurances, mortgage
repayments, and stock-exchange holdings which Margaret had left so neatly ordered under a paper-weight
on the desk. But he didn't touch them. They were
something between a husband and his wife, a wife who
had been alive when he had interviewed Crowther
earlier that day.

'You know him, then?' asked Bell.

'I saw him this morning,' said Morse. 'I saw him
about the Woodstock murder.'

'Really?' Bell looked surprised.

'He was the man who picked up the girls.'

'You think he was involved?'

'I don't know,' said Morse.

'Has this business got anything to do with it?'

'I don't know.'

The ambulance was still waiting outside and curious eyes were peeping from all the curtains along the road. In the kitchen Morse looked down at Margaret Crowther. He had never seen her before, and he was surprised to realize how attractive she must have been. Fortyish? Hair greying a little, but a good, firm figure and a finely featured face, twisted now and blue.

'No point in keeping her here,' said Bell.

Morse shook his head. 'No point at all.'

'It takes a long time, you know, this North Sea gas.'

The two men talked in a desultory way for several minutes, and Morse prepared to leave. But as he walked out to his car, he was called back by the police doctor.

'Can you come back a minute, Inspector?' Morse re-entered the house.

'He says he must talk to you.'

Crowther sat with his head against the back of the chair. He was breathing heavily and the sweat stood out upon his brow. He was in a state of deep shock, and was already under sedation.

'Inspector,' he opened his eyes wearily. 'Inspector, I've got to talk to you.' He had great difficulty in getting this far, and Morse looked to the doctor, who slowly shook his head.

'Tomorrow, sir,' said Morse. 'I'll see you tomorrow.'

'Inspector, I've got to talk to you.'

'Yes, I know. But not now. We'll talk tomorrow. It'll be all right then.' Morse put his hand to Crowther's forehead and felt the clammy wetness there.

'Inspector!' But the top corner of the walls where Crowther was trying to focus was slowly disintegrating before his eyes; the angles melted and spiralled and faded away.

Morse drove slowly out of Southdown Road and realized just how close Crowther lived to Jennifer Coleby. It was a black night and the moon was hidden away deep behind the lowering clouds. Rectangles of light, shaded by curtains, showed from most of the front-room windows, and in many Morse could see the light-blue phosphorescent glow of television screens. He looked at one house in particular and looked up at one window in it, the window directly above the door. But it was dark, and he drove on.

CHAPTER TWENTY-FIVE

Tuesday, 19 October, a.m.

MORSE HAD SLEPT very badly and woke with a throbbing head. He hated suicides. Why had she done it? Was suicide just the coward's refuge from some black despair? Or was it in its way an act of courage that revealed a perverted sort of valour? Not that, though. So many other lives were intertwined: no burdens were shed – they were merely passed from the shoulders of one to those of another. Morse's mind would give itself no rest but twirled around on some interminable funfair ride.

It was past nine o'clock before he was sitting in his leather chair, and his sombre mood draped itself over his sagging shoulders. He summoned Lewis, who knocked apprehensively on the door before going in; but Morse had seemingly lost all recollection of the nasty little episode the day before. He told Lewis the facts of Margaret Crowther's suicide.

'Do you think he's got something important to tell us, sir?'

There was a knock on the door before Lewis could learn the answer to his question, and a young girl brought in the post, said a bright 'Good morning' and was off. Morse fingered through the dozen or so letters and his eye fell on an unopened envelope marked 'strictly private' and addressed to himself. The envelope was exactly similar to the one he had seen the previous evening.

'I don't know whether Crowther's got anything to tell us or not; but it looks as if his late wife has.' He opened the envelope neatly with a letter-knife and read its typewritten contents aloud to Lewis.

Dear Inspector,

I have never met you, but I have seen from the newspapers that you are in charge of the inquiry into the death of Sylvia Kaye. I should have told you this a long time ago, but I hope it's not too late even now. You see, Inspector, I killed Sylvia Kaye. (The words were doubly underlined.)

I must try to explain myself. Please forgive me if I get a little muddled, but it all seems very long ago.

I have known for about six months – well, certainly for six months – perhaps I've known for much longer – that my husband has been having an affair with another woman. I had no proof and have none now. But it is so difficult for a man to hide this sort of thing from his wife. We have been married for fifteen years and I know him so well. It was written all over what he said and what he did and how he looked – he must have been terribly unhappy, I think.

On Wednesday, 22nd September, I left the house at 6.30 p.m. to go to my evening class at Headington – but I didn't go immediately. Instead, I waited in my car just off the Banbury Road. I seemed to wait such a long time and I didn't really know what I was going to do. Then at about a quarter to seven Bernard – my husband – drove up to the junction at Charlton Road and turned right towards the northern roundabout. I followed him as best I could – I say that because I'm not a good driver – and anyway it was getting darker all the time. There wasn't much traffic and I could see him clearly two or three cars ahead. At the Woodstock Road roundabout he turned along the A34. He was driving too fast for me, though, and I kept dropping further and further behind. I thought I had lost him – but there were road-works ahead and the traffic had to filter into single line for about a mile. There was a slow, heavy lorry in the front and I soon caught up again – Bernard was only about six or seven cars ahead of me. The lorry turned off towards Bladon at the next roundabout and I managed to keep Bernard in sight and saw him take the first turning on the left in Woodstock itself. I panicked a bit and didn't know what to do – I turned into the next street, and stopped the car and walked back. But it was hopeless. I drove back to Headington and was only twenty minutes late for my evening class.

The next Wednesday, the 29th September, I drove out to Woodstock again, leaving the house a good ten minutes earlier than usual, parked my car further along the village, and walked back to the street into which Bernard had turned the previous week. I didn't know where to wait and I felt silly and

conspicuous, but I found a safe enough little spot on
the left of the road – I was terrified that Bernard
would see me – if he came that was – and I waited
there and watched every car that came round the
corner. It was child's play to see the cars turning in –
and the occupants as well. He came at quarter-past
seven and I felt myself trembling frantically. He was
not alone – a young girl with long fair hair, in a white
blouse, was sitting next to him in the front seat. I
thought they must see me because the car turned –
oh, only six or seven yards ahead of me – into the car
park of the Black Prince. My legs were shaking and
the blood was pounding in my ears, but something
made me go through with it. I walked cautiously up
to the yard and peered in. There were several cars
there already and I couldn't see Bernard's for several
minutes. I edged round the back of one car – just to
the left of the yard – and then I saw them. The car
was on the same side at the far end, with the boot
towards the wall – he must have backed in. They
were sitting in the front – talking for a while. I felt a
cold anger inside me. Bernard and a blowzy blonde –
about seventeen she looked! I saw them kissing.
Then they got out of the front and into the back. I
couldn't see any more – at least I was spared that.

I can't really explain what I felt. As I write now it
all seems so flat – and so unimportant somehow. I
felt more anger than jealousy – I know that. Burning
anger that Bernard had shamed me so. It was about
five minutes later when they got out. They said
something – but I couldn't hear what it was. There

was a lever – a long tyre-lever – I found it on the
floor of the yard, and I picked it up. I don't know
why. I felt so frightened and so angry. And suddenly
the engine of the car was switched on and then the
lights and the whole yard was lit up. The car moved
off and out of the yard, and after it had gone the
darkness seemed even blacker than before. The girl
stood where he had left her, and I crept behind the
three or four cars between us and came up behind
her. I said nothing and I'm sure she didn't hear me. I
hit her across the back of the head with an easy
strength. It seemed like a dream. I felt nothing – no
remorse – no fear – nothing. I left her where she was,
against the far wall. It was still very dark. I didn't
know when or how she would be found – and I
didn't care.

Bernard knew all along that I had murdered Sylvia
Kaye – he passed me on my way back to Oxford. He
must have seen me because I saw him. He was right
behind me for some time and must have seen the
number plate. I saw his car as clear as daylight when
he overtook me.

I know what you have suspected about Bernard.
But you have been wrong. I don't know what he's
told you – but I know you have spoken to him. If he
has told you lies, it has only been to shield me. But I
need no one to shield me any longer. Look after
Bernard and don't let him suffer too much because of
me. He did what hundreds of men do, and for that I
blame myself and no one else. I have neither been a
good wife to him nor a good mother to his children.

I am just so tired – so desperately tired of everything.
For what I have done I am now most bitterly sorry –
but I realize that this is no excuse. What else can I say
– what else is there to say?
Margaret Crowther.

Morse's voice trailed away and the room was very still.
Lewis felt very moved as he heard the letter read aloud,
almost as if Margaret Crowther were there. But she
would never speak again. He thought of his visit to her
and guessed how cruelly she must have suffered these
last few months.

'You thought it was something like that, didn't you,
sir?'

'No,' said Morse.

'Comes as a bit of a shock, doesn't it? Out of the
blue, like.'

'I don't think much of her English style,' said Morse.
He handed the letter over to Lewis. 'She uses far too
many dashes for my liking.' The comment seemed
heartless and irrelevant. Lewis read the letter to
himself.

'She's a good, clean typist anyway, sir.'

'Bit odd, don't you think, that she typed her name
at the end instead of using her signature?'

Give Morse a letter and his imagination soared to
the realms of the bright-eyed seraphim. Lewis groaned
inwardly.

'You think she wrote it, don't you, sir?'

Morse reluctantly reined back the wild horses. 'Yes.
She wrote it.'

Lewis thought he understood the Inspector's feelings. There would have to be a bit of tidying up, of course, but the case was now substantially over. He'd enjoyed most of his time working with the irascible, volatile inspector, but now ... The phone rang and Morse answered. He said 'I see'. a dozen times and replaced the receiver.

'Crowther's in the Radcliffe – he's had a mild heart attack. He's not allowed to see anyone for two days at least.'

'Perhaps he couldn't tell us much more,' suggested Lewis.

'Oh yes he could,' said Morse. He leaned back, put his hands on his head like a naughty schoolboy, and stared vacantly at the farthest corner of the wall. Lewis thought it best to keep quiet, but he grew uncomfortably restless as the minutes ticked by.

'Would you like a coffee, sir?' Morse didn't seem to hear him. 'Coffee? Would you like a coffee?' Morse reminded him of a very deaf person with his hearing-aid switched off. Minute after minute slipped by before the grey eyes refocused on the world around him.

'Well, that's cleared up one thing, Lewis. We can cross Mrs Crowther off our list of suspects, can't we?'

Chapter Twenty-Six

Tuesday, 19 October, p.m.

At midday Peter Newlove was sitting in his rooms. He was expecting no one. Normally Bernard might have dropped in about now for a gin, but the news had swept the college that morning: Margaret had killed herself and Bernard had suffered a heart attack. And the double-barrelled news hit no one harder than Peter. He had known Margaret well and had liked her; and Bernard was his best friend in that academic, dilettante style of friendship which springs up in most collegiate universities. He had rung up the hospital, but there was no chance of visiting Bernard until Thursday at the earliest. He had sent some flowers: Bernard liked flowers and had no wife to send them now . . . He had enquired, too, about the children. They had gone to stay with an aunt in Hendon, though Peter couldn't imagine how such an arrangement could possibly help them very much.

There was a knock on the door. 'It's open.'

He had not met Inspector Morse before and was pleasantly surprised that his offer of a drink was accepted. Morse explained in blunt, unequivocal terms why he had called.

'And it was written on *that* one?' Newlove frowned at the open portable typewriter on the table.

'No doubt about it.'

Newlove looked mildly perplexed, but said nothing.

'Do you know a young lady named Jennifer Coleby, Miss Jennifer Coleby?'

'I don't, I'm afraid.' Newlove's frown grew deeper.

'She works in the High, not far from here. Town and Gown. Assurance place.'

Newlove shook his head. 'I might have seen her, of course. But I don't know her. I've not heard the name before.'

'And you've never written to anyone of that name?'

'No. How could I? As I say, I've never heard of the woman.'

Morse pursed his lips and continued. 'Who else could have used your typewriter, sir?'

'Well, I don't know really. I suppose almost anyone in a way. I don't lock the place up very much unless there are question papers about.'

'You mean you leave your doors open and let anybody just walk in and help himself to your booze or your books – or your typewriter?'

'No, it's not like that. But quite a few of the Fellows do drop in.'

'Who in particular, would you say?'

'Well, there's a new young don here this term, Melhuish, for example. He's been in quite a few times recently.'

'And?'

'And a dozen others.' He sounded a little uneasy.

'Have you ever seen any of these, er, friends of yours using your typewriter?'

'Well, no. I don't think I have.'

'They'd use their own, wouldn't they?'

'Yes. I suppose they would.'

'Not much "suppose" about it, is there, sir?' said Morse.

'No.'

'You've no idea then?'

'I'm not being very helpful, I know. But I've no idea at all.'

Morse abruptly switched his questioning. 'Did you know Mrs Crowther?'

'Yes.'

'You've heard about her?'

'Yes,' said Newlove quietly.

'And Bernard Crowther?' Newlove nodded. 'I understand he's one of your best friends?' Again Newlove nodded. 'I've been to his room this morning, sir. If you want to put it crudely I've been snooping around. But you see, I often have to snoop around. I take no particular delight in it.'

'I understand,' said Newlove.

'I wonder if you do understand, sir.' There was a clipped impatience in his voice now. 'He often drops in to see you, is that right?'

'Quite often.'

'And do you think he'd come to you if he wanted anything?'

'You mean rather than to somebody else?'

'Yes.'

'He'd come to me.'

'Did you know that his typewriter can't even cope with a comma?'

'No, I didn't,' lied Newlove.

After dropping Morse at Lonsdale College, Lewis had his own duties to perform. For the life of him he couldn't understand the point of this particular errand, but Morse had said it was of vital importance. Something had galvanized the Inspector into new life. But it wasn't the gay, rumbustious Morse of the early days of the case. Something grim had come over him and Lewis found him a little frightening sometimes. He only hoped they got no more letters upon which Morse could practise his misdirected ingenuity.

He pulled the official police car into the small yard of the Summertown Health Centre, situated on the corner of the Banbury Road and Marston Ferry Road. It was a finely built, large, red-stone structure with steps up to a white porch before the front door – one of the many beautiful large houses built by the well-to-do along the Banbury Road in the latter half of the nineteenth century. Lewis was expected and had only a minute or so to wait before being shown into the consulting room of the senior partner.

'That's the lot, Sergeant.' Dr Green handed over a file to Lewis.

'Are you sure it's all here, sir? Inspector Morse was very anxious for me to get everything.'

Dr Green was silent for a moment. 'The only thing that's not there is . . . is er any record that we had er may have had about any er conversation we er may have had with Miss Kaye about her er private sex life. You understand, I know, Sergeant, that there are er there is the ethical side of er the er confidential nature of the er doctor's relationship with the er patient.'

'You mean she was on the pill, doctor.' Lewis stepped boldly with his policeman's boots where the angelic Green had so delicately feared to tread.

'Er . . . I er didn't say that, did I, Sergeant? I er said that we er it is er improper yes improper to er betray to betray the confidences that we er we er hear in the consulting room.'

'Would you have told us if she *wasn't* on the pill?' asked Lewis innocently.

'Now that's er a very difficult er question. You er we er you er you are putting words into my er mouth a bit aren't you, Sergeant? All I'm saying is er . . .'

Lewis wondered what the senior partner would say to a patient who had malignant cancer. It would be, he was sure, a most protracted er interview. He thanked the good doctor and left as quickly as he could, although he was half-way down the porch steps before he finally shook off the er persistent Green. He'd have to tell his wife about er Dr Green.

As they had agreed, Lewis picked up Morse outside Lonsdale College at one o'clock. He told the Inspector about the troubled state of Dr Green's conscience on the problem of professional confidentiality, but Morse was cynically unimpressed.

'We know she was on the pill, remember?' Lewis should have remembered. He had read the reports; in fact Morse had specially asked him to get to know them as well as he could. It hadn't seemed very important at the time. Perhaps, even then, Morse had seen its relevance? But he doubted it, and his doubts, as it happened, were well justified.

As Lewis drove out of the city, Morse asked him to turn off to the motel at the Woodstock roundabout. 'We'll have a pint and a sandwich, eh?'

They sat in the Morris Bar, Morse engrossed in the medical reports on Sylvia Kaye. They covered, at intermittent stages, the whole of her pathetically brief little life, from the mild attack of jaundice at the age of two days to an awkward break of her arm in the August before she had died. Measles, warts on fingers, middle-ear infection, dysmenorrhoea, headaches (myopia?). A fairly uneventful medical history. Most of the notes were reasonably legible, and oddly enough the arch-apostle of indecision, the conscientious Green, had a beautifully clear and rounded hand. His only direct contacts with Sylvia had been over the last two afflictions, the head-aches and the broken arm. Morse passed the file over to Lewis, and went to refill the glasses. Some of the details had appeared in the post-mortem report anyway, but his memory wasn't Lewis's strongest asset.

'Have you ever broken your arm?' asked Morse.

'No.'

'They say it's very painful. Something to do with the

neurological endings or something. Like when you hurt your foot, Lewis. Very, very painful.'

'You should know, sir.'

'Ah, but if you've got a basically strong constitution like me, you soon recover.' Lewis let it go. 'Did you notice,' continued Morse, 'that Green saw her on the day before she died?'

Lewis opened the file again. He had read the entry, but without noticing the date. He looked again and saw that Morse was right. Sylvia had visited the Summertown Health Centre on Tuesday, 28 September, with a letter from the orthopaedic surgeon at the Radcliffe Infirmary. It read: 'Arm still very stiff and rather painful. Further treatment necessary. Continuation of physiotherapy treatment recommended as before – Tuesday and Thursday a.m.'

Lewis could imagine the consultation. And suddenly a thought flashed into his mind. It was being with Morse that did it. His fanciful suspicions were getting as wild as the Inspector's. 'You don't think, surely, that er . . .' He was getting as bad as Green.

'That what?' said Morse, his face strangely grave.

'That Green was having an affair with Sylvia?'

Morse smiled wanly and drained his glass. 'We could find out, I suppose.'

'But you said this medical stuff was very important.'

'That was an understatement.'

'Have you found what you wanted, sir?'

'Yes. You could say that. Let's say I just wanted a bit of confirmation. I spoke to Green on the telephone yesterday.'

'Did he er did he er er,' mimicked Lewis. It was an isolated moment of levity in the last grim days of the case.

Sue had Tuesday afternoon off, and she was glad of it. Working in the casualty department was tiring, especially on her feet. The other girls were out and she made herself some toast and sat in the little kitchen staring with her beautiful, doleful eyes at the white floor-tiles. She'd promised to write to David and she really must get down to it this afternoon. She wondered what to say. She could tell him about work and she could tell him how lovely it had been to see him last weekend and she could tell him how much she looked forward to seeing him again. Yet all seemed empty of delight. She blamed herself bitterly for her own selfishness; but even as she did so, she knew that she was more concerned with her own wishes and her own desires than with anyone else's. With David's – particularly David's. It was futile, it was quite impossible, it was utterly foolish, it was even dangerous to think of him – to think about Morse, that is. But she wanted him so badly. She longed for him to call – she longed just to see him. Anything . . . And as she sat there in the little kitchen staring at the white tiles still, she felt an overwhelming sense of self-reproach and loneliness and misery.

Jennifer was busy on Tuesday afternoon. Palmer had sent her a draft letter and wanted her to look it through. Premiums on virtually everything were to be increased by 10% after Christmas and all the company's clients had to be informed. The dear man, thought Jennifer; he's not so very bright really. The first paragraph of his letter was reminiscent of the tortuous exercises she'd been set in Latin prose. 'Which' followed 'which', which followed yet another 'which'. A coven of whiches, she thought, and smiled at the conceit. She amended the paragraph with a bold confidence; a full stop here, a new paragraph there, a better word here – much clearer. Palmer knew she was by far the brightest girl in the office, and over important drafts he always consulted her. She wouldn't be staying there much longer, though. She had applied for two jobs in the last week. But she wouldn't dream of telling anybody, not even Mr Palmer. Not that it was unpleasant working where she was – far from it. And she earned almost as much as Mary and Sue put together . . . Sue! She thought of Sunday evening when she had returned from London. How glad she had felt to find them like that! She visualized the scene again and a cruel smile played over her lips.

She took the amended drafts to Mr Palmer's office, where Judith was trying to keep pace with the very moderate speed at which her employer was dictating a letter. She handed the draft to him. 'I've made a few suggestions.'

'Oh, thank you very much. I just rushed it off, you know. Put down the first things that came into my head. I realized it was, you know, a bit er a bit rough. Thanks very much. Jolly good.'

Jennifer said no more. She left, and as she walked up the corridor to the typists' room, the same nasty smile was playing about her pretty mouth.

The third of the triad, the undaunted, dumpy, freckled little Mary, worked for Radio Oxon. In the BBC she might have been accorded the distinguished title of 'continuity girl'; but she was in a dead-end job with the local radio station. Like Jennifer she had been thinking of a change, although unlike Jennifer she had few qualifications behind her. Jennifer had some A levels and all her shorthand and typing certificates; she must have been clever at school, thought Mary. Cool, sort of *knowing* all the time ... It worked well enough, the three of them living together; but she wouldn't mind a move. Sue was all right, she quite liked Sue really, although she'd been a bit moody and broody just recently. Men trouble. Had she fallen for that Inspector chap? She wouldn't blame her, though. At least Sue was human. She wasn't quite so sure about Jennifer.

After lunch on Tuesday one of the assistants came in to chat with her. He had a beard, a light-hearted manner, five young children and a roving eye for the ladies. Mary did not positively strive to discourage his attentions.

CHAPTER TWENTY-SEVEN

Thursday, Friday; 21, 22 October

BERNARD CROWTHER WAS, in the words of the ward sister, 'satisfactory', and on Thursday afternoon he was sitting up in bed to receive his first visitor. Strangely, Morse had not seemed anxious to press his claims, and had waived his rights at the head of the queue.

Peter Newlove was glad to see his old friend looking so lively. They talked naturally and quietly for a few minutes. Some things just had to be said, but when Peter had said them, he turned to other matters and he knew that Bernard understood. It was almost time to go. But Bernard put his hand on his friend's arm and Peter sat down again beside the bed. An oxygen tube hung over the metal frame behind Bernard's head and a multi-dialled machine stood guard on the other side of the bed.

'I want to tell you something, Peter.'

Peter leaned forward slightly to hear him. Bernard was speaking more labouredly now and taking a deep breath before each group of words. 'We can talk again tomorrow. Don't upset yourself now.'

'Please stay.' Bernard's voice was strained and urgent as he went on. 'I've got to tell you. You know all about that murder at Woodstock?' Peter nodded. 'I picked up the two girls.' He breathed heavily again and a light smile came on his lips. 'Funny really. I was going to meet one of them anyway. But they missed the bus and I picked them up. It ruined everything, of course. They knew each other and – well, it scared me off.' He rested a while, and Peter looked hard at his old friend and tried to keep the look of incredulity out of his eyes.

'To cut a long story short, I finished up with the other one. Think of it, Peter! I finished up with the other one! She was hot stuff, good Lord she was. Peter, can you hear me?' He leaned back, shook his head sadly, and took another deep breath.

'I had her – in the back of the car. She made me feel as randy as an old goat. And then – and then I left her. That's the funny thing about it. I left her. I drove back home. That's all.'

'You left her, you mean, at the Black Prince?'

Bernard nodded. 'Yes. That's where they found her. I'm glad I've told you.'

'Are you going to tell the police?'

'That's what I want to ask you, Peter. You see I . . .' he stopped. 'I don't know whether I should tell you, and you must promise me never to breathe it to a living soul' – he looked anxiously at Peter, but seemed confident of his trust – 'but I'm pretty sure that I saw someone else in the yard that night. I didn't know who it was, of course.' He was becoming progressively more exhausted each time he spoke, and Peter rose to his feet anxiously.

'Don't go.' The uphill climb was nearly done. 'I didn't know – it was so dark. It worried me though. I had a double whisky at a pub near by ànd I drove home.' The words were coming more slowly. 'I passed her. What a stupid fool I was. She saw me.'

'Who do you mean? Who did you pass, Bernard?'

Bernard's eyes were closed, and he appeared not to hear. 'I checked up. She didn't go to her night class.' He opened his heavy eyes; he was glad he'd told somebody, and glad it was Peter. But Peter looked dazed and puzzled. He stood up and bent over and spoke as quietly but as clearly as he could into Bernard's ear.

'You mean you think it was – it was *Margaret* who killed her?' Bernard nodded.

'And that was why she . . .' Bernard nodded his weary head once more.

'I'll call in again tomorrow. Try to rest.' Peter prepared to go and was already on his way when he heard his name called again.

Bernard's eyes were open and he held up his right hand with a fragile authority. Peter retraced his steps.

'Not now, Bernard. Get some sleep.'

'I want to apologize.'

'Apologize?'

'They've found out about the typewriter, haven't they?'

'Yes. It was mine.'

'I used it, Peter. I ought to have told you.'

'Forget it. What does it matter?'

But it did matter. Bernard knew that; but he was too tired and could think no more. Margaret was dead. That was the overwhelming reality. He was only now beginning to grasp the utter devastation caused by that one terrible reality: *Margaret was dead.*

He lay back and dozed into a wakeful dream. The cast of the scene was assembled and he saw it all again, yet in a detached, impersonal way, as if he were standing quite outside himself.

When he saw them he had known immediately it was her, but he couldn't understand why she was hitch-hiking. They exchanged no words and she sat in the back. She must have felt, as he had, how dangerous it had suddenly become; she obviously knew the other girl. It was almost a relief to him when she said she was getting off at Begbroke. He made an excuse – getting cigarettes – and they had whispered anxiously together. It was better to forget it for that night. He was worried. He couldn't afford the risk. But surely he could pick her up later, couldn't he? She had asked it with a growing anger. He'd sensed, as they were driving along, the jealousy she must have felt as the girl in the front had chatted him up. Not that he had given her any encouragement. Not then, anyway. But he felt genu-inely worried, and, he told her so. They could meet again next week: he would be writing in the usual way. It was half a minute of agitated whispering – no longer; just inside the door of the Golden Rose. There had been exasperation and a glint of blind fury in her eyes. But he understood how she felt. He wanted her again, too – just as badly as ever.

He got back into the car and drove on to Woodstock.

Now that she had the field to herself, the blonde girl seemed even freer from any inhibitions. She leaned back with a relaxed and open sensuality. The top button of her thin, white blouse was unfastened, and the blouse itself seemed like a silken seed-pod ready to burst open, her breasts swelling like two sun-ripened seeds beneath it.

'What do you do?'

'I'm at the University.'

'Lecturer?'

'Yes.' Their eyes met. It had gone on like that until they reached Woodstock. 'Well, where shall I drop you?'

'Oh, anywhere really.'

'You going to see the boy friend?'

'Not for half an hour or so. I've got plenty of time.'

'Where are you meeting him?'

'The Black Prince. Know it?'

'Would you like to come for a drink with me first?' He felt very nervous and excited.

'Why not?'

There was a space in the yard and he backed in, up against the far left-hand wall.

'Perhaps it's not such a good idea to have a drink here,' she said.

'No, perhaps not.'

She lay back again in the seat, her skirt rising up around her thighs. Her legs were stretched out, long, inviting, slightly parted.

'You married?' she asked. He nodded. Her right hand played idly and irregularly with the gear lever, her fingers caressing the knob. The windows were gradually misting over with their breath and he leaned over to the compartment on the near side of the dashboard. His arm brushed her as he did so and he felt a gentle forward pressure from her body. He found the duster and half-heartedly cleaned her side window. He felt the pressure of her right hand against his leg as he moved slightly across her, but she made no effort to remove it. He put his left arm around the back of her seat and she turned towards him. Her lips were full and open and tantalizingly she licked her tongue along them. He could resist her no longer and kissed her with an abrupt and passionate abandon. Her tongue snaked into his mouth and her body turned towards him, her breasts thrusting forward against him. He caressed her legs with his right hand, revelling in sheer animal joy as she swayed slightly and parted them with wider invitation. She broke off the long and frenzied kissing and licked the lobe of his ear and whispered, 'Undo the buttons on my blouse. I'm not wearing a bra.'

'Let's get in the back,' he said hoarsely. His erection was enormous.

It was over all too soon, and he felt guilty of his own reactions. He wanted to get away from her. She seemed quite different now – metamorphosed in a single minute.

'I'd better go.'

'So soon?' She was slowly fastening her blouse but the spell was broken now.

'Yes. I'm afraid so.'

'You enjoyed it, didn't you?'

'Of course. You know I did.'

'You'd like to do it again some time?'

'You know I would.' He was getting more and more anxious to get away. Had he imagined someone out there? A peeping Tom, perhaps?

'You've not told me your name.'

'You've not told me yours.'

'Sylvia. Sylvia Kaye.'

'Look Sylvia.' He tried to sound as loving towards her as he could. 'Don't you think it would be better if we, you know, just thought of this as something beautiful that happened to us. Just the once. Here tonight.'

She turned nasty and sour then. 'You don't want to see me again, do you? You're just like the rest. Bi' of sex and a blow out and you're off.' She spoke differently, too. She sounded like a common slut, a cheap, hard pick-up from a Soho side-street. But she was right, of course – absolutely right. He'd got what he wanted. But hadn't she? Was she a prostitute? He thought of his days in the army and the men who'd caught a dose of the pox. He must get out of here; out of this claustrophobic car and this dark and miserable yard. He put his hand in his pocket and found a £1 note. But for some loose silver, he had no more money on him.

'A pound no'! One bloody pound no'! Chris' – you must think I'm a cheap bi' of goods. You 'ave a bi' of money on you nex' time mate – or else keep your bloody 'ands off.'

He felt a deep sense of shame and corruption. She got out of the car and he followed her.

'I'll find ou' who you bloody are, mister. I will – you see!'

What had happened then he didn't know. He remembered saying something and he vaguely remembered that she had said something back. He remembered his headlights swathing the yard and he remembered waiting for a gap in the traffic as he reached the main road. He remembered stopping to buy a double whisky and he remembered driving fast down the dual carriageway; and he remembered coming up behind a car and then swerving past it and flying through the night, his mind reeling. And on Thursday afternoon he had read in the *Oxford Mail* of the murder of Sylvia Kaye.

It had been foolish to write that letter, of course, but at least Peter would be out of trouble now. It was always asking for trouble – putting anything down on paper; but it had been a neat little arrangement until then. It was her suggestion anyway, and it seemed necessary. The post in North Oxford was really dreadful – 10.00 a.m. or later now – and no one seemed to mind the girls at the office getting letters. And so often he couldn't be quite sure until the last minute. Sometimes things got into a complex tangle, but more often the arrangement had worked very smoothly. They had worked out a good system between them. Quite clever really. No one even looked at the date anyway. Sometimes he had incorporated a brief message, too – like that last time. That last time ... Morse must have had his wits about him, but he hadn't been quite clever enough to see the whole picture ... He couldn't have told Morse the whole truth, of course, but he hadn't deliberately meant to mislead him. A bit, certainly. That height business, for example . . . He'd like to see Morse.. Perhaps under other circumstances they could have got to know each other, become friends . . .

He dozed off completely and it was dark when he awoke. The lights were dim. The silent, white figure of a nurse sat behind a small table at the far end of the ward, and he saw that most of the other patients were lying asleep. The real world rushed back at him, and Margaret was dead. Why? Why? Was it as she said in the letter? He wondered how he could ever face life again, and he thought of the children. What had they been told?

Sharp spasms of agonizing pain leaped across his chest and he knew suddenly and with certitude that he was going to die. The nurse was with him, and now the doctor. He was drenched with sweat. Margaret! Had she killed Sylvia or had he? What did it matter? The pains were dying away and he felt a strange serenity.

'Doctor,' he whispered.

'Take it gently, Mr Crowther. You'll feel better now.' But Crowther had suffered a massive coronary thrombosis and his chances of living on were tilted against him in the balances.

'Doctor. Will you write something for me?'

'Yes. Of course.'

'To Inspector Morse. Write it down.' The doctor took his note-book out and wrote down the brief message. He looked at Crowther with worried eyes: the pulse was weakening rapidly. The machine was working, its black dials turned up to their maximum readings. Bernard felt the oxygen mask over his face and saw in a strangely lucid way the minutest details of all around him. Dying was going to be much easier than he had ever hoped. Easier than living. He knocked away the mask with surprising vigour, and spoke his last words.

'Doctor. Tell my children that I loved them.'

His eyes closed and he seemed to fall into a deep sleep. It was 2.35 a.m. He died at 6.30 the same morning before the sun had risen in the straggly grey of the eastern sky and before the early morning porters came clattering along the corridors with their hospital trolleys.

Morse looked down at him. It was 8.30 a.m. and the last mortal remains of Bernard Crowther had been unobtrusively wheeled into the hospital mortuary almost two hours ago. Morse had liked Crowther. Intelligent face; good-looking man really. He thought that Margaret must have loved him dearly once; probably always had, deep down. And not only Margaret. There had been someone else, too, hadn't there, Bernard? Morse looked down at the sheet of note-paper in his hand, and read it again. 'To Inspector Morse. I'm so sorry. I've told you so many lies. Please leave *her* alone. She had nothing to do with it. How could she? I killed Sylvia Kaye.'

The pronouns were puzzling, or so they had seemed to the doctor as he wrote the brief message. But Morse understood them and he knew that Bernard Crowther had guessed the truth before he died. He looked at the dead man again: the feet were as cold as stone and he would babble no more o' green fields.

Morse turned slowly on his heel and left.

Chapter Twenty-Eight

Friday, 22 October, a.m.

LATER THAT SAME Friday morning Morse sat in his office bringing Lewis up to date with the morning's developments. 'You see, all along the trouble with this case has been not so much that they've told us downright lies but that they've told us such a tricky combination of lies and the truth. But we're nearly at the end of the road, thank God.'

'We're not finished yet, sir?'

'Well, what do you think? It's not a very tidy way of leaving things, is it? It's always nice to have a confession, I know, but what do you do with *two* of 'em?'

'Perhaps we shall never know, sir. I think that they were just trying to cover up for each other, you know – taking the blame for what the other had done.'

'Who do you think did it, Sergeant?'

Lewis had his choice ready. 'I think she did it, sir.'

'Pshaw!' Well, it had been a 50:50 chance, and he'd guessed wrong. Or at least Morse thought he was wrong. But *he* hadn't been on very good form recently, had he? 'Come on,' said Morse. 'Tell me. What makes you pick on poor Mrs Crowther?'

'Well, I think she found out about Crowther going with this other woman and I believe what she said about following him and seeing him at Woodstock. She couldn't have known some of the things she mentioned if she hadn't been there, could she?'

'Go on,' said Morse.

'I mean, for instance, about where the car was parked in the yard. About them getting in the back of the car – *we* didn't know that; but it seems to fit in with the evidence we got when one of Sylvia's hairs was found on the back seat. I just feel she couldn't have made it up. She couldn't have got those things from the newspapers because they were never printed.'

Morse nodded his agreement. 'And I'll tell you something else, Lewis. She wasn't at her Headington class on that Wednesday night. There's no tick for her on the register anyway. I've looked.'

Lewis was grateful for the corroborative evidence. 'But you don't believe it was her, sir?'

'I know it wasn't,' said Morse simply. 'You see, Lewis, I think that if Margaret Crowther had been in murderous mood that night, it would have been Bernard's skull on the other end of a tyre-lever – not a nonentity like Sylvia's.'

Lewis seemed far from convinced. 'I think you're wrong, sir. I know what you mean, but all women are different. You can't just say a woman would do this and wouldn't do that. Some women would do anything. She must have felt terribly jealous of this other girl taking her husband from her like that.'

'She doesn't say she was jealous, though; she says she felt "burning anger", remember?'

Lewis didn't, but he saw his opening. 'But why are

you all of a sudden so anxious to believe what she says, sir? I thought you said you *didn't* believe her.'

Morse nodded his approval. 'That's exactly what I mean. It's all such a mixture of truth and falsehood. Our job is to sift the wheat from the chaff.'

'And how do we do that?'

'Well, we need a bit of psychological insight, for one thing. And I think she was telling the truth when she said she was angry. To me, it's got the right sort of ring about it. I'm pretty sure if she was making it up she'd have said she was jealous, rather than angry. And if she was angry, I think the object of her anger would be her husband, not Sylvia Kaye.'

To Lewis it all seemed thin and wishy-washy. 'I've never cared much for psychology, sir.'

'You're not convinced?'

'Not with that, sir. No.'

'I don't blame you,' said Morse. 'I'm not very convinced myself. But you'll be glad to know that we don't have to depend on my abilities as a psychologist. Just think a minute, Lewis. She said she entered the yard, keeping close in – that is, to her left – and edged her way behind the cars. She saw Crowther at the far end of the yard, also on the left. Agreed?'

'Agreed.'

'But the tyre-lever, if we can believe the evidence, and I can see no possible reason for *not* doing so, was either in, or beside, the tool-box at the farthest right-hand corner of the yard. The weapon with which Mrs Crowther claims she killed Sylvia Kaye was at least twenty yards away from where she stood. She mentions in her statement that she was not only angry but frightened, too. And I can well believe her. Who wouldn't be frightened? Frightened of what was going on, frightened of the dark perhaps; but above all *frightened of being seen*. And yet you ask me to believe that she crossed the yard and picked up a tyre-lever that was almost certainly no more than four or five yards from where Bernard stood with his bottled blonde? Rubbish! She read about the tyre-lever in the papers.'

'Someone could have moved it, sir.'

'Yes. Someone could, certainly. Who do you suggest?'

Lewis felt that his arguing with Morse in this mood was almost as sacrilegious as Moses arguing with the Lord on Sinai. Anyway, he ought to have spotted that business about the spanner from the start. Very bad, really. But something else had bothered him about Margaret's statement. It had seemed so obvious from the start that this was a man's crime, not a woman's. He had himself looked down on Sylvia that first night and he had known perfectly well, without any pathologist's report, that she had been raped. Her clothes were torn and quite obviously someone had not been able to wait to get his hands on her body. It had been no surprise to him, or to Morse surely, that the report had mentioned the semen dribbling down her legs, and the bruising round her breasts. But all that didn't square with Margaret Crowther's evidence. She'd seen them in the back of the car, she said. But had she been right? The hair was found in the back of the car, but that didn't prove very much, did it? It could have got there in a hundred different ways. No. Things didn't add up either way. It beat him. He put his thoughts into words and Morse listened carefully.

'You're right. It's a problem that caused me a great deal of anxiety.'

'But it's not a problem now, sir?'

'Oh no. If that were our only problem we'd have some plain sailing ahead of us.'

'And you don't think we have?'

'I'm afraid we've got some very stormy seas to face.' Morse's face was drawn and grey, and his voice was strained as he continued. 'There's one more thing I should have told you, Lewis. After I left the Radcliffe this morning, I called to see Newlove. He'd been to see Bernard yesterday afternoon and was quite willing to talk about him.'

'Anything new, sir?'

'Yes, I suppose you can say there is, in a way. Newlove didn't want to talk about the personal side of things, but he told me that Crowther had spoken to him about the night of the murder. Very much what we already knew or what we've pieced together. Except for one thing, Lewis. Crowther said he thought *there was someone else in the yard* that night.'

'Well we knew that, didn't we, sir?'

'Just a minute, Lewis. Let's just picture the scene, if we can. Crowther gets out of the front seat and into the back, right? Sylvia Kaye does the same. Now there was precious little room where the car was, and this was certainly not the place or the occasion for old-world gallantry; and I reckon it's odds-on that she got out the front nearside and into the back nearside and that he did the same on his side. In other words they sat on the same sides in the back of the car as they did in the front – he on the right, she on the left. Now whatever peculiar posture Crowther got himself into, I think that for most of the time he had his back to where his wife was standing – in other words she was almost directly behind him. But Bernard hadn't got eyes in the back of his head, and Margaret, as we've said, was probably scared stiff of being seen. And it tends to lead to one conclusion, as I see it, and one conclusion only: Crowther did not see his wife that night. I'm sure she was there, but I don't think he saw her. But he did see somebody else. In other words *there was yet another person in the yard that night,* another person much nearer to him than Margaret ever got; someone standing very near to the tool-kit, and someone Crowther caught a shadowy glimpse of, as he sat in the back of his car. And I think it may have been that person, Lewis, who murdered Sylvia Kaye.'

'You don't think it was Bernard either, then?'

For the first time Morse seemed oddly hesitant. 'He could have done it, of course.'

'But I just don't see a motive, do you sir?'

'No,' said Morse flatly, 'I don't.' He looked around the room dejectedly.

'Did you get anything else from Mr Newlove, sir?'

'Yes. Crowther told him he'd used his typewriter.'

'Newlove's typewriter, you mean?'

'You sound surprised.'

'You mean Crowther *did* write that letter after all?'

Morse gave him a look of pained disappointment. 'You've never doubted that, surely?'

He opened a drawer in his desk and took out a sealed white envelope which he handed across to Lewis. It was addressed to Jennifer Coleby. 'I want you to go to see her, Lewis, and give her this, and stay with her while she opens it. Inside there's one sheet of paper and a return envelope addressed to me. Tell her to answer the question I've asked and then to seal up her answer in the return envelope. Is that clear?'

'Wouldn't it be easier to ring her up, sir?'

Morse's eyes suddenly blazed with anger, although when he spoke his words were quiet and controlled. 'As I was saying, Lewis, you will stay with her and when she has written her answer you will make sure that the envelope is sealed tight. You see, I don't want you to see the question I've asked, nor the answer that she gives.' The voice was icy now, and Lewis quickly nodded his understanding. He had never realized quite how frightening the Inspector could be, and he was glad to get away.

CHAPTER TWENTY-NINE

Friday, 22 October, p.m.

AFTER LEWIS HAD gone, Morse sat and thought of Sue. So much had happened since Monday, but Sue had remained uppermost in his thoughts for almost all the time. He had to see her again. He looked at his watch. Midday. He wondered what she was doing, and suddenly spurred himself into action.

'Is that the Radcliffe?'

'Yes.'

'Accident department, please.'

'I'm putting you through, sir.'

'Hallo. Accident department.' It wasn't Sue.

'I want to have a quick word with Miss Widdowson, please.'

'You mean Staff Nurse Widdowson.' He hadn't known that.

'Susan, I think her Christian name is.'

'I'm sorry, sir. We're not allowed to take outside telephone calls except . . .'

'It might be an emergency,' interrupted Morse hopefully.

'Is it an emergency, sir?'

'Not really, no.'

'I'm sorry, sir.'

'Look, this is the police.'

'I'm sorry, sir.' Obviously she had heard that one before.

Slowly Morse was getting angry again. 'Is the Matron there?'

'You want me to put you through to Matron?'

'Yes, I do.'

He had to wait a good two minutes. 'Hullo. Matron here.'

'Matron, I'm speaking from Thames Valley Police Station. Chief Inspector Morse. I want to speak to Staff Nurse Widdowson. I understand you have your rules about this, and of course I wouldn't in the normal way wish to break them . . .'

'Is it urgent?' *Vox auctoritatis.*

'Well, let's say it's important.'

For the next few minutes Matron coolly and lucidly explained the regulations governing the delivery of personal mail to, and the acceptance of incoming telephone calls by, members of 'my' nursing staff. She spelled out the rules and the reasons for the rules, and Morse fidgeted at his table, the fingers on his left hand drumming the top of his desk in characteristic fashion.

'You see, you have no idea of the volume of official letters and telephone calls that all my departments receive every day. And if we had the additional complication of all personal letters and calls, where would it all end? I have tried and I think I have succeeded . . .'

Morse heard her out. As she had been talking a wildly improbable thought had taken root in his mind. He almost wanted to hear her repeat the tedious catalogue of constraints. 'I'm most grateful to you, Matron. I do want to apologize . . .'

'Oh, not at all. I've enjoyed talking to you. Now, please let me help in any way I can.' She would do anything for him now, he knew that. But the situation had changed. There was just the wildest, slimmest chance now, where before there had been none at all. He rang off as soon as he could, the Matron almost begging for the chance of doing him some favour. But he wanted none: his course was now clear.

Sue was having lunch while Morse was finishing his lengthy call to her immediate superior. She was thinking of him, too. Would she had known him earlier! She knew with a passionate certainty that he could have changed her life. Was it too late even now? Dr Eyres sat next to her, taking every opportunity he decently could of effecting the closest physical contact with the lovely staff nurse; but Sue loathed his proximity and his insinuations and, not worrying about a sweet, she left the table as quickly as she could. Oh Morse! Why didn't I meet you before? She walked back to the outpatients' room at the casualty clinic and sat down on one of the hard benches. Absently she picked up a long-outdated copy of *Punch* and flicked mechanically through the faded pages . . . What was she to do? He hadn't been anywhere near since that wretched night when Jennifer had come home. Jennifer! And she had been fool enough to confide in Jennifer. David? She would have to write to David. He would be so upset; but to live with

someone, to sleep with someone, forty, even fifty years
– someone you didn't really and truly love . . .

Then she saw him. He stood there, an anxious,
vulnerable look in his grey eyes. The tears started in
her eyes and she felt an incredible joy. He came and
sat beside her. He didn't even try to hold her hand –
there was no need of that. They talked, she didn't know
what about. It didn't matter.

'I shall have to go,' she said. 'Try to see me soon,
won't you?' It was after half-past one.

Morse felt desperately sick at heart. He looked at
Sue long and hard, and he knew that he loved her so
dearly.

'Sue?'

'Yes?'

'Have you got a photograph of yourself?'

Sue rummaged in her handbag and found something. 'Not all that good, is it, really?'

Morse looked at the photograph. She was right. It
didn't really do her justice, but it was his Sue all right.
He put it carefully into his wallet, and got up to go.
Patients were already waiting: patients with bulky plas-
ters over legs and arms; patients with bandages round
their heads and wrists; a road casualty with blood
around the mouth, the face an ashen white. It was time
to go. He touched her hand lightly and their fingers
met in a tender, sweet farewell. Sue watched him go,
limping slightly, through the flappy, celluloid doors.

*

It was almost a quarter to two as Morse walked down from the Radcliffe Infirmary to the broad, tree-lined avenue of St Giles'. He thought of postponing his next task; but it had to be done some time, and he was on the spot now anyway.

Keeping to the right-hand side of St Giles' as he made his way in the general direction of the Martyrs' Memorial, Morse stopped at the first snack-bar he came to, the Wimpy Grill, and walked inside. On his own admission the small, swarthy Italian, turning beefburgers on a hotplate, 'no speake, signor, the English so good,' and promptly summoned his slatternly young waitress into the consultation. Morse left amid a general shaking of heads and a flurry of gesticulation; it wasn't going to be easy. A few yards further down he stopped and entered the 'Bird and Baby' where he ordered a pint of bitter and engaged in earnest, quiet conversation for several minutes with the barman, who also as it happened was the landlord and who always stood lunch-time duty behind his bar. Sorry, no. Oh yes, he'd have noticed; but no. Sorry. It was going to be a long, dispiriting business, but one which only Morse himself could do.

He worked his way methodically along the dozen likely places in the Cornmarket below the ABC Cinema, crossed the road at Carfax, and started up the other side. It was at a little ('snacks served') cake shop nestling alongside the giant pile of Marks and Spencer that he found the person he was searching for. She was a grey-haired, plumpish woman, with a kindly face and a friendly manner. Morse spoke to her for several minutes, and this time too there was much nodding of the head and pointing. But pointing not vaguely outside, up alleys or down side-streets; this time the pointing was towards a little room, beyond the shop, wherein the establishment's snacks were served. To be precise, the pointing was towards one particular small table standing in the far corner of the room, with one chair on each side of it, both now empty, and a cruet, a dirty ashtray and a bottle of tomato sauce upon its red-and-white striped tablecloth.

It was 3.45 p.m. Morse went over to the table and sat down. He knew that the case was nearly over now, but he could feel no elation. His feet ached, especially the right one, and he was badly in need of something to cheer him up. Again he took out the picture of Sue from his wallet and looked at the face of the girl he loved so hopelessly. The grey-haired waitress came up to him.

'Can I get you anything, sir? I'm sorry I didn't realize you might . . .'

'I'll have a cup of tea, luv,' said Morse. It was better than nothing.

He was not back in his office until 4.45 p.m. A note from Lewis lay on his desk. His sergeant hoped it would be all right going off a bit early. Please to ring him if he was needed. His wife had a touch of 'flu and the kids were a bit of a handful.

Morse screwed up the note and tossed it into the wastepaper basket. Underneath the note lay the letter that Lewis had brought from Jennifer Coleby. Making certain that it was carefully sealed, Morse placed it unopened into the bottom left-hand drawer of his desk and turned the key in the lock.

He looked up a number in the directory and heard the drumming 'purr purr, purr purr'. He looked at his watch: almost 5.00 p.m. It wouldn't matter of course if he had gone, but he wanted to get things over straight away. 'Purr purr, purr purr.' He was on the point of giving up when the call was answered.

'Hello?' It was Palmer.

'Ah. Glad to catch you, sir. Morse here.'

'Oh.' The little manager sounded none too over-joyed. 'You're lucky. I was just locking up, but I thought I'd better get back and answer it. You never know in this job. Could be important.'

'It is important.'

'Oh.'

Palmer lived in the fashionable Observatory Street at the bottom of the Woodstock Road. Yes. He could meet Morse – of course, he could – if it was important. They arranged a meeting at the Bull and Stirrup in nearby Walton Street at 8.30 p.m. that evening.

It was a mean-looking, ill-lighted, spit-and-sawdust type of pub; a dispiriting sort of place, with gee-gees, darts and football-pools the overriding claims upon the shabby clientele. Morse wanted to get things over and get out as quickly as he could. It was a struggle for a start, and Palmer was cagey and reluctant; but Morse knew too much for him. Grudgingly, but with apparent honesty, Palmer told his pitiable little tale.

'I suppose you think I should have told you this before?'

'I don't know. I'm not married myself.' Morse sounded utterly indifferent. It was 9.00 p.m. and he took his leave.

He drove up the Woodstock Road at rather more than 30 mph; but spotting a police car up ahead he slackened off to the statutory speed limit. He swung round the Woodstock roundabout, the starting point of all this sorry mess, and headed for Woodstock. At the village of Yarnton he turned off and parked the Lancia outside the home of Mrs Mabel Jarman, where he stayed for no more than a couple of minutes.

On his way home he called at police HQ. The corridors were darkened, but he didn't bother to turn on the lights. In his office he unlocked the bottom left-hand drawer and took out the envelope. His hand shook slightly as he reached for his paper-knife and neatly slit open the top. He felt like a cricketer who has made a duck, checking the score-book just in case an odd run made by the other batsman had been fortuitously misattributed to his own name. But Morse had no faith in miracles, and he knew what the note had to say before he opened it. He saw the note; he did not read it. He saw it synoptically, not as the sum of its individual words and letters. Miracles do not happen.

He turned off the light, locked his office door, and walked back along the darkened corridor. The last piece had clicked into place. The jigsaw was complete.

CHAPTER THIRTY

Saturday, 23 October

SINCE BREAKFAST SUE had been trying to write to David. Once or twice she had written half a page before screwing up the paper and starting a fresh sheet; but mostly the elusive phraseology had failed her after nothing more than a miserably brief sentence. She tried again.

My dear David,
You've been so kind and so loving to me that I know this letter will come as a terrible shock to you. But I feel I must tell you – it's not fair to keep anything from you. The truth is that I've fallen in love with someone else and I . . .

What else could she say? She couldn't just leave it at that . . . She screwed up the latest draft and added it to the growing collection of tight paper balls upon the table.

A sombre-looking Morse sat in his black leather chair that same morning. Another restless, fitful night. He must have some holiday.

'You look tired, sir,' said Lewis.

Morse nodded. 'Yes, but we've come to the end of the road, now.'

'We have, sir?'

Morse seemed to buoy himself up. He took a deep breath: 'I've taken one or two wrong turnings, as you know, Lewis; but by some fluke I was always heading in the right direction – even on the night of the murder. Do you remember when we stood in that yard? I remember staring up at the stars and thinking how many secrets they must know, looking down on everything. I remember trying even then to see the pattern, not just the bits that form the pattern. There was something very odd, you know Lewis, about that night. It looked like a sex murder right enough. But things are not always what they seem, are they?'

He seemed to be speaking in a dazed, sing-song sort of way, almost as if he were on drugs. 'Now you can *make* things look a bit odd, but I've not met any of these clever killers yet. Or things just *happen* like that, eh? It was odd if Sylvia had been raped where she was found, wasn't it? I know it was very dark in the yard that night, but cars with full headlights were coming in and out all the time. It's surely stretching the imagination a bit to think that anyone would be crazy enough to rape a girl in the full blaze of motorists' headlights.' He seemed to Lewis to be relaxing a little and his eyes had lost their dull stare. 'Well?' That was more like the chief.

'I suppose you're right, sir.'

'But it looked odd. A young, leggy blonde murdered and raped or raped and murdered. Whichever way round it was, it all pointed in the same way. We've got a sex-killer to find. But I wasn't sure. Raping isn't easy they tell me if the young lady isn't too willing, and, as I say, I discounted the likelihood of Sylvia being raped in the yard. She could have screamed and yelled – unless of course she was dead already. But I'm a bit squeamish about that sort of thing, and I thought the chances of us having to deal with a Christie-like necrophiliac were a bit remote. Where does that leave us, then?' Lewis hoped it was a rhetorical question, and so it was. 'Well, let us concentrate our attention separately upon each of the two components – rape and murder. Let us assume two distinct actions – not one. Let us assume that she has intercourse with a man – after all, there was no doubt about the fact of intercourse. Let us assume further that this took place entirely with her consent. Now there was one shred of evidence to support this. Sylvia wasn't a member of women's lib, but she wasn't wearing a bra, and it seemed to me, if not unusual, well – a little suggestive. We discovered that Sylvia had several white blouses, but no white bras. Why not? No one as conscious of her figure and her appearance as Sylvia Kaye is going to wear a black bra under a thin, white blouse, is she? I could draw only one conclusion – that Sylvia not infrequently went out without a bra; and if she did wear a bra, it would be a black one, because all the girls believe that black underwear is terribly sexy. Now all this suggested that perhaps she was a young lady of somewhat easy virtue, and I think it's pretty clear she was.'

'She wasn't wearing pants either, sir.'

'No. But the pathologist's report suggests that she had been – there were the marks of elastic round her waist. Yes, I'm pretty sure that she had been wearing pants and that they got stuck in someone's pocket and later got thrown away or burned. Anyway, it's not important. To get back to the separate components of the crime. First, a man had intercourse with Sylvia – pretty certainly without too much opposition. Second, someone murdered her. It could have been the same man, but it's not easy to see the motive. The evidence we got at a very early stage seemed to suggest that this was a completely casual acquaintanceship, a chance pick-up on the road to Woodstock. All right. But since it was established that Bernard Crowther was the man who had stopped at the Woodstock roundabout, certain aspects of the case seemed to get more puzzling rather than less. I could well imagine that Crowther was the sort of man who might now and then be unfaithful to his wife; from what we now know, his relationship with his wife seems to have drifted over the last few years from idyllic bliss to idiotic bickering. But if we were looking for a sex-crazed maniac, I felt fairly sure Crowther wasn't the man we were looking for. He seemed to me an essentially civilized man. You remember when you looked at those photographs of Sylvia, Lewis? You remember you said you'd like to get the bastard who did it? But you had a composite picture of the crime in your mind, I think: you were putting together the rape and the murder and *something else – the obvious interference with Sylvia's scanty clothing*. Now I couldn't fit Crowther into that picture; and if Mrs

282

Crowther's evidence was right in any respect, it was surely right at the point where she described what she saw in the car. You made that point yourself, Lewis. What have we got then? First, he makes love to the girl in the back of the car. Second, he may have had a quarrel with her about something. Let's say she's a mercenary young tart and she agreed to make love with him on the sort of terms a common prostitute would ask. Let's say he couldn't or wouldn't pay her. Let's say they quarrel and he kills her. It's a possibility. But I just couldn't believe that if this had been the sequence of events that we should have found Sylvia in the condition we did – with her blouse torn and ripped away from her. Or at least not if we were right in thinking of Crowther as the guilty party.'

Lewis interrupted him quietly. 'You said that you knew who did that.'

'I think you do, too,' replied Morse. 'As the case progressed there seemed to be only one person who had a mind sufficiently warped and perverted to interfere with the body of a murdered girl. A man who had been waiting to see her anyway; a man we know who perpetually tantalized and tortured himself by thoughts of sex; a man who feasted on a weekly diet of blue films and pornography. You know all about him, Lewis. And I went to see him a week ago. His bedroom is cluttered with the whole paraphernalia of dirty postcards, Danish magazines, hard pornography and all the rest. He's sick, Lewis, and he knows he's sick, and his mother knows he's sick. But he's not a vicious type of chap. In fact he's not unlikeable in a nasty sort of way. He told me that he'd often had a dream about undressing the body of a dead girl.'

'My God!' said Lewis.

'You shouldn't feel too surprised about it, you know,' said Morse. 'I'm told that Freud mentions that sort of dream as being quite a common form of sexual fantasy among frustrated voyeurs.' Lewis remembered the film. He'd found it a bit erotic himself, hadn't he? But he hadn't wanted to admit it – even to himself.

'He'd met Sylvia several times before. They usually met in the cocktail lounge of the Black Prince, had some booze and then went back to his house – to his bedroom. He paid for it. He told me so.'

'He had quite a lot of expense one way or another, sir.'

'He did indeed. Anyway, on the night when Sylvia was murdered he'd been waiting since about a quarter to eight. He drank more and more and felt more and more desperate as the time ticked by and Sylvia didn't appear. He went out several times to look for her. But he saw nothing. When he did find her he was sick in mind and body: sick from pent-up sexual frustration and sick from too much drink. He found her quite by chance – so he says – and I believe him.'

'And then . . . you mean he . . . he fiddled about with her?'

Morse nodded. 'Yes. He did.'

'He needs treatment, sir.'

'He's promised me to see a psychiatrist – but I'm not very optimistic about that. I only ever knew one psychiatrist. Funny chap. If ever a man was in need of psychiatric treatment it was him.' Morse smiled ruefully, and Lewis felt his chief was becoming more like his normal self.

'So that's cleared that bit up, sir.'

'Yes. But it didn't help all that much, did it? I was as sure as I could be that Sylvia Kaye was not murdered by Mr John Sanders. She was murdered, so the pathology reports says, between 7 and 8 p.m. or thereabouts. Now we know all that stuff about the murderer going back to the scene of the crime, but I just couldn't believe that Sanders had stood for about two and a half to three hours drinking whisky no more than fifty-odd yards away from where his victim lay murdered. He'd have hopped it, that's for sure. What seemed so odd to me was why she wasn't found earlier. But you cleared that up.'

Lewis was glad to know that he had been of value somewhere along the line, and he knew what Morse was referring to, for he had himself interviewed all the drivers of vehicles parked in the yard that night. The driver of the car beside which Sylvia had been found had earlier parked in an awkward position just outside the yard of the Black Prince; but he had been anxious about blocking other cars and he had immediately taken the opportunity, on seeing a car drive out from the yard, of backing his own car into the space left vacant. His light of course could not possibly have picked up Sylvia's body, and when he got out of the driving seat the body was against the wall on the other side of the car.

'Well,' continued Morse, 'by this time, for one

reason or another we managed to get on to Crowther. Or rather the Crowthers. Perhaps we shall never know the exact part each of them played that night. But one thing I think we can confidently suggest – that as a result of what happened *Margaret thought that Bernard had murdered Sylvia*. Whether she killed herself just because of what she suspected, I don't know, though it was surely one of the factors that drove her to it. But that's only half the matter. I think, too, that *Bernard thought that Margaret had murdered Sylvia*. If I'm right about this, it seems to me to explain a lot of things. Bernard had two overwhelming reasons for keeping quiet. First, his love affair would almost certainly be brought out into the open, with all the consequences that would entail. But second, and even more important, his evidence might well help us find the murderer who, as Bernard saw things, was probably his own wife, Margaret. Oh dear, Lewis, if only they had spoken to each other about it! You don't suspect someone else of a crime if you've done it yourself. And I think each of them was quite genuine in suspecting the other. So we can say with every confidence that *neither of them did it.* And if Bernard had shown any intelligence he would have known how improbable it was that Margaret was actually involved in the murder. He passed his wife on the way back to Oxford! Now we know from Margaret's evidence that she's a slowish driver and perhaps most cars would pass her anyway. But if he left for Oxford *before* her, it is a physical impossibility for him to have overtaken her. Agreed?'

'Unless he called for a drink or something, sir.'

'I hadn't thought of that,' said Morse slowly. 'But it isn't a vital point. Let's go on. Now the key person in the case from the beginning has been Miss X – the Miss X who was with Sylvia in Bernard Crowther's car. What did we learn about her? The most vital fact we learned was something Mrs Jarman heard; and she's utterly convinced that she *did* hear it – I saw her again last night. She heard Sylvia say, "We'll have a giggle about it in the morning." So. We find the field narrowed very considerably, do we not? We investigate the Town and Gown Assurance Co. and we discover some interesting facts. And the most interesting fact of all is that someone tells Miss Jennifer Coleby to keep her mouth shut.' Lewis opened his own mouth, but got no further. 'I know you think I've been anti that young lady from the beginning, but I am now convinced – more than ever convinced – that the letter we found addressed to Jennifer Coleby was written to her by Bernard Crowther. If you want chapter and verse, it was written on the afternoon of Friday, 1 October in the rooms of Mr Peter Newlove in Lonsdale College on the same Mr Peter Newlove's typewriter. That, Lewis, is a *fact*.'

Again Lewis made an effort to protest, and again Morse waved the protest aside. 'Hear me out, Lewis. Jennifer Coleby lied from the word go. In fact of all the people in this case, it's Jennifer Coleby who had the monopoly of the lies. Lies, lies and more lies. But why *should* she lie? Why should anyone be so anxious to mislead us to the extent that she did? I felt sure, fairly early on, that the reason was pretty simple really. The young lady who sat in the back of Bernard's car was his mistress, and everything we learned from Margaret confirmed the truth of his own admission that he did in fact have a mistress. Now I needn't go over all the lies we got from Jennifer; but there was some truth amid the tangled web of all the lies. And the one thing she told us that seemed the biggest whopper of the lot was just about the one thing that was true. *She said she'd got a car.*'

Lewis could restrain himself no longer. 'But she had a puncture, sir. We know all about that.'

'Oh, I don't doubt she had a puncture. We know she did. She rang up the Battery and Tyre people. But if they couldn't mend it, someone else could, eh? If you remember, Jennifer didn't ask the tyre man to call some other time; and she didn't have it done at Barkers. But somebody mended her puncture, Lewis. Perhaps she did it herself? She's not a fool, is she? Perhaps she asked the man next door? I don't know. But you can repair a puncture in five minutes without much trouble, and *Jennifer Coleby is a practical girl and she had to have a car that night.*'

'I don't follow that at all,' said the mystified Lewis.

'You will, have no fear.' Morse looked at his watch. 'I want you to go and pick her up, Lewis.'

'You mean Miss Coleby?'

'Who the hell else?'

Morse followed Lewis out, knocked at the office of Chief Superintendent Strange and went in.

Some half an hour later the door was opened, and Strange stood on the threshold with Morse. Both men looked stern-faced, and Strange nodded his head gravely as the Chief Inspector said a few final words.

'You look tired, you know, Morse. I think you ought to put in for a fortnight's furlough now this is over.'

'Well, not quite over, sir.'

Morse walked slowly back to his office.

When Jennifer Coleby arrived Morse asked her to sit down and then walked over to Lewis. 'I want this to be private, Lewis. You understand, I know.'

Lewis didn't understand and he felt hurt. But he left them together, and walked along to the canteen.

'Look Inspector. I really thought that after your sergeant saw me yesterday that you'd finished . . .'

Morse interrupted her sharply. '*I've* asked you here and *I'll* do the talking. You just sit back and shut up for a few minutes.' There was thinly veiled menace in his voice, and Jennifer Coleby, looking very much on her guard, did as Morse had bidden her.

'Let me tell you what I suspected long ago in this case, Miss Coleby. You can interrupt me if I go wrong, but I want no more of your miserable lies.' She glanced viciously into his hard eyes, but said nothing. 'Let me tell you what I think. I think that two girls were picked up by a man one night and that one of the girls was the man's mistress. I think that this mistress usually travelled by car to see her lover, but on that particular night she couldn't get there by car, and that was why she either had to catch a bus or hitch-hike. Unfortunately, and by sheer chance, she was picked up *by the very man she was going to see.* Unfortunately, too, there were two girls, and he had to pick them both up, and *these two girls knew each other.* Now the whole thing suddenly seemed too dangerous – this is what I think, Miss Coleby, you understand – and somehow they decided to forget their date and wait until the next opportunity arose. I think that this girl, the mistress, asked to be dropped off somewhere on the way. She probably made some perfectly natural excuse – she was a good liar – and she asked him to drop her off. But she knew where the other girl was going – no doubt the other girl had told her – and she felt uncontrollaby jealous that night. She'd perhaps sensed something as they'd all driven along together. You see, the girl who was sitting in the front was very attractive to men. And perhaps? Who knows? The man, the man she knew so well, had been unfaithful to his wife. He had been unfaithful with her! Why not with some other girl? So I think this is what happened. She got out of the car, but she didn't return home. No. She waited for a bus and one came almost immediately. How she must have cursed her luck. If only she'd not hitched a lift! Anyway, she caught the bus and found her way to the place where she knew she might find them. And she did find them. It was dark there and she couldn't see very much, but she saw enough. And she felt a murderous jealousy welling up inside her, not so much against her lover, but against that cheap slut of a girl, a girl she'd got to know but never liked, a girl she now hated with unspeakable fury. I think perhaps they may have spoken to each other when the man had gone

– but I can only guess, and I may be wrong. I think that the girl who had just got out of the car could sense the deadly fury in the other girl's face, and I think she tried to run away. But as she did a vicious blow crashed across her skull and she lay dead in a heap upon a cobbled yard. I think the dead girl was dragged by the arms into the darkest corner of the yard and I think the girl who murdered her walked out into the night and caught a bus that took her home.'

Morse stopped, and there was utter silence in the room. 'Do you think that's how it happened, Miss Coleby?'

She nodded her head.

'We both know who murdered Sylvia, don't we?' Morse spoke so very softly that she could only just catch his words. Again she nodded.

Morse rang Lewis and told him to come in. 'Take a few notes, Sergeant. Now, Miss Coleby. A few more questions, please. Who mended your puncture for you?'

'The man across the road. Mr Thorogood.'

'How long did it take him?'

'Five, ten minutes. Not long. I helped him.'

'How long have you been the mistress of your employer, Mr Palmer?' Lewis lifted his eyes in amazement.

'Nearly a year.'

'Didn't you think it a bit dangerous – telling someone else?'

'I suppose it was. But it meant we could have a room once a week.'

'Palmer told you this morning that I knew?'

'Yes.' She had answered mildly enough thus far. But the old flash blazed in her eyes once more. 'How did you know?'

'I had to guess. But there had to be some reason. It was accidental, really. I checked the night-school register for Wednesday, 29 September, to see whether Mrs Crowther had been present. She wasn't. But I noticed another name on the list, and she *had* been present, a Mrs Josephine Palmer. Well . . .'

'You've got a suspicious mind, Inspector.'

'And when did this business of the letters start?'

'In the summer. Stupid really. But it worked all right – so they said.'

'Can you give me your solemn word, Miss Coleby, that you will say nothing of this to anyone?'

'Yes, Inspector. I think I owe you that at least.'

Morse got up. 'Well, get someone to take her back to work, Lewis. We've taken up enough of Miss Coleby's time.' A flabbergasted Lewis gaped at them like a fish out of water, and Jennifer looked round and gave him a wan, sad smile.

'You're not being very fair to me are you, sir?' Lewis seemed downcast and annoyed.

'What do you mean?' asked Morse.

'You said the case was nearly over.'

'It is over,' said Morse.

'You know who murdered her?'

'A person has already been arrested and charged with the murder of Sylvia Kaye.'

'When was this?'

'This morning. Here!' Morse took out the letter which Lewis himself had brought from Jennifer Coleby, and passed it over. Lewis took out the sheet of paper and read with blind, blank, uncomprehending disbelief the one line answer that Miss Coleby had written to Morse's question.

'Yes,' said Morse softly. 'It's true.'

Lewis was full of questions, but he received no answers. 'Look, Lewis, I want to be alone. You go home and look after your wife for a change. I'll talk to you on Monday.'

The two men left the office. Lewis got his coat and was soon away. But Morse walked slowly to the cells at the far end of the north wing.

'Want to go in, sir?' said the sergeant on duty.

Morse nodded. 'Leave us alone, will you?'

'Anything you say, sir. Cell number 1.'

Morse took the keys, unbolted the main door to the cells and walked along to cell number 1. He put his hands on the bars and stood staring sadly through.

'Hello, Sue,' he said.

CHAPTER THIRTY-ONE

Monday, 25 October

THE DAY HAD broken bright and clear, but by mid-morning a melancholy army of heavy grey cloud had massed overhead; and flurries of light rain were already sprinkling the window panes of Morse's office as, for the last time on the case of Sylvia Kaye, the two detectives faced each other across the desk.

'What did we know about Miss X?' asked Morse, and proceeded to answer the question himself. 'We knew roughly what she looked like, we knew roughly what she was wearing, and we knew roughly what age she was. It was a start, but it could never have got us very far. But we also knew that the two girls waiting at the bus stop not only knew each other but that *they would be seeing each other again the following morning*. Now this, without a doubt, was by far the most important single piece of evidence we ever got, and we acted upon it immediately. Naturally we assumed that we could narrow down the field of our inquiries, and quite properly we concentrated our attentions on the office girls who worked with Sylvia Kaye. Of course, it could have been a friend of Sylvia's, someone she would be meeting at lunchtime perhaps, or someone she would be meeting on the bus. It could have been a hundred and one things. But we didn't think so. And we didn't think so because our suspicions were very soon aroused, and with every justification, by the peculiar behaviour of one of the girls who worked in the same office as Sylvia – Miss Jennifer Coleby. But although we didn't know it at the time, there was someone else Sylvia would be meeting that next morning, and if we'd been a fraction brighter earlier on, Lewis, we might have got on to it more quickly. Sylvia was undergoing physiotherapy treatment at the Radcliffe Infirmary for her broken arm, and she was going for this treatment regularly on Tuesday and Thursday mornings. That is, she would be reporting for physiotherapy to the staff nurse in charge of the Accident Outpatients' Department *on the morning of Thursday, 30 September.* In other words, she would be reporting to Staff Nurse Widdowson.' Lewis got up to close the windows upon which the rain was splattering more heavily now. 'This, of course,' continued Morse, 'meant nothing very much by itself. But we learned that Sylvia didn't have many close girl friends, didn't we? It was interesting. Yes, at the very least it was interesting.' Morse's attention wandered momentarily, and he stared as Lewis had done through the windows to the concrete yard outside, now gleaming under the lowering sky. 'But let's return to Jennifer Coleby. Crowther wrote to her – that's established now beyond any question of doubt. But Crowther didn't write the note *for* Jennifer: she was merely the messenger boy. She's admitted that, and she had no option really. When I wrote to her I didn't ask her to accuse anyone of murder; but I did ask her if the letter was meant for Sue Widdowson, and she confirmed that it was. You'll never know, Lewis, how much I dreaded the truth of all this . . .'

The rain plashed across the yard, and the room was sombre and dark. Electric lights flashed on in several adjoining rooms, but not in Morse's office. 'Just consider a minute, Lewis. *Jennifer had a car.* That was a central fact in the case. And in spite of the temporary trouble she had with a puncture, *she used her car on the night of the 29th.* She said she did, remember? And she did. I didn't believe her at the time, but I was wrong. She met someone that night who saw her car and saw Jennifer Coleby in it. Someone who had nothing whatsoever to do with Sylvia's murder. And that was someone with whom Jennifer was having an affair – her employer, Mr Palmer. So, although the evidence had pointed at almost every stage to Jennifer Coleby, she suddenly acquired for herself a wholly incontrovertible alibi. Up to that point I had felt utterly convinced that the other girl in this affair was Jennifer; but I now had to face the undoubted, unchallengeable fact that whoever it was who sat behind Sylvia Kaye that night in Bernard Crowther's car, it was not, quite definitely *not,* Jennifer Coleby. Who was it, then? Although I was forced to abandon Jennifer as suspect number one – indeed, forced to abandon her as a suspect at all – I stuck stubbornly to my original idea that whoever the girl was, she was Crowther's mistress, and that it was to her that Crowther had sent his message. So let us look at things from Crowther's angle for a few minutes. I think that without a shadow of doubt he must have been a very frightened man. Just put yourself in his shoes, Lewis. He had left Sylvia Kaye alive and well – he knew that – on the Wednesday night. And the next day – what does he discover? He reads in the press that this same girl has been found murdered. But not murdered *anywhere*. Murdered on the very spot where he had last seen her – in the courtyard of the Black Prince. Who *knew* that he'd been there? Just himself and Sylvia – and she could never again say anything to anyone. But Sue Widdowson would have *guessed*, because Sylvia would have told her where she was going. He must have been worried out of his wits, and certainly for an intelligent man he doesn't seem to have been very sensible in what he did. Again and again the thought must have flashed across his mind: would Sue realize how dangerous it would be to say one single word to a living soul? He must have thought she would surely realize this. But still the doubts must have nagged away at his mind. She was the one person who could upset the whole apple-cart – not only bring him under suspicion for Sylvia's murder but throw the whole of his family-life into a turmoil he felt he couldn't face. He just had to make sure, or at least he had to do *something*. He daren't see her. So he wrote.' Lewis showed the familiar signs of unease and Morse nodded his understanding. 'I know, Lewis. Why does he write to *Jennifer*?'

'Why did he write at all, sir? Why not just ring?'

'Yes. I'm coming to that. But first let's be absolutely certain about the *fact* of the matter – and the fact is that Crowther *did* write to Jennifer Coleby. For if we fully recognize the significance of that, we can begin to answer the perfectly valid question you raise. Why not ring her? Why not? The answer is fairly straightforward, I think. *Who* was he to ring, and *where*? Let's assume for the minute that he wants to ring up Jennifer – the faithful messenger girl. At work? No. It was too dangerous. All the girls in the office knew Palmer's views on using his company's phones, and they played it fair because he turned a blind eye to personal correspondence coming in. But more than that. It was also far too dangerous, because all incoming telephone calls – except to the private phone in Palmer's office, which his personal secretary handled – came through the switchboard; and as you well know anyone on the switchboard can listen in with complete impunity to whatever's being said. No. That was out. Well? Why not ring Sue Widdowson herself? Why not ring his mistress and speak to her direct, either at her home or at the hospital? Again it's not difficult to see why he didn't. If he rang Sue up at home, he could never be sure that the other two weren't there, could he? He could risk Jennifer, but not Mary. He must have felt pretty certain – and I'm sure he was right – that listening in, even to a one-sided telephone call, is a temptingly easy and interesting pastime.'

After politely knocking on Morse's door, the young girl with the office correspondence entered brightly and placed the inspector's morning mail into his in-tray.

'Not a very nice day, sir.'

'No,' said Morse.

'It'll probably clear up later.' She gave him a warm and pleasant smile as she left, and Morse nodded in a kindly way. It was some vague consolation to know that life was still going on around him. He stared absently out of the window and noticed that the rain had slackened. Perhaps she was right. It would probably clear up later . . .

'But why couldn't he ring her at work, sir?'

'Ah yes. I'm sorry, Lewis. Why couldn't he ring her at work, you say? I found the answer to that only last Friday. It is virtually impossible for any outsider, even for the police, to get into direct contact with any of the nursing staff at the Radcliffe. I tried it myself, and you might as well ask directory enquiries for a number if you haven't got the address. There's an old battle-axe of a matron there . . .'

'Couldn't Crowther have written to her, though? Surely . . .'

'He could, yes. And I don't know why he didn't really, except . . . You see, Lewis, he'd got into this routine with Sue Widdowson. Let me try to explain how it must have started. As you know, the post gets worse and worse everywhere. But in North Oxford it seems it's particularly bad. It seldom arrives before ten in the morning – far too late for anyone to receive a letter before setting off for work. And even if it arrived early, say at eight, it would still not be in time. Why not write to her at the hospital, then? The answer is that our dear Matron puts her foot down there as well; she positively forbids all private mail being accepted in the hospital.'

'But if Crowther had posted a letter to her home address, she would have got it as soon as she came back from work, wouldn't she?'

'Yes, you're right. But you put your finger right on the central difficulty, and this is why I should think Jennifer Coleby was brought into the picture in the first place. Bernard Crowther, you see, like most of these University fellows, didn't work any regular hours at Lonsdale College. Something would always be cropping up at odd times – disciplinary matters, unexpected visitors, unscheduled meetings – and he could never plan his extra-marital escapades with any more than the hopeful anticipation that he might be free at any particular time in the days ahead. But much more important than this, he had to keep a very careful eye on the day-to-day comings and goings of his own family. Margaret might arrange something, the children might get a half-day holiday out of the blue, or be ill or – well, here, too, there was plenty that could go wrong and mess up the best-laid plans completely. So it seems to me that Crowther often didn't know for certain until the day itself, even perhaps until a few hours before-hand, if and when and where he was going to be free to meet his mistress. But, Lewis, *Lonsdale College is no more than a hundred yards or so* from the premises of the Town and Gown Assurance office in the High.'

'You mean Crowther just walked along and dropped a note in?'

'He did just that.'

'But Jennifer wouldn't be able to contact Sue during the day either, would she? You just said . . .'

'I know what you're going to say. He might just as well have written to Sue's home address. She wouldn't get the message any earlier, because the letter would be lying on the door-mat when she got in. In fact she'd almost certainly get it later. But all this is assuming that Crowther could write *the day before* to arrange a meeting, and as I say I suspect that he very often couldn't. But there's another much more important point, Lewis. You say that Jennifer couldn't contact Sue during the day. *But she could, and she often did.* The two of them met fairly regularly for a snack at lunchtime. They met in a little café next to M and S. I know that, Lewis. I've been there.' Morse intoned the last words in a melancholy, mechanical way, and Lewis looked at him curiously. There was something that Morse had said a few minutes ago. It was almost as if . . .

'Jennifer Coleby must have known all about this then, sir.'

'I don't know about *all.* She knew enough, though. Too much. I suppose . . .' He lapsed into silence for a few minutes, but when he resumed there was more spring and spirit in his voice. 'I don't know how it started, but at some stage they must have told each other about themselves. They tell me that women, and men, too, for that matter, enjoy talking to someone else about their conquests; and some chance remark probably brought the two of them together, and a bond of conspiracy was soon forged. I think there can be no doubt about that. I suspect it was Crowther, perhaps after a couple of misunderstandings and disappointments over meetings with Sue, who suggested the idea

301

of dropping some harmless-looking note addressed to Jennifer Coleby into the letter-box of Town and Gown. I'm pretty sure he had the sort of mind that enjoyed the idea of cryptic messages, and the practice grew and this became their normal channel of communication. He would stroll past and put a letter or a postcard through the front door of the office. Simple – not even out of his way. It probably only happened at first when an unexpected opportunity arose, but as time went on it became the normal practice, so normal that he even followed it for his last and crucial message to her. And quite apart from being a neat and extremely useful device, it must have seemed a godsend to Crowther not to have to write any actual letters as such to Sue. Like most people in such illicit affairs he must have had a dread of a letter going astray, being opened by the wrong person, or being found somewhere. No one could learn very much this way, could he, even if he did find the letters?'

'When did you first think it was Miss Widdowson, sir?' Lewis asked his question with an unwonted gentleness, for at last he had begun to understand.

Morse stared wearily and sadly at the desk in front of him, the fingers of the left hand drumming nervously on the surface. 'I suppose there were the vaguest hints – oh, I don't know. But I wasn't certain until last Friday. Perhaps the first time I began to suspect the truth was when I checked the evening-class register for Margaret Crowther's attendance record. I happened to notice, purely by accident really, that by some divine mischance Palmer's wife was a member of the same class. And it made me wonder; it made me wonder a lot. I thought it most improbable that Jennifer Coleby was the sort of person to grant a lot of favours without getting some in return; and I pondered on the bond that must exist between her and the other girl. In a roundabout way I considered the possibility of both girls being in similar circumstances, in the same sort of relationship with other people. With men. And so I did a lot of guessing, and I thought of Crowther with somebody and Jennifer with somebody; and then Palmer fitting in somewhere perhaps? And then . . . Well, and then I thought of Sue Widdowson, and suddenly the pieces began to click together. Could Jennifer be having an affair with Palmer? So often in this sort of situation it's someone you meet at work; and who was there at Town and Gown but Palmer? He was the only man on the premises. I kept wondering what it was that Jennifer was getting out of the bargain. And it suddenly struck me that there was one thing that she would want above all. Do you know what that was, Lewis?'

'I'm afraid I've no experience in that sort of thing, sir.'

'Nor have I,' said Morse.

'Well, I suppose you'd want a place where you could be alone together . . . Oh, I see. You mean . . .'

'Yes, Lewis. Someone could offer Jennifer a room where she could be alone with Palmer. Mary wasn't out all that much. But whenever she was, the coast was clear, because the other member of the trio could also arrange to be conveniently absent at the same time. And that's what she did.'

'Just a minute, sir.' Some worry was nagging away at the back of Lewis's mind. He was thinking back to the night of Wednesday, 29 September . . . Then he had it. 'But the house would have been free, wouldn't it, on that Wednesday night? I thought you said that Mary had gone to the pictures or something.'

'We'll make a detective of you yet, Lewis.' Morse got up from his leather chair, clapped his hand on his sergeant's shoulder, and stood watching the threatening clouds roll slowly westward. It had stopped raining now and the shallow puddles in the yard lay undisturbed. 'That was another of Jennifer's lies, I'm afraid. Mary was at home that night – she told me so. But even if Mary had been out, I don't think it would have made any difference. I'm pretty sure that Jennifer's job was to drive Sue to meet Crowther. That was her part of the bargain. And on Wednesday, 29 September, they both had their dates – as we know.'

'But why didn't they . . .' Lewis appeared reluctant to continue the sentence, and Morse did it for him.

'Why didn't the four of them take the opportunity of using the house whenever Mary was out? Is that what you mean?'

'Yes.'

'Well, it was a pretty safe bet for Palmer, of course. He lives a good way off and very few people would be likely to know him in North Oxford. Anyway it was a reasonable risk. In fact I know he's been there. I had the house watched all last week, and on Wednesday night Palmer's car was parked in the next road. McPherson found it – I'd put him on special duty.' A slightly pained expression crossed Lewis's face, but Morse ignored it. 'He didn't actually see Palmer go in, but he saw him come out, and I saw Palmer myself on Friday night when I had it all out with him.'

'But it was too risky for Crowther?'

'What do you think? He lived only a stone's throw from the place. No, it would be the stupidest thing imaginable for him to do. He'd lived there for years. Virtually everyone knew him, and he walked along the same street almost every night when he went for a drink at the Fletcher's Arms. People would have started talking immediately. No, no. That was not on from the start.'

'So when they both had dates . . .'

'It was Jennifer's job to give Sue a lift, yes.'

'So if Jennifer hadn't suddenly found a puncture in her tyre that night, Sylvia might never have been murdered.'

'No, she wouldn't.' Morse crossed the room and sat down again in his chair. He had almost finished. 'On the night of the murder, Sue Widdowson was impatient and probably a bit annoyed with Jennifer. I don't know. Anyway she felt she couldn't wait while Jennifer was ringing up about the puncture, and finally finding some decent old boy across the way who might take ages. She thought she'd be late and so she decided to catch a bus. She walked over to the Woodstock Road and she stood at Fare Stage 5 and . . . well you know the rest. She found someone else waiting. She found Miss Sylvia Kaye.'

'If only she'd waited.'

Morse nodded. 'If only she'd waited, yes. Jennifer got the puncture mended in no more than five or ten minutes, so she says. She'd arranged to meet Palmer at the Golden Rose that night. You see she always took Sue to Woodstock and it was convenient for her and Palmer to meet at some pub near by – Begbroke, Bladon, or Woodstock itself. And they met that night, we know that. In fact, in spite of all her troubles, Jennifer was there before Palmer. She bought herself a lager and lime and went out to sit in the garden to watch out for him coming.'

'Funny, isn't it, sir. If Sue Widdowson . . .'

'You're full of "ifs", Lewis.'

'Life *is* full of "ifs", sir.'

'Yes, that's true.'

'But you were still guessing, weren't you? I mean, you had no solid evidence to go on.'

'Perhaps not then. But everything was adding up. Sue and Jennifer were about the same height, same sort of colouring, except . . .'

'Except what, sir?'

'It doesn't matter. Forget it. Dress? I saw the coat that Mrs Jarman described; I saw the same sort of slacks; and Sue Widdowson was wearing them. On Friday night I showed Mrs Jarman a photograph of Sue and she recognized her immediately. No wonder the poor woman couldn't pick anybody out at the identity parade. The girl she had seen at the bus stop just wasn't there.'

'People do make mistakes, sir.'

'If only they did, Lewis. If only they did!'

'But it's still not *proof*.'

'No, I suppose it isn't. But I found something else. When I called at the Radcliffe to see Crowther's body, I got his keys from the ward-sister – they'd been in his trouser pocket. I asked her if anyone from the nursing staff had been along to see him, and she said that no one had. But she said that Staff Nurse Widdowson had asked her how he was getting along and that she had stood at the top of the ward and looked for a long time at the bed where Crowther lay.'

Morse's voice was growing agitated, but he pulled himself together as quickly as he could. Once more he walked over to the window and saw the sun beginning to filter through the thinning cloud. 'I went to Lonsdale College and I looked through Crowther's room. I found only one drawer locked up in the whole place, one of the drawers in his table desk – the bottom drawer on the left, if you're interested.' He turned round and glared at Lewis, and his voice sounded harsh and fierce. 'I opened the drawer, and I found ... I found a photograph of Sue.' His voice had suddenly become very quiet and he turned again to look out of the window. 'A copy of the same photograph she gave to me.' But he spoke these last words so softly that Lewis was unable to catch them.

EPILOGUE

IT WAS DONE.

Lewis drove home for his lunch, hoping that his wife was feeling better. He passed a newspaper placard with bold, large headlines: WOODSTOCK MURDER – WOMAN HELPING POLICE. He didn't stop to buy a copy.

Morse went along once more to the cell block, and spent a few minutes with Sue. 'Anything you want?'

There were tears in her eyes as she shook her head, and he stood by her in the cell, awkward and lost. 'Inspector?'

'Yes.'

'Perhaps you can't believe me, and it doesn't matter anyway. But . . . I loved you.'

Morse said nothing. He felt his eyes prickling and he rubbed his left hand across them, and prayed that she would notice nothing. For a while he could not trust himself to speak, and when he did he looked down at his darling girl and said only, 'Goodbye, Sue.'

He walked outside and locked the door of the cell behind him. He could say no more. He tore himself away and walked along the corridor, and he heard her voice for the last time.

'Inspector?'

He turned. She stood by the bars of the cell, her face streaming with tears of anguish and despair. 'Inspector, you never did tell me your Christian name.'

It was getting dark when Morse finally left his office. He climbed into his Lancia, drove out of the yard on which the puddles now had almost dried, and turned left into the main stream of the city-bound traffic. As he passed the ring-road roundabout, he saw two people standing on the grass verge thumbing a lift. One was a girl, a pretty girl by the look of her. Perhaps the other was a girl, too. It was difficult to tell. He drove on to his home in Oxford.